Christmas at Catoctin Creek

Catoctin Creek: Book 4

Natalie Keller Reinert

Natalie Keller Reinert Books

This is a work of fiction. Names, characters, businesses, places, events, locales, and incidents are either the products of the author's imagination or used in a fictitious manner. Any resemblance to actual persons, living or dead, or actual events is purely coincidental.

Copyright © 2021 Natalie Keller Reinert

Cover Photo: anakondasp/Depositphotos

Cover Designer: Natalie Keller Reinert

Interior Formatting: Natalie Keller Reinert

ISBN: 978-1-956575-07-1

Books by Natalie Keller Reinert

The Catoctin Creek Series

The Grabbing Mane Series

The Eventing Series

The Alex & Alexander Series

The Show Barn Blues Series

The Hidden Horses of New York: A Novel

Chapter One

Rosemary

"Twelve horses!" Rosemary stared at Ethel Hauffmann in dismay. "You're sure there are *twelve?*"

"D'you think I miscounted?" The older woman gave Rosemary a sharp look. Then she shrugged her bony shoulders and glanced back at the dilapidated barn behind her. As if the inhabitants knew they were being watched, a thin whinny floated from the open door. "You don't want 'em?"

Rosemary felt her heart twist at that hungry neigh. Of course she wanted them—Rosemary had never seen a horse she didn't want. That was one reason she'd started an equine sanctuary at her family farm in the first place. And these twelve horses were in need, with no one to stand up for them. She couldn't say no, but . . .

How?

Shivering in the wind blowing off the gray-green Catoctin Mountains, Rosemary ticked over the facts. Notch Gap Farm was full. Her permanent horses, the ones who needed lifetime homes after years of trauma, occupied every single stall. Over the sunny Maryland summer, when she could let some horses live outside day and night, she'd accepted some horses who were suitable for adoption. But now winter was coming on, and the first snowflakes could fall any day now. Or worse, freezing rain. Sleet. The sort of elements she couldn't possibly let horses try to endure without shelter.

"I don't have a single stall," Rosemary said, spreading her hands helplessly. "I don't know what to say."

"Well, I don't know who else'll take 'em," Ethel went on, her tone matter-of-fact. "I figured you was the one to call, being the horse rescuer around here. They're good-looking horses, too. Reckon you could sell them if you wanted. But they're all hungry. Dunno when's they last ate anything besides hay."

Sell them! Ethel really had no idea what Rosemary did. She swallowed back her anger; sharp words wouldn't help her with this woman. Ethel Hauffmann had lived in Catoctin Creek for all of her fifty-six years, and she had been popular for exactly none of them. This leopard would not change her spots now.

Rosemary looked around, as if she might spot a way out of this mess in the jungle of overgrowth surrounding the tumbledown barn, or maybe in the dark fir trees ringing the dilapidated brick farmhouse a short distance away. Wan Christmas lights gleamed bravely through the pearly gray daylight; Mrs. Wayne had decorated early this year. What were the chances of that, Rosemary wondered, when the old Wayne couple hadn't even made it to Thanksgiving? It was a shame.

No one had really known the Waynes very well; they kept to themselves. Like their cousin Ethel, they'd lived in the rolling farmland around the small town of Catoctin Creek for their entire lives. But while Ethel and her quiet husband presided over a fairly prosperous and modern hog and soybean operation, the Waynes continued to rely on feed corn and dairy cattle, as Mr. Wayne's father and grandfather had done before him. This had never been more than a hardscrabble homestead; it was even more desolate than Rosemary remembered on this dark November day.

Of course, Rosemary had only been here once or twice, anyway; as a child, her mother and Mrs. Wayne had shared some duties on various church committees. Even then, the childless Waynes had been secretive and wary of visitors getting in their business. Her mother had warned her that even in a big-hearted farming community like Catoctin Creek, there would be a few loners who wanted to be left alone. Best to just respect them, she'd advised her wide-eyed daughter. Don't ask too many questions.

So she hadn't, for most of her life . . . but now Rosemary wished she'd asked a few more questions before she'd answered Ethel's request to meet her at the old Wayne farm. This wasn't the way she'd expected her day to go.

She'd been planning on going into Frederick and doing a little Christmas shopping, maybe picking up some new twinkle lights for the barn and front porch. With November blowing in so gray and gloomy, she thought it was time to cheer the place up a bit. She'd hummed a little holiday tune as she brushed her wavy dark hair and picked out a silly pair of candy cane earrings her friend Nikki had given her as a gag gift the year before. *Sleigh Ride.* That was everyone's favorite, wasn't it?

"Babe, I'm heading into town," she'd called, and her husband, Stephen, replied from his upstairs office that he hoped she'd have a nice time.

Then her phone rang, and Rosemary's Christmas shopping plans were derailed.

On the phone, Ethel hadn't said how many horses they were dealing with, just that she was handling the Wayne estate and they'd left behind some livestock, and she figured Rosemary was the person to call about the horses.

"Of course," Rosemary assured her, because horses always came first.

So Rosemary had taken off her nice black wool peacoat, bought on a weekend in Manhattan with Stephen, who thought even self-described country mice like his wife deserved to be pampered in the city (he hadn't been wrong—she'd had a marvelous time) and threw on a heavy old canvas barn coat, pulled on rubber muck boots over her jeans, and then drove through the wet countryside towards the old Wayne farm, waving to friends who were out hanging their own Christmas lights and setting up their plastic snowmen on their lawns. It seemed like everyone was bound and determined to cheer up this gray month with extra holiday cheer.

Rosemary hadn't known what to expect. She'd heard about the Waynes' passing, of course. It had been a surprising case. The elderly couple had passed away as quietly as they had lived, and the town of Catoctin Creek hadn't realized they were gone until Dennis Wayne failed to pay his feed store bill on time. Luckily—if there could be luck in such a situation—they had a hired farmhand to care for the animals. But when no one refilled the feed bins, he hadn't bothered to alert anyone. He'd just thrown the animals hay and gone on with his day. And when his last paycheck didn't arrive, he'd gotten into his battered old truck and headed for greener pastures.

That was the story going around, anyway. No one really knew where he'd gone. Just that Elaine from the feed store sent out her son Joe to find out why the Waynes hadn't paid their bill and why they weren't answering their phone, and he'd reported back that he'd climbed onto the porch roof, looked into the front bedroom window, and seen the two of them asleep.

" 'Very asleep?' I asks him," Elaine explained to a court of eager listeners at the Blue Plate Diner, and Rosemary had felt a prickle of horror run up the back of her neck. "And sure enough, he jimmies up that winder and he says, 'Ma, they're stone-cold.' I says, 'Joe, you get outta that house and you call the police.' And of course you all know the police took them to the hospital and checked it out and said they died of natural cause."

Joe had also checked the barns and found the horses in the stalls, hungry and thirsty. He watered them and threw everyone hay. And now it was a day later, and Ethel was telling her the horses should be her problem.

She tugged her coat a little tighter; the wind out here on the flat valley floor was sharper than back in her protected cove, her farmstead carved into the foothills. Time to get a plan in motion before everyone froze. "Well, I'll manage feeding them," she assured Ethel. "The rescue has a line of credit at the feed store, so I can tap into that. I'll make sure they're fed and watered, but can they stay here? Like I said, I don't have room for them at my farm. At least we could keep their stalls clean and turn them out here."

Ethel merely shrugged again. She was an annoying woman, Rosemary thought. No heart to speak of. She was Dennis Wayne's second cousin by marriage, but according to Nikki, who got all the gossip first from her privileged positions as proprietress of both the

Blue Plate Diner and the Catoctin Cafe & Bakery, Ethel had no interest in administering the estate a second longer than was required of her. There were already rumors swirling that she'd take the first offer on the property, whether it was from a farmer or a developer.

She definitely didn't plan to take care of twelve half-starved horses. If Rosemary didn't handle the horses, Ethel would have them shipped straight to auction, and with no history or information on what they could do, they'd go for meat prices. The exact scenario which Rosemary's rescue was supposed to prevent.

"I mean, I'll find a place for them eventually," Rosemary continued, trying to keep her voice neutral. "But at first—"

"No, I don't see any good keeping them here," Ethel interrupted, swiping crossly at a strand of hair blowing in her face. "The outbuildings are falling down. Dennis didn't take care of nothing, as you can see. And if the real estate man I talk to wants the barn taken down, the barn's going down." Ethel shrugged. "I can't say for sure how long it'll even be there. Let's just get the animals gone."

"Give me a few days. I'll find somewhere for them soon, I promise," Rosemary assured her, then turned away, already tired of the woman's callousness. Sure, horses had no place on a dairy farm. Sure, they were an added stress on Ethel. But there was no reason to shrug off their misery when something went wrong. For whatever reason, the Waynes had seen fit to acquire a dozen horses. Now they needed to be fed and housed. It was a simple matter of morality for Rosemary. She couldn't understand why more people didn't see things that way.

Putting a few feet between Ethel and herself, her rubber boots squishing into the late-autumn mud, Rosemary called her husband to tell him why she'd be home late. Stephen was quiet for a moment, absorbing the news. She bit her lip as she waited; Stephen was a very good sport, but he often worried about people taking advantage of her kindness. Would he raise any objections to her taking in the horses?

Well, he'd just have to get over it, Rosemary decided. It wasn't like she had a choice in the matter. Horses in need were her job. They were her calling. And she'd been thinking about expanding the rescue's capacity for a while now. This would just speed things up.

The silence stretched out for several seconds. Then, Stephen asked in a quiet, thoughtful voice, "Would you say there's enough money in the rescue bank account to handle this many horses?"

"For a couple of weeks," Rosemary guessed, hoping it was true. "There's the account at the feed store. And I still have something left from selling Goliath to the school." The large Belgian horse had appeared like a gift over the summer, offered cheaply at an auction where Rosemary sometimes picked up former Amish workhorses. Rosemary bought him and brought him home, then immediately called Sean at Long Pond, where he was putting together the riding school program at the girl's school before the September opening. Rosemary was the head advisor on the program, but she left the horse decisions with Sean and his girlfriend, Nadine. Sean tried him out, and Goliath turned out to be saddle-broken and steady, an excellent addition to the program.

When the school opened for its first semester, both Goliath and Finn, another of Rosemary's rescues, were instant favorites with the boarding school girls. Sean said they'd never seen anything like them. That did not surprise Rosemary. Goliath was a full-blooded draft horse; Finn was half-draft, half Appaloosa. They were nothing like the expensive, lighter-boned warmbloods favored by the horse show set. She was delighted to introduce some new experiences into the girls' lives.

"Can the school use any of them?" Stephen asked now.

Rosemary didn't want to explain how awkward she felt about using her clout in the riding program to place her rescue horses. "I couldn't say off hand," she hedged. "I don't know if any of them ride. Look, maybe we can place some at other rescues. I'll have to call around, see if anyone has openings. But in the meantime, I'm it. I'll have to stay a little later here and make sure they're comfortable. The barn here is . . . not the best."

"Do what you have to do," Stephen replied, as she'd known he would, eventually. "I'll feed our guys tonight."

"Thanks, love." Rosemary was endlessly grateful for his steady temper. If Stephen had freaked out about the horses, she might have, too.

But, knowing his quiet support was waiting in the background, she could handle this challenge.

Before Rosemary went back to Ethel, she called the feed store and spoke with Tricia, the high school girl who propped up the counter on weekends. She confirmed the rescue's credit limit, then ordered feed and hay for delivery. Tricia spoke with the guys in the warehouse and promised she'd have it in an hour. "Special rush delivery for the rescue," she promised.

"Thanks, Tricia." Rosemary pocketed her phone and looked back at Ethel. The older woman was still gazing angrily across the land, looking as if she wished she could give the abandoned farm a kick in the rear. And maybe her dead cousin, too. Rosemary sighed, pushing out another wave of frustration with her breath before walking over to join her. Time for this grump to get out of here.

She said, "The feed store's sending me a delivery. They'll be here in an hour. I can handle things from here, if you want to go."

"Thanks," Ethel said, jingling her keys in her coat pocket. "Oh, by the way, did you hear the latest about the lost hiker?"

"There's an update?" Rosemary had been trying not to think too much about the story. The local news stations had reported a hiker's disappearance a few days ago, and a slow trickle of reporters from the D.C. area had made their way through Catoctin Creek, looking for background information. But the hiker wasn't from their town, and no one had anything to say other than to offer their best wishes. The journalists had scampered off to other towns in the region. "Did they find her?"

"No, but there's a person of interest," Ethel said. "The boyfriend." Her grin flashed, inappropriate and unwanted, and Rosemary felt the same sick feeling she'd gotten when she first saw the news, and again when the news vans pulled into town. Her old fear of leaving her house rose up when she thought about being lost in the woods, and all she wanted to do was drive back behind the gate of Notch Gap Farm and stay there, safe and sound, forever.

It was a terrible impulse, one she had to fight with disappointing regularity.

"It's awful," Rosemary replied absently, looking towards the Catoctins. The mountains rose up several miles to their west, low

Appalachian ridges thickly forested with drab, past-peak fall color. Even though the calendar page insisted they were in early November, many of the trees still clung to their dried old leaves. Their matted crowns of brown and burnt orange looked forbidding against the gray sky. Rosemary hated to imagine being lost up there—and yet at the same time, she found it odd. The Catoctin Mountains were hardly uncharted wilderness. Farmland surrounded the long mountain chain on both sides. Civilization was always nearby. This implied something else was going on with this missing woman; something more than simply wandering in the forest.

That was another thing which bothered Rosemary. If she wasn't lost, where was she?

"Well, I'd better go." Ethel clearly sensed Rosemary wasn't interested in gossiping with her. "Call me if you need anything, but you don't need to give me any updates. Whatever you do with them is fine. I'll let you know if anything changes with the barn."

Rosemary watched Ethel walk across the rutted driveway and climb into her truck. The woman drove away without so much as a wave goodbye.

"What a witch," Rosemary muttered, then turned back towards the rotting barn. The sight wasn't a cheerful one. Gray boards with wide black gaps, a shingled roof peeling back at the corners, an overhang over the barnyard that was slowly sinking towards the muddy ground. The opposite of her own cozy farm, and she hated to think that horses had been locked up in there for what, a week? More? And she couldn't even let them out now. With the threat of chilly rain on the wind, and the sucking mud of the barnyard, and the tumbledown fences surrounding the farm, they'd be in even

worse shape before the next morning if they were allowed out.
They might even end up on the road.

But if she couldn't move them to greener pastures, at least she
could cheer them up with a good grooming and some warming
food. For that, though, she could use a little help. Rosemary
picked up her phone again and called the barn office at Long Pond.
"Hey, Nadine? I know you're busy with the school, but . . . could I
borrow you?"

Chapter Two

Nadine

Nadine showed up within twenty minutes of Rosemary's call. She liked to be needed; it was a reminder she belonged in Catoctin Creek. She wasn't an outsider here. After traveling the northeast for most of her late teens and twenties, working at dozens of stables and farms, she was beyond relieved to have found a place at last in the hometown which she'd never felt a part of in her school years.

And Rosemary was a big part of that—Rosemary had essentially gotten her the job as manager at Long Pond—so she would have made time for Rosemary even if she'd been asleep, or sick with a head cold, or in the middle of a particularly good lunch. She glanced down at her good paddock boots as she slipped out of the shiny silver truck with the Long Pond logo on the door; the ground wasn't exactly leather-friendly. Maybe she should have slowed down long enough to put on a pair of Wellingtons. But Rosemary was coming out of the barn, her usually serene face anxious, and Nadine knew she was right to have gotten here in a rush.

She squelched over to meet Rosemary. "Got here as fast as I can. Jeez, it's *freezing* out here. Makes my day so far feel like summer. Why's it colder here than at Long Pond?"

"This place has absolutely no protection from the wind." Rosemary gestured to the lonely, gray-brown pastures and stubble fields surrounding them. "This has to be an awful place all winter, I'm sure."

"The Waynes *could* have planted a windbreak," Nadine observed, looking at the ramshackle brick house beyond the barn. "Just for giggles."

"I don't think this was a happy place. I don't know what was going on out here, but the Waynes were never outgoing people. I can't think of a time I saw them at the Blue Plate or at the spring fundraiser...I can't even remember them at the Christmas carnival, and no one missed that."

"Hey, I remember the Christmas carnival!" Nadine's childhood had its ups and downs, but she still savored the memory of those carnivals held on the field behind the volunteer firefighters' station just off Main Street. She remembered the smell of funnel cakes sizzling in oil, the sound of church choirs singing Christmas carols from a holly-draped stage, the rattle of the midway rides, throwing golf balls at fish bowls to win a goldfish of her own. Those carnivals had been the highlight of winter for her. "Whatever happened to those? I don't think I've been to one since I was seven or eight."

"No money to run it," Rosemary said with a little shrug. "The same reason everything else gets cancelled."

"Other small towns manage them," Nadine grumbled. She had so few positive childhood memories; it annoyed her that they had snatched the Christmas carnival away when she was so young. "I wonder if the school could put up some cash. Want to help me present it to the admins?"

"Interesting idea." Nadine could tell Rosemary wasn't really listening. She looked distracted, probably mentally listing all the work ahead of her. Twelve horses could easily be a full-time job. Nadine handled twenty-two back at Long Pond, but she had Darby to help her, and the girls who joined the barn program as their physical fitness requirement, and still more who were joining the small but growing Horsemanship Club. And Sean, though he was generally an afterthought, since he spent most of his time in the arena, either riding or teaching.

"Yeah, it's not the right time," Nadine said apologetically. "Sorry, I just get excited sometimes."

"You're so high-energy." Rosemary gave her a fond look, then snapped back to work mode. "Listen, can you help me get these horses cleaned up and blanketed? They're all hayed and watered, and no one's in any danger of colic, but it's going to freeze tonight and that barn is missing half its boards. And I've got the feed delivery coming in half an hour, so we'll have to give them a small dinner."

"Of course, I'll help." Nadine fell into step beside Rosemary and they trudged through the mud to the barn door. "Gosh, this is a wet November. Makes me want to hole up next to a fireplace for the next six months." She remembered something. "Did you hear the latest about the woman in the mountains?"

Rosemary seemed to hesitate before replying, "Yes. I heard they were investigating the boyfriend."

"Yeah, it's always the boyfriend." Nadine glanced at Rosemary. "You okay? You look a little pale."

"Oh, just cold," Rosemary said, trying to brush off Nadine's concern. "I've been out here for an hour."

"Cold, that's for sure. Feels like we might get a white Christmas."

"Hah! *That* won't happen." Rosemary's voice was assured.

"Didn't it happen last year?" Nadine challenged, amused.

"One time isn't a pattern."

Nadine couldn't help but grin. "Better than a zero chance, though, wouldn't you say?"

"Take it from me." Rosemary tugged open the creaking barn door. "A cold November means a warm December . . . oh. Hello, there."

Nadine leaned over Rosemary's shoulder and laughed. "Oh, boy. One of *them.*"

"Chestnut mare, beware," Rosemary muttered. "I hate stereotypes, but—"

"Everything happens for a reason," Nadine finished, still chuckling. Then she addressed the large chestnut horse in the narrow barn aisle. "What are you doing in the aisle, mama?"

The mare snorted at them and shook her head. She was a pretty horse—or she ought to be, anyway. That ratty forelock and the witches' locks in her mane weren't doing her any favors; and she had enough mud caked on her thick winter coat to officially qualify her as more dirt than horse. But her bold white blaze was pretty impressive, and the way it dropped across the mare's left eye, coloring the iris blue instead of brown, was a sure attention-getter.

Nadine wondered what her story was. She knew a few girls who would go bananas for a horse with a blue eye.

"She's pretty," Nadine said. "Very fancy."

"She looks like trouble," Rosemary said, clearly not impressed. "Scoot in and let me close this door before she gets out."

"So you typecast the chestnut mare with the blaze," Nadine laughed, slipping into the barn's narrow aisle. The rutted clay seemed to slide beneath her boots. She held out a hand to the mare, who considered her warily. "That doesn't seem like you, Rosemary."

"I guess I'm just expecting the worst, in general, today." Rosemary pointed at the ground. "See that plastic bag? About ten minutes ago, it was full of carrots. The one treat I had in the truck for them."

Nadine laughed and picked up the damp bag. Five pounds of carrots, gone. The mare shifted her head to look at the bag fluttering in the dim glow filtering from the dusty lightbulb overhead, and Nadine saw the telltale orange slobber on her lips and chin. "Well, you're a big old piggy, aren't you?"

The mare made a chewing motion, her molars working beneath her taut jaws. Pretty easy to translate that language. *More carrots?* she was asking.

"I like her." Nadine decided.

"She's trouble." Rosemary put her hand on the mare's chest, asking her to back up. "You need to get back in your stall, miss."

"Could be." Nadine stuffed the plastic bag into a blue barrel overflowing the hay twine and rolled up feed bags. "Maybe good trouble? I like a sassy mare every now and then."

"Well, you're welcome to her."

"You think? What's the plan for these horses?" Nadine didn't hate the idea of taking the chestnut mare back to Long Pond. She might make one of the girls a cool project.

Rosemary maneuvered the mare into a dark stall and closed the door. "Listen, if you have the stalls and you think the horse can work in the program, you're welcome to *any* of them. I have no idea what I'm going to do with these horses. I wanted to expand the rescue since I started taking in rehab projects instead of just lifelong rescues, but this is not the way to do it."

"Don't worry. We can figure out twelve horses." Nadine glanced around the gloomy barn. The lower level of a bank barn could be cozy or depressing, depending on the farm owner's management style, and the Waynes had clearly used cobwebs in all of their decorating. The horses nosed through hay in stalls that were mostly built of patchwork old lumber, the walls just high enough to keep them from wandering around and harassing one another. Nadine wondered what the point of all these horses had been. The Waynes had grown corn and run dairy cattle—all of it done half-heartedly, as far as Nadine could tell. They didn't need a herd of horses in any way, shape, or form. "Do you have any idea what they were doing with all these horses?"

"I really don't," Rosemary sighed, tugging at the red loops of a big trash bag. Nadine spotted the duct tape label on it: *BLANKETS.* "But they haven't been abused or starved. Look at them—they need cleaned up, sure, but no one here is skin and bone. And these rugs—" She tugged out a few musty green horse blankets. "They're not new, but they're not rags, either. And there are brushes and supplements in the feed room. It's like they had a purpose for them, but didn't tell anyone. Which would be just like the Waynes. They never talked to anyone."

"Are their feet taken care of?" Nadine peered over the wall of the nearest stall, where a dark bay horse with big, sloping shoulders was eating hay. He shoved his nose at her companionably as she tried to get a look at his hooves. "This guy is wearing shoes! And they're not old, either. So his feet have been done recently."

"So weird." Rosemary opened another bag of blankets and tugged them out, brushing aside a few small spiders. "The chestnut's hooves are pretty recent trims, too. I wonder if Kevin's been shoeing them."

"Oh, worth asking Nikki about. She can find out for us. You want to go over to the cafe when we're done and find out?" Nadine wondered if Nikki had any blueberry muffins left. Might as well make the most of a rare evening away from the school.

"You know what? That sounds like exactly what I need. Even if she doesn't know, I could use a quick catch-up with Nikki. We've all been so busy." Rosemary handed Nadine a horse blanket. It was heavy and smelled of dust and horse hair. Nadine sneezed. "That should fit the horse you're standing by," Rosemary went on. "It's a seventy-six. Bless you, by the way," she added absently, digging through the blankets, checking the size labels and sorting them into piles.

Nadine went into the stall, noticing the old brown shavings had been freshly picked clean, and tossed the blanket over the bay horse's back. He ignored her as she worked, buckling up the chest and reaching beneath his barrel to grab the straps hanging down the far side. "I think this guy's a Standardbred," she said as she worked. "Got those big old leg bones and that crazy shoulder."

"Look under his mane and see if there's a brand," Rosemary called from the neighboring stall. "If he raced, there'll be a freeze brand."

Nadine flipped up the horse's heavy, black mane. Sure enough, there were fuzzy white markings just below the line of his crest. "Yeah, he's branded alright. I don't know if we could ever read it, though."

"Too bad," Rosemary said. "But at least we know his breeding. That's helpful when we're trying to re-home him down the road."

"I've never ridden a Standardbred." Nadine let the horse's mane fall back over his neck. He turned to look at her, and she ran a finger down the squiggly white stripe that ran between his eyes and over one nostril. "Super cute, though."

"Good, so you'll take that one, too." Rosemary's voice was absent.

Two free horses, no questions asked? Nadine shook her head as she left the horse to his hay and went back to the blanket pile, tugging out one she thought would fit the next horse in the row. She'd have loved that as a kid. She'd have found some way to keep a horse, working off board in an empty pasture or something, if only she'd known how to find one. Instead, she'd had to wait until she was a teenager with a driver's license and could use her mother's lack of attention as an opportunity to sneak out and ride dangerous horses for work instead of going to school. Well, either way, she figured. She had her equestrian life now. She had a good job and a dresser drawer full of expensive riding breeches and a boyfriend who was just as passionate about horses as she was. Twelve-year-old Nadine would be seriously impressed.

She tried to channel that lifelong passion for horses every day when she dealt with girls who didn't want to be at Long Pond. The group of department heads they all called The Admin often sent Nadine girls who were having trouble fitting in, assuming that the magic of horses would fix them, and Nadine tried her best to use barn chores, grooming, and even riding lessons to help the girls find self-confidence and a feeling of belonging. It stuck for a few of them. Others found their passion elsewhere, on the lacrosse field or in the chemistry lab. Long Pond wasn't lacking for expensive facilities where a teenage girl could find herself—or lose herself—in hard work.

Nadine didn't let her feelings get hurt when a girl didn't manage to fall in love with horses after a week of after-school sessions spent in the barn; she sent them off to their next assignment with lots of well wishes and a reminder they were always welcome if they changed their minds. Since school started two months ago, she'd gotten six girls working their way through the extracurricular rotation, but just two of them had stayed on, one of them signing on for lessons with Sean and one of them content to stay on the ground, helping Darby and Nadine with stall cleaning and grooming.

It was one of the most satisfying parts of her day, seeing those girls in the barn, learning about horses and growing more confident in themselves. More fit, too—that was why barn work counted as their phys. ed. requirement. She had a new girl slated to start soon—Addy Doyle, who apparently absolutely hated Long Pond, according to the email Admin had sent down about her. Nadine buckled a blanket onto the cheeky chestnut mare, glancing again at that wild blue eye, and wondered if Addy would be the next new equestrian of Long Pond.

If she kept adding girls on, she *would* need more horses.

It was all very interesting timing, Nadine thought.

Chapter Three

Nikki

The Catoctin Cafe & Bakery was pleasantly empty in the
evenings. Nikki only left the front door unlocked and the
open sign turned on because she used that time to work on the
books, whether it was orders or actual accounting for one of the
restaurants, and she didn't mind filling coffee cups and gossiping
on the side. Preferred it, as a matter of fact. Since Kevin had started
making rounds without Gus, the old blacksmith who was teaching
him the farrier trade, he worked late every night, and she was tired
of sitting upstairs without him, poring over spreadsheets all alone.

And, of course, she'd never close her door if Rosemary wanted
her support. They'd been best friends since they were little girls. If
Rosemary needed help, the rest of the world could just sit and
wait, as far as Nikki was concerned.

So when Nadine and Rosemary came in, shivering and muddy,
at half past seven, Nikki just picked up the bag of coffee beans and
poured them into the grinder. Time for a fresh pot. Her years of
working at the Blue Plate Diner had taught her a lot about the
amount of coffee consumed in an average crisis. She closed her

laptop while the coffee machine started rumbling to itself. Business could wait.

Rosemary explained what they'd been up to. By the time she was finished, Nikki could feel her eyebrows arching all the way to the loose auburn curls falling around her forehead. "Twelve horses, and of course she doesn't call Caitlin! Who probably has plenty of room over at Elmwood? Oh, no, Ethel called *you,* the woman with a full barn, because she knew you'd never say no."

Sitting at the round table in front of the dining room's broad picture window, Rosemary shrugged off Nikki's complaints. "Caitlin *doesn't* have room. Since she leased Elmwood to that fancy horse show trainer, she has next to nothing to do with the place. Nadine doesn't even work there anymore."

Nadine, sitting across from her, offered a small smile. "It's true. I don't. And Ellen hired Richie and Rose to groom for her. Caitlin lives at the house and that's it. To be honest, I think she might be moving."

"Moving?" Nikki went back behind the counter and pulled down heavy white mugs for the coffee. "Excuse me, where is she moving to? I haven't heard a thing about that."

"I think somewhere in town?" Nadine looked sorry she'd brought it up. "I heard her talking about buying a smaller place. She was at Connie's place."

"If the ice cream parlor is getting the town gossip, Connie Foltz is going to have to start calling me with updates." Nikki tugged the pot out of the coffeemaker with a little too much force. She was only half-joking about Connie getting the gossip. People *relied* on Nikki—relied on her to know the latest on everyone in Catoctin Creek—comings and goings, births and deaths, marriages and divorces, the works. That was why Elaine brought the news about the Waynes straight to the Blue Plate. She knew who the queen was in this town. Nikki shook her head, pouring coffee. "I gotta tell ya, I just don't know about Caitlin. Too busy building empires. I mean, yes, she's doing amazing things for Catoctin Creek, but, yeah. She's still *Caitlin.*"

Rosemary lifted her eyebrows.

A little too pointedly, Nikki thought. "Fine," she admitted. "I owe Caitlin for helping me get this house." She looked around the cafe's dining room; it had originally been the big front parlor of the Schubert house, and the shining wooden floors, wide front windows, and soaring ceiling with white-painted trim was part of the cafe's sensational charm. The woodwork glowed beneath the Edison bulbs hanging above the counter and the warm globe lighting above the tables where customers sat and exclaimed over Nikki's baking.

This cafe was a realization of Nikki's dreams, and she never could have afforded it if Caitlin hadn't given her an exceptional deal.

"I know we've had our differences with Caitlin, but she has done a lot for us," Rosemary reminded her.

"I know, I know." Nikki put coffees in front of each of them, and the tray with a little milk jug, a saucer of rough brown sugar cubes. Embarrassing, getting called out by Rosemary, although nothing new. Rosie was the sweet one in their relationship, even if Nikki was the baker. And she really *was* thankful for Caitlin's help in acquiring the Schubert house. She still woke up and felt a moment of shock when she realized she was on the second floor of the graceful Queen Anne house at the far end of town, instead of back in the loft bed of her old garage apartment, about to start another grind at the Blue Plate.

And she wasn't the only one in Catoctin Creek to benefit from Caitlin's recent shift into real estate investment. The entire town was changing: Connie Foltz reopening the old ice cream parlor, with its antique tiles and whimsical pressed-tin ceiling; the two antique shops now open on Main Street, and an expensive bed-and-breakfast in a lovely turreted Victorian back on Brunner Lane. All of it funded in some way by Caitlin. She even helped the prospective business owners find and apply to historical preservation grants, or assistance for women starting small businesses.

And the outside world noticed. While the cafe still saw little weeknight traffic, their weekends were growing stronger every month. Catoctin Creek was getting more buzz in blogs and weekend newspaper supplements. People from D.C. and Baltimore and beyond were coming to stay in the quaint town which hadn't quite been "discovered" by tourists yet.

Of course, the missing hiker story was putting the town name into the world for the wrong reasons, but Nikki was confident that would blow over. Who could get lost in the Catoctins, for heaven's sake? They were a series of long hills surrounded by farms. Barely mountains at all. That woman would turn up in a few days, hale and hearty. Nikki was sure of it.

She put a plate of round, buttery cookies between Rosemary and Nadine and pulled up a chair to sit between them. "At least it's a nice, quiet Sunday night and we can talk this out. You said you thought Kevin might have some goods on the horses. What do you want to know, exactly?"

"I want to know their backstory, if I can find it out," Rosemary said, picking up a cookie and examining it from all angles. Her chipped fingernails looked red and sore, probably from the cold and wet outside. "Obviously, I'm going to have to find somewhere to put them, but I'm hoping they can be adopted out quickly. That would be easier if I knew what their backgrounds were. If I knew for sure they had been ridden, for example."

"Someone has been trimming and shoeing them," Nadine said. "Fairly recently. So we thought maybe Kevin would know . . . maybe he said something to you yesterday, when the news broke."

"You'd think so," Nikki sighed. "But I never see him for more than a few minutes at night. With the hours he's working, I'd swear he's handling every client in Gus's book and then some. Gus claims that he's still working, but I'm not entirely sure I believe him. He stays far away from here, obviously. He knows what I'd like to say to him."

She was so tired of Kevin's constant work. When he'd moved to Catoctin Creek, ostensibly to find a fresh course for his life but also because he was intent on pursuing *her,* Nikki had obviously hoped he would find happiness in his new career. She just hadn't realized that his life's work would involve working thirteen-hour days as a journeyman farrier, just a man and his dog, driving from farm to farm, trimming and shaping and nailing on shoes. Sometimes Nikki sat in her empty cafe and felt a little cheated. She hadn't counted on spending so much time alone when she finally had a partner.

"He takes Grover every morning and they're out the door and that's usually that," Nikki finished, aware the other two women were watching her warily—she must have that grumpy expression on her face again. "I feed him supper and then he falls asleep on the sofa."

"He's a great farrier," Nadine ventured. "I think you should be proud of how far he's come. I mean, he's only been doing it for like a year."

"And he's supposedly taking over for Gus, slowly, but did Gus work days like this? You know, I could probably hire someone part-time to give me a break with this place, but I just haven't seen the point." The coffeemaker chimed and Nikki hopped up to get refills for everyone's cups. "As for the horse issue," she said over her shoulder, "can you fundraise to build a new barn? If you wanted to expand anyway, why not go for it?"

"I did," Rosemary said. She picked up another cookie and sighed at it. "But now the ground is about to freeze. No one's going to take on a project until spring as it is. And the horses need to be placed *now*."

"Nadine, are you taking any?" Nikki refilled the younger woman's cup. "Between you and Sean, you should be able to handle a few more horses."

"I'm going to try," Nadine said. "But of course, any horses we want to add to the program have to be cleared by the faculty heads and ultimately the headmistress. They're considered a pretty big expenditure, obviously. So they really have to serve a purpose right away. I think I can make a case for training them as community service, but it would really help if they were rideable right away."

A bell rang, interrupting her. They glanced as one towards the door. A couple were coming inside, slowly shedding layers of cold weather gear. They were clearly out-of-towners. Nikki sighed to herself. They'd probably read that blog post about her chocolate-peanut butter layer cake; it had been making the rounds on social media and she'd even fielded a few calls asking about the recipe. Her eyes lingered on the pair for a moment, wondering where they were from. Their expensive knits and fleece-lined booties said some place with a lot less mud than western Maryland in November. "Let me go serve these two, and I'll be right back," she promised. "Talk amongst yourselves."

"I should really get going," Rosemary said regretfully. "Stephen fed everyone at home, and he'll be getting dinner for me as well. Can I grab some dessert for him, Niks?"

"Of course you can. Help yourself." She glanced back at the couple, who were making encouraging noises near the bakery case. "Be right there!"

"Go, don't let me keep you," Rosemary said. "Only, is there any lemon meringue in the back?"

"For you, always." Nikki laughed. "You never change."

Nikki served the couple—they did, in fact, want the chocolate-peanut butter cake they'd read about online—and then started cleaning up the place for the night. It was nearly eight o'clock, and she felt like closing. When the bell on the door jingled once more, she glanced up with resignation and was a little surprised to see a young woman she didn't know.

The weekenders they saw in Catoctin Creek were generally older couples—well-heeled D.C. beltway types, heading out to the country to find horse brasses and reclaimed wood for their shabby chic farmhouse interior design. Or whatever it was people called their decor these days. Nikki couldn't keep up with trends. She was too busy.

This woman standing before her counter was much younger than the normal weekender—maybe thirty—and her outfit was more city sleek than L.L. Bean. Black and gray wool. Heeled boots. Sleek ash-blonde hair. She hadn't driven out here hoping for a hike and deal on estate china.

And that made Nikki suspicious.

"Is it alright to order a latte?" The woman asked cautiously. "I know it's late, but I didn't see hours posted."

"I close when I'm done working," Nikki said. "I'll make you a latte. And anything else you want, barring a sandwich. I don't feel like cleaning the panini press again."

"That's no problem," the young woman laughed, sounding a little startled by Nikki's frankness. "Maybe just something sweet. I ate back in the city, but I'm pretty easily tempted by sugar and everything in this case looks incredible."

"It's all incredible," Nikki said with a smirk before disappearing behind the espresso machine. "And it's all made here."

"Amazing. All amazing. This seems like an amazing town, though. So I guess I'm not surprised that the most beautiful bakery in the world is here."

"You're getting the fancy new version of Catoctin Creek." Nikki tamped down the espresso. "Just last year, this was still barely a wide spot in the road. We've been doing a lot of work to spruce the old girl up."

"Wait, you're Nikki Mercer, right?" The woman's face suddenly lit up with recognition. She had bold blue eyes, lined dark to make them stand out even more. When she widened them, they were almost cartoon-princess enormous. "You run the Blue Plate Diner, too."

"Yeah?" Nikki poured the espresso shot into a paper to-go cup. No more dishes tonight. "You know that's an odd way to introduce yourself to someone, right?"

"Oh, I'm so sorry. I'm Kelly O'Connell. I'm up here from Arlington. I'm a reporter with WDCN."

"Mm-hmm." So, Nikki had been right to be suspicious. She congratulated her instincts on being correct, as usual. "So I guess you're here to cover the missing woman?"

"I am," Kelly confessed, dipping her head so her straight blonde hair fell over the face. "But I'm not here looking for quotes or anything. Just wanted to get a feel for the place. Look around and understand what she was doing up here."

Nikki lifted her brows. That didn't sound right at all. Reporters didn't show up looking for a *vibe*. They were looking for facts. Right? She put the latte on the counter. "Did you decide on a sweet?"

"Oh—a maple pecan roll, please." Kelly O'Connell of WDCN News gave Nikki a hopeful smile. "I imagine you'll get more traffic from people like me. You might want to keep your bakery case well-stocked. This cafe has an urban kind of feel. I think folks from the city will like it."

"I'll try not to take that as an insult," Nikki said, but she gave Kelly a grin anyway. She knew what she meant: hardwood and Edison bulbs were part of city canon these days. "Thanks for the warning. I guess I better make more muffins in the morning."

"Oh, there will be muffins?" Kelly's round eyes sparkled with anticipation. "I'll set my alarm."

Nikki started to ring up the sale as she answered. "There *will* be muffins. Blueberry, lemon poppyseed, and apple spice. But you better stay away from the poppyseed if you're going to be on TV afterwards. I don't mess around with my fillings."

"Good advice," Kelly said, passing her credit card across the reader. "Thanks. It was really nice to meet you."

"You too," Nikki said. "Feel free to sit for a few minutes. I have some stuff to clean up back here. No rush." Why crowd her out? There was no one upstairs, anyway. Kevin was still out somewhere, driving a country road or shoeing someone's horse.

She watched Kelly walk to a table by one of the wide front windows. There wasn't much to see; the interior lights hid the house's wraparound front porch and the lawn that sloped down to Main Street. But the woman still glanced through the glass as if she was seeing something beautiful in the November night.

Or maybe, Nikki thought, she was just looking at her own reflection. It was pretty enough.

~ele~

Nikki hung around in the cafe after Kelly left. The place was clean, but the silence of their rooms upstairs wasn't appealing enough to make her close up her laptop and climb the stairs. She crumbled a piece of cake with her fingers, nibbling bite by bite as she punched in numbers on her spreadsheets, making two restaurants hum along.

When she finally spotted the headlights of Kevin's truck pulling into the gravel parking lot behind the house, the clock told her it was just before nine o'clock. By now she was worn out, and in desperate need of some food that hadn't been baked with several pounds of butter, but she gave Kevin twenty minutes alone upstairs to settle in for the evening. She figured everyone needed a little bit of decompression time. Luckily, she got hers sitting in an armchair off to one side of her empty dining room, playing games on her phone.

When she finally opened the door at the top of the stairs, she heard Kevin hop up from the sofa and run into the kitchen, while Grover's paws clicked on the hardwood. "Hello, puppy," she sighed, giving Kevin's fluffy yellow dog a good pat and a scratch around the ears. "Did you have a nice day at farrier school?"

The dog did a quick, happy spin and then he took off for the kitchen.

She smiled to herself, pausing to take off her shoes and leave them on the landing. By the time she made it to the living room—a former bedroom at the end of the upstairs hall—Kevin was putting a pizza box on the coffee table. The cardboard was warm from the oven and smelled of garlic and cured meat.

"Picked this up from town on the way home," he announced, as proudly as if he'd made it himself, then leaned in to give her a kiss. "Hungry?"

Nikki sighed with contentment. She instantly forgave him for another late evening of work. Seriously, pizza could work wonders on a mood. "You are the best man in the world."

"I am," Kevin agreed. "Would you like a glass of wine?"

"I would like *two* glasses of wine," she said, picking up a slice of pizza. It burned her fingers, but she chanced a bite, anyway. Spicy sausage—*delicious*.

"So, a bottle for the table." Kevin hustled back to the kitchen and returned with an open bottle of red and two glasses, Grover tagging at his heels. "I stayed late at Elmwood with the new trainer...she's exacting, let me tell you. Two horses I had to leave

unfinished and promised Gus would come over and look at them."
He shook his head. "How was cafe life today?"

"Well, you missed drama with Rosemary, unfortunately. And I
just met a reporter a little while before we closed. She thinks more
journalists are going to end up here."

"Not exactly the press Catoctin Creek could use," Kevin mused,
turning the TV down as a detergent commercial came on, a
woman gushing about stain removal power with way too much
enthusiasm. "And how is Rosemary? What happened?"

"Oh, poor girl. She's swamped. You remember the Waynes out
on Route 9?" Nikki shrugged as Kevin shook his head. "No, you
wouldn't. Although Gus might know them. Someone was
trimming their horses' hooves, apparently. She and Nadine came
over to ask about that. They're trying to figure out where the
horses came from, and why the Waynes had them at all."

"Maybe Gus kept them on as clients," Kevin suggested. He'd
taken over almost half of the clients in his mentor's book, but Gus
wasn't ready for full retirement yet. That was what Gus and Kevin
said, anyway. Town gossip said that Gus's wife wasn't ready for
him to hang around at home all day, bugging her.

"Well, either way, Ethel Hauffmann is socking Rosemary with
all twelve of their horses. So she has to find a place to keep them,
because the Wayne property is falling apart. And I hear Ethel's
dying to sell it to a developer, which means the barn goes in the
end."

"God. Twelve horses out of the blue. That's a lot."

"Yeah. Nadine's helping her take care of them, but the bottom
line is, her barn is full."

"That's true," Kevin muttered. He took a sip of wine, his gaze going distant. Nikki knew he was running through his client list, wondering if he knew anyone with space to take twelve horses. But even if winter wasn't coming on, taking on that many horses would be a pretty huge ask. Plenty of commercial boarding stables had fewer than twelve stalls in total. "I'll have to ask around, see if anyone has interest in taking one or two of them."

Nikki reached for another slice of pizza. "I get the impression Long Pond might take a couple. If we can place a few more, maybe Rosemary can find a way to keep the rest at her farm. I was thinking Stephen might have some ideas, too. Can you talk to him tomorrow?"

"I presume Rosemary will be talking to him . . . right about now, actually."

"Yeah, but the conversations you have with your wife and the conversations you have with your best friend are really different. And you and he have the same business-y background. See if you two can get together and come up with some brilliant fundraising idea that can get a barn extension built. It's for charity, so it shouldn't be *that* hard, right? Not like pulling teeth to get a bank loan."

Kevin laughed. "You know it's hard to get money just like, in general, all the time, right? But especially at Christmas?"

"Well, maybe it shouldn't be." Nikki shrugged, taking a gulp of wine. "Here we are, heading into the holiday season, we've got horses in need of help and a person willing to do it, and oh, by the way, we've got a bunch of reporters driving up here from the nation's capital. I'm just saying, if we want attention and money for a local charity, this is probably a good time to ask for it. Maybe we need to put on some big attention-grabbing event."

"An event?" Kevin reached for another slice of pizza. "Like a charity auction?"

"No," Nikki said, feeling reckless. It must be the wine. "Like something *big*. Like—like a carnival. Remember the Christmas carnival? No, you're not from here." She hiccuped and put her fingers to her lips, smiling sheepishly. "Oops, got a little too excited for a minute there."

Kevin studied her for a moment. He was smiling in that maddening way he had, as if he just adored her so much, he was going to burst with pride. It made her want to kiss him and pull his hair and steal his lunch money, all at once. He said, "You're really a pistol, you know that?"

She smirked. "A *pistol?* Who taught you to say that? Some old farmwife? No one calls anyone a pistol anymore."

"It's a good word for you," Kevin said, leaning back to sip at his wine. "It's very accurate. I have to believe, as usual, that you can do anything you've set your mind to do. So if you say I'm going to talk to Stephen and come up with a brilliant fundraiser idea, then you're probably right."

She smiled at him, tipping her head back on the sofa. The wine and pizza were making her sleepy in record time tonight. "Thanks, Kev," she said dreamily.

"But there's an even larger chance that you're going to come up with the idea before I do."

"No. I'm too tired. I run two restaurants, remember? You do this for me."

"No problem. I'll bounce over to their farm tomorrow."

Nikki squeezed his free hand. "You're a good guy to have on my side."

"I am but a tool in your belt, fair Nikki. But, uh . . . got any other compliments for me? I could use some praise. I had a lot of horses to get under today, and more than one of them tried to shit on me. This job can be hard on a man's ego."

"Okay. Umm, you're also a good provider." She nodded at the pizza box. "My hero, and all that."

"Anything else? Anything at all."

"And I love you," she told him, and then she hit him with a throw pillow, just to make sure he wouldn't get a big head about it.

Chapter Four

Nadine

S ean was trying to rearrange the living room when Nadine came in.

Her first thought was to shriek. *Again, Sean, really?* Luckily, Nadine was long practiced at controlling her emotions. So instead of yelling at her boyfriend, who was *clearly* going through something, she simply exhaled slowly, then reminded herself to unclench the fists she'd made the moment she walked in the door and seen his mess. Okay. Rearranging the living room was becoming a weekly thing for him. But they could work through this.

She hung up her coat on the hook by the door—luckily those hooks were screwed into the wall, or no doubt Sean would have moved them several times by now—and slipped off her paddock boots, still flecked with dried mud from working with Rosemary at the Wayne farm. Now, Rosemary had a *real* problem, Nadine reminded herself. Nadine just had a boyfriend who was having some kind of weird reaction to moving back into a small space.

They'd spent the summer in the Long Pond farmhouse, a beautiful old home built by German immigrants in the way-back-when, probably one of the first houses in the area. Nadine had enjoyed the change from her old shoebox apartment above the barn at Elmwood, but she'd been happy enough to downsize in September, moving into a one-bedroom unit in the school's newly built employee housing.

Sean, apparently, hadn't handled the change as well. One summer of spacious country living had evidently broken his brain. Before he'd moved to Catoctin Creek to work at Elmwood, he'd lived in what was essentially a mansion, from what Nadine could tell from photos. And to the manor-born go the vices, Nadine supposed. You can take the kid out of the mansion, but can you take the mansion out of the kid?

Now he was obsessed with trying to change their small living room space, as if somehow he could add square footage by constantly shifting the sofa between the two walls that weren't interrupted by the apartment door or the kitchen bar.

Nadine's policy had been to roll with it, hoping he snapped out of his obsession soon, but on days like this, coming home to an overturned living room was more than she could handle without a few long, deep breaths and a mental reminder that she loved him, really, seriously. Her legs ached, her feet were sweaty and cold, and she needed to get out of this tight sports bra ASAP. Then, she wanted some place to relax.

"Sean," she said, as soon as she felt able to modulate her voice. "Baby. I am going to shower, but then I will need a place to sit down."

"One second," Sean panted, sliding the coffee table under the window. "I'll get the books off the sofa and back on the shelves. I'll be done before you know it."

The bookcase was now next to the kitchen bar, she noticed, whereas when she'd left this afternoon after lunch, it had been across the room, next to the window overlooking the barn and arenas. She looked at the stacks of books on the couch. It was going to take more than one second to put all of those back. Nadine shook her head slightly and went into the kitchen to fill the kettle. She was cold all the way through. Only tea could save her now. Tea and a hot, hot shower.

"Sean," she called over the running water, "why are we doing this again? Is everything okay?"

"Everything's fine." Sean blinked at her through the hatch between the living room and the kitchen. "Why do you ask?"

"Babe. Because this is the third time in two weeks you've torn up the living room."

He grinned and raked his hands through his tawny hair. "Oh, I messed up last time. You know what I forgot to account for?"

"What?"

"The Christmas tree."

It was Nadine's turn to blink. "Oh, right." She hadn't even considered the upcoming holidays. She looked over the living room again, imagining the bulk of a fir tree crowding in there, and shook her head slightly. Christmas. Oy.

It wasn't that she was against the idea of Christmas; far from it. Nadine liked the holidays, it was just that life was just *really* busy, and she hadn't noticed the weeks running away with her. They'd spent the summer building the program for the coming school year, as well as managing operations and teaching at Elmwood; then, just as the first girls began moving into the school's new dorms, Caitlin had leased Elmwood to an old acquaintance of Sean's from his horse showing days. For a brief moment in late August, Nadine thought maybe she'd gotten control of her life back. She'd signed up for a few courses from an online college, and she was ready to poke away at her own education.

Then school began for everyone else, and she realized she'd just traded one kind of busy for another.

She didn't really mind; Nadine had always preferred a full schedule to an empty one. She just had absolutely nothing left at the end of a day to spend on trivial things like keeping track of the year as it went racing past. She was a little surprised that Sean had any brainpower left to devote to things like planning Christmas decorations. Of course, he spent most of his working day teaching and riding. She was the one who dealt with the nitty-gritty of the business, the scheduling, the ordering, the finances, the vet visits, and a thousand other needs which horses required every day.

To his credit, Sean *did* handle domestic things like flipping the calendar and adding things to the grocery list when they ran out, and he packed up their dirty clothes to go to the school laundry every Thursday. He even dragged her away from work to get coffee or dinner out once in a while. He was turning out pretty decent at being one half of a couple, which was a surprise to everyone who had ever met him, but Nadine figured he just hadn't had a chance to discover his homemaking side when he'd been a spoiled rich kid living on the show circuit and supported by a series of maids and grooms.

She doubted this domesticity would extend to cooking a Christmas dinner, though. He better not try to rope her into some kind of holiday extravaganza. Nadine regarded cooking as a necessary evil, not a party. And she still didn't think their living room was big enough to accommodate anything larger than a table-top tree. "You weren't planning a big Christmas, were you?" Nadine asked him warily.

Sean started hefting books. He cast her an astonished look. With his sandy hair falling over his eyes, he looked like a child who had just heard Santa wasn't coming. "What? You don't want to celebrate Christmas?"

"I just assumed we'd let the school handle the heavy lifting. Decorations and trees and things. I think there's a committee for the holiday celebration, actually. Maybe you should join that. It seems like it would be a good outlet for you."

"There has to be one," Sean said thoughtfully. "Some of the kids will stay over through the holidays. They'll need a lot of celebration here to make up for it."

"Staying at school over Christmas? Okay, that's rough." Maybe Nadine hadn't enjoyed a particularly privileged childhood, but at least she'd been home for the holidays every year. Sometimes her mom didn't even have a jailbird boyfriend hanging around, and Nadine really felt like she'd gotten the best present of all: her mom, all to herself. This year, though, her mother would be in Florida. She'd gotten a job as a caregiver to an elderly woman who wintered in some retirement community in Sarasota. Nadine was genuinely happy for her mom, and only a little, privately sorry for herself. "I think I heard some kids talking about putting stockings up on the stalls," she continued, pulling down the box of tea bags as the tea kettle readied itself for a whistle. "But I figured I'd get Darby to handle all that."

"Darby would probably love to take on holiday duty in the barn," Sean agreed. "She gives me that vibe. Like she just enjoys a good party, in general." He huffed a little under the weight of some pretty sizable riding manuals. They'd done some collecting over the summer, bringing home vintage horsemanship books to decorate the farmhouse, showing off for the parents of prospective students who came to tour the school. Nadine thought it had been a waste to drag all those handsome books back to this small apartment, but the school administration had seen no need to keep them once they took over the farmhouse for their offices and reception centers for parents and donors. So Sean brought them back to the house . . . and that was another chunk of their tiny living space gone.

"So, that works. Darby will decorate the barn. And you'll decorate the apartment?" She looked at Sean hopefully. "Understated and minimalist, yeah?"

He pulled a sad face. "Just me? I thought we'd do it together?"

"Oh. Well, sure. I'm sure I can find some time for that." Beside her, the kettle whistled. *Finally.* "Tonight, though, I have to run through my English assignment for this week. Can you maybe order us something from the dining hall for dinner?" She smiled and shrugged apologetically.

Sean put the final stack of books away with what she thought was unnecessary emphasis. "They're having lasagna in the dining hall," he informed her darkly.

"Oh," she said again, blinking. This was not bad news to her. "Why is the school lasagna bad news?"

"I'd rather eat grilled cheese for dinner than eat the school lasagna."

"Well . . . we have cheese. And bread." Nadine looked suggestively at the refrigerator.

Sean leaned on the kitchen counter and looked at her. His eyes twinkled. "Are you asking me to make you a grilled cheese sandwich?"

"I am." She blew him a kiss. "And maybe you could put some tomato on it?"

Sean sighed. "And bacon?"

"Well, if you're offering . . ."

"Fine. Go, shower and do your homework." Sean put his hands on his hips and turned back to the living room. "Honestly, I think it looks good."

Nadine thought she'd trip over the coffee table in the middle of the night until she remembered it was there, but she nodded. "Really nice." She started down the little hall to their room.

"Oh," Sean said suddenly. "I meant to ask you, what did Rosemary want?"

She paused in the hall, suddenly too tired to even discuss it. Maybe if she pushed it all out in one breath. "Someone dumped a lot of horses at an old farm north of town, and she needed help cleaning them up so we could get rugs on them."

"Good grief, really? How many horses? Are they okay?"

"Twelve. And they're just a little hungry and stir crazy, I think. Someone was feeding them up until a few days ago, from what I understand. It's too bad our barn is almost full; she has no idea where to put them and the property is literally falling down."

"And here we were so proud of ourselves for filling the barn this summer."

"I know!" Nadine leaned against the wall, thinking of their horse-filled summer prepping the riding school for its first semester. "We have three stalls. I think we can take a couple."

"You think? I doubt it."

"Why? We just need to see if they're safe to ride. There's a cute Standardbred gelding, and a really flashy chestnut mare."

"Is that what you want in your life? A flashy chestnut mare?" Sean winked.

"Wait until you see her. She's just got a special something, and I don't just mean the blue eye. And honestly, even if they're not riding sound, couldn't it be good for the girls? A charity thing, like community service?" Nadine lifted her eyebrows at him. "Learning to take care of rescued animals . . . that's got to be worth a few points on their GPAs, right?"

"I guess it could be." Sean looked thoughtful. "You want me to see if I can put together something for Admin?"

"Thank you. Those three stalls we've got would help Rosemary out a lot. And I think that there's some potential for the girls who don't want to ride."

"Your horsemanship club."

"I'll take as many girls as I can get," Nadine said, thinking of the way her little collection of misfit students bloomed when they realized horses didn't judge them for their past or their families or their inability to part their hair in the middle. "Plus, if you're using all the horses for lessons, at least I'll have some projects for them to learn on the ground with. So it works out."

"I'll see what I can do."

Nadine padded back over and gave him a kiss. "You're very considerate, you know that?"

"I know," Sean said, pretending to grumble. "The most considerate man in Catoctin Creek."

"I'm lucky I saw you first. No one ever would have known how nice you were when you first came to town," she told him sweetly, and patted his cheek before she went to the bedroom.

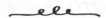

Bent over her laptop, Nadine tried to make herself care about the paper she was supposed to be writing. She really wanted a college education, but sometimes she had to wonder if it was more about personal vanity than an actual desire to learn anything. Was she just hoping people would take her more seriously if she had a degree? She was still a professional barn manager at the end of the day; this was her chosen career and she already had the job. Maybe all this homework was a waste of time.

Still, she felt better about herself after she'd done some schoolwork, so there had to be something to it. At least she was reading books she'd only heard other people talking about before, and figuring out some math problems which had previously looked like gibberish on a page. Maybe she'd never actually make it all the way to a bachelor's degree, but she'd give herself a little personal polish, anyway. Hold her head a little higher amongst the highly educated faculty and parents during school functions.

After an hour, she'd made some serious headway on the paper and was feeling peckish. It was eight o'clock already, so Sean would be more than ready for her to come out and eat. She sniffed the air, checking for bacon, and thought she detected it. "Okay," she told her laptop. "It's quitting time."

But before she closed the laptop, she noticed she had a new email in her work account. She clicked and read the email, her lips pursing a little more with every line.

Hello Nadine,

I hope this finds you well. My name is Kelly O'Connell and I'm a reporter with WDCN news. As you probably know, a missing hiker in the area has been receiving a lot of attention in the news recently. I've checked some records and found that she's connected with the riding program at your school. Would you have a few minutes to talk to me? It can be off the record if you prefer; I am just looking for a little more information on Monica Waters.

Kind regards,

Kelly O'Connell

Nadine read the email a few more times. It didn't magically make more sense with any of the repeated readings. She carried the laptop into the living room, where Sean was indeed cooking up a pan of bacon. He'd finished tidying the living room, too, Nadine noted with some relief. Confusing, but tidy. That was something. "Sean?" she called, raising her voice over the sizzling bacon. "Do you know anything about the missing woman?"

"The one in the woods? Not a thing," Sean shouted back. "One sandwich or two?"

"Just one, thanks."

"Okay. Why is your forehead all scrunched up like that? Did they find her?" Sean made a face. "Is it yucky?"

"No, I don't think they found her. I just got a weird email from some reporter. She says the missing woman is connected with the riding program."

"The riding program *here?*" Sean switched off the bacon and the sound in the apartment decreased immediately. "Excuse me? I have no idea who that woman is. What's her name? Monica something?"

"Monica Waters." Nadine looked at the laptop again. "I don't know who that could be, though. She must be mistaken."

"She must. Since we're the riding program, from start to finish."

"Unless she's a parent?"

"Wouldn't one of the kids have told us if their mother's picture was all over the news because she disappeared in the mountains?"

"True."

"Anyway, why did this chick email you?" Sean demanded huffily. "I'm the head of the riding program."

"For some reason, she thought Barn Manager sounded like the right person. Odd. I wonder if that means she's connected to one of the horses. Sound like anyone we bought a horse from?"

"No. I know every single person we bought a horse from." Sean shook his head. "I'm sure if her name had come up before, we would have noticed it when they first reported she was missing. Plus, someone would have called me freaking out if a mutual friend was the subject of a national news story."

"Hmm." Nadine put the laptop down on the coffee table and flopped onto the couch. "I wonder if she had something to do with Goliath, then. That's the only horse we have with no real connections."

Sean flipped a sandwich with great skill. "That could be," he said idly, eyes on the pan. "Rosemary said he came from an auction, right?"

"Yeah, one of those Pennsylvania Amish auctions. Cart horses and stuff." Nadine thought about pulling up his file—they had scanned documents in the school intranet, *very* official stuff—but she was tired of her computer. And everything. She was just plain tired, she realized. "Well, it's probably nothing. If I think of it tomorrow, I'll ask Rosemary about it, but I can't think anymore tonight. And she's probably exhausted, too. We dealt with all those horses and then she had to go straight home and do it all over again with her own barn. I know Stephen feeds, but does he do all the stalls and everything? Doubt it. At least I had Darby and the students to handle our horses."

"Here," Sean said, bringing a plate into the living room. He set it on the coffee table. They didn't have a dining room or room for a dining table in their small living room, so they made do with the coffee table. "Eat this nice sandwich I made you. And then I'll give you some ice cream."

"There's ice cream? Oh, Sean." Nadine was briefly overcome. "What did I do to deserve you?"

"You put up with me when I was a total dick," Sean told her seriously. "But then, instead of an award, you just had to keep me. So I don't know how that all adds up. For me, it worked out."

"Well, I'm glad I settled for you," Nadine teased, tilting her head coquettishly at him. "My mother said you'd be a lot of work, and she was right, but you've turned out pretty great."

"Funny," Sean said, sliding onto the sofa next to her. "My mother said the same thing about you."

"And that," Nadine told him, "is why we keep our parents two thousand miles away."

"Too right," Sean said fervently, and he dug into his sandwich like a starving man.

Nadine thought about the mysterious email again as she fought sleep after dinner, watching a movie with her head tucked up against Sean's shoulder. It had to be something to do with Goliath, she decided. And boy, she hoped it would not be a problem. They'd worked hard to convince the Admins that they should add a horse with no paper trail to their string. If the horse dragged some missing person scandal into the school, she was going to hear about it from the big bosses.

And no matter how old Nadine got, she still didn't like getting called up on the carpet at school.

Chapter Five

Rosemary

Rosemary liked the way her horses turned their heads the moment she walked into their barn. Stephen's head swiveled, too. He looked handsome under the warm yellow glow of the overhead bulbs, his dark hair under a black knit cap, his short beard showing off the sharp lines of his jaw. Rosemary paused in the doorway and took in her lovely old barn, her adorable horses, her gorgeous husband, and had a moment's sense of peace.

Stephen had been filling water buckets; he kinked the hose and waved with his free hand. "Hello, you. Go inside and warm up, I'm almost finished out here."

"I can help," she protested. "I'm already in my barn clothes. What needs done?"

"Absolutely nothing. Go on, go inside. Check the Crock-Pot, there's a chicken stew in there."

Rosemary felt her mouth watering. "With dumplings on top?"

"You better believe it. Your mother's recipe, right out of the box on the counter."

"You're a hero," she said, meaning it. Her mother's chicken and dumpling stew was perfection on a cold night. "I'll go get cleaned up."

By the time she came downstairs again, wavy dark hair wrapped in a towel and flannel pajamas buttoned to her chin, Stephen was in the old-fashioned kitchen, dishing stew out into wide soup bowls. He paused to give her a slow, lingering kiss. "Mmm," she murmured, lips close to this. "You taste like chicken. Oh, and herbs."

"That's what all the girls say."

She studied him as he set out the bowls and cutlery on the kitchen table, admiring the way his skin was flushed above his damp beard. He'd washed off in the kitchen sink; she could smell the lemon scent of the hand soap she kept in her mother's old china soap dispenser, shaped like a chicken and sitting on the kitchen windowsill since time immemorial. Stephen had adapted to plaid work shirts and heavy jeans after moving to Catoctin Creek, but he still kept his beard trimmed, his hair short and his fingernails clean, always ready for a New York City boardroom at the drop of a hat. She liked the way he could be both—it was a trait she didn't possess. She was all farm girl, through and through.

"So," he said, pouring iced tea into a glass for her. "What do you think of the horses?"

"The Wayne horses?" She considered the horses she'd left blanketed and snug for the night in their drafty old barn. "Honestly, they're really not in terrible shape. It's lucky. They've only been completely abandoned for a day or two. Some of them still had water in their buckets when Joe found them, apparently. And Ethel was nice enough to water them again before she demanded I come out and take charge of them." Rosemary heard the waspishness in her voice. "I shouldn't be hard on her. She knows nothing about horses, and she didn't know her cousin was dead. It must have been an awful surprise."

"Did she seem sad?"

Rosemary shrugged. "No, but who am I to say?"

Stephen sat down across from her. "You're so forgiving. I'd be calling her every name in the book right now."

"I guess it won't help anything, so why bother? The real question is how I'm going to take care of the horses. Tomorrow I'm going to see if I have any contacts with room, but . . ." Rosemary shook her head. "It's a tough time of year, and everything is so expensive right now. I'm afraid I'm on my own here."

"Well, I've put in calls to all sorts of charitable types in New York," Stephen said, scooping up some dumplings on his spoon. "Someone will put us in touch with some grant organization you haven't tried before. You can get emergency funding that way."

"And what am I going to use it for? I need stabling. We can't build a barn tomorrow. Or even in the next few months. That's the real issue—" Rosemary pointed her spoon at the window, in the general direction of the pastures behind the house. "Space."

Stephen shook his head and swallowed. "We'll figure it out. Is there such a thing as temporary stabling?"

"Actually, there is. Big tents." She considered the idea for the first time. "I *suppose* it could work."

"There. We're already figuring things out."

Rosemary hesitated, then admitted, "Nikki thinks I should run a fundraiser. But I don't know what that would look like. I mean, we do the spring fundraiser every year. I don't see how we could add another one. Maybe something with a Christmas theme?"

"The holiday angle seems like a reach. No one thinks of anyone but themselves at Christmas," Stephen said.

"Maybe not in New York," Rosemary replied primly. "But in Catoctin Creek? I'd like to think we can take care of each other."

"Oh, please." Stephen's eyes twinkled at her. "We're going to do the city versus country thing again? If the good farmers of Catoctin Creek are so generous, why did Ethel hand you the responsibility for her cousin's horses without even considering asking for help from the rest of the town? I think in your head, you think she could have walked into the Blue Plate and announced that she needed money for her dearly departed relative's horses, and everyone would just pull cash from their wallets. Maybe you should try that."

"Okay, it's not that simple," Rosemary allowed, smiling slightly. "But I do think we could find a way to ask the town for help. I just haven't thought of it yet."

After dinner, she presented the lemon meringue pie with a flourish. "The benefits of an emergency meeting at Nikki's place," she said.

"Oh, that's the stuff." Stephen flicked off a piece of crust and popped it into his mouth. "Sweet baby Jesus, the amount of butter in her pie crusts . . ."

"Did I say you could have a bite? I'm pretty sure I'm not generous enough to share, being from this selfish little backwater town." Rosemary grinned at him.

"You said it with your eyes," Stephen assured her. "Your eyes said, 'Eat some pie, my dearest darling husband.'"

"What kind of look says that?"

"A look of love," Stephen guessed, taking another bite. "What's that wedding quote? 'Love is kind, love is giving, love is a parade,' something hokey like that. Well, remember that saying when it comes to baked goods. Love is sharing your pie."

"Did you marry me because I'm good friends with a baker?"

"Rosemary. I'm astonished by you. I make all my decisions based on pie." Stephen took down some plates. "You don't?"

"I make all my decisions based on what will create the most trouble in my life," Rosemary sighed. "Hence, the barn full of horses. And you. The troublesome husband who eats all the pie crust before I even slice the pie."

"Listen, I didn't choose this life," Stephen informed her. "There's a whole curse. It has to do with the butter. Did I never tell you the tale of the Italian witch of Canarsie and my hapless mother, hexed in the Little Italy Ferrara's while she tried to buy the last pound of butter cookies?"

"What was her name, this Italian witch?"

"Uh . . . it was . . . Strega Nona. Strega Nona the witch."

Rosemary snorted with laughter. "Strega Nona! You'd think a guy from Brooklyn would know a few more Italian names than that . . ."

"Are you stereotypin' me?" Stephen put on his most stereotypical Brooklyn accent. "Sounds like you're stereotypin' me."

"Oh my gosh." Rosemary shook her head, still laughing. At her elbow, her phone buzzed, and she picked it up, reading the text on the screen. She narrowed her eyes and read it again.

"Something weird?"

"Two words from Nadine."

"Horse emergency?" Stephen guessed, not without merit.

"Christmas carnival," Rosemary read. She looked at Stephen. "Seriously, stop eating the crust off that pie and cut a slice!"

He obeyed, expression meek. "So . . . Christmas carnival? Is that code?"

"You know, I think she might be right."

"So you're not going to tell me . . ."

"Sorry. Listen. The town used to have a Christmas carnival. Nothing fancy, just a midway and food and games, up at the volunteer firefighter's field. It came up somehow tonight. I don't remember why, and Nadine asked about putting one on, but I brushed her off. Too focused on taking care of the horses at that exact moment, I guess. But I don't know why we didn't think of it when we were talking to Nikki about ways to fundraise."

"You can't think of everything at every moment," Stephen supplied. He put a slice of pie in front of her. "Eat that."

"I need to talk to Nadine about this idea," Rosemary sighed, looking longingly at her phone.

"Tell her you'll go see her tomorrow," Stephen said. "Tonight, give your brain a little break."

───── ✎ ─────

Nadine was showing a bored-looking tween girl how to muck a stall when Rosemary arrived at the Long Pond barn. "Take a break," Nadine advised her, stepping around the wheelbarrow in the stall doorway. "There are hot chocolate packets in the tack room."

The girl breathed an obvious sigh of relief, tugging out her phone before she even left the stall. The sound of her fingers tapping on the glass surface was surprisingly loud in the midmorning quiet of the barn.

Rosemary concealed her amusement until they were a few stalls away, walking towards the warmth of Nadine's office. "She looked like she was being tortured and you just let her off the rack," she said as she took off her coat. The barn was shut up tight against the windy day outside, and the horses warmed it even more with their bodies. "You're really ruining her life with chores, huh?"

"Well, she's going straight back to them after you leave," Nadine said with a smirk. "Some of these girls are so spoiled at home, I don't even think they'd know how to clean their own rooms. Boarding school's a blessing for them, even if they don't know it yet."

"I used to dream about going away to a riding school when I was a kid." Rosemary settled down in a plush chair near the heater. Nadine's office was located at the far end of the graceful center-aisle barn the school had built over a section of the Kelbaughs' old corn field, with one window facing into the indoor arena and another facing out over the outdoor riding arena. Movement in the outdoor ring caught her attention, and she saw a rider cantering over a line of jumps, his movements graceful as the horse skipped over the fences. "Good grief, why is Sean riding outside on a day like this?"

Nadine glanced out the window as she settled into the leather chair behind her tidy desk. "Yeah, he's giving everyone a few more schools out there before the footing freezes. He says they get all pent-up when they work in the indoor constantly. This is after he spent an entire winter at Elmwood refusing to ride outside, mind you." Nadine laughed and shook her head.

"Well, he's getting better every year, I guess?"

"He's *definitely* a work in progress." Nadine rolled her eyes. "So, you got my text last night and you thought about it."

"I got your text. Your very short text. Two words? Stephen couldn't stop me from muttering about it all evening."

"I wanted it to percolate in your brain. Honestly, so glad you didn't text me back, because I was exhausted. But the idea just came to me while I was watching TV." Nadine cocked her head, as if remembering something.

"Everything okay?"

"Yeah." Nadine shook her head. "Something random happened last night, but honestly, I think it's nothing. Let's talk Christmas carnival. Did it percolate?"

"It did! It percolated into a single question."

"Which is?"

"How?"

Nadine leaned back in her chair, a knowing smile on her face. The office made the slim young woman seem older, more mature than her mid-twenties. Rosemary was technically her boss—she was on the school board as an advisory to the equestrian program —but she found she rarely felt that way. She just made herself available to answer questions or provide advice. And the hands-off approach seemed to work. Nadine was clearly thriving here. Sean was doing pretty well, too.

"The key is, we have to get together a committee to do the heavy lifting for us," Nadine said, shrugging, as if pulling together a last-minute committee of locals right before the Christmas rush would be no big deal. "So I think like, who is good at what? Everyone has some strengths. Here's how I see it breaking down: we've got Elaine from the feed store to do budgets, we've got Ronnie from the Farm Bureau to organize the site. Mickey down at Trout's Market can find food trucks and get the church ladies to come and set up their kitchens. And then we just have to find midway rides. We pick some dates, we book the stuff, and we tell everyone all profits go to Notch Gap Farm to care for the rescued horses of Catoctin Creek. Simple."

"Sure." Rosemary shrugged, feeling like Nadine had just listed six months' worth of work. "That's simple."

"Listen, all of them do this every spring for the fundraiser. And that's not nearly as much fun as the Christmas carnival could be. That's just people in a school gym buying jam and sticking money in jars. We could offer rides! Games! Music!"

"When do you expect to put all this on?" Rosemary asked, feeling weak. "It's already the fifth of November."

"Oh, we can do it the second weekend of December, maybe? That gives us six weeks."

Rosemary had an idea that putting on a carnival would take more than six weeks, but maybe there was something to this whole youthful-enthusiasm-energy Nadine was giving off. The girl was practically sparking with it. "Okay. What do you want me to do?"

"You go home and work out exactly what you want to get out of this," Nadine told her. "What the horses need, what it will cost, how the town can help. We need an appeal with solid, concrete goals everyone can rally behind."

"Right. And the school?"

"Yes. Include us," Nadine said, standing up again, as if she had too much enthusiasm for this project to sit down even for a minute. "We're going to make a splash with Long Pond's equestrian program. This isn't just about teaching rich girls to ride. This is going to be a community service project that changes lives."

Rosemary stared at the young woman. She'd once considered Nadine a sort of protege. But now Nadine's goals were far outreaching her own humble ones.

It was a beautiful thing, really.

—ee—

Leaving the barn, Rosemary and Nadine spotted the tween girl who had been learning to clean a stall when she arrived. The student was huddled up on a small stack of hay bales, looking miserable.

"Everything okay, Addy?" Nadine asked.

"No," the girl replied sulkily, the single syllable drawn out of her as if it was on a string.

"What's wrong?" Rosemary asked.

"I'm cold," Addy told her, frowning.

"Farmwork warms you up."

"Addy's new to horses," Nadine told Rosemary confidingly. "New to animals, I think, right, Addy?"

"I'm not allowed to have pets at home," Addy declared. "My brother's allergic. To everything. If he was around a dog, he could *die.*"

"Oh, gosh," Rosemary glanced at Nadine. "That's, um . . ."

"Annoying," Addy finished. "Just like my brother." She looked around the barn and shrugged. "Horses smell different than I expected."

"Bad, different?" Rosemary inquired. If a person thought horses smelled bad, they were a lost cause from the start.

"No, not bad." Addy looked at her fingernails. "They're fine. Just different."

Nadine took over. "Think you can get through that stall on your own? I want to check in with Mr. Casey about afternoon lessons."

"Yeah, I can do it." Addy dragged herself back into the stall and picked up the manure fork with languid movements, like a lizard who'd been out of the sun too long.

"Is she learning to ride, or just horsemanship?" Rosemary asked as they headed to the barn door.

"Just horsemanship for now. It's her first day. We'll see if she changes her mind about horses—a few of them have, so far. She's another one of the girls who got sent to me because they weren't fitting in. Some of these girls are real go-getters, some are normal." Nadine grinned. "The normal ones are the sore thumbs here, unfortunately."

Sean was still cantering his tall chestnut gelding around a course of jumps, and they leaned against the arena railing, watching him correct the horse's stride by making slight adjustments to his own position. Sean called himself a recovering rich kid these days; he'd realized how much of his youthful success in the show-ring was related to the top trainers he rode with and the exceptional horses they had mounted him on. Fortunately, he was naturally talented. Some kids would have learned to pose in the saddle and never really advanced on their own. Sean had actual chops to back up his pretty riding.

"He looks a million times better these days than when he came to Catoctin Creek, don't you think?" Nadine shielded her eyes against the slanting sunlight. "I'm so proud of him."

"You should be." Rosemary shifted her gaze past Sean to the mountains rearing up behind the farm. The *school,* she reminded herself, shaking her head slightly. She still thought of Long Pond as a farm; she was nearly always astonished when she walked past the farmhouse and saw the school buildings stretching out behind it, taking over for the cornfields and pastures she'd known all her life. It wasn't a terrible development; her brain just didn't seem to want to keep up with the changes. She supposed it was natural enough wishing things would just stay the same, always.

But of course, everything changed, whether she wanted it to or not.

Chapter Six

Kelly

K elly had never had a muffin this delicious in her entire life.

She was willing to go on the record about it—she was absolutely dying to tell someone about it, as a matter of fact. She crumbled up another bite in her mouth and sent a text to Deepa Jones, the dining columnist who did quick review pieces for WDCN from time to time. They needed to send Deepa and a van up here and interview the crap out of that curly-haired woman behind the counter.

The cafe was cute, too, set in this lovely historic mansion. The whole damn town was cute. Catoctin Creek—what a precious little piece of alliteration! It would have annoyed the old Kelly. The more grumpy, frustrated Kelly.

But she was trying to put that Kelly in the past. She was trying to perk up, seriously. And if Monica's disappearance hadn't convinced her to shake her life up, she knew something else would have. She had a chance now.

Paying off her student loans—yeah, that happened!—gave Kelly a new perspective on life. She didn't have to be Kelly O'Connell of

WDCN News anymore. That pigeonhole, that fetter, that weight on her shoulders? Gone. And now, her future might just open up. Between this newfound freedom and the frightening realization that yes, it really could all be taken away in moments, Kelly O'Connell was ready to shed her former self before she missed her chance.

The old, grumpy, unimpressed Kelly would have been bored in Catoctin Creek, anxious to get back to her busy life around D.C. Sales at new boutiques, making sure she was spotted at restaurant openings, showing up at gallery openings for artists whose work she hated. She'd embraced it all. Because what choice had she had? She was a person with a recognizable face, a household name. She reported on the biggest stories in town, and Washington, D.C. was no small town. She even anchored when Gregory Allan wasn't in the big chair, twice a year for his vacations, and when he was occasionally sick. She was a woman on the move, a woman with a future, a woman in a hurry.

She was sick of that woman.

The new Kelly was trying to be more open to things that were cute, pretty. Even romantic. So when she woke that morning and looked out at the sunrise unveiling the foggy forests just outside town, she didn't immediately and sarcastically think, *Yeah yeah, another country sunrise, start the presses.* She just tried to take it all in. See what this sincerity thing was all about. Irony was so played out, and cloaking herself in ten layers of artificial disdain had never done Kelly any good. If it had, she wouldn't be sitting here.

Of course, then she wouldn't be eating this muffin.

Man, life was hard to figure out sometimes. Better to just let it happen.

Another new move. The old Kelly was your classic over-thinker. Ruining her life, one carefully deliberated chess move at a time.

Not again.

She picked up her latte, took a meditative sip. She'd been so impressed with the latte she'd gotten here last night, she'd asked about the beans from the woman behind the counter. Nikki Mercer. Tired-looking woman, curly hair with the most astonishing corkscrews tumbling from the big clip she tried to hold it back with, unmanicured nails and old scars on her hands. Kelly admired her, wanted to adopt her, or be adopted by her. This was a woman who had a dream and went for it, even if it cost her. She could just tell.

The beans were roasted just on the other side of the mountain, Nikki had told her, at some little roaster in some other tiny town. These Maryland mountaineers stuck together, she guessed. It was going to make the coming week interesting—well, however long she was up here. She'd asked the station to book the Airbnb for two weeks and expected to only need it for a week. She'd figure out Monica's deal quickly once she was here; Kelly was confident of that. But maybe Monica would turn up today, before Kelly even got started.

Maybe Kelly would be heading home this evening.

Kelly nodded to herself at the thought. She could find herself back in Arlington just as easily as she could here, right? Because she hated this case, everything about it: hated dealing with cops, hated thinking about a woman lost in those dark woods beyond the town, hated the intimate knowledge of who Monica was being spilled to all the world. Hated standing in front of a camera and telling spectators in their living rooms about the details of someone's personal life as if they had any stake in this story at all. What business was it of theirs, if the missing woman was a jogger or a swimmer, a painter or a collector, a teacher or a doctor or a marketing executive or a museum curator? And why did they need to know what she was doing in the mountains, or who her boyfriend was, or what he was doing the night she was last seen? Most of what passed for news reporting was satisfying voyeurism, Kelly thought. Again. She was tired of that, more than anything: of satisfying the perceived needs of a public who *surely* had their own problems they'd be better off thinking about.

But she was guilty of it, too. She was guilty of all of it. She'd told the stories, but she'd watched them, too. Voraciously. Trying on other people's lives and problems, then discarding them.

Kelly looked up as the cafe door opened with a little jingle of bells and a swoosh of cold air. A dark-haired woman in a long tweed coat and beautiful brown leather boots came into the cafe. Nikki greeted her like an old friend, and Kelly couldn't help but lean hungrily towards the warmth between them. They were clearly close; Kelly wished for such friendship with every fiber in her being. So what if she'd just spent a decade—the entirety of her twenties—mowing other women down in her quest to get ahead in her job? It had done her no good. She was allowed to turn over a new leaf. She could learn how to be a friend.

She stuck her thumb against the crumbs on her plate, pressing the pad down to catch as many as she could, then popping it into her mouth. The flavor was fantastic, the texture crumbly and rich with all the butter which had gone into it; she should have another. She should just fill up on muffins and then go back to the rental cottage that WDCN corporate travel had booked her into, a tiny garage or an old barn or something. Despite these earthy beginnings, the apartment had the most gorgeous gourmet kitchen, and a lovely loft bed. She could stay there forever, maybe. Never go back to Arlington. Who needed the city? She'd just eat muffins and lounge in her bed.

And maybe a bellyful of muffins would stop Grayson's voice before it even started, repeating over and over the last words he'd said to her: *There's nothing real about you at all.*

Oops, there it was. Too late. She'd have to stop at one muffin and go to work like a big girl, after all. Working was just as effective at shutting up his voice, the one which had echoed for two whole long years in her tired, tired mind.

She didn't know how Monica could stand it, but maybe he had never spoken to her like that.

Kelly nearly laughed aloud. Of *course* he had.

"I just have to go feed those horses," Nikki's friend was saying. "Yeah, things are moving along. Nadine might be able to take a couple, if we can convince the administration they'd be good for the school. I obviously don't want to abuse my position by arguing for them, but I'm short on options. I have got to get them off that property. It's dangerous, and I can't be driving up there twice a day. I have enough going on as it is."

"What did Stephen say about it?" Nikki leaned on the counter. She was careless with her voice, Kelly noticed. She didn't worry about who might hear it. Maybe that was a country thing. No one in D.C. wanted to be overheard. People like Kelly might be nearby, taking notes.

"He didn't say a lot. I think he's just worried there won't be enough money to feed them all for more than a week or two. And he's right. I have to sit down and figure out the numbers. Maybe I can get an emergency grant."

"Rosie-marie, I believe it's time to ask the town for help," Nikki said.

Rosie-marie? Kelly tilted her head. That was an odd name.

"It's funny you say that." The friend laughed, but it was a fragile sound, Kelly thought. "Nadine has some crazy idea in her head about a Christmas carnival. She had me at the barn this morning talking about it."

"Crazy idea? Crazy genius, I think you mean."

"So she already talked to you."

"Of course she did." Nikki's voice was arch. "She knows the real power-players in this town. She called me first thing this morning."

"Well, it's great. If it can be done. There's just one thing . . ." the friend said, trailing off uncertainly.

"Yeah?"

There was silence for a moment. Kelly huddled over her phone, just in case one of them looked around and noticed her. The listener; the eavesdropper.

"The town doesn't owe me anything," the friend said eventually. "It's as simple as that."

"You're not asking them to give you something for nothing. And anyway, every spring fundraiser, they show up for you and donate. And it's not just because you bring along Mighty-mite for the kids to pet."

"It might be because you're strong-arming them when I'm not looking."

"It might be," Nikki agreed. "I hadn't thought of that. But I can strong-arm them in this, too. In fact, it would be my pleasure."

"So, you think I should do it."

"We should do it, Rosemary."

Ah, Kelly nodded to herself. Rosemary. That made more sense as a name.

"Think about it," Nikki said.

Then the bells over the front door chimed. Kelly forgot she was pretending to look at her phone and turned reflexively. Luckily, Rosemary and Nikki did, too, which meant they were facing away from her.

Kelly's breath caught in her throat as she saw the newcomer. A tall, dark stranger stood in the doorway. And what a sight! With his long, sweeping brown overcoat and wide-brimmed hat, he looked just like an apparition from the past. A gangster, maybe. Did this house have ghosts? It probably did! Crap! Kelly was very, very afraid of ghosts. She felt her fingernails bite into her palms as she clenched her hands beneath the table.

"Close that door, William," Nikki scolded. "You're letting all that wind in."

Nikki wouldn't be afraid of ghosts, Kelly was sure of that.

The apparition tugged the door shut and removed his hat, revealing a flesh-and-blood, scowling face. Long-jawed and long-nosed, handsome in an old-fashioned, patrician kind of way, the man looked disagreeably at the women by the counter. "Well? Can I get a decent cappuccino in this town?" he demanded.

Kelly unclenched her fists and let her shoulders relax. He wasn't the ghost of a gangster at all. Just a middle-aged guy with a bad attitude. Which, she had to admit, made a lot more sense than a spirit entering the cafe through the front door. Obviously a spirit would simply waft through the wall.

"I don't know, William, can you?" Nikki challenged. "It depends on how nicely you can ask me."

The newcomer scrunched up his face in a scowl. "Can you *please* make me a cappuccino, dear sweet Nikki Mercer, who never let me copy off her spelling tests even though I always asked nicely, but apparently things have changed, and she now responds to honey?"

Rosemary burst into laughter, and Kelly very nearly did, too. Another old school friend? These people never left home. Kelly had abandoned her southern Virginia hometown as soon as the first college acceptance letter had come in . . . at least, mentally, she had. She'd survived that last summer in her parents' house by working every shift she could at Patsy's Wings and Things, although a fat lot of good that chunk of cash she'd taken with her to Princeton had done in the end.

She wondered if Patsy's was hiring. She could go back and make a fresh start. Maybe her tiny hometown would be just like Catoctin Creek.

No, that wasn't likely. For one thing, her parents were still there. Working, reading, puttering in the yard, asking her if she was happy. The worst question in the world, and their favorite.

"I suppose with that kind of sweet request, I'll *have* to make you a cappuccino," Nikki was laughing. "But I'm charging you double to make up for the damage you've done to my gas bill. I swear the temperature dropped twenty degrees when you stood there making a dramatic entrance."

The guy's face relaxed now. Once the scowl was gone, he was really handsome, in a grizzled and tired kind of way—which was not nothing, Kelly reasoned. Most movie cowboys could claim good looks by meeting the same criteria. Not a Hallmark movie cowboy, mind you. But a real, dark gunslinger flick. "I'll pay it, and gladly. Hey, Rosemary. It's good to see you. But I couldn't even count on you for a gasp of surprise and delight?"

"We knew you were back in town," Rosemary said. "You call in to the feed store to make sure they have enough dog food. Elaine tells us everything, you know."

"Even when we don't want her to," Nikki added.

"Oh, to be sold out by the feed store every time!" William's laugh was attractive, too—lighter than those thunderous features would let on. "I guess buying a hundred pounds of dog food gives a person away."

"Well, if you're gonna travel with four huskies . . ."

"You'd have me on the road *alone?* Someone might abduct me!"

There was silence in the cafe.

William looked around. For a split second, his eyes met Kelly's, and she felt a warm flutter from her head to her toes. Then they danced back to Rosemary and Nikki. "Did I say something wrong?"

Nikki busied herself with the espresso machine. "You didn't hear about the lost hiker?"

"I just came back last night." William looked mystified. "Someone's lost? Someone we know?"

"No, an out-of-towner." Rosemary took over the story for Nikki as the milk frother hissed. "She's been gone for almost a week. Went on a hike from the Cascade Falls trailhead and hasn't been heard from since."

William whistled. "Well, that's a shame. Sorry I made that joke. I haven't been paying any attention to the news. Just me and the boys, on the open road, singing Beach Boys tunes."

Kelly wondered if *the boys* were the huskies or actual people.

"Where are the boys now?" Rosemary asked.

"Back at the house, eating my furniture."

The huskies, then.

"You better be joking . . ."

"I am. I put them in the mudroom while I'm gone. I need to hustle back, though. They've been in there a long time. Might actually eat through a door or something, knowing them."

"You can call ahead if you're ever in a big rush." Nikki reached across the counter and casually slipped his phone from his shirt pocket. She held it up to his face. "Here, unlock this with your big old nose and I'll put my number in."

William obligingly put his face to the phone, unlocking it so that Nikki could type in a phone number.

When she was finished, he accepted his coffee from her and pulled a crumpled bill from his pocket. She snorted and took the money, shaking her head as she unrolled it on the counter. "You still carry cash like a toddler, William Cunningham."

"I spend like one too. Nothing in my truck but candy, bubblegum, and baseball cards."

They snorted with laughter, but Kelly figured *that* joke was inside. She sighed involuntarily, and the threesome looked her way.

"Kelly O'Connell of WDCN News," Nikki said. "Come on over here and meet the town playboy."

William snorted as Kelly stood up, resisting the urge to pat her hair flat. "More like the town recluse, but Nikki's too mean to introduce me correctly."

"Too mean?" Rosemary asked. "For telling the truth? I remember when you brought three girls to Homecoming."

"You could have been the fourth," William reminded her, grinning. "The offer still stands. Go out with me?"

"The answer's still no." Rosemary rolled her eyes. "Anyway, didn't anyone tell you I'm married now?"

"What?" William gasped as Rosemary waved her subtle gold ring at him. "Good grief, Rosemary! And all this time I thought I'd have you to fall back on!"

"That's what happens when you skip a winter at home. Where were you last year?"

He shrugged. "You know, a man goes to the Baja, a man gets distracted by all the swaying palm trees."

Nikki snorted. "You should have stayed."

"And miss out on the gossip? I *had* to come back. This town's like a magnet."

Through all this banter, Kelly stood awkwardly a few feet away, wishing Nikki had never summoned her—or that she'd just waved from the table and gone back to her phone. Like a normal person.

"Guys," Nikki said, rescuing her. "Say hello to Kelly."

"Hi, Kelly," William said obediently.

"It's nice to meet you, Kelly." Rosemary held out a hand. "What brings you to Catoctin Creek?"

Kelly had a sudden impulse to lie. Something about William's presence made her feel foolish, as if he'd figure out in an instant that she'd come here because of an ex-boyfriend. But that was crazy. He knew nothing about her. "I'm a reporter," she admitted.

"I'm here to investigate the missing hiker case." It was easier to leave Monica's name, her personal connection, out of it.

"Oh, wow," Rosemary said, her hand going to her mouth. "Do you have—have you heard anything we haven't—"

Kelly was about to reply when she felt William's eyes on her. She glanced up at him—really up, he was *tall*—and saw him frowning. The expression immediately got her back up. Kelly was used to people not wanting her around; part of the joy of being a television news reporter was always showing up where one wasn't wanted.

But this guy had just walked into this cafe and the women had greeted him like an old friend, but he clearly didn't live here year round, or even every year. So, who didn't belong where? And what was this guy's story, anyway? She felt her brows coming together as they stared each other down.

William was the first to look away, his jaw working as if he was choking back something he wanted to say to her. Kelly was instantly suspicious.

"I don't know anything special," she told Rosemary, flicking her gaze back to the kind woman in front of her. "I just want to do everything I can to make sure she's found."

"Well, I wish you well. I'm sure if you need anything, anyone in the town will be happy to help you."

It was a pleasant idea. Kelly knew it wasn't true. Small towns didn't welcome reporters. She was just being kind. "I'm sure they will," Kelly assured her. "Thank you."

"Well, I should go." Rosemary gave her a little wave. "Apparently, I'm working on a Christmas carnival. And I have twelve horses to take care of."

Kelly wished Rosemary a nice day and went back to her table. As she lifted her coffee cup to her lips, she watched the threesome extending their goodbyes. Her eyes lingered on the tall man at the center of their little group. She knew she had to find out more about this William Cunningham, a man with four huskies and a potentially guilty conscience.

Chapter Seven

Nikki

William didn't hang around much longer. Nikki was sorry he left so soon; she always liked it when his face showed up in town again. Some years he didn't come for more than a few weeks, and he'd remained absent all last winter. Other years, he came in autumn and stayed through late spring. Whenever he arrived, though, William was always gone before Memorial Day. He joked that he wasn't allowed in town during the summer months. Nikki often wondered what the real reason was, but she never asked.

By the time he left and Rosemary followed, taking a box of lemon-raspberry bars with her, Kelly had gone back to her table by the window, nursing her coffee. She was clearly trying to focus all her attention on her phone, but Nikki could see through an eavesdropper at a hundred paces. She marched over and picked up the empty muffin plate, watching with grim amusement as Kelly tried not to cringe.

"I guess you want to know everyone's backstory now," Nikki said, standing over her. "You heard just enough to titillate, right?

The three girls at Homecoming story is true. The spelling test story is only partially true, though. I let him copy sometimes, when I thought the words were too hard for him. William's a terrible speller."

Kelly glanced up and gave her a tentative smile. "I couldn't help but listen. I'm sorry. It's kind of my job."

"No, it's not." Nikki glanced around at her quiet cafe, then she slid into the seat across from Kelly, setting the empty plate down again. "Your job isn't to eavesdrop. But don't worry, that's what country diners are all about. Just because this place is a bit fancier than the Blue Plate doesn't mean the rules about gossip change. So I'll trade you. No hard feelings for eavesdropping if you tell me what you're really doing in Catoctin Creek."

She watched the girl draw back in her chair. "I don't know what you mean by *really*—"

"You're the only one here this morning." Nikki spread her hands, taking in the entirety of the empty cafe. "And I did a little snooping last night, and my old garage is the only booked rental in town. Yes," she added, looking smug. "You're staying in my old apartment. The kitchen's nice, isn't it? You're welcome. I tested just about every recipe on the menu using that kitchen."

"I promise you I didn't lie about who I am." Kelly licked her lips, looking furtive. "I'm really a reporter with WDCN and I'm really covering the missing hiker story."

"I believe that part. But I don't know why you're really here. No one else sent a reporter to stay. A few have passed through, but they're stopping in all the towns around the state park, all the way up to the Pennsylvania state line."

"Well," Kelly said, "I guess I had a feeling."

Nikki snorted. "You can do better than that."

Kelly sighed. "Between you and me?"

Nikki's eyebrows went up. "Between you and me. Bakers' honor."

She took a breath. Whatever it was, she wasn't dealing with it well. "Her boyfriend is my ex-fiancé ."

Nikki leaned back in her chair. Now *that* was a surprise. "Her— the missing hiker's boyfriend? Seriously?"

Kelly nodded. "Her name is Monica Waters. And he—Grayson —has gone out with a few girls since we broke up. It was two years ago, so I'm kind of old news, not even worth interviewing at this point. But yeah, I—" she swallowed hard. "I feel invested in this. I want to find Monica. And that's why I'm really here, as quick as I could get the assignment. I know she didn't go far from the trail. She's around Catoctin Creek."

The bell on the door sang out its brassy *ding*, and Nikki's eyes flew to the person walking in. Her shoulders relaxed as she recognized the new entry. "Hey, Caitlin," she called, "you're here early today." Then her glance went back to Kelly's face. The young woman faced her with obvious nervousness. "I don't know much about your line of work, but I'm not sure you're the right person for this assignment. A little too close?"

Kelly's cheeks went red. A blushing reporter—*that* had probably gotten her into trouble on the job. But she held her chin high despite her obvious embarrassment. "No one is going to dig as deep or find as many leads as I am. *Because* I'm invested. I'm not just here to get my check. I want to know where she is, and I'm going to find out."

"Well, you better be careful," Nikki said, standing up. "This is a typical small town here. They're not going to want to answer a lot of questions."

Kelly smiled at her. "Honestly? I'm used to people who don't want to talk to me."

Nikki was startled. What a bleak thing to say. But she accepted it as a close to their conversation. "Let me know when you want a refill," she said, and headed back behind the counter.

ele

Nikki felt a little guilty when Kelly finally asked for a second latte, took her cup, and skedaddled for the door. But at the same time, she was pretty sure the girl had no business coming up here and rooting around for the missing hiker. *Way* too close to the case. And what if the boyfriend really had done it—whatever *it* was? She could be next in line. Nikki had listened to enough murder podcasts to know how these things worked. She shook her head. *Men.*

"Who's the city girl?" Caitlin came over from the table where she'd been tapping away at her laptop. Her phrasing surprised Nikki. Most of the time, Nikki considered Caitlin a convert to urban life, even if she did live in her family farmhouse and spend most of her days shuttling between investments around Catoctin Creek. Caitlin just *seemed* like a city girl, born in the wrong place and not quite ready to remedy it yet. But if Nadine was right, and she was thinking of moving, that would be an unsurprising change.

"That's a reporter, here about the missing hiker," Nikki said, pretending it was all she knew. "You heard anything new about her?"

"Nothing," Caitlin said, shaking her head. "Nasty business. Hey, listen, can I get a cortado? Do you know how to make that?"

Nikki rolled her eyes. "Sure. You can have a cortado." In a town where most people would have a hard time figuring out the difference between a latte and a cappuccino, trust Caitlin to order a drink that wasn't even on the handwritten coffee bar menu. Luckily, Nikki liked to experiment with her espresso machine. She figured she could barista with the best in Brooklyn at this point. "How's the real estate game treating you?" she asked, pouring milk into a pitcher.

"Not bad. I'm looking at the Wayne place this afternoon."

"Oh, no kidding?" Nikki eyed her over the espresso machine. "To do what? Tell me you're not building a subdivision, Caitlin."

"Do you really think I'm that evil?" Caitlin shook her head, her smooth hair sliding back into place like it wasn't even real. "Although between you and me, Ethel Hauffmann would sell that place for six houses per acre if she thought they'd get the zoning pushed through. But I'm thinking five-acre farmettes. Easier on everyone, keeps the area agricultural, brings in some new blood, but not *too* many new people. What do you think of that idea?"

"I suppose it's fine," Nikki said, dipping the steam wand into the milk. It squealed as it went to work, giving her a moment to consider the potential new residents Caitlin would bring into the area. They'd probably be fairly well-off, upper-middle-class, ex-city folk. She pursed her lips, thinking of the foot traffic in the cafe. It would double—triple? The weekenders from D.C. loved this cafe; they far preferred it to the hokey charm of the Blue Plate Diner.

She could start offering full breakfasts, maybe, if she converted the empty back sitting room into a second dining room . . .

"Someone's counting her chickens," Caitlin laughed as Nikki switched off the steamer. "Come on, you like the idea, don't you?"

"I don't think it's your worst," Nikki said with a shrug. She slowly poured the milk into the espresso, even adding a little lucky clover design she'd learned from a YouTube video. "Sounds like you'd be bringing in customers for me, and for Connie, too," she added. City people loved fancy ice cream, and Connie lived for crazy flavors. Last week she'd been experimenting with a cranberry sauce flavor for Thanksgiving.

Caitlin nodded. "And for the market, and for the salons, and for who knows what stores haven't been opened up yet. You know the Trouts want to expand, and Hazel McKinley has been dreaming of opening up a quilting and knitting shop for years. The Wesleys are living in Frederick now, but I ran into Ashley the other day and they'd like more space than they've got in town, and her wife is looking for a place to open a local co-op, selling farm goods and crafts and honey, that kind of thing. All these little places could thrive if we bring in more traffic, you know?" Caitlin looked down at her coffee and smiled. "And look at *you*, the budding barista!"

"Budding?" Nikki snorted. "I'm already an expert."

"This is beautiful. I hate to drink it." Caitlin took a sip anyway. "And delicious. So, you're on my side?"

"Do I have to take sides?"

"Honey, this is Catoctin Creek. You absolutely have to take sides. And I expect you to be on mine. If I try to get the zoning changed, there will be *words.*"

Nikki imagined two factions at the zoning board meeting, shouting across the volunteer firefighters' hall. "Sounds exciting. But it turns out, I have a little request of you, too."

Caitlin's smile was devilish. "Do tell."

"You heard about Rosemary and the Wayne horses, right?"

"Tragic," Caitlin said, taking another sip. "A big problem."

"Rosemary needs temporary stabling for the winter and she needs a barn extension built next year. For situations just like this. And if we keep adding residents with five acres, they're going to buy horses and there will be more situations with bad fits, retirements, that kind of thing. She will need to expand."

"I agree. What's my role?"

"We're talking about putting together the old Christmas carnival again. All proceeds to benefit Rosemary's rescue."

Caitlin forgot to take a tiny sip of her hot cortado. She threw it back, made a sort of lugging sound, then choked. Finally, she looked into her cup in dismay. "Well, I killed the lucky clover," she said around a cough. "I'm sure that's not a sign or anything. But, hey! A Christmas carnival! I remember the old ones. They were a lot of fun. Maybe a little basic but, I guess that's just what this town needs."

Nikki narrowed her eyes. "So? Are you on our side with this?"

"Of course!" Caitlin said, waving her free hand. "Anything you need. Just ask."

"We'll be taking you up on that," Nikki warned her. "Nadine's spearheading this, but the girl is busy. She can't do everything on her own. And you know how Rosemary is with crowds and strangers. I'm not going to ask her to get on the phone and ask for quotes from ride companies or something."

"Nikki, I'm telling you that I am glad to help," Caitlin said, all traces of her former flippant self suddenly erased. She leaned forward, one hand on the counter, and met Nikki's eyes. "You and Rosemary are my oldest friends, even if we don't always remember our school days the same way. I am here for both of you."

Chapter Eight

Kelly

There was no way to hang out in the bakery after that conversation with Nikki, so Kelly took a second latte to go and headed out into the crisp morning. She knew more caffeine wasn't the right choice; nine o'clock was awfully early to be on her fourth shot of espresso. But she wanted the vigor in her veins; she wanted to feel like she could do anything, and anyway, it was very good coffee.

She walked up Main Street, glancing into the windows of the shops facing the cracked sidewalk. Catoctin Creek was still only half-awake, she thought, a hamlet that was on its first baby steps towards its inevitable tourist-town rejuvenation. The result would be a revision of history, a place that was only half-real, but at least it would *look* alive. There were the usual suspects of an aging country town which had been quietly decomposing: the flyblown blinds in the window of the farm insurance agency's abandoned local branch; the faded posters of extinct hairstyles in a shuttered salon. But the small grocery store was already bustling with morning shoppers, and the Blue Plate Diner, a squat, sixties-era building which sat alone in a gravel parking lot, was doing a booming business.

"Nikki must hate this," Kelly murmured to herself, watching the breakfast trade through the diner's plate-glass windows. All that effort to build the beautiful bakery at the end of the street, and the locals were here, eating bacon and eggs and buttered white toast. But maybe the diner was like the grocery store: a necessary place for the locals, for the residents who would never change, no matter how many tourists spilled into their town looking for antiques and artisan cheese. Maybe Nikki was just hedging her bets.

Smart, to have her feet on both sides of the stream. If she were nimble enough, she could hop to the other side when one began to collapse.

And her friend, Rosemary? Kelly pondered what she'd heard. Too many horses, a riding school, a rescue. In the midst of doing research on the town before she'd driven up, Kelly had heard of the fancy school that had moved into town, bringing a staff of new residents mostly pulled from New York City—all of whom probably crowded the bakery for breakfast on weekends, now that she thought about it.

Rosemary probably had something to do with that. Fiddling around with a small charity, rescuing animals, asking for money from the newcomers to town. Well, it made sense. If they were going to show up and start using the town's resources, they ought to contribute.

So, there was nothing too interesting or surprising going on there, nothing which made Kelly pause in her footsteps. It was

William Cunningham who had her attention. He looked at her like a man who was waiting for trouble.

He looked like a man who could *cause* a lot of trouble.

Good trouble?

Kelly shook her head, irritated with herself. Okay, there was something to his flashing brown eyes and his mane of dark brown, gray-streaked hair. Something which awakened her instincts and held her attention. She suspected it was mostly his looks, though. He might have the face of a desperado, but his eyes gave away his thoughts, so he couldn't be *too* dangerous.

The real problems out there were the men who could hide it all. Men like Grayson, keeping a woman guessing and squirming, on his hook for years. She clenched one fist in her pocket, willing him out of her mind. But, of course, she was only in Catoctin Creek *because* of Grayson, so it was hard to forget about him. Every step she took was a reminder that he'd hurt her, dumped her, and then, two years later, done something to his present girlfriend.

She didn't know what, not exactly.

Kelly didn't believe that Grayson was capable of doing someone physical harm; she didn't think he had Monica tied up in the forest or that he'd killed her and dumped her body in a quarry or anything like that. She believed Monica was out there, and on her own, and had chosen to disappear into the mountains of her own free will—but that her will had been manipulated by a man who was well practiced in the art of gaslighting. She didn't know Monica, of course, but she knew what Monica was going through. She'd buried herself in her work to escape Grayson's deceptions, his cutting remarks, his smooth suggestions that she wasn't good enough, wasn't real enough, just plain wasn't *enough*. What was so different between vanishing into a career and vanishing into the forest?

She stood on the corner of Main and Catoctin, beneath the Victorian turret over the ice cream parlor, which was definitely part of the new and improved Catoctin Creek—there was that telltale word, *artisanal*, in the window lettering—and regarded the town. A nice place as any to disappear, she figured. Maybe if she waited long enough, Monica would just turn up. And if she could be the first person to talk to the woman, she could help her understand what she'd gone through, why she'd felt the need to run away from her life.

It probably wouldn't be that simple, though. The caffeine hummed in her veins, giving her the energy she'd been looking for. Maybe it wasn't *real* energy; maybe it was just the shakes and an unquiet mind, but either way, Kelly was going to milk it for everything it was worth. She turned on her heel and headed back towards her apartment. How odd, to think it had been Nikki's. But she supposed everything in this small town was shared in some way. The really interesting part was seeing the way she fit into it, already, almost as if she'd already become part of the interwoven web of Catoctin Creek.

If so, it was the most she'd ever belonged anywhere in her entire life.

"The reporter."

Kelly whirled. There was no mistaking that gravelly voice; even though she'd just met him, William Cunningham had a way of sticking with a person.

For her, anyway.

He came up the sidewalk with a brown grocery bag under one arm, the coffee cup from Nikki's cafe in his free hand. His long coat hung open despite the frigid morning. And he looked down his nose at her as if he had something to say.

"Hi," she said, because the silence growing between them was awkward enough to force it. "I was just walking home."

"Home?" He lifted an eyebrow. "I thought you said you're from the city."

"The apartment," she corrected, hating him. "Are you always this much of a stickler for correct verbiage?"

William's stern expression cracked at that. "No," he said, grinning at her. "I'm just kind of a crusty old jerk."

Kelly burst into surprised laughter. "You *are*, too! I didn't want to say anything, obviously, but . . ." She let her voice trail off, grinning back. He had a nice smile.

"Again, that's what I get for living with four dogs. They never notice I have no manners." He shifted the grocery bag, moving its weight around. She heard cans clinking together.

"That must be heavy. I'll let you go—"

"No, it's fine." The grin remained on his face, warming her from the inside out. "Just some essentials until I get my kitchen in working order. You can't abandon a three hundred-year-old house for a year without expecting some heavy repairs, I guess."

"Three hundred years!" Kelly gaped at him. "That must be one of the oldest houses in the state."

"It is. Although it's not quite three hundred years old. I *might* have exaggerated." He gave her an odd look. "Or I might be lying. Can you tell, Miss Bigshot Reporter?"

Kelly felt all the warmth sink right out of her toes and dissipate onto the cracked sidewalk beneath her fleece-lined boots. Oh, it was going to be like that, was it? Right back to the distrustful attitude he'd given her in the cafe? Fine. "It's *Ms* Bigshot Reporter," she informed him. "And I do a thing called fact-checking? So I guess if I were to report on your house for any reason, I'd call the county and get hold of the tax records. They're public," she added. "Anyone can do it."

He was probably some anti-government nut who hated the idea of anyone knowing his private business, too.

But to her surprise, William didn't launch into a tirade about the deep state. Instead, he nodded, as if he'd sized her up and was impressed with what he'd seen. "Well, your diligence is appreciated," he said. "Keep up the good work." And he moved to pass her on the sidewalk.

Kelly automatically stepped to one side, giving him room, but her mind was racing. If she was to believe her instincts, there was a *lot* William didn't want her to know. And Kelly O'Connell had very good instincts. It was one of the reasons she'd become a successful reporter, a job which had never even been on her shortlist of careers.

She frowned after him as he walked down the sidewalk to his parked truck, a big, battered Chevy with a cap over the bed. Her observations were automatic, reflexes of her job: the Maryland license plate, the bumper stickers naming a couple of breweries out in Colorado and Wyoming, the reddish clay under the fenders that all the November rain hadn't managed to wash away.

He put the grocery bag on the passenger seat, slammed the door, and looked back at her. Even from thirty feet away, she felt the force of his gaze. Very carefully, Kelly took a bite of her inner cheek, pressing her molars down on the skin. The pressure satisfied something deep within her; some demand she couldn't name. For a while, she'd done it too hard, and scarred the inside of her mouth. She had learned to be more careful.

But now, as he let his eyes rake her up and down, she ground down the way she used to. The way she had when Grayson had proposed, the way she had when she'd told him to get out of her life.

The way she had at the most emotionally frightening moments of her life.

William got into the truck and it started with a rough bang. She turned her head away, looking into the empty ice cream parlor as if she was ready for a cone at this early hour. The menu on the back wall was written in swirling, colorful chalk. "Cranberry sauce," Kelly murmured. "Weird."

She went on staring at the menu until he was gone, the truck's loud growl disappearing down Main Street. She didn't feel any better about William Cunningham now than she had after their brief meeting in the cafe. He was a secretive man.

And she was here because of secrets.

Chapter Nine

William

The driveway had definitely been overgrown during the past year. The day before, William had been forced to climb out of his truck and snap back tree branches and brown, grasping vines, just to get to the house. If he'd come home back in September, the way he'd planned, he'd have needed a machete to break some of the thicker growth back. But Labor Day had come and gone and he still hadn't felt ready to return home. So he'd lingered out west a little longer. And it had worked out. Now, with the countryside in the grips of this November cold snap and the weeds dying off, he could break the stalks off with his hands.

Now, the rough remnants of the weeds scraped alongside his truck, but there wasn't much more damage to be done to the exterior of this old warrior. William patted his dashboard affectionately, listening to the engine growl as the truck ascended the final hill before the driveway gave way to the overgrown lawn of Hilltop House.

He winced at the sight. Oof, this place was a mess. A year spent alone was not good for a house, especially one of a few centuries' vintage. Just as he'd said to Kelly.

For a moment, his jaw stiffened, thinking of the blonde-haired reporter he'd met in town. She'd looked at him as if he had some secret she wanted to ferret out. Well, it was a nosy profession. But she was going to have to learn to mind her own business in Catoctin Creek. He wouldn't worry about seeing much of her; he only went to town for necessities, anyway. He parked his truck in front of the house's wide front porch and tried to put the girl out of his mind.

He had plenty of real problems to worry about. Keeping Hilltop House intact was chief amongst them. He hated that he'd left the house for so long; it was disrespectful, and it went against all of his principles. But every time he'd tried to come back, over the past year and a half of traveling, the thought was enough to make him break into a sweat. It happened sometimes; there was a reason he didn't live here year round. But he'd let it go on for too long this time around.

But now he was back, and he was going to dedicate himself to working on the house. He was going to do right by Hilltop House. At least, until he felt the need to leave again.

The dogs set up a barking din from the mudroom out back as he climbed out of the truck and hoisted his bag of groceries. The front porch was reached by three very rotten stairs, so he went around the side of the house, noticing new gaps in the mortar between the sun-mellowed red bricks and sagging eaves heaped with pine needles. He shouldn't have let the place sit without a caretaker. He hadn't even meant to. He never did. He just didn't know who he could trust to sit with his house full of ghosts for a season or three while he wandered.

William paused with his hand on the mudroom door, ready to let out his raucous pack of huskies, but something was wrong; some instinct stilled his hand. His eyes roved over the backyard, taking in the brown morass of weeds, piles of plants which had been killed in the season's first frost and huddled over in death. He'd arrived so late last night, he hadn't seen the place for the mess it was. But in the clear light of this cold morning, it was surprisingly easy to see the path that had been beaten through the tangles of weeds.

Someone had walked through this yard, and very recently.

He flicked his eyes around, searching from the fir trees ringing the house to the dark woods beyond the yard, their interlocking branches marching right up the slopes of the Catoctin Mountains. Nothing. He turned around, taking in the leaning stone barn and its little family of outbuildings, and the overgrown pastures where horses and cattle had once grazed. The property bordered the state park on the west side, but that was a long walk through thick forest, and no trails led down to the fence. There was no easy option for anyone to find this place by accident.

William frowned, hoping whoever had been wandering through the property was gone now. Because the dogs were about to tear down the door, and he had to let them loose, and while they weren't bad dogs, he wasn't sure just what they'd do if they found someone they didn't like out there when they were this hyped up.

Barking, scrabbling at the wood. The door actually shifted under his hand, reminding him that huskies were heavy dogs. If he didn't want to replace the door frame, he had to let them out.

And William had enough repairs to make.

"Well, here you go," he grunted, swinging the door open and stepping back.

Black and white flashed past him as his pack of huskies tore out the door, flying into the weed-strewn backyard. William smiled as he watched them race around, biting at each other and barking rapidly. "Crazy mutts," he muttered.

Lola, Trina, Didi, and Bob: they were his best friends, his travel companions, and his hiking buddies. They were also sisters and brother from the same litter, because William wasn't good at picking things. He wanted everything, and he'd been raised to *get* everything—kind of like the way he'd taken three girls to Homecoming. He shook his head at the memory. He couldn't believe Rosemary brought that up in front of the reporter.

The reporter. Kelly O'Something. Back in the cafe, she'd looked at him with such suspicion, he'd nearly taken a step backwards. Run out the door. Anything to get away from that piercing gaze. She had pretty blue eyes, maybe a little pale if he was being completely honest, but they'd taken one look at him and hadn't liked what they'd seen. She hadn't been so bold on the street, though. Nervous, when she was alone. William shook his head. No good in replaying their conversations over and over. She could go sniffing around Catoctin Creek all she wanted. He'd be up here, getting work done and sitting by the fire and—"Lola!" he shouted. "Stop humping your brother!"

And wrangling dogs.

William spent the day cleaning out Hilltop's huge kitchen. The renovations at the house had stopped in the eighties, right about when his parents stopped bringing the family to western Maryland for the Christmas holidays. William remembered the first holiday they hadn't come; he'd been ten, and he'd been heartbroken.

He knew from phone calls and letters that his grandparents had still come to Hilltop House for the holidays, and so had some of his cousins. He hadn't been able to understand why the Willowdale branch of the family remained at their chilly Chesapeake compound for the entirety of the Christmas and New Year holidays, despite the obvious superiority of the Hilltop sledding hills, and then didn't even go back to Hilltop for their usual visits throughout the year. No Presidents Day weekend, no spring break—they spent *that* in Florida, bumming around on boring beaches—and worst of all, no summer vacation.

His grandparents always invited them to come up, but his parents refused to go back. William couldn't understand it. Who would give up this magnificent family farm in the mountains? There were horses, and cows, and a couple of sheep. There were rabbits in a hutch in the barn. There was a creek with crayfish hiding beneath rocks, threatening to pinch small boys' toes. There were trees to climb. And most of all, there was his family: a whole rabble of Cunninghams and assorted other cousins and aunts and uncles, all gathered in the family home beneath the Catoctin Mountains.

Occasionally his parents relented, acknowledging he had no place in their feud with his grandparents, and let him come back for summer. In the gap between his sophomore and junior years of high school, armed with a driver's license and a battered old Honda of his own, William stayed. He could get himself to school in Catoctin Creek. Reluctantly, but not willing to fight with him anymore about it, his parents signed off on the move and his grandparents let him stay through the next two school years, allowing William to spend his final two years of high school attending Catoctin Creek High School.

Then he went to college, his grandparents embarked on a world tour with a few of his aunts and uncles, and they never came home again. The world was a dangerous place. In their will, his grandparents left William the family house, but no explanations.

So William didn't know how it all went together, the falling-out with his family and this time capsule of a house, but there was no doubt that the years matched up. They'd stopped updating the place right around the time his parents stopped coming. The off-white appliances, worn linoleum, and hideous brown tiles were an affront to his architectural education, but he'd never cared enough to change it. Coming home to Hilltop House had been enough.

But this winter would be different, he'd vowed, mapping out the changes he'd make as he'd driven himself and the dogs back from Colorado. This winter, he was going to restore the kitchen of Hilltop, and maybe the dining room, as well. Bring it back to its Federal-era beauty. Or at least, a contemporary edition of how he imagined it must have looked like back then.

The dogs weren't impressed with his newfound mission. All morning, they flooded in and out of the kitchen, tails wagging, eyes expectant, waiting for him to pick up a ball and throw it, or grab a walking stick and head out into the forest for a chilly hike. Lola, the huntress of the family, sought to appease him, bringing in her finds from the overgrown wilds of the yard and pastures: an ancient leather man's shoe, a deer antler, a bright red knit cap. This last item caught William's attention, and he prised it from her jaws, thanking her for the gift with a piece of carrot. But there wasn't much to learn from the dripping-wet hat, except that Lola was probably leading her pack far too deeply into the forest and finding hiking trails.

"Am I going to have to drop everything and build a new fence?" William asked his dogs, and they bounced around, throwing themselves over one another's backs in an effort to please him.

Yes, definitely, you are!

"Don't make me do it." William threw everyone bits of carrot and tried to get back to work. He was prying up the ugly reddish linoleum on the floor, and it was dirty, backbreaking work. But it was still better than digging fence post holes. He let Lola take the hat back and left them to their wanderings. There wouldn't ever be anyone within two miles of this house, anyway. Especially not in November. The hat had probably been blown here, or dropped by a bird taking it back to their nest.

Or lost by whoever had been wandering around the backyard before he'd gotten home this morning.

William dropped the linoleum and went to the fridge, pulling out a pitcher of water. He'd filled it at the spring house this morning. It was always a relief to open the wooden door beneath the house's southwest corner and see the water still bubbling up from its well, spilling into a moss-covered drain. The drain led the water outside, and it would emerge in a stream several dozen feet from the house, tumbling down the hill and through the pastures. When William was a kid, he'd loved to play in the stream, and know the sparkling water originated somewhere inside his house— although he hadn't understood then that it came from beneath the ground, or that some wise Cunningham in the eighteenth century had found the spring and decided to build his house on top of it.

It wasn't until he was much, much older and the sole heir of Hilltop House that he realized he was in possession of a water system which never froze, even in the coldest winter. Pretty great.

The Hilltop House well was actually a local legend, which had found its way into several magazine articles and a few books about the history of the Catoctin Mountains. There was never much to say about the Cunninghams, who, despite being some of the first English settlers in the region, kept to themselves and out of the papers, believing as always that making a fuss was not the refined thing to do.

At least William knew where he got it from. You couldn't fight six generations of family tradition, right?

He drank straight from the pitcher, savoring the crisp, clean flavor of the water. Outside, Lola was barking. No surprise there. Trina and Didi joined in; but they generally followed their sister in everything. It wasn't until Bob started barking with his rusty voice that William grew curious. Bob was the quiet one. When he started talking, he really wanted to be heard.

William glanced at the shotgun leaning in a corner by the mudroom door. He hesitated, then picked it up. It was November, after all. If they'd found a bear, it would be woozy, and angry at being woken up. He wouldn't kill an animal without cause, but he'd damn sure be ready to scare it away. He'd learned that much while spending his summers out in the Rockies.

Be ready for anything.

The dogs were barking at the old dairy. He saw them as soon as he burst through the mudroom door, wagging their tails as they frantically ran in circles around the half-hidden stone building a few hundred feet from the house.

"Oh, no." William quickened his pace, half-running across the uneven ground. They'd had bears in the dairy before, and he hadn't checked to be sure the door was locked tight this fall. Another reason he absolutely must get a caretaker for next summer. He was going to work on the ad tonight. He'd line up some college student before all the good ones were snapped up by farms and estates in Ireland and England and France . . .

"Dogs! Stop that barking!" he shouted. Lola turned and looked at him, and he'd swear her expression was astonished. As if he'd just given her the most ridiculous command she'd ever heard.

Lola had never really regarded him as smarter than she was.

Trina and Didi backed away from the dairy, leaving Bob to continue barking at the door. The dairy's front door faced the barn, away from the house. The windows on two sides were covered with old newspapers, but there was nothing to see inside; William had emptied it out two summers ago, bitterly disappointed to find the old creaming pans and pitchers were long gone and the space had been used as storage for broken chairs and boxes from the house.

He approached the door cautiously, the shotgun at the ready. If a bear had broken down the door, he was willing to concede that was the bear's business, but how exactly was he going to approach having a bear hibernating a few hundred feet from his house all winter? It was going to be problematic. William again saw himself digging fence post holes and bit back a groan.

Bob wagged his tail furiously and barked a few more times, but now he was giving William encouraging looks, his blue husky eyes fixing on him briefly before glancing back into the dairy. *Come on, Dad,* his expression said clearly. *Come and see what we found!*

"Okay," William murmured. "Easy there, Bob. Let's just back away, okay?"

He walked a dozen feet past the dairy, then turned around, squinting against the late afternoon sun to see into its shadowy depths.

The door was closed.

"Oh," William said. He glanced back at the dogs, who crowded around the door, tails going a mile a minute. Lola barked sharply, her ears pricked as if she'd just heard movement inside.

Animals don't close the door behind them.

William glanced down at the gun in his hands. This wasn't going the way he wanted at all. If someone was in there, a human and not a bear, he couldn't go bursting in with a shotgun. Whoever was in the dairy knew he was out here, and if they were armed, they'd shoot him the moment he opened the door.

He nodded slowly, knowing what he had to do.

"Come on, dogs," he called loudly. "Let's go on back to the house." And he trudged past the dairy again, close enough for his footsteps to be clearly heard inside, just inches from the paper-wrapped windows. He whistled, again and again, until the dogs followed.

Back in the house, the dogs looked at him with clear disappointment. He doled out kibble, hoping an early supper would do the trick. But he knew he'd failed his pack today. They'd

found trouble, and told him about it, and he'd called them liars—
or as good as, anyway.

William sighed and threw himself down on the old sofa in the
front living room. The last rays of sunlight were shining through
the dusty windows, casting a warm, golden glow on the room—
and the cobwebs in every corner. William shook his head at the
mess and opened his phone, flicking around to see what was going
on in the world outside. He thumbed past several national stories
he didn't want to know a thing about, then paused on a local
update. *Boyfriend Questioned in Missing Hiker Case.*

William read the story, then started searching out older ones,
reading the case of the missing Monica Waters with greater and
greater concentration. Thirty-one years old, athletic, a physical
therapist—the stats were fairly bland, but they told Willam what
he needed to know: it was highly unlikely she'd gotten lost in the
woods. It was much more likely, according to the police, that
Monica had been the victim of foul play.

Or, William thought grimly, she's living in my dairy.

Chapter Ten

Kelly

K elly had never liked hiking. Too many opportunities to slip on loose rocks, turn an ankle crossing a cold creek, or get bitten up by no-see-ums and mosquitoes. Maybe she'd just had bad experiences with it, but the woods and Kelly were not friends.

So she faced the Cascade Falls trail head with some trepidation. It was bad enough knowing her ex fiancé's girlfriend had stepped off on this very trail last week and then apparently vanished from the face of the earth. Even a real nature lover would feel some serious trepidation about that kind of association. Still, she knew what she had to do. This wasn't just for Monica—a woman she didn't know, but could absolutely empathize with. This was for herself, as well.

A couple of state park rangers were hovering near the trailhead map, drinking coffee and chatting as they soaked up the few rays of sunshine finding their way through the treetops. A man and a woman, they stopped talking as she approached, feeling like a walking target in her new boots and dark jeans, with the crease from the store shelf still running up the legs. They would probably stop her, she thought, probably put an end to this nonsense before it started.

She lifted her chin, ready to be told she couldn't go into the woods.

"Be careful out there, miss," the man said. He was very young, baby-faced, with a razor scrape on his chin. Kelly wondered why he didn't grow a big, scary, mountain man beard. It would look great with the uniform and that wide-brimmed hat all park rangers seemed to wear. He continued, "You might have heard of a missing woman in the woods. This is the trailhead she got lost from. So we're warning everyone to check their cell phone battery and make sure they've got a map."

The female park ranger produced a folded piece of paper. Kelly took it and looked at the rudimentary map: a few dark lines, a few dots to indicate points of interest. Sure, super helpful, she thought. Aloud, she asked, "How long should I allow myself to hike the whole trail?"

The woman glanced at her partner, as if to say, *We got a novice here.* "Okay, first thing, it's not a loop," she explained. "When you get to Cascade Falls, you either turn around or you join the Cascade trail. That leads to the other side of the mountain. And *that's* how you can get lost. There's a whole trail system up there. Do us all a favor and don't go a step past the falls, okay?"

Kelly hated being talked down to, but she knew she deserved it this time. "Got it," she agreed, pocketing the map.

The male ranger wasn't satisfied with her yet. "You could end up in Pennsylvania, or West Virginia," he told her. "Anywhere in the Alleghenies. The trails just keep going. You could end up on the Appalachian Trail and find yourself in Maine."

"We'd find you before you got to Maine," the woman said wryly.

"Well, yeah. I'm just saying. It's denser out there than the news is leading people to believe."

"They want a body," the woman sighed. "Media's all the same. Sensation sensation. Can't accept someone might just be lost in the woods."

"They don't know anything about anything," the man agreed.

"Well, I guess I'll see you shortly," Kelly said brightly.

"Two hours," the woman said, as if realizing they hadn't answered her only question. "That's how long. You should be outta there and on your way back to civilization by lunchtime."

"Perfect," Kelly said. "I'll see you then."

"We go to lunch at twelve," the guy said. "So you might miss us."

"Okay." *I'll try to cope with my disappointment.*

They looked at each other for a minute. Then the park rangers stepped aside, and Kelly stepped off onto the trail.

—ele—

She panted her way up the slowly rising trail, hating the woods more with every passing minute. The way the dark clumps of fir trees would gather over the trail, pawing at her with their furry branches. The way roots would seem to rise out of nowhere and trip her as she gained elevation. The way the topmost branches of the canopy were still clinging tightly to their dying summer leaves, blocking out the wan November sunlight. The way the underbrush would make some *snap* in the distance, causing her to whip her head around, her loose hair catching in grasping branches as she tried to find the source of the sound. Once she saw a deer, its gray-brown coat fading into the tree trunks like an optical illusion, but generally the forest kept its secrets.

It was welcome to them, if only it wouldn't scare her.

The rumbling sound of Cascade Falls was welcome, the first background noise she'd heard in an hour. The trail led to the base of the falls, and for a while she just stood near some mossy rocks, watching the water hurl itself over the mountainside. It was pretty damn majestic, she had to admit. She could see why people wanted to make this hike. She decided to see what it looked like from the top and followed the path running alongside the waterfall. It was steep, but park rangers had shoved rocky steps into place, creating an almost-natural staircase. She supposed that it still counted as part of the Falls trail. Probably she wasn't veering off into territory beyond her map unless she actually went past the top of the waterfall.

Even with the helpful rocks, Kelly labored up the steepest climb near the top of the falls, wondering why her daily gym workouts weren't enough to make this kind of work feel easier. By the time she was at the top, she had stopped taking in the rushing waters roaring past the trail; she was too busy concentrating on the rushing and roaring in her ears, courtesy of her thudding heartbeat.

But she was able to sit down on a sun warmed slab of rock near the summit, and that suddenly made the whole ordeal worthwhile.

Through a gap in the trees, she could actually see over the valley: the brown and green strips of farmland and forest, the cluster of houses that must be the village of Catoctin Creek, and even beyond that. Through a hazy midmorning sky, she could see the rounded humps of a lone mountain to the southeast. She wondered what it was called. Idly, Kelly pulled her phone from her coat pocket, thinking she'd just look up the name of the mountain.

No service.

She sighed. "They couldn't warn me about *that*? Losing service is pretty freaking significant, park rangers."

Then she heard a crack in the brush behind her.

Kelly felt as if someone had poured a bucket of icy water over her head. She was suddenly freezing, despite the warm patch of sun, despite the sweat she'd worked up climbing the falls. There was another snap, and she felt frozen in place. She couldn't have turned around if she'd tried.

It's just a deer, she told herself. *Just a deer, just a deer, just a deer.*

But what if it wasn't?

She didn't *really* believe that Grayson had done something to Monica. That was the real point of coming out here, she'd told herself so again and again. To see where she'd been, to prove that she had just gone for a walk in the woods and decided not to come home. She'd feel something out here if something was wrong. If Grayson had been here, with his simmering resentment and his pocket full of ill intentions. And he wasn't here now, either. He had been questioned. He knew he was a person of interest, so he'd be lying low at home, being very, very careful . . . wouldn't he?

He wouldn't be out here in the woods, stalking her. That was absurd. Grayson wasn't a murderer, or even a crazy person. He was just a jerk who treated his girlfriends badly. That wasn't so unusual. Grayson was *definitely* not hiding in this forest, waiting for her to stumble into his path.

But, Kelly's reporter brain reminded her, someone else might be. *Crack.*

Kelly tried to steady her breathing. That had sounded farther away. As if whatever was in the forest was leaving her vicinity. *Crack-crack.* Yes. It was definitely moving away from her.

She waited as long as she could. Then she got up, smiling shakily to herself. Well, *that* had been crazy. A little bit of an over-reaction. Definitely just some deer wandering around. She was dusting herself off, congratulating herself on surviving not just the climb but the scary noises, when she heard another rustle in the bushes, just a few feet away.

Without pausing to look, Kelly turned and ran.

She didn't know how far she'd gone. Surely not far. She wasn't that fast a runner. But she'd had to take some precautions, just in case whoever had been following her decided to take up the chase. So Kelly had ducked off the trail, zig-zagged through some fir thickets, and jumped down a few fairly steep banks. In doing so, she'd found herself racing along the topmost ridge of the mountain, with trees falling off in either direction from her, the slopes spilling downwards around her.

And now, of course, she was lost.

"I'm an idiot," Kelly said aloud. Not too loud, just in case, but enough for the words to have shape and meaning. She needed to hear them to understand them. She was a bona fide, certifiable idiot. Off the trail, without phone service, in the forest. "Way to go, Kelly."

But here was the thing: all civilization was downhill. If she skidded and slid her way down these slopes, she'd eventually find humans. A road. A barn. A town. *Something.* It was the thing she'd never understood about Monica's disappearance: these mountains might be desolate, but they were like islands, popping up from settled territory. Surely there was no way to be lost, and stay lost? You'd find people again very quickly.

Unless the people you found were the problem, Kelly thought grimly, looking around for the best way to start picking her way down the mountainside.

The sun shifted as she walked, slid, and cursed through the woods. Noon came and went, and she wondered what the park rangers would think when they came back from their lunch break and saw her car was still in the parking lot. "They'll probably be all *we warned her,* and shake their heads," Kelly muttered, pushing branches aside. "But again, if they'd mentioned my phone wouldn't work, I definitely wouldn't have even gone into the woods . . ." She stopped short, her monologue cutting off. There was a fence in front of her.

She was still in the forest, and the ground was still sloping ever downward, but here was a barbed wire fence, rusty with age, running through the trees. Which probably meant she'd found the edge of state land. If she wanted to get out of here, she could either walk along this fence line, or take her chances with whoever owned the property on the other side.

Suddenly, this felt like a very worrisome crossroads. Kelly had enjoyed plenty of time to think of all the ways she could meet an unfortunate end in these woods. Prominently among them was "crazed mountain hermit with shotgun," and she figured her chances of running into one of these characters was going up exponentially the moment she left the relatively protected lands of the state park.

But then again, if she followed the barbed wire fence, she could end up just walking the perimeter of the park for miles. And there were only a few more hours of daylight. The coming night would be below freezing; she absolutely wouldn't make it through a night out here in just her puffy coat and these extra-thick hiking socks she'd bought. Plus, she was starving, and thirsty, and heartily sick of trees in general.

Mountain hermit it was then.

Kelly dropped to her knees and cautiously pulled the bottom strand of barbed wire up as far as it would go. She'd have to wriggle under it. She was halfway under the fence when she realized she couldn't keep holding the strand up with one hand; she'd have to switch hands to get to the other side. As she tried to change hands as quickly as possible, the barbed wire snapped down on her back. The ripping sound of her puffy coat splitting open made her decide once and for all: if she survived this experience, she wasn't just going to let the police handle Monica's case however they liked, she was never going back into the forest again. She wasn't even going to *drive* through the forest. Any forest. Forget trees forever.

She'd really liked this coat.

And what was on the other side? Nothing. More trees. Kelly stood, brushed the pine needles and loose leaves from her clothes, and set off again.

She'd only been walking about fifteen minutes when she heard the dogs barking.

She'd only been waiting about fifteen minutes when she heard the bag clinking.

Chapter Eleven

Nikki

Nikki glanced over at Rosemary, bent over a laptop at a corner table, and wondered how she was getting on. She hadn't meant to leave the poor girl to do all that research on her own. But the day's lunch trade had finally picked up, and she was hopping to keep up with the orders. After Kelly had left, the morning had been calm enough; Nikki had even taken out the box of Christmas decorations and gotten as far as hanging up a single strand of lights around the front window when the bell over the door had started ringing.

And ringing.

And *ringing*.

What had started as a quiet morning humming Christmas tunes and hanging up some decorations had turned into one of her busiest days of the year so far.

She tripped over her box of decorations and shoved it with one foot, hiding it beneath the shelf where she kept extra boxes of cup lids and straws. The holiday spirit was just going to have to wait for this lunch rush to end. *Ping!* Nikki glanced over her shoulder;

the panini press was finished. She set down the coffee mugs she'd been about to run over to the corner table and rescued the sandwiches before they began to burn.

The bell over the door rang. Even more people. Every dining table was full; there were a few hardy souls sitting on the front porch, waiting for their meals to go. Nikki couldn't believe the traffic in this place. And on a Monday!

What was more, she knew the cafe wasn't cannibalizing the business over at the Blue Plate. Lauren sent her the numbers every day at two, six, and eight. They were steady—even rising over last year. Catoctin Creek was just busier, and the cafe attracted different people than the diner.

Right now, a pair of park rangers were eating chicken salad sandwiches at the table by the big window, an antique-shopping couple were exclaiming over every mouthful of her baked potato soup, and some local women were chit-chatting over ham and Swiss baguettes.

Nikki was extremely pleased with the way things were going for her little cafe, and her little town, too. But she was really, really tired.

When Rosemary had come in for a pick-me-up after taking care of the Wayne horses, she'd wanted to talk to Nikki about the carnival idea. Nikki had listened to her idly, but her mind was elsewhere. She felt so guilty about it, she decided to take charge of the conversation.

"Have you figured out what businesses are going to get spots?" she asked.

Rosemary had looked at her blankly. "Spots?"

"Like, a tent, or a booth. Who is handling that? Vendors and local businesses, food trucks . . ."

"I'm not sure. Nadine's going to ask some people."

"When?"

"I guess today? Or after school hours?" Rosemary had looked so confused, Nikki took pity on her.

"Listen, you're just overwhelmed with the idea. Take my laptop and go look at the website for the holiday fair over at PenMar. Here—" Nikki dug out a legal pad and put it on top of the laptop. "Take notes on what they offer, what they charge, and how they sign folks up for it. Categorize everything and I promise it will start to take shape. This is exactly how I figured out the cafe idea. I just looked at a ton of menus and catering forms and reverse-engineered."

Once Rosemary was settled with the laptop and the legal pad, Nikki brought her tea and kept the cup full. Tea was safer. Too much coffee and the poor girl would get even more jangled-up.

The antiquing couple finished their soup and stood up, throwing a few dollars on the table. Nikki watched them go before she moved to clear the table. They stepped around the strand of Christmas lights she'd left hanging in the doorway, batting at the dangling decorations. Nikki winced. She'd have to get back to the Christmas decorations or someone was going to trip.

"You doing okay?" she asked Rosemary on her way back to the kitchen, dishes in hand, dollar bills in her pocket. "Everything coming together?"

"It is, thanks." Rosemary smiled gratefully at her. "It's still a lot but I'm starting to see all the moving pieces."

"Send a text to Nadine so she doesn't do the same thing," Nikki advised her, and Rosemary made a terrified face, grabbing at her phone.

The kitchen was still steamy from the last run of the sanitizer, and Nikki rinsed the soup bowls before dropping them into the wash sink to soak. The lunch dishes were really adding up. Nikki considered the possibility of hiring a part-time dishwasher. And if this kind of lunch business continued, she'd need counter help, too. Maybe it was time to hire help, anyway. She'd been waiting until the cafe's fortunes were a little more certain, but she was just bone-tired these days. Her feet ached before she even got out of bed in the morning, and her shoulders seemed to draw together behind her neck if she didn't pay attention, giving her a hunched-over appearance that Kevin had commented on more than once.

But this was a good kind of tired, she reminded herself. And eventually the cafe would turn a profit, maybe not as efficiently as the Blue Plate, but still enough to hire someone to handle the counter in the evenings, clean the kitchen up, take over for her on the occasional weekend.

Kevin had been making tiny noises about going on vacation over the winter, and so far she'd had to say no, because there wasn't anyone to cover for her. But maybe it was time to go ahead and make that first hire. Just rip that band-aid right off.

"It's good trouble," Nikki told herself aloud, and she drew a smiley face on the steamed-up steel cabinet doors above the wash sink.

A radio squawk drew her out of the kitchen, and she found two sheriff deputies standing before the bake case, looking at the assortment of sliced pies and cakes and dessert bars with child-like enthusiasm. "Afternoon," she called, arranging herself behind the case. "What can I get for you?"

"A magical diet version of that chocolate cake," the younger deputy said, patting her flat stomach.

Nikki rolled her eyes, but politely, in a *yeah, right?* kind of way. She heard way too much of words like *guilt* and *sneak* and *skinny* when people were admiring the bakes she spent so much time on. She didn't spend all her time creating food so that people would feel bad about eating it. "There's no diet on earth that's worth skipping my triple chocolate cake," she assured the woman, who was in stunningly good shape. "You all having a good day out there?"

"Just about," the second deputy said, a middle-aged woman with dark, curly hair escaping from her hat. "The Waters case is tough on everyone, but it's about to get crazier. So we decided we need some pastries to help us deal with it."

"Oh, no. What now?"

"A big press conference with the sheriff and the FBI tomorrow," the younger deputy whispered. "Right here in town."

Nikki's jaw dropped. "You're joking."

"Nope. You know how it is. They want to keep the national media talking, in case that turns up any leads outside of Maryland."

Nikki glanced at her discarded strand of Christmas lights. "Are you saying tomorrow is going to be very, very busy?"

"I'd say by tonight," the younger deputy assured her. "The media vans are going to start pulling in any minute, now that they've announced the presser." She leaned over the case. "I can't! I give in. Can I get a slice of that cake? And do you have ice cream?"

"You better believe it," Nikki said. "A la mode is my love language."

Rosemary looked up when the police were gone. "Um, so they said the FBI are heading into town?"

"That's what they said." Nikki sat down across from her and sighed. "I don't love this look for our town."

"I thought you said it was an opportunity to get press," Rosemary pointed out. "For the carnival."

"Well, maybe some press *is* bad press." She pressed her lips together, thinking. "You think he murdered her?"

"Who, the boyfriend? No. I don't."

"What makes you think so?"

"That reporter. Kelly. Didn't you tell me she was the guy's ex?"

"Yeah . . . so?"

"So if she thought he was capable of murder, she wouldn't be up here. She'd be hiding somewhere until he was behind bars." Rosemary looked quite convinced. "I'm telling you, there's no way she came up looking for some vigilante justice. I saw that girl! She's like a twig. A very expensively dressed twig. With nice hair," she added.

Nikki wondered what the girl like a twig was doing today. She'd kind of expected her to come back for lunch, but maybe she was still embarrassed about their eavesdropping chat earlier.

"Anyway," Rosemary went on. "Look at this. It's the company that does the midway rides for the PenMar festival." She pushed her laptop over to Nikki. "I sent them an email, and they said they have availability with their small kit for our dates next month."

"Rosemary! Good for you." Nikki glanced over the website. "What's the small kit?"

"A carousel, a big slide, and one of those crazy school buses that goes up and around." Rosemary's smile slipped a little. "It's not much . . ."

"No, but it's perfect to start. If we have vendors, food, a couple of rides, and some entertainment, that will be plenty. After all," Nikki said, pushing the laptop back to her. "We're replacing nothing with something. People are going to appreciate that."

"Yeah," Rosemary said, her smile back in full force. "I think you're right."

Chapter Twelve

William

By late afternoon, the dogs were still barking like mad every time they went outside, but William had made up his mind to ignore them. It wouldn't do any good to go out there and mess around by that dairy again. Whoever was in there didn't want to be found. Whether it was Monica Waters or some drifter or even some crazy criminal, they hadn't made themselves known to him. They clearly had reasons for staying hidden.

And in any case, *he* didn't want to be the one doing any finding. Not getting involved was a signature of the William Cunningham brand. He kept to himself; he minded his own business; and he appreciated the same treatment from others. He had tried trusting people, and they had taught him that people do irrational, ridiculous, hurtful things and never offer any explanation at all. So William was fine with just avoiding them.

If the person in the dairy had any sense, they'd wait and get out tonight, while the dogs were inside and asleep.

Sure, William knew there were other, more socially accepted ways to handle an intruder in his outbuilding. But calling the cops didn't sit right with him. His summers wandering the west involved more trespassing than he'd like to admit. A person could spend a lot of time on public land while driving through the Rockies and down into the empty landscapes of the southwest, but sometimes a long trek or a whim to see a particular view from a particular mountaintop or even a flat tire had left him holing up on private property. He'd slept in caves overlooking magnificent empty vistas—empty other than the *No Trespassing* signs nailed to every withered tree and collapsing fence post in sight. But he left no trash, he took no artifacts, and he killed neither plants nor animals. So, no harm done, that was how William saw his stays on private property, and he figured he could apply that policy to others, as well. Hopefully, whoever was in there didn't mess up his nice clean dairy.

With his mind set at least partially at ease about any potential responsibility re: his trespasser, William devoted his entire day to the kitchen renovation with renewed energy. He finished tearing up the linoleum, unplugged the old refrigerator and removed the door, then hauled both pieces out to the bed of his truck. Next, he called the dogs in, put them back in the mudroom, and got into his truck. He had a new fridge lined up in Frederick. He'd pick that up, plus some food to stick in it, and be back to Hilltop House before sunset. The dogs could wait, and maybe it would give his trespasser time to decide if they were going to leave during daylight or wait for the night.

The errands went smoothly, and on the way home, his route took him through the center of Catoctin Creek. He slowed as he passed the Blue Plate Diner. He hadn't tasted the fried chicken special there in years; something about the biscuits, made with

Nikki's aunt's secret recipe (or so she claimed) alongside that plate of golden-fried chicken and pile of creamy mashed potatoes was part of his childhood summers at Hilltop House. His grandparents would bring them all down and—no, he wasn't going to think about that now.

And anyway, his inner thriftiness urged him to go straight home; he had a cooler full of meat and dairy for the shiny new fridge resting in the back of the truck, plus half a dozen full grocery bags on the seat next to him. William figured at this point he could resist the average platter of fried chicken or meatloaf without too much difficulty; sometimes he thought he'd had enough country cooking, enough rib-sticking entrees served with mashed potatoes and two vegetables, to last a lifetime. It turned out there was a limit to how many roadside diners and truck stop buffets a man could enjoy.

But if he managed to drive past his memories of meals at the Blue Plate, he couldn't quite resist the quaint wooden sign in front of the Catoctin Cafe & Bakery. Not when he knew what goodness waited within. To say nothing with meeting the friendly eyes of an old pal. He pulled the truck onto the side street and parked in the little gravel lot behind the house.

As he entered the cafe, Nikki looked up from wiping a table and smiled at him. "Back again so soon?"

William appreciated her easiness with him. Some people didn't know how to talk to him; they walked on eggshells around the man who only came to Catoctin Creek in winter and disappeared the rest of the year for who-knew-where. "I don't know, Nikki. You might keep me in town year-round with this place open."

"But not down off your mountain every day. Surely not."

"Well, no. I was looking for a few days' worth of provisions." He grinned. "Maybe I'll just come down once a week."

Nikki laughed and flicked her damp towel at him as she went behind the counter. "So, did you hear about our Christmas carnival?"

He lifted an eyebrow. "They're bringing that back?"

"Who do you think *they* is, William?" Nikki shook her head, but she was still smiling. "You know what I found out recently? We're the adults now."

"Oh, you think?"

"I know. Maybe you missed that while you've been out wandering the country, but we grew up and took over the town. And it's doing pretty well. You should stick around and see it."

"So you're taking over the town, and you're going to bring back the carnival. It sounds like a lot of work."

"Well, we're going to do it. Rosemary and me and Nadine, and whoever else we can round up." Her voice was defiant, as if he'd told her she couldn't do it. But William was no fool. He knew better than to tell Nikki Mercer she couldn't do something she'd set her mind to doing.

He watched her pop a bakery box into shape, her fingers deft and practiced. Nikki had always been so—so—*proficient*. She got things done. He had been more laid back, letting things go until the last possible minute, trying to make do with whatever he had on hand instead of planning ahead. Impossible to plan ahead, when his parents had ripped the carpet from beneath his feet as a child. He'd never trust anyone again, not completely. He wasn't a total fool. A memory of childhood sparked, the easy days before the feud. "Hey, remember when we tried to build a treehouse at Rosemary's place?"

"Yeah. Someone didn't bring the nails." She flicked her eyes up at him. "What was it you said? You thought we could just sort of *prop* it up?"

"I didn't want to hurt the tree!"

"And Rosemary agreed with you, and while you were trying to lean some boards on slanting branches, she fell out of the tree and her parents thought she broke her ankle and that was the end of tree climbing on Notch Gap Farm."

"Her mom was so mad at me." William smiled at the memory. "It's good to see her out and about again."

"Stephen's been good for her. She was in kind of a holding period for so long—you remember what she was like. I swear we all went to work trying to fix that girl," Nikki chuckled. "Caitlin forced her into teaching some horsemanship classes, and because of that, she works with the school now. I think she and Nadine are going to involve the school kids in the Christmas carnival somehow . . . and hey," Nikki narrowed her eyes at him, and William resisted the urge to take a step backwards. "What's the Cunningham Foundation up to these days? Think your bosses could find a few dollars for this carnival? It's benefiting Rosemary's rescue, so the money's going straight back into the town."

William winced. The idea of getting involved in something . . . even if all he was doing was sending an email to the board of his grandparents' charity fund, he'd still have to represent the foundation in some way. Nikki would probably force him to get a big check for a photo op, just to watch him squirm. "Can't I just donate the money directly to the rescue? Wouldn't that be more effective than spending it on a carnival? We could go right to the source, so to speak."

"No, William. The point of the carnival is that it will raise *more* money, from *more* people, than if we had a few fundraising organizations send in some cash. We'll get some donations to get this thing off the ground, then everyone else can have fun, spend, and support Rosemary's rescue. The whole town wins. Doesn't that sound better than a few businesses writing checks to Rosemary?"

William still liked his idea better. But he wasn't exactly a joiner. "What do I have to do? Besides hand over some cash to the carnival fund?"

Nikki smiled smugly. "Be helpful. Earn your keep around here. Like I said, this town is on the up-and-up. We need everyone pulling their own weight if we're going to make it."

"What, I don't pay my bills like everyone else?"

"Not nearly enough of them, if you're gone half the year." Nikki started filling the open box with pastries, not consulting him on what he might want, just making very good guesses about muffins and croissants. "Maybe you need to find a reason to stick around if you want all of us to keep on loving you. Unconditional adoration doesn't last forever, my dear William."

"Maybe it should," he grumbled, leaning against the counter. He looked around the quiet cafe. Sunset was filtering into the front window, golden light catching dust motes as they danced above the warm wooden floors. A new memory sparked; a younger one, this time. "You know, I ran into that Kelly girl out on the street this morning. After we left here."

"Oh, yeah?" Nikki didn't look up. "Do you want this last sugar cookie? It's three days old."

"Yes, of course I do. Yeah, so I talked to her for a minute. She's a suspicious one. Eyed me up and down like she thought I was a serial killer."

"Maybe she does think you're a serial killer. I mean, she's here looking for her—for a missing woman."

William heard the pause as she corrected herself. He looked her over, watching her close the box with exaggerated concentration. "What were you going to say?"

"When?"

"Just now."

"I said what was I was going to say." Nikki pushed the box across to him. "Half-price. I just gave you all the stuff I was going to throw out in the morning."

He shrugged and took out his wallet. "That's a deal."

"Don't worry about Kelly," Nikki told him, accepting his money, straightening it out with that exasperated look she was always giving him. "She's here for her own reasons, not just digging into this missing hiker situation. I think we should leave her alone to do her thing. She'll be in and out of here in no time."

"She seems like the kind of person who might stay," William said. Then he wondered where the words had come from. It was really, truly, none of his business what Kelly O'Something did with her time in or out of Catoctin Creek. He was just here for the winter. Just here to fix up his house. Just here to honor tradition, or habit, or obsession—whatever it was that kept him coming back.

Nikki eyed him, that old expression of hers which suggested she knew than the other person did about their feelings. "Watch yourself, Will," she said gently. "That girl isn't here for any of us."

Chapter Thirteen

Nikki

A pretty girl could do a number on any guy, Nikki figured. Even one as checked out as William. She watched him head out of the cafe, his eyes still soft and confused. He had a way of getting inside his own mind, and it showed on his face. Nikki didn't think he knew about it; she wasn't going to be the one to point it out. At this point, when they were all in their mid-thirties, there was no changing some characteristics.

She sighed and threw herself down into the corner armchair. Surely no one else was coming in tonight. They'd all gorged themselves at lunch; between the huge business the cafe had done today, and the past-their-prime pastries she'd boxed up for William, she was going to have to get up early in the morning and bake some extra batches of just about everything. Dusk fell, then full darkness, shrouding the dining room in shadows, but Nikki didn't notice. She had fallen fast asleep.

The bell rang, waking her from a dream about a gigantic cupcake order—really, it was more of a nightmare—and she sat up with a start, her head swimming as she looked around the dimly lit cafe. She realized she'd forgotten to turn on the lights over the dining room tables, and was just scrambling to her feet when she saw that it wasn't a customer coming into the store, but Kevin, with Grover padding at his heels.

"Oh, thank god," she sighed, sinking back into the armchair.

Grover trotted over to see her, tail wagging, and she sank her fingers into his fluffy, golden coat. "Did you have a nice day with Daddy?"

Kevin leaned over her, smelling of cold and horse and smoke, and gave her a kiss. "It's so funny when you call me Daddy," he said teasingly. "I never thought you'd be that type."

"It's just how we are with pets," she said, smiling languidly up at him. "They're our children. How was your day?"

"Busy." Kevin looked around. "Busier than yours? I hope not."

"No, honestly, this place was a zoo earlier. Things died off in the early evening. I had some deputies in here at lunch telling me it was going to be drama central tonight, but thank goodness, they were wrong."

Kevin frowned and leaned over the bake case, picking at some leftover croissants. "Why did they say it was going to be busy?"

"They told me that the sheriff was having some press conference here tomorrow, and all the media would be descending on us tonight. You see any news vans on your way home?"

"None," Kevin said. "No, wait—I did see a WDCN van up by the Falls trailhead."

"That's probably that Kelly person," Nikki said dismissively. "The girl who was in here."

"I thought you said she came alone."

"That's true, she did come alone." Nikki frowned. "Well, maybe they sent up reinforcements. I haven't seen her since breakfast. She must be doing a report for the evening news or something. You know, I kind of think William is into her."

"William?"

"I've told you about William Cunningham," Nikki insisted. "I know I have."

"Maybe. Yes. Of course." Kevin was distracted, looking over the bake case with admiration in his eyes. "Hey, we need dessert tonight. Are you going to close up now?"

"Yes. Let me lock up and finish things while you shower. Then I'm coming up with a vat of leftover baked potato soup and some baguettes."

"Mmm, that sounds amazing. Hey, how about apple pie? That would go good with soup and bread. It's cold out there tonight." Kevin flicked Grover a piece of croissant. The dog caught it and wagged his wavy tail. "Grover and I had a very chilly day."

"Sure, just take the pie upstairs while I close things up, okay?" She got herself up, pulled a pie from the case, and handed it over to Kevin.

He leaned over for a kiss before disappearing through the door to their staircase, and Nikki went through the rest of her closing routine, checking the locks on the windows, putting the chain and deadbolt on the front door. The drooping Christmas lights were still hanging by the door, her decoration plans not even close to finished. She pushed them aside so she wouldn't trip in the morning when she came downstairs in the darkness to start baking. Maybe tomorrow she'd manage to get them hung.

Or maybe she wouldn't. If she had to do extra baking in the morning, things would run late, even if she got up early. And if tomorrow's breakfast and lunch rushes were anything like today's . . . if the deputies were right and more reporters made their way into Catoctin Creek for a press conference . . .

Nikki pressed her hands to her lower back, where a sudden muscle spasm twinged with vicious delight. She'd been getting these odd pains in the curve of her spine lately. *Now is not the time to get old,* she warned herself. *Wait until you can afford to retire somewhere warm.*

Somewhere with less baking.

And fewer horses, she thought grimly, glancing towards the door to their staircase. She could hear Kevin's footsteps overhead, the old house creaking as he made his way into the bathroom. A pipe clanged and moaned as he switched on the shower. She imagined the icy cold of the bathroom, which never seemed to receive any heat from the registers, the shock of steam rising up from the claw-footed bath tub which dominated the small, wood-paneled room. He'd be fresh and clean when she went upstairs, his red-gold hair slicked back from his forehead, his boyish smile trained on her as she limped past, feeling a hundred years older than he did, to take her own shower.

She shouldn't be angry that Kevin had an easier time of life than she did. It had always been that way, even when he'd come to Catoctin Creek lost and trying to find his way. He was a happy person, and joy came easily to him. It was usually one of his charms, one of the quirks of his personality which made her love him so much, but on nights like this, when she was stiff and sore from falling asleep in an armchair as she waited for him to come home, it just made her resentful.

"Well, this is the life you chose," Nikki reminded herself. "And if it makes you mad sometimes, that's just hard luck."

She had switched off the lights to the bake case and was about to make her retreat up the stairs when headlights flashed outside and she heard the crunch of tires on gravel. With a sigh, she went back to the door and pulled the curtain aside to see if it was friend or foe showing up this late in the evening.

A news van. Nikki wrinkled her nose.

Ugh, so it begins.

She began unlocking the door again, resigned to her fate. But just this one, she told herself. She wasn't getting caught up in some late-night burst of traffic. For one thing, her feet were too sore to put up with the extra work.

A woman wearing an extraordinary amount of makeup and a trim power suit ran up to the door, waving to Nikki. She opened the door a crack, wincing at the cold air which came swirling inside. "I've just closed, sorry," she called.

"Oh, damn," the woman said, stopping short on the walk. "Any coffee left at all? We just drove up from Richmond and we're exhausted."

"The coffee pot is cleaned out for the night . . . but I could make you Americanos," Nikki offered. "And there's cold milk. But I'm afraid I'm not getting steamed milk on anything I'd have to wash. You get it, right?"

"*Totally* understandable, yes!" The woman looked prepared to accept the leftover granules in the coffee filter. "Please, please. Three? And I'll pay you double for any cookies you've got."

Nikki let her into the cafe and locked the door behind her. "There's no need for that. I won't price-gouge you on cookies. You don't mind waiting in the dark, right? If I turn on the lights, someone else might show up. You know what they say, no good deed goes unpunished."

"Not at all." The woman beamed, clearly ecstatic at the idea of coffee and cookies. Nikki couldn't really blame her. Was there anything more cheering?

With just the kitchen light shining through the open door, Nikki set up cups beneath the espresso maker and pulled shots, then topped them with hot water. She set the to-go cups on the counter, pushed forward the basket of sugar by the register, and pulled a bottle of half-and-half from the refrigerator. "Arriving for the press conference tomorrow?" she asked, placing cookies into a box.

"Oh, no," the woman said, stirring milk into the coffees. "Didn't you hear? There's another missing woman. She went hiking today and didn't come back."

"What?" Shocked, Nikki dropped a cookie through suddenly bloodless fingers. It split on the floor at her feet.

"I know! They just announced it around sunset. We were on the road immediately. We're heading up to the trail parking lot right now. They're setting up a command center. Everyone's sleeping in their vans because there aren't any rooms in town." The woman sighed. "I am *not* looking forward to the bathroom situation."

"Did they say who it is?" Nikki had a sick feeling she already knew the answer.

"A reporter from WDCN!" The woman shook her head. "Came up here to cover the *first* missing hiker story. Can you believe it?"

Chapter Fourteen

William

Nikki's shaming always got to William.

She didn't really mean it to come across that way; she just treated him like a brother, same as she always had. But when Nikki teased him, he saw the truth behind her words. She'd told him at Homecoming that he shouldn't act like he was doing all those girls a favor by not choosing just one for a date; he shouldn't have brought *anyone* and shown the seniors of Catoctin Creek that no one was good enough for William's undivided attention. She'd been laughing when she'd said it, but her eyes had been serious, and William heard the unspoken truth: he was being a pompous asshole. He took her advice; William didn't ask anyone to prom. He went with friends and he had a great time.

That was the thing about Nikki: she was usually right.

And her teasing made him feel better, oddly enough. Like he was safe at home, back where he belonged. Sometimes William wished he'd never gone to college at all, never left Hilltop House. He should have stayed here and waited it out. Maybe his family would still come back each summer. Maybe his parents would give in and leave their leafy suburbs. Maybe he wouldn't always feel so alone. At least in Catoctin Creek, he had the company of the people who hadn't left.

As often as he could bear it.

Sunset was streaming across the road ahead of him, shadows of half-bare trees clawing at the blacktop and the brown grass along the verges. William's truck whined slightly on the slow rises of the countryside, as around him the farms were growing more rolling, the people growing more stubborn. The stoic, hardworking farmers of western Maryland: somewhere along the line, the Cunninghams had wandered away from their roots, become businessmen and later, businesswomen, but they'd never truly given up their home. And Catoctin Creek had always accepted them. *Him.*

They'd always loved him in Catoctin Creek; love hadn't been the problem. This was the one place where William had felt truly loved, embraced by his family, his friends, and the entire town. The Cunninghams weren't demonstrative on their own. Each individual family, on their own, could be accused of being rather cold. They were the sort of people who put work and academics first: solid things, with measurable results, that a person could rely on.

But in those golden summers and sparkling Christmas holidays at Hilltop House, the porches spilling over with children, the sitting rooms and kitchen full of chattering aunts and uncles and cousins and grandparents, William had known that as a group, they were strong enough to let go of their usual standoffish demeanors. As a clan, they knew where they stood, and the outside world couldn't threaten them. Hair literally came down; the sleek, tight knot that was his mother's daily coiffure became a long braid, and later just a tangle of curls, as her shoulders unknotted and her laugh lines deepened. At Hilltop House, the Cunninghams and their many offshoots could be real at last.

That was why he'd cried every August when they went home to the suburban Colonial in Willowdale, although his mother had thought all that fuss was about going back to school, that he was complaining about another hard year of putting his nose to the grindstone—a family talent which poor William hadn't inherited.

Everyone else in his house assimilated into their old lives quickly. His mother's hair went back into its strict twist, and his father's tie went back around his taut neck, and William's school uniform was set out each night and checked carefully for wrinkles or stains. He polished his shoes every evening, the pointless chore leaving him feeling put upon and disappointed, aware that the rigidity in his back, the tightness in his jaw, was just like his father's. The resemblance frightened him. Was this what life was going to be like? *Forever?*

He'd left to make sure that feeling wouldn't stick. Stayed in Catoctin Creek, tried to be that better version of himself year-round. And for a little while, he'd succeeded. And then he left. The Cunningham hunt for glory: it didn't skip a generation after all. *Stupid.*

He should have stayed.

Now he drove back up the overgrown driveway, wondering what had happened to it all. So many mysteries: the family fight, the end of holidays spent at Hilltop House. The unexpected loss of his grandparents, then two of his aunts and uncles. The bitter realization that he'd ended up with the house, but not the people who made it a home. He started to recognize that his parents had held themselves back from that exuberant lifestyle because opening up to emotion was exactly how a person could get hurt.

They were still in Willowdale, of course. Not in the same Colonial where he'd grown up; a few years back, they'd moved into a new condo with granite counters and a view of the Chesapeake from their broad balconies. William sometimes saw them right around the holidays. And sometimes they went on a Christmas week cruise around the Caribbean, and then he didn't see them. He understood that his parents weren't icy because they didn't love him; they were icy because that was who they'd chosen to be.

He couldn't live that way, but he couldn't open himself up again, either. Not to all the hurt that waited for him.

So he lived alone.

The truck rattled up the rutted driveway. When the trees cleared and Hilltop House came into view, William felt that brief moment of lift, the same sensation that had warmed him since he was a child and the house had been full of his favorite people, good cooking smells, the promise of a perfect holiday.

Too bad it was empty.

Or rather, it *should* be empty—

William leaned forward, peering through the windshield. Was there someone sitting on his front porch? There *was*.

Who the hell was that?

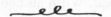

A girl.

Okay, a woman.

There was a woman on his front porch, sitting on the stairs with her hands in her lap. She straightened as the truck approached, and he could see the trepidation in her face as he parked a few feet away. She scrambled to her feet, and William noticed the leaves in her pale hair, the dirt smudging her jeans, the white stuffing slowly leaking from the back of her black puffy jacket.

Someone was having a bad day.

The moment William realized the woman on his porch was Kelly O'Something was a strange one. His heart did a little double-thump, as if it was trying to escape his chest. And his hands clenched on the truck's steering wheel, as if he was trying not to wreck. And his mind went very, very clear, for just a moment, as if he finally understood what on earth he was doing out here in the frozen wilds of western Maryland.

Waiting to save Kelly.

Then the clarity was gone, and he shook his head quickly, as if he could retain—or dissipate—that strange thought. Where had that come from? The brain was a strange organ, for sure. He must have gotten some wires crossed there; some neutrons did a little two-step and mixed up his present and his past and his over-active imagination . . .

She was staring at him, her eyes huge in her pale face. He was thirty feet away, but he knew the exact shade of blue in her irises.

That was something, wasn't it?

William slowly slid from behind the wheel, his jeans catching on the torn leather of the seat. When his boots hit the ground, they made a squelching noise. The ground was still damp, despite the day's earnest sunshine. Cold rose up from the earth as if someone had left a refrigerator door open just underground.

Refrigerator. He had a brand-new refrigerator in the back of the truck, and bags of groceries which were waiting for him to install it.

The distraction was enough to propel William around the truck, over to the porch, a safe distance from Kelly. From the back of the house, he heard the dogs barking like crazy, longing to get out of the mudroom to help him deal with the trespasser. Good thing he'd shut them up when he'd gone out.

"Hey there," he said.

"Oh, my god," the woman gasped, her voice hoarse. As if she'd been shouting. "You're the man from town. William. This is your house?"

"You're the reporter," he said, ignoring her question. Of course it was his house—why else would he be up here? "Kelly O'Something."

She pushed back her hair with a slim, white hand. He remembered how sleek and perfect that hair had been this morning. Not anymore. She'd been through something today. "O'Connell," she corrected him. "Did you know you don't have cell phone signal out here?"

"I'm aware." He kicked at the ground, unable to meet her incredulous stare. What, it was so crazy to run into him twice in one day?

Well, three times, he guessed.

"You probably want a ride back into town," he continued, when she didn't respond.

"Or to the trailhead parking lot, where I left my car." She crossed her arms over her chest. Another white ball of stuffing popped from the back of her coat and drifted off on the frigid breeze. "It's freezing out here, so . . ."

"You can go inside and warm up for a few minutes," William suggested, wondering why it had taken him so long to realize she was probably half-frozen. "I actually have some things to unload. If you want to just wait a bit, maybe you can clean up and have a snack while I get this done, and then I can give you a ride out?"

"That would be fine, thanks." She took a few anxious steps from side to side. "And maybe I could . . . er . . . use your washroom."

"Oh, of course." William took out his keys and hopped over the rotten steps onto the porch. He glanced at her muddy hiking boots, glad she hadn't accidentally put a foot right through the wood when she'd climbed the steps earlier. "How long you been out here?" he asked, fiddling with the door lock.

She looked around as if reading the sharp angle of the sun. "A couple of hours. There were barking dogs earlier, so I climbed a tree, but then they sounded like they were shut inside, so I came down. Found the house."

"You climbed a tree!" William was impressed. "Did you really?"

"Yeah. I remember how to climb trees," Kelly said. "I'm not a hundred years old."

"Didn't say you were." William shrugged.

He gave the front door key a wiggle while he shoved the door knob at the same time, and the big front door gave way with a groan and a squeak. "Perfect," he grunted. "Someday I'll fix that." As the door opened, the dogs' uproar was even easier to hear. They were going nuts back there.

"Are the dogs loose?" Kelly's face grew even more pale, if that was possible. "They sound mean."

"They're not," William assured her. "Those dogs are more than likely going to lick you to death, as long as you're with me. And maybe even if you aren't. They're my road buddies, not killers."

Kelly followed him through the front hall, her hiking boots hitting the creaking old floor with little determined thuds. He heard her pause as each doorway opened off the hall, glancing into the rooms that opened off to the right and left. He knew what she was thinking: *This place was beautiful, once.*

She was right. He was ashamed he'd let it reach this point, practically decaying under their very feet.

But he was working on that now.

She spent a few minutes in the downstairs bath, and once she emerged, William led her straight to the kitchen at the back of the house, imagining as he entered how much nicer this big, bright room would be once he'd gotten the drab reds and browns exorcised from its cabinets and floors. The dogs pounded against the mudroom door, howling with frustration. Kelly hung back in the kitchen doorway, her hands clutching the scarred wooden frame. "I don't know about this," she said, her voice wobbling with fear—and probably exhaustion, he thought.

"Trust me," William said. "Tell you what, we'll do it one dog at a time. Then you'll have four new best friends."

He opened the door just an inch, and a dark muzzle appeared. Lola, of course. She'd be first to everything. He opened the door a little more, to let her squeeze through, and as she leapt into the kitchen, blue eyes shining brightly, William tried to slam the door shut again.

Too late.

Four huskies went leaping and skidding across the torn-up linoleum, their claws dragging at the rips and remnants William had piled on the old stone flags underneath. For a moment they spun around his legs, whining and yelping with the sheer ecstasy of seeing him again after four whole hours spent apart. But then Lola remembered the stranger. The alpha dog spun and froze in place, her gaze locked on Kelly.

The other dogs whipped around as if Lola had given them an unspoken command.

William supposed he couldn't blame Kelly for turning and running. All of those uncanny husky gazes fixed on the girl must have been too terrifying for words. But it wasn't the right approach to meeting the dogs, either. As she skedaddled down the hallway, the dogs let loose a rafter-shaking volley of barks, then took off after her, leaving William alone in the kitchen.

He sighed as a door slammed down the hall. The dogs were barking like banshees, covering up the click of the house's old-fashioned locks, but he'd bet she locked herself into whatever room she'd chosen for refuge.

William went down the hall, clicking on the overhead light as he went, then pushed the dogs aside, telling them to shush with a few sharp commands. They sat down and awaited his pleasure, tails wagging frantically. On the other side of the closed door, he heard scuffling sounds, as if Kelly was pushing a chair up against the door.

"Kelly?" he called through the door. "It's okay. I promise they won't hurt you."

"I'm fine in here, thank you."

He tried the door handle. Locked, as he'd assumed. She was a smart cookie; her instincts would have kicked in the moment she'd slammed the door. Turn, lock, run. "Okay, then. You want to sit in there while I get my truck unloaded?"

There was a moment's pause. He imagined Kelly checking out her surroundings for the first time. She'd picked the library. While there was nothing on the shelves from the past fifty years, if she liked classic literature or odd old instructional titles on business and farming and Maryland government, she was in for a treat. Plus, the wing chairs were comfortable. The only downside was that there was nothing in there to light a fire. He hadn't gotten around to laying firewood and starters in all the downstairs rooms yet.

And the furnace at Hilltop House hadn't run in some years.

William waited for her verdict.

"I'm fine in here," she repeated eventually.

"Well, read whatever you want," William told her. "The light switch is by the door." The evening was already growing dark; the sun had slipped behind the mountaintops while they'd been dealing with Lola and her pack. "I'll be sure the dogs are put away before I come back to get you."

Silence.

Okay, then. William figured she could sit in there and pout about the dogs if she wanted.

Lola was just trying to be friendly, but if a girl couldn't understand that . . .

He shook his head and went back down the hall. It was going to take at least an hour to get the fridge installed and the groceries put away. He'd deal with her after that.

Chapter Fifteen

Kelly

There were a *lot* of books in this room.

Kelly was getting definite fairy tale vibes from the space. Dusty volumes crammed onto shelves that reached to the high, coffered ceiling. The all-important sliding ladders. Leather and plush wing chairs deep enough to disappear in. A few brass lamps and one huge, slightly tattered, badly faded Persian carpet spread across the floorboards, presumably to quiet one's footsteps as one crept across this cathedral of reading. She could imagine a lot of studying had gone on in this room.

And maybe some canoodling, too; there were shadowy corners and shelves with convenient candelabras at about shoulder height, where Kelly could imagine a little necking going down. Plus, she noticed, a few scattered diaries with crabbed and elegant script handwritten in their crackling pages, and even a splendid, if desiccated, feather quill discarded on a shelf by the tall windows overlooking the mountains, which seemed to rise from just beyond the overgrown lawn.

To Kelly's generally unromantic eye, this was a space perfect for secret assignations, doomed love affairs, and promises that could not be kept. She wasn't sure why; it was just *so* atmospheric, so moody and elegantly shabby. It made her want to read a romance novel and imagine herself in a gown, breasts pushed up to her chin with some medieval marvel of corsetry, being wooed in secret by one of the King's men.

She was sleep-deprived, though, so that was probably feeding the delusion.

In truth, she supposed, she was being held captive in the forgotten library of some mountain man's moldering mansion. Which, if pleasingly alliterative, was not great. Those freaking dogs, for starters. Who ran around with a pack of wolves? And he hadn't ever seemed too pleased to meet her. When they'd been introduced at the cafe, she'd noted the distrust in his eyes. It had been more annoying than anything. Another guy who hated the media. Great. Like he was so unique in thinking journalists were evil. He probably did all his own research on the internet, too.

Not that there was internet here.

She'd checked; no Wi-Fi networks to be found in this pile of bricks. And definitely no signal. Earlier in the afternoon, while she'd been stuck in a tree waiting for the wolves to disappear into the house, she'd found one measly bar of cell phone signal. But it hadn't proven strong enough to get a text or a phone call out. As far as the outside world was concerned, Kelly O'Connell was probably dead. Or just lost. Which was kind of embarrassing. With apologies to her friends and family, Kelly would prefer they reported her as endangered, as opposed to lost. The sad, pathetic truth: Kelly couldn't stay on the trail.

Her wanderings eventually took her to the tall casement windows, and she peered curiously; evidently night had fallen while she'd been exploring her surroundings, dusk enveloping the weedy lawn and the somber fir trees leaning over the house like a dark sea surging over the shore. She was glad she'd already found the old-fashioned button that turned on a single wan lamp near the library door. There was just enough light to read, if she could find the concentration to peer at some antique tome, but after some perusals of the dense old books on the shelves, Kelly finally decided she preferred simply languishing in a leather wing chair, thinking about how much her feet hurt. She really should have broken in those new hiking boots before she went out and got lost on a mountainside in them. But who had the time?

A knock at the door turned her head with a snap. "Yes?" she called, trying to keep her voice even.

"Can I come in?"

"Of course you can," she scoffed. "It's your house."

"Well, it's locked."

"Oh, right." She'd forgotten that she'd locked him out. A bold move, she supposed, locking the man out of a room in his own house, but then again, he kept wolves around. "No dogs, right?" she asked through the door, her fingers on the lock.

"They're back in the mudroom," he said patiently. "But they wouldn't hurt you—"

"I don't care." She opened the door and looked up. "Good grief, you're tall. I keep forgetting."

He hadn't seemed this tall in the cafe, but maybe she'd just been distracted by the conversation she'd been eavesdropping on for such a long time. Or maybe she hadn't been standing so close to him, then, making it less noticeable. And their conversation on the street had been from a few feet apart. So that made sense.

Well, she was just inches from him now. Kelly was keenly aware of the way William towered over her. His broad chest was level with her nose. She lifted her face and saw his pointed chin just above the top of her head. She saw the faint line of his stubble, a dark beard breaking through tanned skin. Suddenly, Kelly's fingers tingled, as if she was rubbing them over those renegade bristles. Her heart made a sudden, confusing lurch against her ribs.

She took a step back, as much so she could look him in the eye as to put some physical distance between them. And her hands? She put them firmly behind her back where they couldn't do anything insane. "Sorry about locking you out," she muttered, suddenly embarrassed.

He rubbed his chin, smiling. Kelly had to twist her fingers together. "No, no, I probably would do the same thing. It's been a little, um, wild out here, hasn't it?"

"You said it," she sighed. "Well . . . come in, I guess?"

William laughed. "Thanks."

She stepped aside, and he strode into the room, throwing himself into one of the wing chairs with a tired sigh. She watched him lift his long legs over the chair arm, effortlessly graceful in that lanky frame. "It's not easy moving a fridge all by yourself, you know," he told her, sighing. "You should have come out and helped me."

"Me?" Kelly cautiously took a seat in the chair facing him. She sat on the very edge; the cold leather squeaked a protest beneath her. The noise almost made her leap up again. Her nerves were completely out of control, she decided. This man was not good for her. "What would you expect me to do, exactly? I couldn't move a fridge."

"Cheer me on," William suggested. His deep brown eyes twinkled, the tan skin around them folding into creases that suggested a smile. "Or at least open the front door for me."

"You could have left all the doors open. It's already freezing in here." She felt a sudden shiver at the words. She'd been so cold, for so long, she'd forgotten about it. And the moment she'd seen William, she'd felt warm all over. But his reminder let the chill of the room seep back into her bones.

"God!" he exclaimed, heaving himself out of the chair with such violence, she nearly got up and ran away again. "I'm still all warmed up from work, but you must be an icicle. Hang on one second."

Kelly watched him race from the room. His movement was so effortless and balanced for such a tall man; there was nothing ungainly or clumsy about him. And he'd shed his coat, leaving just a flannel shirt that hugged his broad shoulders. It was the first time she'd seen him without a coat. It was quite warming, really. Kelly bit her lip, shaking her head at herself. Okay, William Cunningham was a really, really sexy guy. She could admit that and move on, right? She wasn't here to get mixed up with some village black sheep.

She had to focus on finding Monica, preferably while not getting herself killed in the woods, either from her own stupidity or by the hands of some deranged person. Pursuing William, the sexy mountain man, was not on the agenda.

The floorboards in the hall squeaked, announcing William's imminent return, and Kelly tried to arrange herself in a nonchalant pose before he reentered. Unfortunately, she found that she'd forgotten how to sit. What did people *do?* What she arrived at was some sort of half-lounging posture, draped partially over one fat arm of the wing chair, her legs crossed saucily. It wasn't good, but she was pretty sure if she tried to change position now, she'd fall out of the chair.

William paused in the doorway, gazing at her. "Are you okay?"

Evidently he thought she'd had a stroke and keeled over in the sixty seconds he'd been gone. She gripped the arm of the chair, straightened, and cleared her throat, feeling foolish. "Yes. I'm—I'm just tired, I guess."

"Of course you are. Well, this will warm you up. I should have thought of it before." William held up a box with wire caging. "Space heater." He eyed the yawning space between the chairs and the lone electrical socket on the wall next to the door. There was enough room there to dance a waltz. Or play a vigorous round of Twister. Kelly decided she was up for either, but she wasn't quite sure how to bring it up. William frowned at the gap. "We'll have to do some rearranging first, though. Let me move that chair?"

Kelly obligingly hopped out of her chair, noticing as she did so that her feet were nearly numb with cold. It was almost a blessing; her feet didn't hurt nearly as much now. She let William drag the chairs across the floor, wincing a little as the chair legs squealed against the hardwood. From down the hall, a few yelps let her know the wolf pack felt the same way.

"You're hobbling," William said, watching her trip across the floor. "What happened?"

"My feet are numb," she admitted. "And I think they're blistered." She sat down and pushed off her boots, holding her socked feet towards the glowing space heater. "I spent a little more time wandering through the forest than on my typical workday."

"Yeesh." William gave her a sympathetic smile. "Glad that's over. Sit down and I'll make you some tea, okay?"

This was good. Warmth, and tea, and the low-level hum in her bloodstream that he seemed to inspire just by sharing this space with her. Kelly flexed her toes and wondered if she could just stay here forever, let the outside world spin away without her.

But of course, she couldn't. Reality pricked at the back of her thoughts, taking over her dreams of escape. She might be on her way out of the journalism world, but she wasn't done yet. And she still had to deal with the potential that she'd become a *second* missing hiker from the Cascade Falls trail. The rangers—her car— people were going to be looking for her.

"I have to get back," she reminded William. "People will be looking for me."

"But you just said your feet are numb and blistered. What am I going to do, drop you off by your car and say good luck with the pedals? Listen. It's freezing out there, and it looks like rain," William went on, shaking his head. "Tell you what—I'll make you some tea, and then I'll drive down the lane until I find some service and I'll call the park ranger office and let them know you're safe."

"Will they send someone to get me?" Kelly had some vague idea that she'd done something wrong and would have to complete an exit interview about her foolishness, at the very least.

"Well . . ."

She tilted her head. "What?"

"Here's the thing about that. I'm not giving them my name or address. I'll just let them know you're safe and you'll be back in civilization ASAP. But no one's coming up here for you."

"What? Why on earth not?" She sat upright, suddenly afraid of what he might say next. Oh, damn, was William a serial killer after all? She should have guessed—weren't people always falling for murderers? That was how people got murdered, for heaven's sake. They all had some sexy vibe, probably. Piercing brown eyes the color of a fall forest after a rainy day—Kelly stopped her thoughts, with an effort, before they got out of hand.

"It's not because of you," William said, holding up a hand as if to stop her from running away. "It's—there's someone else here, on the property, and they don't want to be found. At least, I think there's someone else here. They might be gone now."

Kelly pulled her feet underneath her, wincing at the pinprick feeling of blood returning. "What are you talking about? Who is here?"

"I'm not sure." But William's gaze shifted away from hers, and she recognized that guilty expression from earlier in the day. When he'd found out she was a reporter, and he'd immediately behaved as if he had something to hide.

He couldn't possibly mean Monica is here somewhere, can he?

Kelly felt every fear she'd worked through this afternoon rushing straight back to her brain. Marching out into the forest looking for answers like she was some big-shot bounty hunter or something. And now here she was, curled up on his wing chair with her shoes off, practically *begging* to be tied up and murdered. She didn't know this guy! So he was really tall and had nice eyes and a kind smile! What did that matter? He was standing here refusing to give his address to the police so that she could be rescued—*uh, kind of a red flag, Kelly!*

"I don't know who's here," William repeated, sighing. "I know that sounds crazy, but there's someone in the dairy and they clearly don't want to be seen by me. So I'm leaving them alone to figure it out."

Kelly shook her head, staring at him as if it was the first time she'd seen him. Certainly the undercurrent of arousal he'd inspired by his presence had completely left her system now. "You're insane," she whispered, and he winced.

"I might be," he agreed, looking straight into her eyes again. "But I'm definitely harmless."

"Insane, but harmless," she repeated. She studied his face. There was guilt, sure, but it was the guilt of a child who stole a lollipop at the grocery store. Suddenly, she remembered his conversation with Rosemary and Nikki. His silly chatter. Bubblegum and baseball cards. A big kid. "Yeah, I can buy that. Insane but harmless."

She didn't know if she meant insane in a *you're definitely a murderer* way or if she'd moved back into a more gentle, *you're a very crazy space cadet* kind of way. She hadn't made up her mind yet. But she did feel marginally less like she was about to be chopped up into pieces, which was nice.

William stood up, his height unfolding gradually above her. "Listen, let me make you some tea. It'll be five minutes. Can I leave you here for five minutes to warm up? And then I'll go deal with the phone situation."

Slowly, Kelly nodded. She didn't have a *lot* of choice. Her feet really hurt too much to run away again. Every minute she stayed off of them, she was more aware of how much damage she'd done. And he didn't *seem* like he was going to murder her. He seemed nice. Much nicer, in fact, then he had back in the cafe, when he'd been pretty rude.

"It's fine," she agreed finally. "Thank you. But, um, the person in your dairy, William. That's a little weird, right? Can we agree that's weird?"

"It's weird, but I promise you I'm not involved. At all. The dogs barked, and I went to see, and it was clear that someone was in there and didn't want to be found. The way I see it, if someone doesn't want to be found, I have to respect that. I just got back last night, after all. They didn't know I was going to show up and want my land back all of a sudden, right?"

Kelly had never heard logic like this before. It sounded admirably giving and ridiculously naïve. Sort of a mix of charming and dismaying. "But there could be an ax-murderer in your dairy," she pointed out.

"And I could be an ax-murderer up in this house," William pointed out. "See? It works both ways."

She sighed at his word choice. This guy. What was with this guy? "Please don't give me a reason to go running into the darkness by putting ideas in my head."

William leaned forward and, to her intense surprise (and shocking delight) ran his fingers familiarly over her messy hair. "Don't go running into the night, city girl. It's cold out there and I don't want to have to go chasing you."

Again, Kelly thought, watching him leave the room, not great with the ominous-sounding phrasing. But she was beginning to understand that William wasn't dangerous.

Just a little out of practice with talking to people.

He came back about five minutes later, as he'd promised, with two mugs of tea and a bag of mini chocolate chip cookies. Kelly burst into surprised laughter when he came into the room, a mug in each hand and the bag clenched between his teeth. "You should have trained your wolves to be butlers," she snorted, carefully taking the bag from his mouth and brushing the top edge along the side of her chair, drying it as casually as she could.

"Wolves?" William sat down next to her. "Ahhh, that's nice. I've been on my feet all day today, too. Getting back here always means a big transition from driving. It's getting harder on my back and legs every year. Getting old," he added contentedly, handing her a mug of steaming tea.

"You don't sound too mad about it." Kelly watched for signs of aging like a witch leaning into her enchanted mirror, clutching angrily at every slightly paler hair, certain each one would be her first gray. Her mother's dark hair had gone snow-white at age forty-five, which had been quite a startling change for all of them, but especially for her father, whose pale blonde hair had simple gotten more pale, as if fading from years of sunlight. Kelly figured that genetics were not her side, and had an idea that thirty-one was the start of her last full decade as a natural blonde.

"I figure getting old is a privilege not everyone is granted," William replied. He sounded suddenly far away, and Kelly glanced over at him. She wasn't surprised to see him gazing into the distance, eyes unfocused.

"Is this your family house?" she asked, figuring she might as well get some answers. Her reporter's brain liked to know exactly what was going on around her, at all times. The mystery here was driving her crazy.

"It was," William answered, still at a distance. "Now it's mine."

His words made her blink. Sore subject, she decided, when he didn't elaborate. "And I got the impression earlier today, back at the cafe, that you travel most of the year?"

"That's right." He came back then, smiling at her. "I live in the truck, mostly. I camp. Sometimes I rent a cabin, if I can find one cheap enough. Me and the dogs, we stick together, go all over the west. Following the snow-melt, then running away from the first snowflakes. This year we spent the summer in Wyoming, and then drove south until October...started back from Colorado two weeks ago and of course you saw we just got back."

"So you're a nomad."

"A part-time nomad."

"But why, when you have this house?"

"Because the house is empty," William said simply.

She looked around. "It's still empty now. You could go south, if you were just following good weather."

He shook his head. "I don't mind it so much in the winter. Except for Christmas. I hate it at Christmas. But for the rest of the winter, it's fine. And if I didn't do any work on the old girl, she'd fall down. It's on the National Register of Historic Places, so I'd probably get in a lot of trouble, aside from feeling bad about it."

Kelly took a cookie from the bag and inspected it. The little hard ones. "Will you judge me if I dunk this in my tea?"

William shook his head again, smiling. "A judgment free zone."

"Good." She dipped the cookie in her mug. "You know, I don't really like Christmas, either."

"Ah, a fellow Scrooge!"

"It's not that, it's just...it's never really been for me. My parents are really bookish. They would rather just sit in...well, in a room like this, if they could fit one into their rancher, but I think the ceilings are eight feet, not sixteen." She grinned, then bit into her cookie, taking a moment to savor the softness, the sugar and the tea spreading across her tongue. "Christmas vacation was always just a time for them to take a little break. Read some books they'd bought for each other. I wanted to get out and see things, but they were tired. They still are...they're professors, they teach at the University of Virginia. Christmas is their one downtime for months, I guess."

"Do they still just sit and read at Christmas?"

"They do. It's so still and quiet there. I take extra shifts at the station and tell them it's mandatory." They were so proud of her, they didn't even complain. "It was awful."

"You work through Christmas to avoid reading with your parents." William smiled. "Well, you can always spend the holiday with me, and we can sit and hate it together."

She found herself smiling back. "A nice idea. The bitterest Christmas ever."

"What would your ideal Christmas be?"

She thought about it. Dunked another cookie, thought some more. For some reason, no answers swam to the surface. "You know, I'm not sure anymore. But I *think* it would be really over the top. The lights, the carols, the marshmallows in the hot chocolate, the works."

"Phew." William shook his head, looking pained. "I don't know that I could manage *that*."

"How disappointing," she joked. "Here I thought you were about to be my Christmas elf and grant my wishes."

"I don't think that's an elf's role," William mused. "Elves make toys, they don't grant wishes."

"Well, they tell Santa what I want and *he* grants the wishes... right?"

"No, because you tell Santa in a letter...or face to face."

"Face to face?" Kelly raised her eyebrows.

"At Macy's," William clarified. "On Thirty-fourth Street in Manhattan. That's the only place you can really meet Santa Claus."

"How dare you? I have it on the best authority that I met Santa six times between the age of two and eight, and every single time he was right outside a Dillard's in the Charlottesville mall. You're telling me that was a *faux* Santa?"

"That was a Santa imposter," William told her gravely. "I'm so sorry you had to hear it from me."

"Lies! And to think I trusted you." Kelly tossed a cookie at him, and William caught it deftly.

"You trust me now?"

Oh, embarrassing. She wanted to curl in on herself, form a tiny ball, and roll out of the room. "I mean...sure, I trust you."

"No more insinuating I want to chop you up and bury you in the backyard?"

"William, you really have to work on your phrasing around a lady," she sighed, shaking her head. "That kind of thing is too specific. It infers you've been thinking about how you'd do it. Like you're looking at me and just considering the best way to get rid of me."

"I'm sorry," he said, instantly contrite. "I assure you, when I look at you, I'm not thinking about that at all."

And his eyes flicked up and down her as if he was drinking her in as quickly as possible.

Kelly felt a shiver run from her warmed toes to her hot cheeks, and once again, she had to curse that blushing skin of hers. She turned her head, hoping her hair would hide the embarrassing rush of blood beneath her skin, and as she did so, she saw her discarded phone resting on the table near the door. The outside world came flooding back. "Oh no," she sighed, tugging her feet from beneath her. "We still haven't told anyone I'm here!"

"Do you really want to?" William's question was so quietly posed, she had to turn and look at him for a moment, trying to determine if he'd spoken at all.

"No," she admitted finally. It felt good to know the answer, even if she was pretty sure it was the wrong one. "I like being a ghost. There's nothing out there I want to go back to. Not yet, anyway."

"I'll make the call," William promised her. "But only to make sure no helicopters swoop over here tonight. The dogs would hate that. They're dogs, by the way. Not wolves."

"I probably knew that," Kelly said. "I have some logical areas of my brain."

"So I'll go call," William repeated, as if convincing himself. He stood up and placed his teacup on the table.

"I'll come with you," she offered.

"I'd rather you wait here," he said gently. "So as not to get cold again. I don't need you getting sick."

"What do you need me to do?"

He looked at her, those deep brown eyes meltingly soft. "I need you to be here when I get back."

"I'll be right here," Kelly whispered. "I promise not to run away. Or lock you out," she added, smiling almost shyly.

They looked at each other for a long moment, and Kelly thought he was taking her measure, deciding if he wanted to say anything else. A flood of words rushed through her brain and were discarded just as quickly. Without thinking, without stopping to ponder, she stepped forward, tilted her chin up, and looked into his eyes.

William's hand came to her cheek, warmth flooding from his fingers, so that for a moment she wondered how a man could be so incredibly hot, like a furnace raged inside him. Then his mouth came down to meet hers, and she gave in to his kiss without another thought.

Chapter Sixteen

Nadine

Filling stalls with shavings wasn't Nadine's usual job, but the empty stalls in the barn needed to be prepped, and she wanted to have them ready for the Wayne horses as soon as they could get them moved over. Plus, it was her idea. No reason to burden Darby with her brainwaves.

Once she'd pushed the community service angle to the faculty heads, they'd agreed that she could take in three of the abandoned horses, as long as she felt they had a decent probability of joining the riding school in the future. Nadine had felt bad about only taking the horses with the most potential for riding and jumping work, but Rosemary brushed away her concerns. "Of course I want the school to get horses they can *use*," she assured Nadine. "One of the toughest things in the world is convincing people that horses who can't be ridden still have value. That's why I take in unrideable horses for life. So no, I'm not going to ask our school admins to figure that out in their very first year. Horse rescue is a long game."

Of course, Rosemary was sweet and forgiving about everything, so Nadine had no doubt she'd have said something similar even if she was annoyed. But the truth in Rosemary's words was easy to recognize. Horses had to have jobs. It was very difficult to justify their expensive upkeep if they didn't give back. A sad, unassailable fact.

Darby was walking along the other stalls, checking water and hay levels for the night. She paused outside the stall, watching Nadine shake out a fat plastic bag of bedding.

"You want me to do that?" she asked.

Nadine looked up, spitting sawdust from between her lips. She studied her assistant for a moment. Darby was twenty, with the stick figure most of the wealthy school girls aspired to, but surprisingly strong. She could lift two shavings bags onto her shoulders and still manage to sprint down the barn aisle when she saw a horse shoving an unlatched door open—Nadine had seen her do it. "No, that's fine," she said finally. "You've been doing the heavy work all day."

"I don't mind." Darby crossed her thin arms over her chest, leaning on the stall door. "I'm not against this, you know. It's just three more horses. So if you need help, just ask."

"Maybe you can come with me to the Wayne farm in the next few days and pick up the horses."

"Of course. I'd be happy to." Darby fiddled with the stall door latch for a moment. When she spoke again, it was with a decidedly nonchalant air. "So, um, I heard something about a Christmas carnival to benefit the horse rescue. Is that really happening? The girls are all talking about it like it's a done deal."

Nadine wiped sweat from her brow. "How on earth do they know about it already?"

"You know teenagers. They have ears like bats."

"Well, I'm trying to get something rolling, along with Nikki and Rosemary. Rides and food, and I'm going to talk to Sean about bringing the horse show club to do an exhibition. What do you think of that?"

"They'll love it. Plus, I was thinking . . ." Darby flicked at a loose wisp of hay, stalling. "Maybe the project horses, the rescues you're bringing in—the girls could do little in-hand exercises with them. Right? Like walk them, show off their manners, maybe have them go over a bridge and a tarp."

"Like an in-hand trail class? Darby, that's a great idea!" Nadine started to spread the shavings with the manure fork. The stall filled with the scent of fresh pine. "Seriously," she went on, "I love it. What a fun way to get the new students excited about working with the horses. As many as we can get, anyway." She already had plans for Addy Doyle to take on one of the horses as her project. She hadn't decided who was best for the other two yet. Addy just seemed . . . well, she seemed the most lost at Long Pond, for lack of a better word.

Nadine didn't like to see any of the girls feeling lost.

"Thanks," Darby said, smiling broadly. "I'm glad you like it. Well, I'm done with the barn for the evening. I'll come back down for night check around nine."

"Perfect. Thank you, Darby." They switched off on night check, giving everyone the opportunity for uninterrupted evenings at home, rather than coming back down in their pajamas to check the horses before bed.

"No problem. Hey," she added as she started to walk away, "did you hear about the second hiker?"

"The second—no. What are you talking about?" Nadine came to the stall door, resting the manure fork on the concrete barn aisle. She had a sudden feeling of dread fill her, ice-cold and metallic on the tongue.

"Oh, you won't believe it. Some reporter went hiking on the Cascade Falls Trail and disappeared. Same trail as the other woman." Darby raised her eyebrows. "Pretty crazy, right?"

Nadine didn't know what to say. It couldn't be . . . "Was her name Kelly?" she asked finally.

"I think that's it, actually. Wait, you didn't know her, did you?"

"Rosemary was telling me about her. She met her at Nikki's cafe." Nadine shook her head, feeling as if she had actually met Kelly, knew her. "This is getting too weird." *And too close to home.* "I don't like it. We have to keep the girls close. No trail rides, okay? Everyone stays in the indoor. And anyone who goes out to the pasture gets an escort. Or at least someone in the barn watching them."

Darby nodded. "I think that's a good plan."

Nadine picked up the rake she'd left in the doorway and smoothed out the shavings, even though they were already flat. As she scraped and raked, she murmured, "I can't believe it's come to this. In Catoctin Creek, of all places."

Her phone rang as she finished up the job. Nikki, sounding tired but determined. "Come down to the cafe when you're done with the barn," she commanded. "Bring Sean. Emergency carnival meeting. Dinner will be served."

"Emergency?" The word was alarming.

"Oh, you know what I mean. Last-minute. Just, come on."
Nikki hung up.

Well, Nadine thought, sliding her phone back into her pocket.
At least she didn't have to figure out what they were eating for
dinner tonight.

Chapter Seventeen

Rosemary

Rosemary hadn't even been certain the old fairgrounds out behind the volunteer firefighter station were still available. She'd been concerned they might have been sold, and she'd tried to line up some back-up sites, just in case she couldn't get access to the land.

"Nope, not sold," Kevin told her. He was hunched over one of her horse's hooves, filing away. A dusting of hoof shavings was falling over his steel-toed boots like a miniature snowstorm. Nearby, Grover was contentedly chewing on a sliver of hoof. "I went up there and asked myself. You know Chuck, at the fire station. He says they manage the land. I said, 'Manage? Looks like it's abandoned,' and he told me it would be fine once they ran a bush-hog over it. I asked him how soon he could get it cleaned up and he said they'd fit it in next week."

Rosemary stared at the back of Kevin's neck. "That's incredible! Just like that? No fees or anything?"

"Nah, all free. I told him it was for charity, for this place, and he said as long as we could cover the liability insurance, it was all ours."

"The liability insurance," Rosemary echoed. "Oh, no. That sounds important."

"No worries. Ronnie's on it. I stopped in at the farm bureau office on the way here. He's got a guy."

"He's got a guy." Rosemary shook her head. This was really happening.

She'd never heard of anything coming together so quickly. It had just been a few days, and the carnival was going from theoretical to a real date on the calendar. Could this be the very definition of a Christmas miracle?

If so, the horses deserved it. She had a tent barn arriving in the next few days; it would provide shelter for the nine horses remaining. Despite her best efforts to shop the horses to potential rescues, no other rescue in the region had room to take any horses in. "It's a tough time of year," she heard, over and over.

And she knew it was. Rosemary had been in this game long enough to understand that late autumn was when people who hadn't been able to afford to buy a load of hay for winter confronted their skinny horses for the first time; when unrideable ponies with cute color patterns got sold at auction as Christmas presents; when everyone and their brother were out asking for donations or trying to buy advertising space on social media. The giving season could be a very trying time to try to get people to give.

That was what made the carnival such a fantastic idea. They were giving something back to the people. The whole *portion of proceeds goes to charity* approach could be a lot more palatable than asking for a check.

Kevin straightened, groaning a little as his spine unraveled from its bend, and let the horse's hoof slip to the ground. "That heel's looking good," he told the mare, giving her a friendly pat on the neck. "You sure are growing some nice new feet, missy."

"She's been a work in progress for years," Rosemary said, momentarily distracted from the carnival. She felt proud of the little mare for getting a compliment. "Gus has been practically begging her to grow out those heels."

"Looks like she finally agreed." Kevin stretched from side to side. "Oh boy, this job is going to kill me yet."

"No regrets, I hope." Rosemary handed him his coffee mug. "Since you gave up your entire life and career to be a farrier."

"Too late now," he said cheerfully, and took a long drink from the mug. "No, no regrets. It's hard, though, working your way into this business. I'm still a lot slower than Gus. Can't get through as many horses in a day. I spend hours more working every day than he does. Seems like speed pays the bills, which is kind of funny, since I was hoping for a slower life when I left the city."

Rosemary laughed. "The country life has a way of grinding out your hopes and dreams, doesn't it?"

"Or at least reshapes them." Kevin picked up the hoof rasp again, tossing it skillfully. "But I'll get there, eventually. And with Nikki working night and day, it hardly matters, right? Both of us are just investing every minute we've got into our futures. Whenever that is."

"She must be busy today," Rosemary said. "I haven't heard from her all day."

"Wrecked. I texted her earlier, and she said she borrowed a waitress from Lauren to deal with all the customers. Between the reporters and the gawkers and the antiquers . . ." He shook his head. "Weird week in Catoctin Creek, huh?"

"Weird everything," Rosemary admitted. "I'll be happy to see the end of these little mysteries. The horses, these hikers . . . did they say what happened to Kelly, yet?"

"I haven't heard," Kevin said. "But I'm sure she's fine. Nikki said she was a very capable looking woman."

He picked up the mare's hoof again and began to file away.

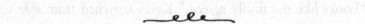

Despite Kevin's description of her day, Nikki still called an emergency meeting of the carnival committee at the cafe that evening. "Dinner provided," she told Rosemary when she called, "so bring Stephen and don't worry about feeding him after."

They arrived at the cafe around seven, and found an impressive crowd gathered there: Nadine and Sean, of course, but also everyone else who had been roped into helping put on the carnival: Elaine and Ronnie from the feed store, Mickey from Trout's Market, Chuck from the volunteer fire department, Connie from the ice cream parlor, and even a newcomer to town, Vicki Hodgekiss, who had opened Kiss and Tell Antiques on Main Street at the end of summer. Kevin was putting out cartons of fried chicken and biscuits on the tables, which had been pulled close together for ease of conversation. His hair was wet and slicked back, fresh from the shower, and he grinned at Rosemary as she took in the scene, her eyes wide, from the doorway.

She looked up at Stephen, hardly able to believe what was happening. "They're doing all of this for the horses?" she whispered.

He squeezed her hand. "Your horses are bringing this town together. Pretty impressive, wife."

"Thanks, husband," she said dryly. "I just hope it's not all going too smoothly to last."

Just then, the door bell jangled behind them. Rosemary stepped out of the way, looking over her shoulder, and saw a tired-looking man looking around the room, eyes wary. He wore a blue suit beneath his winter coat. "Did I stumble into a private party?" he asked. "I just wanted to grab a coffee."

"I can get you a coffee," Rosemary said. "No—it's no problem," she added when he tried to wave her away. "I can see a full pot behind the counter, and we all know each other here."

Nikki was hustling behind the counter, putting together paper packets with a stapler and gritted teeth. "Who is that?" she hissed. "I turned off the *Open* sign an hour ago."

Rosemary shrugged, pulling a paper cup from the dispenser. "Probably another reporter, to be honest. I heard you were busy with them all day."

"I was. The vultures. Well, maybe someone can spare a minute to cover our carnival."

"Probably not until they find the missing hikers," Rosemary sighed. She poured the coffee, then turned to get a lid from the counter. She nearly spilled the coffee as she saw Nikki sway on her feet, clutching at the counter to remain upright. "Nikki! What's wrong?" She put down the cup and grabbed at her friend.

"Nothing," Nikki muttered. "Shhh—don't get anyone freaked out, please."

"Are you sick? You're sweating!" Rosemary swiped at a bead of sweat on Nikki's forehead. "Do you have a fever? Maybe it's the flu

—"

"No, no, it's nothing, I swear. I had a stomach cramp. I took a pill. Everything's alright. Just let it go, okay?" Nikki's voice was low. "I promise you, Rosie-marie, I am fine. Just kind of wiped out from this day."

Rosemary looked over Nikki with a critical eye. "I'm going to keep watch on you, girl," she said finally, and put the lid on the coffee cup. "Do you want me to charge him for this?"

"No. Just give it to the guy and we'll get started." Nikki had closed her eyes; her fingernails were still digging into the counter top. That must be *some* stomach cramp, Rosemary thought, aching with sympathy. She knew Nikki was used to working through every kind of illness, never taking a sick day unless she was either contagious or simply unable to get out of bed. She hoped the carnival wasn't going to add too much strain on top of the bakery and the management of the Blue Plate. But she was pretty sure it would.

"Thanks, what do I owe you?" the man asked, accepting the cup from her gratefully.

"On the house," she said. "On account of us closing early and all."

"No, I'm happy to pay."

"Are you in town for the missing hikers?" Rosemary asked, studying him.

"Yeah, just arrived from D.C."

"I have a favor to ask," she said. "See if you can get your station to do a story on our Christmas carnival, will you? That's what we're planning tonight. I know everything is sad and awful, but it's for charity and we still need some eyes on that, too."

He nodded. "Sure, I can pitch that. Hopefully this story will be history in a day or two, anyway."

"Hopefully," Rosemary agreed.

"And hey," the reporter paused in the doorway. "Where can I get a plate of that fried chicken? Please tell me the restaurant's open."

"Oh, yes. The Blue Plate, just down the street. They're open. You'll probably want to do a story on your dinner, too, once you taste that chicken."

"I don't doubt it," the reporter said, grinning. Then he went out into the night.

Rosemary turned and surveyed the cafe. Everyone was seated, Nikki included, flipping through the pages of the booklets she'd passed out. Rosemary slid into the seat between Nikki and Stephen, feeling eternally lucky ·to be surrounded by such incredible people.

But she was going to keep a close eye on Nikki. Maybe her best friend thought she needed to protect Rosemary all the time, but she didn't even realize Rosemary was keeping watch over her, too, for all these years.

"So which idea is the most exciting?" Stephen asked. They were driving back to Notch Gap Farm, bellies full of chicken and biscuits, heads full of stars. There was a lemon meringue pie in a box on Rosemary's lap, but unless she was very much mistaken, they wouldn't be touching it before the next day.

Lemon meringue could make a nice breakfast, though.

She looked at the moon, nearly full now, shining through the crowns of the trees. The forests were finally shedding their summer cloaks, going bald for the season. She thought about winter fully setting in, and all the complications it would bring: icy water troughs, wet horse blankets, muddy barnyards and pasture gates, the prospect of snow, in general. It was very hard to feel excited about anything, when faced with all that. "I don't know," Rosemary sighed, trying to come up with something. "I'm impressed with Sean and Nadine's idea for a riding exhibition. It's a fun way to include the school in the town."

"And Nadine's idea to do a makeover on one or two of the rescue horses?" Stephen prodded. "Are you okay with that?"

"I am." Rosemary hadn't been sure at first—they knew nothing about these horses, and she didn't want to push them too hard by putting them into the loud, bright spectacle of a carnival.

But Nadine pointed out that they'd be living in the hustle and bustle of the Long Pond stables for over a month by the time the carnival rolled around, and during that period, the horses would be exposed to a lot of noise and movement they hadn't experienced at the Wayne farm. Everyone would have an idea of how the horses would respond to a festival environment well before the event itself.

So Rosemary allowed herself to shrug away her concerns. "Nadine seemed really passionate about it, and I trust her to do the right thing by the horses. I'm going to put aside my own concerns this time. Anyway, those three horses are really for her to handle, not me. I can't micromanage her."

"You're probably the world's best boss." Stephen chuckled and slowed the truck, preparing to turn into the farm's half-hidden driveway. "I bet Nadine forgets you're her manager most of the time."

"Please, *I* forget it," Rosemary confessed. "Once I started turning over those adoption horses instead of just keeping every horse that comes into the barn, I completely ran out of time to worry about the school. So Nadine handles everything and gives me the credit. At the last board meeting, I didn't even bring notes. I had to stop by Nadine's office and pick up her binder to share out what was going on in the barn." She sighed at the memory; she'd been embarrassed to do that to Nadine, although the younger woman swore she didn't mind.

"Do you plan on doing adoptions again? Once you're done with this intake, I mean," Stephen added. "Obviously these horses will get adopted out."

"I think so," Rosemary mused. "I thought life would get easier if I went back to just running a sanctuary. But I guess the Wayne horses are a reminder that my job is bigger than that. If I can do rescue and adoptions, I should be doing it."

"There are definitely more horses in need than the ones you can keep forever. And you've been doing a great job finding homes for horses all around the county." Stephen gave her hand a quick squeeze. "You're amazing."

"Oh, please." She shook her head at him, and watched the headlights pick out the bridge over the creek, then the house and barn overlooking the lawn and woods. "I'm surrounded by amazing people. Believe me, that helps. I can't believe everyone who came to that meeting tonight! And the way Nikki organized it! She's running two businesses as it is. And honestly, Stephen, I don't know that she's one hundred percent right now. She looks really rundown."

"Did you ask her about it?"

"I did, but you know how prickly Nikki is." They pulled up in front of the house, and Rosemary did her customary look around, making sure the lamp above the barn door was lit, and the kitchen light at the back of the house was on. The little things that told her the house and barn were operating properly, all systems go, and set her constantly worrying mind at ease.

Stephen opened her door and held out a hand. Rosemary handed the pie box to him. She loved the way he always hurried to open her door, whether they were going or coming. People said New Yorkers were rude, but born-and-bred city boy Stephen had the most chivalrous habits she'd ever seen. He took the pie box, hefted its weight as if testing it. "Well, the pie feels correct," he joked.

"Yeah. I was afraid she was catching the flu, but she said it was nothing."

"Probably just all the extra work catching up with her. People like Nikki won't stop for rest until they're forced to. She'll get sick and Kevin will make her go to bed and she'll get the nap her body's craving, most likely."

They walked up the porch steps together. Though the night was teeth-chattering cold, Rosemary paused before going into the house, turning to look back at the frozen moon rising over the trees. She'd forgotten about the lost hikers during their meeting tonight, and now the memory flooded back, making her feel guilty. How could people be lost in such settled land, she asked herself for the hundredth time. And then she went into the farmhouse where the Brunner family had lived for two hundred years, locking the door behind her. But she left the porch light on.

Just in case someone needed to see it tonight.

William

Chapter Eighteen

William

S he made him feel whole.

That was the only thing William could think, over and over again, after that first kiss. And after the second, and the third.

And after an hour's time, he thought it again. And after another hour, when they'd just about seemed to slake their thirst for one another, he thought it again, and he *almost* said it out loud, but he stopped himself. Because she'd already warned him that his unedited thoughts made him sound like a serial killer, and he knew he'd better watch that tendency.

She could still hoof it and go disappearing into the night if he scared her. Kelly had made one thing abundantly clear: she wasn't afraid to run away.

Still, at a certain point he realized he was hungry, the dogs were probably hungry, Kelly was probably hungry, *and* he'd never made that promised phone call. Which meant the park rangers might be alarmed, and if they had, in fact, realized Kelly had not come back, they'd have already informed the police—and in that scenario, the helicopters were probably getting gassed up right this instant. So he reluctantly leaned back on the chaise lounge where they'd found their make-out session to be the most comfortable, letting Kelly hover over him, her tangle of blonde hair tumbling over her shoulder and onto his chest.

"What is it?" she whispered, and he loved the huskiness of her tone, loved watching the swollen contours of her lips.

"I hate to let reality intrude," he murmured back, "but I never told the park rangers you were safe."

Her eyes widened. "Oh, no. That's probably bad. What time is it?"

They both turned as one to look at the carriage clock on the mantel. "Past eight?" she moaned. "It's been dark for hours. They thought I'd be back by noon. Everyone's going to think I'm dead. Or kidnapped."

"Or just lost," William suggested.

"Oh, be real," Kelly snapped. "No one really thinks Monica Waters is lost. Everyone thinks her boyfriend killed her and hid the body."

Something shifted inside William. Something guilty. "Really? That's what they're saying?"

"That's what they're *thinking.*" Kelly sat up and straightened her blouse, hiding the delicious promise of her breasts from him. "And that's what they'll think about me, too. Although Grayson will probably have a pretty solid alibi this time, so that should help him out, anyway."

"Grayson?" He'd never heard the name before. "Who is that?"

Kelly gave him a look which he couldn't quite interpret. Pity? Disappointment? Astonishment that he wasn't capable of keeping up with a simple news story? All of them were fair, he figured. She turned away from him, her voice going cold. "That's my—that's *Monica's* boyfriend. The one the police would love to pin for her murder. If they can, which so far they haven't been able to do."

"Or if she's been murdered at all," William said quickly, but he was focused on the way she'd stumbled over Monica's name. She'd said *my*.

She'd almost said Grayson was her boyfriend.

"And we don't think she was murdered," he added. "I don't, anyway."

Kelly shook her head. "I didn't think she was, either. But it's been nearly a week. And even I managed to find my way out of the woods without too much trouble. I'm not saying Grayson had any part in her disappearance, really, but where else could she be?"

William's eyes went to the window. The dairy couldn't be seen under the cover of darkness, of course, but he felt like he could look straight out to the little stone building. If the trespasser was still in there, what were they using for light? For warmth?

"Plus, it's freezing out there," Kelly continued. "Hey—what are you looking at?"

"Nothing," William said, shifting his gaze back to her.

"Anyway, this is why I hate working in the news. It's always bad news. The girl is always dead. And I have to tell everyone, and they pretend they care, but really they want to list all the ways the woman was in the wrong, all the ways she shouldn't have pissed off her man or made some stranger upset or had the nerve to go outside alone." Kelly stalked over to the table where they'd left the cookies and snatched a few out of the bag. Anger-snacking, William thought. "I'd rather do *anything* than go back to that apartment and pull together a story about how nothing good has happened in Catoctin Creek today, though, so I guess being dead through the evening broadcast has kind of saved me that misery, anyway."

"Don't say you're dead," William protested. "It makes me nervous. Look, I'll go make the call."

"I'll come with you," Kelly decided. "I'd better be on the phone, too, or they're going to think I'm—*deceased*—anyway. I'll say this for you, William," she sidled closer, and her face warmed to him again, "you know how to get a girl's blood flowing again."

— ♦♦ —

William insisted on bringing the dogs with them, so before they could leave, he had Kelly sit quietly in a chair in the kitchen while he led each dog over to meet her. They strained at their collars and slathered ferociously as they tugged to get at her, but once she figured out that they were just overjoyed to meet her, relations warmed considerably. The dogs gamboled around them as they walked down the driveway, Kelly snug in one of his wool sweaters and a pair of fleece-lined lady's gloves he'd found in a drawer.

"Whose were they?" she'd asked, smoothing the black leather with one hand before tugging the second glove on.

"Probably a cousin's," William hedged, not sharing that there hadn't been a cousin in this house in fifteen years. Hey, he'd shaken them thoroughly before bringing them downstairs. Only one moth had fluttered out. "Comfortable?"

"Nice and comfy," she said. "Thank you." And she'd snuggled up against him, letting him wrap an arm around her shoulder. "You're so warm," she told him. "It's like bringing along my own furnace."

They had to walk at least a half-mile to find service. William knew a spot close to the main road where he swore his phone would find two bars. It was cold, but companionable; watching the moon rise, pointing to the high clouds coming to overtake, listening to the breeze rattle the dry leaves still clinging to the tree branches. There was rain in the forecast; more cold, autumn rain that would bring muddy fields and damp houses, but at least tonight the change in weather was a pretty thing to watch, the clouds like ethereal paintings reflecting the light of the moon. Even if it was only hours before the first drops fell from the sky, William felt lucky to be out tonight, with this woman by his side.

Luckier, somehow, than he had felt in a long, long time.

He marveled at her presence, at the sudden influence she had on his mood, on his very body. His skin begged for her touch; his eyes sought out her gaze so often, he was embarrassed by it. What had started as an odd premonition just this morning had turned into a feverish obsession by nightfall. *Was this normal?* William wondered. Or was he just reacting to a kindred spirit with the same over-the-top dramatics he reacted to everything?

You take everything so hard, his mother had complained. *Not everything is life or death, Will.*

He had always begged to differ.

When they reached the last bend before the main road, William paused and pulled out his phone. He felt Kelly's eyes on him as he held it up. He thought he'd always feel it when she was looking at him.

But this time she wasn't gazing at him with desire or even with approval. She looked damned annoyed as he made a few half-turns, holding up his phone.

"Huh," he said, looking at the screen.

"Huh?" she repeated. "That doesn't sound good."

"It's not picking anything up." He shook his head, frowning at his phone. Really, phone? Tonight? "Try yours."

Kelly took out her phone and did a quick replay of his movements. Her brows came together. "Huh."

"Yeah." William scratched at the bristle on his jaw. "I—um—I don't know what's wrong. Maybe the tower is down?"

"Do you know where it is?"

He looked at her, puzzled. "Do I know where the phone tower is? No, I don't track their movements."

"It wouldn't *move*, William. God." Her voice was sharp.

They faced each other in the moonlight, both ready to start a fight if the other person so much as made a single wrong move. William felt the tension in his shoulders and neck tightening, along with the sudden desire to be alone, as he usually was. What was this girl doing in his driveway, in his house, anyway? She should go back to where she came from.

But Kelly proved more resilient to stress than he was. She was the first to back down.

"I'm sorry," she said, laughing softly. "Of course you don't know where the tower is. You don't care about how to get in touch with people. That's okay. It's not your thing. For me, my job, it's important that I always be in range. I can tell you the best places for video chats along with the dead zones for voice calls in like six different counties around D.C."

"How very useful," William huffed. "I guess we have different priorities."

"That's what I just said." Kelly glared at him, as if she'd given him a chance and he'd blown it. "Listen, are you planning on being a jerk now? Because I can start walking."

William took a deep breath, trying to still his own temper. Weird, the way it just flared up. He was usually so calm . . . but he was also usually alone.

Being with other people for a long time took reserves he wasn't sure he had anymore. Even people he liked. Even people he *wanted.*

"No," he said, breathing out. "I'm sorry. Listen, we can go back, get the truck, head towards town." He hated the idea even as he said it. If he took her into town, he might as well take her to get her car and go home. And he wanted her to stay.

He couldn't believe how much he wanted her to stay, even if it was taxing him to have someone else around for so long. Her voice in his house, her presence—it changed everything, somehow. He didn't want to be there alone tonight.

"That's probably for the best," Kelly was saying, but he could see the reluctance on her face. It buoyed his depressed spirits just a little. She wanted to stay with him. That was something, right?

"Hey," he said, his voice pitched low. "Kelly, listen, I—"

She turned her face up to him, her bold eyes glistening in the moonlight. "I get it, mountain man. You're a hermit. You're not used to other people."

"How do you—"

"I just know, okay?" And she pressed a kiss against his lips.

William sighed, sliding his hand around her back and pressing her close to him. For a moment, there was no night, no need to call off the cops, no mystery person in his dairy. There was only her.

And then Lola went racing past, barking her head off. The other dogs followed closely behind, baying like bloodhounds. Their kiss broke off abruptly and William stared after the dogs, startled.

"What on earth—" Kelly began.

William felt his heart start to pound out of control. "Wait right there," he gasped, taking off after the dogs. "I don't want them to go all the way to the road!"

The dogs were faster than him, of course, but William was a strong runner. Year-round, for sure, but especially in the first few weeks after he came back from the high elevations and steep tracks of the Rockies—he always returned with far more muscle and lung capacity than was needed for the low tumble of the Catoctins. He had no problem pacing the dogs for the first few hundred feet, and by the time he'd settled into their stride, the dogs realized he was coming along and slowed their gallop to accommodate him.

He convinced Lola to stop just a few feet before the road, and the rest of the pack skidded to a halt behind her. William breathed a sigh of relief as they nosed the brush at the end of the driveway. He didn't expect anyone to be driving by; the road was generally quiet at night. But he still didn't want them too close, just in case. These dogs were his family; he couldn't imagine losing them. William called the dogs over and gave them all a good rub around the ears. They panted up at him, those uncanny husky eyes shining in the moonlight, simply overjoyed with the turn the evening had taken. And then, as if nothing had ever called them down to the road at all, they went jogging back up the driveway towards the house.

William watched them for a minute, letting his breath slow, wondering why his dogs had just given him an impromptu half-mile sprint. And then he took out his phone and held it up. Two bars. It was enough.

He had to look up the ranger station number, though, and he couldn't get the data for a web search. Finally, he gave up and called a number from his address book—the last number he'd entered in, and the only number in Catoctin Creek he had.

The Catoctin Cafe & Bakery.

"Catoctin Cafe, hello?"

William frowned at the voice. If this was Nikki, she sounded terrible.

"Nikki? That you?"

A sigh. "William?"

"How did you know?"

"You have a Colorado phone number. When did that happen?"

"Oh, over the summer. I changed my plan and the whole number thing got mixed up. It's not important. Listen—oh, I'm sorry. Are you okay?"

"I'm fine." Nikki's voice cracked. "Why are you calling me? If this is a call-ahead order, forget it. I'm closed. Even to you."

"No, no." William looked up at the moon, clawed through by black tree branches. When had they started losing their leaves? Just today? The sudden cold snap must have done it. "I needed to tell someone, and I don't have any numbers, but I've got Kelly here."

There was a brief silence. "Kelly?"

"Kelly O'Connell, the reporter."

"The *missing* reporter! What do you mean, you've *got* her?"

"I mean she was lost, and she found her way to the house, and she's here with me now."

"Well, you better just bring her straight back to town and tell the police where she is," Nikki snapped, her voice recovering its usual bravado. "What are you telling me, for?"

William's gaze drifted back up the driveway. It was too dark to see her, but he knew she was there, waiting for him. By now, the dogs would have gotten back to her. He hoped they'd wait with her, make her feel safe and comfortable. "She's going to stay here tonight. And there's no signal up at the house. I had to walk down to the road to call anyone at all. You're the only local number I've got, besides calling 911."

Nikki's sigh could have blown down tall buildings. "What do you want me to do with this information, William?"

"Can you please call the park ranger station and let them know she's safe and accounted for?"

"William, do you have any idea how big a deal this is?"

"No," he said truthfully. "Can I continue not knowing?"

"Why is she staying overnight with you?"

He didn't answer.

"The boy who took everything . . ." Nikki challenged him.

"No, it's not like that. She wants to stay. I offered to take her home. She asked to stay here tonight. Seriously."

"And where is she now?"

"Up the driveway, waiting for me. I ran down to the end . . . the dogs . . . no phone signal . . ." His explanation faded, sounding ludicrous even to his own ears.

William waited while Nikki considered his request. When she spoke again, her voice was so tired, he barely recognized it. With a flash of alarm, William wondered if Nikki hadn't told him something about herself. Was she sick? They were all in their thirties now. Bad things could happen to them. And that would only get more likely as the years passed, faster and faster. William's heart seemed to flutter, the idea of losing all he held dear in Catoctin Creek suddenly pressing down on his chest, his shoulders, his head. If he could find some stability here, even for a moment, what would it matter? Everyone would still leave him in the end. One way or another.

"I'll handle it tonight," Nikki said, casually breaking through his personal panic. "But bring her back in the *morning*, William. You have to. This isn't a game. Not with the other woman missing."

A twinge of guilt, again. But Monica wasn't his story to tell . . . if she was really in his dairy, which she might not be. There was still a chance a bear was hibernating in there. Or a serial killer, to take up Kelly's favorite refrain.

"Thank you," he said. "Really, Nikki. Thank you."

"You owe me," Nikki told him grimly, and she hung up.

William realized he hadn't asked again about her health, hadn't been forceful enough about it. But then again, when had force gotten anyone anywhere with Nikki Mercer? She'd never tell what she didn't want to share.

It was constants like that which kept him coming home every winter.

Footsteps came crunching down the lane, the sound of boots breaking the dead underbrush he'd driven over with his truck the day he'd come home. "I told her," William said. "I mean, I told Nikki, at the bakery. And she's going to tell the rangers. They know Nikki around here; they'll trust her word if she says everything is under control."

"Thank you." Kelly's face was pale in the moonlight. He wanted to kiss her again, but more than that, he wanted to hold her close, feel her warmth pressed against him. Well, if she had any. She looked pretty cold.

"Let's get you back to the house," he said gently. "I'll start a fire in the living room and then I'll make us something to eat."

"You cook, too?" Kelly slid a gloved hand into his. "And here I thought you were just the average handsome hermit living in an abandoned house with your pack of wolves."

"Even hermits have to eat," he reminded her. "In fact, we have to cook more than most, because we don't live close to restaurants."

"Or humans?"

"Or humans," he confirmed.

"Maybe you'd like for me to get out of your hair," she suggested. "Leave you alone to live in your solitude?"

"Absolutely not," William said, with feeling.

Chapter Nineteen

Nikki

"I know," Nikki said. "Mm-hmm. Uh-huh. Well, that's what I'm telling you. Okay. Thanks, Don."

She put the phone down and looked at the ceiling. Don down at the park ranger station was deeply annoyed, but that wasn't on her. And she had enough problems, without borrowing some from everyone else in town. She groaned, rubbing at her side. The muscles in her lower back and side were cramping again, halfway between a backache and a stitch. Nikki felt as if she'd just gone for a long run and gotten herself dehydrated. In fact, now that she really thought about it, it seemed like for the past few days, she couldn't drink enough water to keep her body happy. She was up all night peeing, and up all day drinking, and still her body craved more, *demanded* more. She took the glass she'd left on the coffee table and drained it.

Kevin came into the living room with a thick piece of chocolate cake. He set the plate before her. "You look like you could use some chocolate."

"Kev, you have no idea," she sighed, leaning forward to snag some icing with a finger. "Thank you. Today was just never-ending. First the media circus coming through, like I was their private catering company. Then the carnival meeting, which admittedly I did to myself, but I do feel better that everyone got the information from one place, instead of letting this damn town play telephone like it usually does. But then the phone starts ringing, right when I think my day is through." She cleared her throat experimentally; her voice sounded raspy to her. "And do you hear my voice? Do I have a cold or something?"

"You just sound tired, and please don't take that the wrong way." Kevin sat down beside her. "The meeting was impressive, by the way. You really pulled everyone together. And at the last minute. It was smart; I heard about six different stories about the carnival on my rounds today. Word sure gets out fast around here."

"The way Rosemary had gotten all those contracts together, and Nadine was working on funding along with school stuff, we had to just pull the trigger and make sure everyone was on the same page. I couldn't let the rumor mill give everyone bad information, or we'd have people running in all different directions." Nikki paused long enough to taste her cake. The rich, creamy frosting seemed to melt on her tongue, an explosion of sugar. *"Gosh,* I'm glad I'm a good baker."

"Me, too. So, um, who was that on the phone?"

Nikki laughed. "You waited long enough to ask. Was it killing you?"

"The whole time I was washing the dishes, I was wondering how long before it was okay to ask."

"Anytime, babe. No secrets here. That was Ranger Don up at the state park. Well, that's who I called. It was *William* who called me." Nikki took another bite of cake. "I was just the messenger in this one, and I made sure I had the story straight from William before I passed it on."

"I can't believe I haven't met William yet," Kevin said wonderingly. "He seems to be turning this town on its head, to be honest."

"He's always been a bit of trouble." She rolled her eyes, thinking of William. Those puppy-dog brown eyes, so mournful. That wide mouth, turning down as he over thought yet another situation. William probably wouldn't have believed it if she told him, but he was a bit of a drama queen. He sort of willed crazy things to happen, with his mere presence.

"What kind of trouble?" Kevin was leaning forward, ready for the scoop. That man did love gossip. He was perfect for the farrier job. Carrying tales from barn to barn all day long . . . Nikki swallowed another bite of cake. "Well, he has the missing reporter at his house, so . . ."

"No! The girl from Arlington? Who went hiking and disappeared? I'd say six months ago but apparently everything on earth has managed to happen just today."

"Yup." Nikki took a bite of cake with a big smear of frosting on it and nearly burst into tears. Not just because she was such a good baker, although that definitely played a role. No, because right now she wanted to cry about everything. This morning she'd cried over the Dixie Lily logo on a bag of flour. Her hormones must be broken or something.

"Yeah," she went on, once she'd recovered herself. "Apparently, she ended up at his house, and now she doesn't want to leave. Or that's what he thinks. It could go either way with William. He's always been a bit entitled, though he'd never admit it."

"That sounds worrisome." Kevin bit his lip. "*Should* we be worried? Is he holding this girl hostage?"

"No, he's a sweetheart," she sighed. "Just . . . broken. You know. Like all the best ones are."

"That's right—hey! Am I broken?"

"My city boy who gave up a financial career to stand under horses and hope they don't poop on his head? No. Not broken at all, my love." Nikki filled her mouth with cake before smiling at him, baring her teeth through the frosting and crumbs.

"That's repulsive and I love you," Kevin told her.

"I'm going to teach this move to our kid," Nikki said, and then she put down her fork and burst into tears. For real, this time.

And for the life of her, she had no idea why.

"Nikki?" Kevin slid onto the couch beside her, his arms going around her. She felt Grover's fur pressing against her arm on her other side, his warm puppy breath close to her ear. "Nikki, what's wrong?"

"Nothing," she sobbed. "Nothing, I don't know. I'm just really tired. It's all a lot, you know?"

"I'll run you a bath," Kevin was promising, "and I'll get you a glass of wine, and I'll put on some soft music, and—" he kept rambling as he stroked her back, offering up every relaxing cliche he could think of, while Nikki tried to make herself stop crying through sheer force of will. She *was* just tired, she insisted to herself. *She* was just burned out. She needed a break.

And then everything she'd been feeling for the past few days blended together in her mind, and Nikki bit back a shocked gasp.

Chapter Twenty

Nadine

Not long after sunrise, Sean joined Nadine on the drive over to feed the Wayne farm horses breakfast. The day seemed determined to be disagreeable; frost crackled beneath their feet as they walked to the truck, and a gray layer of fog roiled around the farm, wrapping thick fingers through the trees.

Nadine shivered beneath her puffy coat. This November was really stealing into her bones. "So cold! I don't know, maybe we should open a Florida campus. Don't you have friends in Wellington? Can we talk to them?" She was only half-joking.

Sean wrapped one arm around her shoulders and gave her a squeeze. "Didn't you tell me last year that you *didn't* want to go to Florida?"

"Hmm . . . that doesn't sound like me. You must be thinking of another one of your girlfriends."

"Nope, you're the only one of my girlfriends who has ever wanted to stay up north all winter." Sean opened the truck door for her. "Unfortunately for me, you're also the one I like best. So here we are."

"Funny how things work out for the worst, isn't it?" Nadine teased.

"You said it, sister." Sean shivered all over, then winked at her. "Guess I just have to freeze for love."

At the Wayne farm, they found a barn full of hungry horses, whinnying and slamming their hooves against their stall doors. Stephen and Kevin had come out the preceding afternoon and done some basic repairs to the fences, so they gave everyone a quick breakfast of grain, then let the horses out into the small barnyard, with piles of hay spread out to keep them from arguing too much. Then they got busy mucking out. The stall floors were damp beneath the bedding and needed to be aired out and dried while the horses were turned out.

"This place is gross. We have got to start moving them," Nadine griped as they struggled to shove wheelbarrows across the cracked, uneven barn floor. "Not only does it stink of urine, but the wind goes right through the walls. They might as well be out on that cornfield all night."

"Do you know which horses we want for the school? I've barely had a chance to look at them." Sean started picking through a dirty stall, his nose wrinkling at the smell. The barn had decades, maybe centuries, of dirty animal baked into its stones and clay. Nadine suspected the odor would linger here long after the barn had been torn down.

"Yeah, I have a few in mind," she answered. "We can look at them after we've cleaned up. The weird thing is, they're not bad horses, not any of them. I just can't figure out why the Waynes kept a dozen decent horses. There's not even any tack or harness in this place. They just had a lot of horses who all look pretty capable of having jobs."

Sean only grunted in reply. She didn't mind. There wasn't much to say about it. No one understood the elderly Wayne couple's motivation in anything they'd done over their last twenty years out here, living alone on this desolate farm. Nadine didn't really like thinking about it—didn't want to stop and ponder if they'd been happy together, and that was why they'd chosen to live like hermits, isolated from the town and the other farmers living nearby, or if there was some darker reason why they'd hidden themselves away. She was too new to happiness, to her pleasure in Sean's company, to her satisfaction in her work, to be willing to spend too much time considering the alternatives.

Happily ever after was the only future she wanted to consider right now.

"So it's settled? The black-and-white mare, the bay Standardbred gelding, and the chestnut with some Arab in her?"

Nadine laughed at Sean's characterization of the no-name horses. "Yes, those are the three." They watched the horses tease one another over hay for a few more minutes. Of the twelve, those horses stood out the most to both of them—and they'd need horses who stood out to make a good impression with the schoolgirls and the faculty heads alike. These were people who were used to import records and bloodlines which went to the nineteenth century. They were all too likely to turn up their cultured noses at rescues with no history.

But Nadine knew they were good people, despite all that. After all, *she* was a rescue with no history, and she was doing just fine at Long Pond. She stepped into the shelter of Sean's arms. "Can we come and get them tomorrow?"

"Yeah, I have a break around eleven. Bring Darby. We don't know how they'll load."

"Of course. I already talked to her." Nadine couldn't help smiling. "It's exciting, right? I love our horses, but it's nice to feel like we're doing some good."

"You like saving cast-offs."

She glanced up at him. "Like you?"

His grip tightened around her shoulders. "Exactly like me. Remember when I first came to work here? I had no idea what I was doing. Just wanted my old life back. Sometimes I think horses must feel that way when we show up and tell them surprise—we want them to live somewhere new, do something differently! They're like, 'what the hell, man?' "

"That's so true. It must be so confusing, being a horse."

"Even more confusing than being a human, and that's saying something."

"Hey Sean?"

"Yeah?"

"You're doing pretty good at your new life. In fact . . ." Nadine lowered her voice, as if to share a secret, "I like you a lot more now than when I met you."

Sean laughed, the sound rumbling against her ear.

Before they headed back to work, they put the horses back into their stalls, placating them with huge piles of hay meant to last until Rosemary came to feed them that night. Nadine was closing up the barn doors when Sean pointed across the barren fields. "Look," he said, "the mountains are finally breaking through the fog."

Nadine looked at the mountains and shivered. She'd always loved the Catoctins, but now they seemed connected with so much bad news. "I hope they found Kelly. And hey—we never figured out how Monica Waters was connected to the school."

"Oh, I looked into that." Sean said airily. "She isn't."

Nadine waited, but Sean didn't elaborate. "Just going to leave it at that, then?"

"Look, there's absolutely no record of a Monica Waters in any of the school files. I asked Maggie to check. She spent like an hour searching the databases."

"Did Maggie ask why you wanted to know?" The school receptionist was a terrible gossip. If she went to Nikki's cafe on her lunch hour, word would be out in ten minutes that Sean and Nadine were looking for Monica's name in the horse files. And if a reporter overheard any of that, they'd show up. Nadine hated to think how the admins would react if she got the school embroiled in this case.

Sean was less concerned, shrugging away her question. "Of course she asked. She thought she was doing her part to help find a missing woman, so she was more than happy to do it. I think otherwise she would have told me to do it myself."

Probably true. Maggie had turned away Nadine for less. "Well, there must be something else," Nadine decided. "Something we're missing that isn't on a paper trail."

"And how exactly do you expect to figure it out?"

Nadine sighed, admitting defeat. "I don't."

"Let's talk about something else." Sean started back towards the truck. "The Christmas carnival. I like your idea for including the horse show team."

"Thanks," Nadine said absently. She was still thinking about Monica and Kelly.

Sean peered at her. "Hey, are you okay?"

Nadine leaned against the truck, her eyes on the muddy ground at her feet. "I'm freaked out, okay? This isn't a good look for Catoctin Creek, and both these women are just a little older than me. It's pretty scary to think they could just disappear right outside our town. And they knew each other, and, well, one of them was emailing me. I don't want to be . . ." She shut her mouth before she could admit the truth to Sean.

She was afraid if there was something sinister going on in town, she was going to get caught up in it next.

After all, who else had Kelly contacted in town? Nadine had no way of knowing, but no one else had come forward. Whereas *she* had been asking around about Monica Waters, and Sean had told Maggie about it, which was as good as standing up in the Blue Plate on Fried Chicken Night and shouting the news through a megaphone.

Nadine had no idea what was going on, how Monica and Kelly were connected, or how any of it had been traced back to her or Long Pond, but she did know she *didn't want* to be part of this exclusive little club she'd found herself in.

And she wasn't going anywhere near the woods behind Long Pond, that much was for certain.

Sean wrapped his arms around her. "You're not in any danger," he told her. "Don't get yourself all worked up about this, please. I won't let anyone get you."

She let herself give in to his embrace, but deep down, Nadine wasn't comforted. Sean could make all the promises in the world about how he'd protect her from the world, but she knew that in their relationship, she was the protector. Finally, she pulled away. "Thanks, baby," she told him, patting his hand. "It's good to know if someone tries to abduct me, you'll come galloping up on a snow-white show jumper and challenge him to a puissance."

"There's no fake brick wall too high to keep me from you," Sean assured her soberly. "Better keep Galway tacked up just in case. He's our best jumper."

Chapter Twenty-One

Kelly

K elly woke up feeling warm.

It was a delicious sensation, considering she'd been so cold most of the previous day. The hike had kept her fairly warm, but once she'd been lost, all that wandering had nearly frozen her through, especially once her coat was punctured and started trailing fluff all over the place. Sitting in a tree for hours certainly hadn't helped her circulation. Then there'd been the cold wait on William's porch, and the unheated library where she'd been holed up for two hours while he redid his kitchen appliances or whatever he'd been up to, and then finally that long walk down the driveway in search of signal.

That dark driveway had been so scary, and that moon didn't help, and she still had the slightest fear, just hovering in the background, of the dogs, although they were getting along pretty well now. When they'd come galumphing back up the driveway without William, she'd had to resist the urge to scurry up another tree, but then Lola had shoved her snout against Kelly's hand and she'd realized there was genuine affection there.

These dogs fell in love fast.

She wondered if their master wasn't a bit similar. She'd caught the way he'd looked at her tonight: hungrily, as if she was the answer to a starving man's last wishes. She had never been the subject of such covetous glances. The sensation was almost dizzying.

And at last she saw William again, a welcome shadow on the moonlit lane. He swept her back to the house, deposited her onto an old sofa in the front room, tossed a quilt over her, and built a fire in the cold fireplace in record time. Seriously, Kelly had never seen anything like it. "You're quite a Boy Scout," she told him admiringly, and he laughed and said his grandfather had taught him the knack of it.

"In this very fireplace," he went on, looking around the living room as if the jumping shadows from the fire were illuminating some beautiful old scenes for him. Kelly had looked around, too, hoping to see what he saw, but all she perceived was a neglected room with moth-eaten curtains and graceful antique furniture which would probably be priceless if someone just polished it up.

"Tell me about this house," she'd begged. "There must be so many stories."

"After dinner," he promised. "You stay there and get warm, and I'll find us some food."

"Don't take too long," she called after him, laughing, "I'm half-starved after the day I've had, and all you've given me so far is cookies!"

His laugh echoed down the long hallway.

Kelly snuggled up in the quilt and waited for the fire to warm the room, but it was a big space and the wind had no trouble ferreting its way in through the gaps around the old windows. She tipped her head back on the sofa and watched through the wavy glass as the moon slowly disappeared through increasingly opaque clouds. It would be colder, and yet more cozy, when the raindrops began hitting the glass.

Well, cozy, assuming the roof didn't leak.

Looking for something to take her mind off the impending weather, she reached around the arm of the couch and tugged open the drawer of the little end-table there. It squeaked at first, sounding so like a mouse she dropped the handle like a hot coal, but after nothing fuzzy emerged, she cautiously reached for it again and gave another encouraging little pull. The drawer opened, revealing a tantalizing pile of old photos, a thick hardbound journal, and a pile of truly ancient cough drops.

Kelly's eyes went round. The cough drops were gooey and had stuck to the topmost photo folder, but she found the photograph inside wasn't damaged. The photo itself was beautiful, presumably a family image with a husband and wife, and two bright-eyed children: a girl in pigtails and a boy with a crew cut. She gazed at the sepia-toned photo for a few moments, noticing the way the father resembled William, with his long jaw, lined forehead, and high cheekbones. "So handsome," she murmured. "Good looks run in the family."

Then she heard footsteps in the hall. Kelly dropped the photo folder back into the drawer and shoved it shut again, anxious that William might think she was spying on his personal things.

Although she thought he might take better care of obviously old family photos. Those cough drops needed to be cleaned up. It was a wonder the living room wasn't full of ants. A drawer full of cough drops was definitely how you got ants.

"Here we are," William said, entering the room with a heaped tray. "Obviously I didn't have time to cook you a three-course meal, but I present to you sourdough bread from Nikki's bakery, locally made cheddar, some red grapes that probably should have been marked down, and two Milky Way bars. One of those is mine, now, so don't get greedy." He set the tray down on the coffee table, then reached into his coat pocket and pulled out a bottle of wine. "Ta-da! Everything we need for a fireside feast."

Kelly clapped her hands. "Bravo, bravo! But—" she glanced at the tray. "I think you forgot glasses?"

"Oh!" William struck his forehead in mock anger. "How could I be so foolish? One moment, mademoiselle!" And he went trundling back down the hall.

Kelly had to laugh, but her stomach was growling and she couldn't wait for him to come back to get started. She was already wrist-deep into the bunch of grapes (which were fine, really, just a few wizened ones to avoid) when he returned bearing two wine glasses.

"You just had to get grape juice into you immediately, huh?" He grinned, pouring wine for them. "Let me slice this bread. Nikki's got a way with crusty things, and I don't want the knife to slip on you."

"Crusty things?" Kelly laughed. "Sounds like you're talking about yourself."

"You think I'm crusty?" He put his hand to his heart. "After I made you this meal? I'm wounded."

"You're not exactly Mr. Outgoing," she pointed out. "When we met at the bakery, I kind of thought you were going to yell at me. Tell me to go back where I came from."

"But I didn't even know where you came from."

"I don't think you cared."

He frowned in concentration, drawing the knife through the fat loaf of bread. "I'm not good at meeting people. I spend a lot of time alone. All of it, in fact."

"Sometimes I wish I didn't meet anyone. Maybe we should figure out a half-and-half thing. You ever thought about being a reporter?"

William barked a sharp laugh. "God, no! In fact, that's exactly why I wasn't thrilled to meet you—"

"So you admit it—" Kelly smiled at him.

"Well, you did say it was obvious, didn't you?"

"I suppose so." She accepted a plate with bread and cheese piled on it. "Look, the whole reporter thing was just an unhappy accident. Don't judge me for my job. I started out pulling together stories and fact-checking right out of college, and my student loans were more compelling than my real life plan."

"Which was to . . ."

"To be a historian." Kelly finished, confessing her deepest, darkest secret like it was nothing.

William raised his eyebrows.

Kelly felt blood rising to her cheeks. It was a silly kind of dream job, to want to just rummage around in old papers and records all day, drawing out conclusions about the way people lived and worked and thought once upon a time, but it was exactly what she'd always wanted. Her minor in creative writing and her father's connection with a newspaper in Richmond had gotten her a paying job straight out of college, and, like she'd said, once the student loan bills started arriving, the allure of actually *paying* them became her main inspiration for work. And then she was successful. A career change was awfully hard when the career paid well and people wanted her to do more of it. "I know it sounds ridiculous," she began, but William interrupted her before she could launch into a defense.

"No, it sounds fascinating," he told her. "I'm surrounded by history, and I honestly don't understand much of it. And every summer, when I travel, that just compounds. The things you see out west: abandoned mines, tumbledown shacks, indigenous rock paintings. The whole world is filled with things which you can't just naturally understand. They have to be studied. They have to be explained. I should take you with me next summer and let you be my tour guide."

Kelly put a lot of bread and cheese into her mouth to avoid shouting, 'Yes, please, let's do that!' which was her first, embarrassing impulse.

"And then there's this house," William went on. "You know this is the oldest house in the county? Well, outside of Frederick. The oldest *farmhouse,* is what I should say. It's changed a lot over a few centuries, but there are still original walls and a few interior pieces that haven't been updated since Washington was president. I don't take the best care of it, but I keep it going because . . . because . . ."

She swallowed, took a sip of wine, waited.

But William didn't finish his sentence. The silence stretched around them, broken only by the snaps and crackles of the fire, and the occasional stretch and sigh of the dogs watching them eat. Even without his story to fill the space between them, Kelly felt a deep peace. It was something she'd never expected to find in Catoctin Creek, and she had a little rush of gratitude, as if she could thank the town itself, not the people, but the place, for giving her this feeling.

Peace had eluded her for so long.

"I don't know if I'd ever leave this place," Kelly said eventually. "I haven't felt this calm and centered in a long, long time."

William lifted his arm, hesitated, then put it behind her, carefully resting it along the carved back of the sofa.

Kelly smothered a smile, opting for more bread, and let the contentment of the moment wash around her. They'd kissed with unbridled passion in the library, but she knew all that fevered energy had come from a place of fear and relief, overwrought emotion intermingling in both of them. She wanted to put down her plate and her goblet and climb on top of William right now, get them into a slow and serious make-out session that would while away half the night . . . yet something told her to be patient, and wait for him to catch up. He was a delicate soul, this gruff mountain man.

Finally, William spoke again, in a voice low and gravelled. "So, I have to leave every year," he said, as if admitting a weakness. "The summers here used to be full of life. This house was absolutely bursting at the seams. I can't bear how quiet it sits now. So I pack up the dogs and I hit the road."

She looked at him, but William was staring into the fire, seeing something she couldn't. "You used to have a lot of family here," she guessed, keeping her voice soft. "They don't come anymore?"

"Gone," William whispered. He turned to his head, his eyes boring into hers. "Scattered. Where does everyone go? Why does everything change? We have good things and then people just . . . they just give up. They move on." He bit down on his lip for a moment. "I never could. I'm not like that."

Kelly's breath caught, and she reached out, touching his hand. William's skin was hot and dry; she wrapped her fingers around his and tried to ignore the way the touch sent her pulse racing. "I'm sorry," she said gently, because there was no way of knowing just what he meant, and no platitudes which he hadn't heard before, she was sure. And then, hoping it wasn't presumptuous to say so, she told him, "I'm here for you, though."

He leaned forward so quickly she gasped, but her shock was swallowed up by his kiss, his arms wrapping around her, his hard fingers pressing the back of her neck as she lifted her chin and stretched her neck to meet him, giving in to his demands, making a few of her own.

That had been last night.

And now here she was, slowly awakening to find herself in a bed with rumpled sheets, a thick duvet kicked to the curving wooden foot of a beautiful sleigh bed, fat feather pillows under her head. There was a smoky smell of fire, and a more distant, damp smell of dog. She sat up, wrinkling her nose against a sneeze, and looked around.

The pale, watery light of a rainy morning was kind to the bedroom, which was spare and yet snug, with a dark wooden bureau topped with an old-fashioned white jug, a low fire smoldering in a fireplace with a white mantel and frame, and cream-colored plaster walls. The sleigh bed she found herself in was elegantly carved, and the mattress was soft, though the frame itself a little squeaky. She tested it with a little bounce, listening to the springs squeak rustily, and then heard a dog bark outside the bedroom door.

Well, Lola had given her away. She heard footsteps downstairs, and then on the tread of the staircase. Kelly felt a little nervous bounce of anticipation. *Here comes William!*

Chapter Twenty-Two

Rosemary

"I don't believe it," Rosemary said blankly. "You're . . . really?"

Nikki nodded, looking down at her cup of tea. She'd actually sat down this morning, something she rarely did while she was working at the cafe. Rosemary supposed that was as good a sign as any that Nikki was absolutely feeling different now.

This was going to be hard for her.

Rosemary reached out and took her friend's hands. "Nikki, this is really good news. You used to talk about having a big family, remember? When we were kids and we'd play House? You always had six children. Are you still up for that number?"

Nikki laughed, which was the reaction Rosemary had hoped for —something to draw her out of this uncharacteristic funk. "I absolutely do not want six children—we were very idiotic, Rosemary. Did you forget that part? But you're right. I do want kids, still. And I want Kevin's kids. Think how goofy this baby is going to be. Cute and goofy, like a puppy." She snorted, laughed some more, and then wiped at the tears suddenly leaking from her eyes. "But I really hate the crying. Where did this come from?"

"Hormones make you crazy," Rosemary said, squeezing her hands sympathetically. "And what did Kevin say? Was he excited?"

"I didn't tell him."

"But I thought—"

"I just said 'our kids' completely off-handedly and then I started crying and I scared him so much, he went and got the whipped cream and started dolloping it all over my cake until I dried up. And while I was sitting there waiting, I realized something must be up. And then he made me chamomile tea, to counteract all the sugar, he said, and then he made me go to bed. So there was no chance to talk about what I thought."

"And you listened to him?"

Nikki nodded, a watery grin fighting free.

"Well, then he definitely knows something up."

"Maybe, maybe not. He says I'm working too hard. He probably thinks that's all it is. But you know, intuition . . ." Nikki shrugged. "I went to the twenty-four-hour drugstore out on the highway to Frederick this morning, like, the *moment* he left for his rounds. I couldn't buy a test in town, obviously."

"Of course not." The entire town would know by nine a.m. if Nikki Mercer bought a pregnancy test at the Walgreens just outside town. "Well, any idea where he's working today?"

"At Elmwood. Why, you want me to go accost him at his place of business? Maybe shout out the car window, *You knocked me up!* and see what he does?" Nikki cracked herself up.

"No," Rosemary snorted, shaking her head, "but you *could* take him lunch. Remember the way you used to get him a sandwich, and you two would eat together?"

"That was before I had a *second* restaurant," Nikki pointed out. "And he was practically an intern for Gus at the time. He was mostly watching, not working. Now he'd say he was too busy to stop very long."

"Well, I think he'd like the gesture," Rosemary insisted. Sometimes Nikki just did not see the forest for the trees with that man. She would always be the kind of woman who had to schedule dates once in a while. *Especially* if there were going to be kids around the house. Kids! Nikki! Rosemary had to pause to get herself together before she could continue. "I think his romantic side would be tickled pink. And you know how big his romantic side is."

"Sometimes I think it's his only side," Nikki admitted.

"Let me stick around through lunch here," Rosemary suggested. "I know how to make coffee and heat up sandwiches. Everything else is already made. You rest for a bit, then take Kevin some lunch and give him the good news. It'll be so adorable. I wish I could come with you."

"Fine," Nikki sighed, although she didn't sound as if she found the idea adorable at all. "But I had a meeting with Mickey Trout today at twelve thirty. He's coming over to finalize all the catering for the carnival. Can you handle that?"

Rosemary squared her shoulders. More work? She laughed at more work. Hah-hah-hah. "Of *course* I can. Now, let me get you some more tea, okay? Sit tight."

She went behind the counter and turned on the electric kettle. While she was standing there, the bell rang and two strangers came into the cafe, draped in scarves and wet coats. They stamped and shivered on the mat by the door, while Rosemary sent dagger looks at Nikki, warning her to *stay seated.*

Nikki shrugged and picked at the muffin on her plate with a little gesture which said, *it's your funeral.*

"Good morning ladies," Rosemary said as the women struggled out of their winter weather gear. "What can I get for you today?"

"Lattes, please," one of the women said, unwrapping her scarf. She grimaced at the raindrops studding the fabric. "With something spicy in it, something warming."

"Gingerbread?" Rosemary suggested, looking over the syrups next to the espresso machine.

"Perfect, yes!"

"Two of those," the other woman added. She was heavily made-up, with bright red lips and dark black eyeshadow. Rosemary suspected they were another TV news crew. The first woman, who was light on the face paint, must be there to run the camera. They made a cute duo, actually. "I think I'm frozen all the way through," she went on, tugging her coat tightly around her. "You have anything warm to eat?"

"Everything's baked fresh, and it can be warmed up," Rosemary assured her. "I'd go with the lemon-blueberry scones, but that's just me. I'm obsessed with lemon."

"Citrus," the first woman sighed. "We can pretend we're in Florida."

"We should be so lucky." The reporter nodded. "Two of those, please."

Rosemary bustled around behind the counter, feeling like she was back in her schoolgirl days, playing Restaurant with Nikki. They'd never expected their lives to lead them to this, she thought, placing the scones on plates. Nikki hadn't known she loved cooking until she inherited the Blue Plate and all that came with it. And Rosemary hadn't intended on starting a horse rescue until she'd inherited the farm much sooner than she'd ever expected. They'd both been thrown into their current lives, she mused, without planning to be in them at all.

And yet it had all worked out.

Hadn't it?

She glanced at Nikki again. Her friend was hunched over her tea, her elbows positioned on either side, digging into the tabletop. She looked utterly miserable. So miserable, in fact, that Rosemary had to question whether it was "just" hormones, or "just" a queasy stomach, or "just" a thousand other things that a pregnancy could do to an already stressed person's system.

She was a little afraid that Nikki was on the verge of, or maybe the process of, burning out on her life. And now was not the time for dramatics. Nikki needed solutions.

Rosemary brought the reporter and her assistant their scones and lattes, and made some light small talk with them. They were here to cover the Monica Waters case; yes, they had heard that Kelly O'Connell was apparently safe and sound; sure, as far as they knew, WDCN was just sending someone else to cover the story because this O'Connell person was apparently having some sort of mental breakdown.

"It's because of the boyfriend, you know," the reporter said confidentially.

Rosemary felt her eyes get big. "The—which boyfriend?"

"The fiancé," the assistant corrected her. "Kelly O'Connell's ex-fiancé is the boyfriend."

"Wait, the one they've been questioning?" Rosemary was sure she'd heard wrong.

"Oh, he's in the clear now. A couple of friends stepped up and there's security cam footage of him at work and then at a restaurant in Rockville on the day Monica went on the hike. It wasn't him. But yeah, same guy. Weird, right?" The reporter tasted her scone and made a happy face. "Oh, this is fantastic. Thank you. Did you bake this?"

"No, no—Nikki did." Rosemary gestured. Nikki picked up her head and attempted a smile that was more of a grimace. "And now I think she's going upstairs for a little nap."

"No, I don't think so." Nikki pushed herself upright.

"I think so," Rosemary insisted, giving her a steely eyed look. "I think a nap is just what the doctor ordered. Speaking of which, I'm going to make you a doctor's appointment."

Nikki made a face at her and dragged herself out of the dining room.

Rosemary turned back to the women. "Sorry about that. She's just a little . . ."

"No worries," the camerawoman said. "We all get cranky this time of year. Christ, look at that rain coming down. I really hope that woman isn't out in this."

"There's no way," the reporter said, shrugging. "She's holed up somewhere, I'll bet you. They'd have found her by now if she was in the woods."

"Holed up?" Rosemary lifted her brows. "What do you mean? Like she found a cave or something?"

"No, no." The reporter sipped her latte. "First of all, *yum.* Thank you. But listen, we see this kind of thing in women

Monica's age all the time. They freak out. They're in the wrong career, they're with the wrong guy, they have too many bills, they've got stress coming out of their ears, and they just . . . they flip out. That's not a respectful way of putting it. I'm sorry. There's a term and I'm blanking on it."

"A nervous breakdown," the assistant suggested.

"Basically, yeah. A nervous breakdown. This chick has a high-stress Washington job, she's making deals, she's selling out the environment—oh yeah, you haven't seen the half of what I've seen, we're just not reporting on it because it's not sympathetic and in a missing-woman case you've got to run with a lot of empathy, people are freaking out as it is—but believe me, Monica Waters is no angel. And the chances are? She didn't mean to end up as a lobbyist thug." The reporter grinned at Rosemary's surprised expression. "Yeah. It's the money, it sucks you in. Anyway." Another sip of the latte. "Mmm. Anyway, yeah, add her life drama and then her family had this big horse farm in Pennsylvania that went bust last year, and from what I hear, that really cut her up, too."

"Wait, really?" A customer had entered the cafe, but Rosemary had to get the last of this story wrung out of the reporter before she could leave. "A horse farm?"

"Oh yeah, a big trotting horse farm in the family for generations. Stallions and fillies and whatnot. It was like three hundred acres, white fences, the whole bit. Gone. Horses to auction. Done. And from what I hear, her mental health took a big hit when she found out."

"Oh my goodness." Rosemary remembered what Nadine had said—Kelly had asked about Monica Waters, saying she was connected with the school riding program. Could it be something about one of the horses? She'd sourced several over the summer from Pennsylvania, although Goliath was the only horse from an auction, and he was no Standardbred racehorse. But still . . . "What was the name of the farm, do you know?"

"Not off the top of my head. Kalissa, do you?" She looked across the table.

The assistant shook her head. "No, but I can find it for you. Let me give you a call later, okay?"

"That would be great," Rosemary said. "Seriously, thanks."

Rosemary manned the cafe counter for the next two hours, and she had to admit, she enjoyed the break from her usual day. She even found the time to hang up the Christmas decorations Nikki had hauled down and left behind the counter, but clearly never had time to put up. Twinkle lights, pine garland, holly berries and leaves: with Rosemary's neat hand and attention to detail, the cafe dining room was soon transformed into a Christmas scene straight out of a movie. She was casting cautious glances at the dark fireplace at one end of the room, wondering if she ought to just go ahead and light a fire to finish the effect, when Nikki came downstairs.

She stopped in the doorway and looked around the dining room. "Rosemary, my god. Look at this place."

"Thank you," Rosemary said, smiling playfully. "I think so, too."

"I mean, this is really incredible. I kept meaning to do it, but I couldn't find the energy, and you know that's probably when my first inkling was that something was wrong."

Rosemary walked over to her friend and put her hands on her shoulders. "Nikki, look at me. There is nothing *wrong*. You aren't sick. You're not dealing with a problem. You are going to have a baby, and it's going to be wonderful. Can you repeat that after me?" She ignored the jingling of the bell on the cafe door, focusing all her attention on Nikki.

Nikki gazed back at her as if hypnotized. "I am going to have a baby, and it's going to be wonderful," she repeated, and a slow smile spread over her face as the words began to make sense. "I am going to have a *baby*, and it's going to be *wonderful!*"

"Yes, that's it!" Rosemary leaned in and gave her a hug, careful not to squeeze her too tightly. "And I'm going to be an aunt."

Nikki laughed at that, and Rosemary laughed along, but they both stopped short as another voice echoed across the empty dining room. "You're going to have a baby?"

Kevin's voice was hoarse with disbelief.

Rosemary closed her eyes, her chin still resting on Nikki's shoulders. "Oh, *damn,*" she said. "Who said you could come home for lunch?"

<hr>

"So you gave the game away?" Stephen chuckled and handed up a feed bucket to Rosemary. "That must have been awkward."

"Oh, you know Kevin." Rosemary shook the grain, mixing in the powdered vitamins she'd added. All the Notch Gap Farm horses were on their own unique cocktails of supplements to deal with their individual issues, be it scurf-prone skin or slow-growing, shelly hooves, or even general anxiety. She would do the same with the Wayne horses once they arrived, and she'd gotten them checked over by the vet. "He was so over the moon with excitement, he didn't even look at me. Just grabbed Nikki and kissed her so hard I thought I was going to have to tear him off her for her own safety."

"A baby Kevin." Stephen shook his head, thinking of it. "I don't know if the world is ready for this."

"To say nothing of a baby Nikki. At least she'll have a cheerful attitude as she takes over the world?"

"She?"

Rosemary shrugged. "I mean, that's just how I think of it in my head. A little girl with Nikki's curly hair." She accepted another bucket from Stephen and stirred in a supplement for horses with COPD. "I haven't said anything to her. I don't know that Nikki would prefer one over the other."

"And what about the cafe? And the Blue Plate, and the carnival, for that matter? Has she said anything about that?"

"No," Rosemary sighed. "Only that she's freaked out about having to deal with it all. I feel so bad about the carnival, when I'm the one who put it on her plate."

"But it's going to be over and done with in a matter of weeks," Stephen pointed out. "Whereas running the cafe and the Blue Plate will be the real issues for—well, forever, frankly."

"Well, the Blue Plate is mostly Lauren's at this point. She manages it, she hires and fires, she does the ordering and keeps everything running. Nikki can probably even afford to give her a raise to keep her on if she has to. The bakery, she could manage if someone would help her part time, I think. I wish *I* could."

Stephen closed the feed bin with a clang. "Well, we both know you can't. Not regularly, anyway. Obviously you can drop in and help from time to time, but Nikki needs a long-term solution."

"I know. It's not like she can just pop the baby out and go back to her regular life." Rosemary sighed and started stacking the buckets. In the stalls behind her, the horses set up a racket, banging on stall doors with their hooves and neighing like they were in a Noisiest Horse competition. "You guys are a bunch of toddlers, you know that?" She started dumping grain into feed bins, with Stephen taking on the horses in the far aisle.

She still had to get over to the Wayne farm to feed; Nadine was dealing with that tween student of hers who hated everything and was planning on giving her a private horsemanship lesson that evening. Addy, that was the girl's name. Nadine said she was going to let the girl choose one of the rescue horses as a project, teach her some tricks and basic ground manners, clean her up, and put them both in the carnival as a school showcase. It was nice; Rosemary was glad Nadine had plans for the three horses she'd taken.

It was just about figuring out the other nine now.

There wasn't time to handle Nikki's problems as well as her own, but she'd do everything she could to make sure her friend got through this life change without drama.

"Do you want me to do water buckets?" Stephen asked, handing her a stack of empty feed buckets.

"Please, and I'll get the hay started." She put the buckets by the feed room door and started snapping open hay bales with her pocketknife.

"Have you heard from William?" Stephen asked as he uncoiled the hose. "Any updates on the reporter that he abducted but definitely didn't abduct, according to the crazy rules of this town?"

"They're not crazy. We just know who we can trust. And no, I haven't heard anything else. I did see Don from the park service this afternoon while I was still running the cafe counter, and he said they had booted all the reporters out of the trail parking lot, because they wouldn't stop doing newscasts from in front of her car, and he thought that was an invasion of her privacy, or something. Or he just thought it was ridiculous, and he was sick of them, so he used that as an excuse," Rosemary added thoughtfully. "Don's never been a fan of the media."

"I've noticed country people rarely are," Stephen said dryly.

"Well, when you want to keep to yourself and just help your neighbor when you're asked, and a bunch of news vans are pulling up, and people won't stop asking questions about things that are none of their business, can you really blame us?"

"Oh, so now it's *us*. I thought you liked this Kelly character."

"I mean, I don't *hate* her. I don't really know her, either. And I'm not rooting for more news reporters to set up shop in town, either. They need to figure out where the hiker is and get out of town, in my opinion." Rosemary started tossing hay over the stall walls. "Although I admit I could use a little coverage of the carnival to get more people to come out. I haven't figured that part out yet. Nikki said she asked some guy to cover it, but I haven't heard from him."

"Maybe Kelly will stick around long enough to cover it for you."

"Why would you say that?" Rosemary threw hay into the stall next to Stephen. "You think she doesn't want to just figure this out and go home, too?"

"I don't know. A woman who spends twenty-four hours out of sight at some hilltop mansion with a handsome hermit?" Stephen waggled his eyebrows. "I'm just saying that it feels like a lot of people come to Catoctin Creek and never want to leave. Sounds like she might be one of *us.*"He used the word teasingly.

"Us, meaning you and Kevin?" Rosemary grinned. "Interlopers from the big city?"

"Add in Sean, if you want to expand the net," Stephen said. "And I'm sure there are others. I'm sure you weren't all born and bred in Catoctin Creek."

"Most of us were," Rosemary reminded him. "Remember me the next time you're on Brunner Lane. That was named for my great-grandfather."

"But that would make for a lot of inbreeding, if you weren't trapping outsiders constantly, that's all I'm saying. You get guys like Kevin and Sean and me. We're just helping you keep the gene pool from getting too muddy."

"Well, Kevin certainly is," Rosemary mused. "So, what you're saying is, you think William is up there at Hilltop House seducing Kelly?"

Stephen put the hose into the next water bucket, batting away a horse's inquiring nose. "That is exactly what I think."

Chapter Twenty-Three

William

Just knowing she was upstairs gave him a sense of peace.

He knew it was too much.

He knew it wouldn't last.

He knew he was just lonely.

But was there any harm in indulging, just this tiny bit, in these daydreams?

Having Kelly in the house allowed William to engage in all sorts of ridiculous flights of fancy free. He'd been coming back here for ten years, and in every year of that decade, the winters had gotten longer and lonelier. But what on earth could he do about it? He couldn't just up and abduct someone to live with him, and in all those years, he hadn't figured out how to meet anyone who would come back to Hilltop House and keep him company. Someone who wouldn't make him crazy, someone who wouldn't find him maddening. He had always been sure that someone didn't exist.

Maybe he could have hired a temporary companion; or maybe, in a slightly less depressing turn of events, he might have managed to meet someone on a dating app who was into reclusive men who had never gotten over losing their family not once, but twice. (Who could get over that, though? And how could he not be completely broken? A woman wouldn't just have to daydream about fixing guys to want to be with him, she'd have to be a *professional*.)

But he hadn't done any of that; he'd just waited, preferring to daydream over everything else that might have been real—it was too hard, wasn't it, to actually meet someone, to put all those hopes on the line, to get to know her and fall in love with her and then be abandoned, either quietly and unceremoniously or in a massive fight, plates shattering, hearts breaking. Who could deal with that? Who could face that kind of rejection? William hadn't been raised to choose; he hadn't been raised to be turned down. He had always gotten everything he wanted, and then when he hadn't, he had been utterly, miserably unprepared.

And so now she was here. Kelly O'Connell, or the way he liked to call her in his head, Kelly O'Something, the way he'd remembered her after that morning at the bakery. When had that been? A day ago? A week? A lifetime? He couldn't remember a time when he hadn't been dazed with thinking about her, that sheet of ash-blonde hair, those smoky blue eyes, those perfect pink lips.

He cracked an egg into a cast iron pan and watched it sizzle. He wished he knew how she liked her eggs. Or if she ate eggs. William was seized with momentary panic; then he remembered the way she'd crumbled and eaten the muffin at Nikki's bakery. She wasn't a vegan. Okay. One less concern.

Bacon snapped in a second pan and Lola whined from beside him, licking her formidable chops. "Too hot," he warned her, but the other huskies mistook his words for a promise of imminent snacks and came walking up, their tongues hanging between their enormous white teeth. "I'll save all of you some bacon," he promised. *"And* the grease." It wasn't enough to send them back to their cushions in the corner of the room, but at least he had acknowledged them. Lola sat on her haunches and the other dogs followed suit, still watching him closely.

The dogs liked Kelly too, William thought, dropping slices of the same dense sourdough they'd eaten last night into the toaster. That had to be a good sign. Not that Lola was a particularly difficult dog to get along with, and her word was law with the other three, but still, if she hadn't liked Kelly, there was no way that girl would be upstairs right now.

In his bedroom.

He'd taken her to *his* bedroom, spare and beautiful, the room his parents had once slept in and which his grandmother had bequeathed to him that year he'd first come alone. It had been her brother's, the first William Cunningham—the first William *Makepeace* Cunningham, an old family name turned into a middle name, and little Will used to wonder if the first William hated that middle name as much as he did. But he doubted there were as many English majors running around in back those black-and-white days, over-educated brats to point at him and sing, *William Makepeace, William Makepeace, William Makepeace Thacker-raaaaay,* which was such a specific type of youthful trauma, he wasn't even sure he'd be able to explain it to a therapist even if he ever managed to make himself see one.

Breakfast came together all at once: the toast popped up, the bacon was crisping, the egg yolks were perfect, the kettle was whistling. He heaped everything onto a plate, snagged a mug and the sugar bowl, and placed it all onto the tarnished silver tray he'd used to serve their bread and cheese dinner last night. *Last night*. The events of the night before swam in front of his vision as he climbed the stairs, careful not to step on any dogs milling around his feet. He hadn't spent an evening like that with a woman in years.

Not ever, if he was being honest.

At the bedroom door, he was faced with a terrible conundrum: two full hands, a closed door, and no idea if the woman inside was even awake. Luckily, Lola sat at his feet and gave a short, piercing yap, annoyed by his hesitation. From behind the door, he heard an exclamation.

William cleared his throat. "Lola says good morning and breakfast is served," he called, his words running together.

"Oh my," Kelly exclaimed, and he heard the bedsprings creak as she got out of bed. His heart was hammering in his chest. The door opened, and when he saw her standing before him, looking like a miniature in his flannel pajamas, William nearly dropped the tray.

"Whoops," she said, steadying the tray as it dipped to one side. She smiled at him, tousled hair falling over her eyes. She was so sexy in the morning, he almost forgot about how sexy she was during the day, all put together and made-up. Kelly could beguile him no matter what time of day, or how tangled her hair was.

God, he was in so deep with this girl.

This girl he barely knew.

"Sorry about that," he said, his morning voice a growl in his chest. "I didn't know how you took your eggs, so I just . . ." He gestured at the plate.

She looked at the plate and burst into delighted laughter. "One of *each*?"

"Well, just fried and scrambled and that one is poached," he said, feeling foolish.

"Getting the right egg order is so important," Kelly said seriously. She looked back up at him. "Luckily, I like eggs every way and twice on Sunday."

"Oh, good."

"But I'm not *huge* on scrambled, if I'm being honest . . ."

"Well, that's alright." William hoped he wasn't blushing, but his cheeks were suspiciously warm.

"So maybe you'll come in and eat them for me?" She opened the door all the way and stepped back, gesturing for him to come in.

"I—yes, of course." William hadn't thought for a second about where he'd eat his breakfast. He'd been too fixated on giving Kelly the perfect breakfast in bed experience.

But now she was sitting on the bed, patting the turned-down sheets, and taking the mug of tea from the tray and placing it on the bedside table so it wouldn't spill as he set down the tray. He hadn't thought to bring two forks, but she pushed the fork to him. "I'm going to be disgusting and eat my eggs on top of this toast," she informed him. "But you eat the other piece of toast. I only need one piece to be this gross."

"It's not gross," he protested, but she *did* make a mess as he watched, fascinated. She scooped up the poached egg with half a slice of fat sourdough bread and let the yolk soak into the crust. Then she dropped a little crisp of bacon onto the whole thing and took a bite.

"Mmm," she moaned. "Perfection."

William was so busy watching her eat, he barely remembered to take a bite of his own eggs.

He'd never seen someone enjoy food so much before.

Kelly was a pleasant breakfast companion, sharing her tea with him and insisting that he eat as much bacon as he wanted. She even gave a few bites to the dogs, even though William assured her they had their own share cooling down in the kitchen. They sat on the bed talking long after the plate was empty, just chatting about nothing in particular: the rain falling on the windows, the peculiar pearl color of the clouds, the possibility that it would snow before Christmas, their mutual love of sledding.

"The sledding must be incredible here, too," she said, getting up suddenly and walking to the window. The view overlooked the side yard to the east, the tangle of yard giving way to the stone barn and the overgrown pastures, and then the slopes of the valley falling away from Hilltop House's surrounding land.

"I mean, just look at this hill here," she went on. "And that pasture is so steep—oh! Oh my god!"

William jumped up, the plate sliding to the floor, although luckily it landed on the duvet and didn't shatter. Lola jumped to lick it clean, her patience paying off as it so often did. "What is it?" William gasped, ignoring the dog as she lapped the grease and yolk from his grandmother's good china. "Was it a bear?"

"A person," Kelly said, her hand to her mouth. "I swear I saw a person running from the barn to that little building." She whirled, frantic eyes seeking William's gaze. "Is that the dairy? Wait—was that the person you think is living out there? Did I just see your secret person?"

William was at the window in a moment, but it was too late; whoever Kelly had seen was already disappeared back into their safe place. He leaned his forehead against the cold glass. "I don't know. Are you sure it was a person?"

"I'm sure." Kelly's voice was brittle. "You know this is crazy, right? You can't just have a person squatting in your outbuildings. Especially with everything going on around here. Someone's going to think you're up to something. What are you thinking?"

He turned, feeling that old stirring of irritation. *This* was why he didn't like people around him all the time. They questioned him. They wanted answers. They couldn't just let well enough alone.

If he didn't mind having some person on the run hiding in his dairy, why the hell should she?

"Don't worry about it," he said gruffly. "This is nothing. One time in Colorado, I shared a cave with three other people and never once knew their names or why they were there. But I think one of them might have been a bank robber. There was dye all over his hands, and the next day I heard on the radio—but it didn't matter. We were just people who didn't want to be found. We didn't bother each other; we went our separate ways."

Kelly was looking at him strangely now, and William knew he hadn't said the right thing to placate her. But honestly? Whatever. She could take him or leave him—this was the man he was. And she'd leave him. He already knew it. He could be crazy about a woman and still know he couldn't make her happy. William was always honest with himself.

Except maybe about how much these things could hurt.

"That's *crazy*," Kelly repeated, her blue eyes widening as she realized he was serious. "You can't just live like this."

"Like what?"

"Like—like nothing matters!" Her voice rose, nearly a shout. "This live and let live nonsense—it's not real! People hurt other people all the time, and they have to be held accountable for it. You can't just excuse them for being a bank robber or a murderer because you don't feel like asking questions or turning them in."

"Of course I can." William shrugged. "I simply mind my own business. You should try it."

Kelly's enraged gasp told him everything he needed to know about how well *that* was going over. Well, what did he expect? She was a reporter. They weren't exactly known for leaving things alone, even things that were none of their business.

"I need to get back to town," Kelly said, her voice more faint now. "I need to get my car. How far away is the trail head from here?"

"It's about five miles." William began picking up the plate and mug from their breakfast. They'd been so happy just a few minutes ago. How had it all gone wrong? Inevitable, though, wasn't it? "I'll give you a ride. Just get ready and come downstairs when you want to leave. I'll be working on the kitchen." He went to the door and paused. "Sorry if I offended you."

"Oh, my god," Kelly murmured, shaking her head. Her hair had fallen over her eyes, and William felt a sudden yearning to see the expression in them. But she looked away, and he didn't think she'd let him touch her right now. "You didn't *offend* me. You just . . . you confound me."

"Fair enough," William said, and he headed downstairs. He knew the way this story ended. She'd be gone soon, and oddly enough, the knowledge gave him peace. Eased the tension of realizing he was falling in love, that this woman could shatter him into pieces. With her gone, he could just go back to his normal life. Whatever that was worth.

Chapter Twenty-Four

Nadine

"Easy, easy, easy—there. See? She likes that spot. Keep rubbing her there for a few minutes."

Addy scrunched up her face. "This is a weird place to touch a horse."

"Right between her front legs? No. It makes perfect sense. Horses can't itch themselves there." Nadine found deliberate misunderstanding was her favorite way to derail the schoolgirls when they were trying to make things awkward. And they *always* were. For example, teaching a fourteen-year-old girl, who had never been exposed to horses before this school year, how to clean a sheath? That was bound to be a traumatic experience for everyone involved.

Luckily, this lesson was just about showing Addy where most horses' sweet spots were. Absolutely no need for things to get gross. No matter how hard Addy tried to make it seem that way.

"No, I mean, putting my hands between her front legs, it's like . . . never mind." Addy evidently realized that if she kept talking, it was going to make her look like the weirdo. Which was Nadine's intention. "And wait—what is she doing with her nose?"

The black-and-white pinto mare they'd brought back from the Wayne farm was stretching her neck out as far as it would reach, with her head fully extended, and her upper lip out even farther. She was wiggling her lip frantically. Nadine put her palm up and let the mare rub her lip against it while Abby stared in consternation.

"She's trying to do mutual grooming," Nadine explained. "If she were with another horse, they'd stand almost head to head, with their chests close together, and rub each other's backs with their noses. So when you rub a horse in the right spot, that really itchy spot, this is their reaction. It's like a reflex." The mare's teeth clicked together, pinching Nadine's palm, and she yanked her hand back. "Sometimes it gets a little rough," she admitted, rubbing her palms together. "But it's a pretty cool way to show a horse you're affectionate and a good person for them to hang out with."

Addy looked impressed. "Wow. The only problem now is my arm is getting tired."

"That's okay, you can go ahead and take a break."

Addy straightened from where she'd been bent alongside the mare's barrel, flexing her hands experimentally. "Okay, so I rubbed her belly. Now, what?"

They were working on the very basics. Addy had never been around horses before, and Nadine wasn't sure just what the mare was used to. She was clearly okay with being handled; Nadine had been all over her with a grooming kit, combing out her mane, curry-combing her body, picking up her hooves and cleaning them out. The mare hadn't objected to any of it, although the blue-eyed chestnut mare had failed a similar test, revealing herself to be touchy and ticklish. Nadine was keeping the chestnut mare for a more advanced student, possibly even saving her for Darby to work on, and the bay Standardbred gelding was a little creaky. He was older than she'd first realized, and she thought he had some arthritis issues they needed to work on. Rosemary had agreed to swap another horse for him, but Nadine hadn't selected a new one yet.

That left the black-and-white mare for Addy to work with.

This was going to be their Christmas carnival project: Addy was going to polish up this mare, teach her some manners, and show her off at the fair to show everyone not just what the school was doing with horses, but what their money was going into. They'd be the warm-up act for Sean's horse show club, who would go into the ring afterwards and put on some jumping and drill team equitation for the audience. It was a nice way to draw in more people to the carnival, and keep the focus on horses, reminding everyone that they were donating to help the Wayne horses and Rosemary's rescue.

"Now," Nadine said, placing the grooming kit next to Addy, "you can start cleaning her up. Grab the curry comb and start swirling it around her coat in circles, like this." She mimed the action and Addy followed, clumsily at first, but slowly gaining the hang of it. "Good," Nadine told her, stepping into the aisle to give her room. "All over—and watch out for tickles."

"How will I know—" The mare flicked her tail and stomped, moving away as Addie tried to run the comb over her flank. "Oh, got it."

"Quick learner." Nadine pulled out her phone and flicked around, keeping one eye on the teenager while she checked her email. Nothing from Kelly. She'd finally emailed her back last night, telling her they'd gone through all the school files and couldn't find any mention of Monica Waters in any of their documents. The whole situation was weird. Evidently, Kelly hadn't deemed it worth replying to. Or maybe she was just too busy up at Hilltop House.

When she'd talked to Rosemary earlier and found out that Kelly wasn't only safe and sound, but had apparently holed up with that guy William Cunningham overnight, she'd been amused, but now she was starting to feel annoyed. It was rude of a person to come to town, send emails that stirred up all kinds of questions and worry, and then just not follow up on them. She'd spent a lot of her own time and Sean's trying to figure out the email Kelly had sent. The least the woman could do was reply and say thanks for checking.

Addy had made it all the way around the horse and was looking at Nadine for direction, so Nadine set her up with the body brush, showing her how to whisk dirt away from the horse's body with quick, upturned strokes.

"Do you like doing this?" Addy asked her, wielding the brush without much early success.

"Grooming horses? Yes. A lot. I think it's very calming for both horse and human—"

"No, like, teaching people to groom horses. Aren't you tired of me yet? All this basic stuff, and I never even asked for any of it. And I'm not good at it. You must wish you were doing something else."

"Are you trying to get out of it?" Nadine was amused. Kids were always trying to psych her out, make her think they knew what terrible burdens they were. They didn't get that this was her *job* now. She wanted them in her barn, learning from her. She liked them. But it took them all forever to figure that out. "Maybe you think I'll just shrug and sign off on your horse assignments and forget the whole thing? You want to go do science lab with this period instead? Mrs. Hartwell can—"

"No, no, it's not like that." Addy adjusted the brush in her hand and attempted to stroke the mare's hair in the wrong direction; Nadine reached out and corrected her before she could annoy the horse. "I mean—I don't *mind* it so much anymore. Not like I did at first. I just don't want to be a nuisance, I guess."

"I see. No. You're not a nuisance. This is something I really, truly enjoy—whoops, see this swirl here on her flank? Horses are very sensitive there. Anyway, I'm not going to be standing over you every single minute. Tomorrow you'll be grooming her by yourself."

"Uh, I don't think so!" Addy eyed her like she was a crazy person.

"I know so. Trust me on this. It's not rocket science. You figure out what each horse likes and doesn't like, and you build it into your routine. Just watch her as you brush her. Start cataloging her reactions to things. When she reacts, you respond. It's simple."

Addy considered this as she drew the brush down the mare's neck, glancing cautiously at the mare's head with every downstroke. "And you said she doesn't have a name, right?"

"Nope. What do you want to call her?" Nadine leaned against the wall, eyebrows raised with interest. This had been the moment she'd been waiting for: seeing if Addy would choose to name the horse, and if she did, if she'd choose a pleasant, positive name, or something derogatory. One of the last girls to flunk out of the horse rotation had suggested every horse in the barn be renamed "Dumb-butt." Nadine hoped the girl was enjoying Mrs. Hartwell's science lab option more than mucking out, because she clearly wasn't cut out for the equestrian life.

Addy bit her lip, thinking. The decision process was lengthy; at one point she actually stepped back and looked the mare all over, appraising her as if she was trying to interpret a painting in a gallery. Then she looked at Nadine, her mind made up. "Don't laugh," she warned.

Nadine held her hands up. "I would never."

"I'd like to call her Bertha."

Nadine felt her eyebrows reaching to her hairline. "Um, okay. That's not what I would expect . . ."

"My grandmother's name was Bertha," Addy said.

Nadine noted the *was*. "Oh, I see."

"And she was just really . . ." Addy had no words. "I just think it would be a good name, and she would have liked this horse."

"Okay," Nadine agreed. "Bertha it is."

After the lesson, she sent Addy off to clean up for lunch hour and went in search of Sean. He had just finished riding Galway, the big gray jumper that was the darling of the horse show club. Every girl wanted a shot at Galway in their lesson; Sean reserved the horse for the very best riders, though.

He had Galway in the wash-rack and was stripping his tack. The heat lamps were on overhead, and steam was rising from the horse's sweaty back. Nadine wordlessly filled a bucket with warm water and grabbed a sponge, getting to work on the horse while Sean slid the saddle onto a rack in the aisle. "Tough ride?" she asked.

"A little bit of a tune-up," Sean admitted, giving Galway a cookie. "He ran out of a fence in a lesson yesterday. It's tough keeping a horse this smart in a lesson program. We might want to consider a lease to one of the advanced girls. I think he'd do better with one rider."

"Oh, that's going to cause a riot," Nadine said, smiling ruefully. "But you're probably right. Better for the show team, too."

"I have high hopes for that show team," Sean told her, flashing a grin. He gave Galway another cookie. "The carnival will be a nice little test for them. See how they behave under pressure. The experienced girls will be fine, but there's a few green ones, no shows under their belt."

"Good way to find out who freaks under stress before there are points on the line?" Nadine guessed.

"That's it, exactly. How about your community service project? That new girl managing okay?"

"Really nicely," Nadine smiled, thinking of Addy. "She named the pinto mare Bertha."

Sean snorted.

"No, it's cute! For her grandmother, she said."

"Don't worry, I won't laugh. It just took me by surprise. A barn full of Galways and Goliaths and we have a Bertha now."

"That's what we want," Nadine told him, squeezing the warm water down Galway's arching neck. "A bit of variety."

She had just finished with the horse's bath when her phone chimed with a text. Nadine plucked it from her back pocket and read the message, her mouth falling open a little more with every word.

Sean was staring at her when she looked up. "What is it?" he asked.

"Nikki is . . ." Nadine looked at her phone again, unable to believe what she was reading. She shook her head. "Nikki is *pregnant.*"

"Whoa!" Sean picked up a cooler and threw it over Galway's back. "Didn't expect that news."

"Yeah, me neither." Nadine leaned her head against the wall of the wash-rack. For some reason, the idea of it made her stomach feel uncomfortably fluttery. As if the news had some effect on *her* insides. She supposed it was only natural—a friend was pregnant. It brought up all kinds of . . . well, she didn't want to say *fears,* that didn't seem right, but . . .

She and Sean had never talked about children.

What would happen if she were to suddenly—she didn't even want to think the words in order—what if there was a positive pregnancy test in her life?

What if she wanted one?

"Better her than you, right?" Sean joked.

Nadine looked at him and saw the lines in his forehead.

He was freaked out by this news, too.

Okay, she thought. *This is fine.*

Just one more thing to worry about—discussing the future with Sean. Great. Super. She forced a smile. "Yeah," she said. "Better her than me."

Chapter Twenty-Five

Kelly

T he man was crazy. She'd had her suspicions, of course; the way he was just living up here alone, the way the house was clearly falling down around his ears, those four insane dogs that trailed him everywhere . . . nothing about William Cunningham was ordinary.

And maybe she wasn't looking for more ordinary in her life, but goodness, she definitely didn't need utterly crazy.

Kelly brushed off her hiking clothes from the day before, wishing there was something to do about the spatters of mud and bits of dry leaf clinging to the fabric. Her puffy coat was ruined. There was no other word for it: the nylon was ripped in a neat four-inch tear and the stuffing had been spilling out ever since she'd gotten caught on that fence. But she tugged everything on anyway, leaving William's pajamas folded neatly on the bed—somewhat regretfully, as they were *very* cozy PJs.

Downstairs, she heard William clanging away in the kitchen. Working on the floor again or something, she thought, annoyed. Despite her brave words, the wet morning wasn't exactly compelling Kelly to leave the shelter of Hilltop House, and she found herself wandering through the rooms on the lower floor rather than heading straight into the kitchen to demand her ride. There were five rooms in all, each of them imposingly large, with high ceilings and a series of windows of wavy, antique glass looking over the property. She felt a bit like Jane Eyre, exploring a grand house while the master bustled about with his own inscrutable oddness and the mad wife was locked up just beyond her reach. But of course, whatever drifter he'd let stay on the property wasn't his mad wife . . . she hoped.

Anything was possible.

"Well, yes," Kelly murmured to herself. "Anything is possible, but *anything* is a strong word. Do you really think William has an insane spouse locked up in his dairy?"

She didn't. Not to mention the fact that she'd seen the person. Kelly let her fingers run through the dust on an antique sideboard in the formal dining room and considered what she'd witnessed. A slim figure darting from the barn to the little dairy—nothing too revealing there. But now that she thought about it, the figure *had* to be a woman, or a very small, very slight man. Certainly a possibility, but . . . Kelly took a deep breath and pushed into the kitchen.

William looked up at her, slightly pop-eyed. He was trying to move a huge cabinet, but when he saw her, he gently lowered it to the ground. Lola and the other huskies thumped their tails against the floor in greeting. She ignored them, getting straight to the point.

"William, is the person outside Monica Waters?"

Slowly, William picked up a rag and started to wipe his hands. He was using far more concentration than necessary.

That was all Kelly needed to know. "This is not okay," she told him. "A lot of people are looking for her. Her *family*—"

"Look, I don't know for sure. I haven't seen the person, okay? As a matter of fact, you're the only person who has."

"How can you let her stay out there?"

"I already told you, it's none of my—"

"And I told you, that's absurd! This is a national missing person case, for one thing. The FBI questioned Grayson! Don't you care about other people at all?"

William eyed her. "Why do you keep calling him Grayson? Why not, 'the boyfriend,' like everyone else says it? Do you know the guy?"

"I just happen—I know his name—I'm a reporter," Kelly fumbled.

"Uh-huh. You know him. Tell me."

She didn't owe him anything. Except, of course, for bringing her in from the cold, feeding her, and making love to her. Well, she was willing to pay him back for the first two things, but the last thing had to be considered a gift, for many reasons. Kelly looked at the floor. "He's my ex. We were engaged."

William put down the rag and moved with exaggerated calm to the refrigerator. It was new and shiny, a tower of gleaming stainless steel. It was also mostly empty. He took out a pitcher of water and poured himself a glass. "You know where this water comes from?" he asked, à propos of nothing.

Kelly folded her arms. She really wasn't into guessing games from weirdos. Or otherwise. "The sink?"

"It comes from a spring underneath the house."

She blinked at that, unable to avoid a spark of interest. "Wait—there's a spring under this house?"

"That's right. The first Cunningham in western Maryland found the spring and built the house right over top. It's in that corner—" William pointed to the wall beyond the fridge. "But you have to go outside to get to it. Some modernizing great-grandma of mine bricked up the door to the spring room in the early twentieth century and I haven't found the time to restore it yet. Still, it's just outside the back door here, and that's better than walking to a frozen stream or to a well in winter, don't you think?"

"But isn't there running water?"

"Of course there is," William paused and drank from his glass, eyes closed. "But it isn't the same as just dipping a pitcher into the spring, either."

"That's amazing," Kelly admitted, "but it doesn't change anything—"

"I don't invite people up here," he interrupted. "This house is special. It's not for the world to trample over. And so all I ask is that people leave this house alone. A few deliveries from people I trust in Catoctin Creek, like the feed store folks. But otherwise, I ask that no one comes up here and disturbs me, and my house. We're two broken old things, and we don't want to be bothered while we try to put each other back together."

Kelly's anger flared. "Listen, if I'm *disturbing* you—"

"I don't want the news here," William went on, as if she hadn't said anything at all. "I don't want the police here. I sure as hell don't want the FBI here. I want Miss Waters out there, if *that's* who is out there, to figure out what she's doing and get out of her own accord. I'm not calling in the authorities and having them tramp all over my property and my house to chase out a girl who is doing what she wants with her own free will. You got that?"

She closed her eyes. He was unreal. Slowly, she said, "But, William, that's not possible. No one can just do whatever they want. And you—you can't be afraid of other people's messes. This town seems pretty happy to get involved in each other's business. Why can't you be like that?"

He shrugged, and she felt a surge of fury. Giving up was not the answer. Not *ever.* If there was one rule Kelly lived her life by, it was this: keep going, no matter how tired you are. But William hadn't done that, had he? He'd just stopped. And she didn't know how she could deal with a person like that, a man in stasis.

"I'm just not," William said finally. "It's not who I am. I want to be left alone, and I want to leave other people alone."

Kelly shook her head. "That's not good enough for me, William. I think you owe your community more than that. You don't even know how lucky you are to have this place."

"I don't know if I'd call it luck."

"You wouldn't know luck if it slapped you across the face."

They looked at each from across the kitchen. Lola yawned, her tongue flicking from her mouth.

"Well, that's a shame," William said finally. "Are you ready to go?"

"No," she said. "I want to know if that's Monica."

"You want to clear your ex-boyfriend's name," William said, shrugging. "But that's not your job."

You have it wrong, she thought. Instead of correcting him, she turned away. "I'll be waiting by the front door," she said, leaving the kitchen. If William thought she couldn't turn her back on this case because of some pining love for Grayson, he was dead wrong. And she'd prove it.

By leaving.

She seethed silently all the way back to the Cascade Falls trailhead. It wasn't a quick drive, either—the six miles between Hilltop House and the trailhead parking lot were all tight turns, steep climbs, and slick drops, and the rain was still falling with great purpose, slapping against the windshield whenever they drove from beneath a canopy of trees.

William didn't have anything to say, either. He left the radio on some classical station and a concerto rose up between them, but even that wasn't enough to mute the tension in the truck cab. They'd had a beautiful night together, and now they were enemies, and Kelly thought the music accentuated this fact, rather than detracting from it. As if they were in the third act of an opera, the part where everything goes to hell.

At the trailhead parking lot, he parked the truck a few spots away from her car and they sat silently for a moment, each taking in the mess. There were cups and napkins and general trash all over the place, presumably left by the news crews who had killed time here earlier, when she'd been presumed missing. "You know, I thought a person had to be gone forty-eight hours or something to be missing," William said, the first thing he'd said on the entire drive.

"The usual rules don't apply when another woman went missing on the same trail," she said frostily. "But I suppose you're going to blame this mess on me."

"I *could* say you shouldn't have gone out there alone when you didn't know the first thing about hiking, and were slightly afraid of being murdered," William said. "But why bother telling you what you already know?"

Fuming, Kelly twisted the door handle and hopped out of the truck. She felt in her coat pocket for her keys, mercifully still locked within a zippered inner pocket. The icy rain streamed down her neck as she turned to look at William one more time. Something within her ached at the idea of leaving him like this, sending him back to his empty house while she returned to a life she didn't even like. Why were they doing this again?

Oh, right, because he was crazy. "Thanks for the ride," she said, and shut the truck door, blotting out the sight of his long, sad face.

William drove away.

For a few minutes she stood in the rain, watching the place where his truck had disappeared. She was a little astonished he'd left without even making sure her car turned on, but another part of her wasn't surprised at all. He'd decided she was the enemy. Which was crazy, because she wasn't even sure what war he was fighting.

With a sigh, Kelly got into the car and turned it on. She waited a while for the heat to warm her numbed fingers, and then she turned the little car towards town. First stop, she decided, was to the apartment for a hot shower and fresh clothes. Second stop would definitely be the bakery, for some coffee and hopefully a refresher on the local gossip.

Oh, lord, and she'd better call her parents.

Chapter Twenty-Six

Nikki

Nikki woke up with a start and immediately realized it was late afternoon. She glanced at the time on her phone and groaned—four o'clock. She'd slept for three hours. She ran her hand over the cool spot where Kevin had been earlier. He must have laid down with her just long enough to see her happily back to sleep, then gotten up to head back to work.

Work. So much work. She put her hand on her forehead and ran through the list of things she'd meant to do today. There were the plans for the extra baking to take to the carnival; a special order of white chocolate-raspberry cookies for Mrs. Grissom's sixty-second birthday; tomorrow's bread baking to set up; she was supposed to make an order from High Rock Coffee Roasters, as they were nearly out of beans . . .

She hadn't done any of it. Instead, she'd slept away most of the day. This couldn't be how things went on now. Just because she was pregnant.

Oh, good lord, she was *pregnant*. What a realization to wake up to. Nikki looked down at her stomach, ran her fingers over the skin, warm under her pajamas. "What am I going to do with you?" she asked, not unkindly. Just a little bewildered.

After a moment lost in contemplation, Nikki put her feet on the cold floor and sat on the edge of the bed, trying to will herself to stand up. She wondered how she could still be tired after a three-hour nap—which came following a two-hour nap that morning. What she really wanted was a cup of coffee, but she probably couldn't drink caffeine anymore, right?

That was another thing she had to do: set up a doctor's appointment to make sure she actually knew all the rules. Finding a doctor and getting an appointment would be bad enough, then she'd have to actually *go* to the doctor, probably pretty regularly. Have tests done. Come home and look at the empty bedroom next to this one. Figure out how to fill it. Buy nursery furniture. Baby clothes. Diapers. What else did babies need? Probably loads of things. She'd need bigger clothes for herself; a bigger bra—she squeezed her chest and winced. Her breasts were already bigger. That had been one of the first tip-offs that her hormones were doing something new and unfamiliar. Along with all the crying, of course. She'd always been fairly slight, and honestly, she was quite surprised Kevin hadn't noticed the change before she had.

Kevin. Working from dawn to well after dusk shoeing horses. Shoeing *horses.* Was that a stable job, no pun intended? Sure, they were in farm country, but it wasn't horse country, it wasn't like the posh places down in Virginia where every country house had two or three horses, sometimes far more, grazing their manicured paddocks. They were just a few years past considering riding horses an affectation around here; the new trainer at Elmwood was a help, but it would be awhile before show horses were the norm in this very traditional community, and all the while Kevin was trying to make his living and potentially feed a family while scraping hooves and hammering out horseshoes like they were still living in the nineteenth century . . .

Nikki let herself fall backwards on the bed and closed her eyes. She couldn't get up yet. Couldn't face all this.

There was a tap at the hall door.

She opened her eyes.

"Coming," she called.

When they'd first set up the downstairs as dining rooms and kitchen, they'd had to make a tough decision about the lovely staircase in the front hall. Eventually, they'd walled it in and put a door at the bottom, with another at the top, on the landing. Nikki had felt terrible doing it, but none of the updates were permanent and she'd needed some way to keep their upstairs rooms from being invaded by cafe guests.

Now she dragged herself down the hall to open the upstairs door, expecting to see Rosemary on the landing, or perhaps a delivery person who had been sent up by Rosemary. Assuming she was still downstairs, of course. Four o'clock—Rosemary needed to get back to her farm and feed her horses. Nikki couldn't keep her here all day.

She opened the door and was surprised to see Caitlin standing on the other side, a brown paper bag in one hand, a coffee cup in the other.

"Caitlin! I didn't expect to see you here!" Nikki plucked at her shirt, wishing it wasn't straining so hard across her front. Without a bra, she felt really vulnerable.

Caitlin's eyes slid down to her chest, then up again. She gave Nikki a knowing smile. "I think you need some soup and bread," she said. "And some green tea. Can I come in?"

Nikki stepped back. "Please, be my guest."

Caitlin moved into the upstairs kitchen and settled down at the kitchen table with the bag, pulling out a carton of soup and a plastic spoon. A chunk of baguette that Nikki had baked herself early that morning followed, set on a brown paper napkin. "I know green tea is disgusting," Caitlin said apologetically, "but I filled it with honey, so it should be as sweet as lemonade at this point."

Nikki settled herself into the chair opposite. She thought Caitlin looked rather like a Cheshire Cat, those perfect teeth sparkling at her in the pale luminosity of the cloudy afternoon. "Did Rosemary tell you?" she asked, picking up the spoon. She hadn't realized she was hungry until she smelled the herbs in the broth. For some reason, they made her absolutely ravenous.

"I guessed, and Rosemary blushed." Caitlin laughed. "I came in to get some lunch and grab a quiet corner to do some work, and I was surprised to see Rosemary behind the counter when she has so much going on."

Guilt settled over Nikki again. "I can't rely on her, obviously. It's not right."

"No, we need to find you someone permanent," Caitlin agreed. Nikki noted the use of the word *we*. Caitlin was already taking over, and this wasn't even her business. Incredible, the way that woman's mind worked. "In the meantime, Nadine is downstairs handling things. Sean can manage the horses back at the school just fine without her. He's got Darby and all those kids to help him."

"But who will come and work here? I can't just have Rosemary and Nadine alternate as my interns, Caitlin."

"Don't worry about that right now," Caitlin suggested. "The right situation will turn up."

Nikki was suddenly too hungry to care. She dipped her baguette into the broth and took a fierce bite. Caitlin laughed. "That's the Nikki I'm used to. You're going to be an incredible mother, you know that?"

But Nikki wasn't thinking about being a mother just then. She was thinking only of soup, and bread, and honeyed tea. The basics of life, she figured. That was going to have to be her focus for a while.

Until she could handle dealing with everything else.

<hr/>

Kevin brought home dinner from the Blue Plate, along with a message from Lauren. "She says that you're not allowed to even think about the Blue Plate, so, I guess pretend this dinner didn't come from there," he said, laying out plates on the kitchen table.

"So you told her?" Nikki didn't know if she was hurt or relieved. "Does everyone in town know?"

"Just the essential players," Kevin assured her. "I told Lauren because she needs to know what's going on with the business. And you needing some extra downtime falls under that. Apparently Caitlin knows because she can get any secret out of Rosemary? And Nadine knows because Rosemary needed help sorting out the horses and the cafe."

"I'm putting more work on everyone, and at the worst possible time." Nikki slouched at the table.

"On the plus side, your boobs look fantastic."

She glanced down at her chest. "I guess they do. I ordered some new bras."

"See? Everything has a silver lining. Also, we're going to have a baby, so that's pretty great."

She smiled up at him, her heart suddenly lighter than it had been all day. When she'd told him the news—properly, sitting down, not just him overhearing it from across the cafe—he'd looked rather shell-shocked. Now, though, he'd clearly had some time to do some thinking. And judging by his expression, Kevin had come around to the idea of fatherhood pretty quickly. "You're really happy about it?"

"Are you kidding me?" Kevin took the iced tea pitcher from the fridge and set it on the table, then gave her a kiss on the top of her head. "I'm absolutely thrilled! We're going to have a *baby*. And I can't wait to fight over names with you. Do you want to start right now? I have some doozies picked out."

Nikki shook her head. "No, I'm too tired and I know you're going to say something absolutely insane."

"I'm just saying, I don't see why we *can't* name a girl Marigold," Kevin said lightly, sitting across from her and pulling the plate of biscuits his way. "And if it's a boy, well then, I like Thor."

"No, stop." Nikki laughed and tugged the biscuit dish back. "Please, I'm begging you, no names right now. I can't . . . I can't absorb all that right now."

Kevin's gaze softened. "Hey, take all the time you need. But there's no need to worry. We're going to take care of things."

"We?" Nikki cocked her head. "Just who is *we?*" But she thought she already knew.

"All of us." Kevin spread his fingers wide. "The town. Catoctin Creek. We're going to handle this. Just like we're handling Rosemary's horse rescue, and Kelly O'Connell, and—"

"Wait." Nikki was glad of the distraction. "I need the latest on Kelly O'Connell. Stat."

"Oh, she was *just* downstairs talking to Nadine," Kevin said, as if he didn't know he should have led with this information. "She's talking about taking leave from her job, actually. Pretty interesting. I don't know if she's planning on staying here or what."

Nikki shook her head. "That girl is going through some stuff, huh? Comes up here to deal with her ex's missing boyfriend, disappears in the forest, turns up at William's place, refuses to come back, now she's wandering the town and giving up her job."

"Big-time drama," Kevin agreed. He bit into a fried chicken breast and closed his eyes in contentment, Kelly forgotten. "Oh, happy day," he murmured through a full mouth. "Happy, happy day."

Nikki figured as a pregnant woman she was probably expected to live on salad with grilled chicken breasts or something, but she had to give in to the fried chicken—there was just no ignoring the stuff. And it brought her comfort. One bite, and she immediately felt better about life in general. Of course, she thought, a few other things probably deserved some credit for her growing sense of optimism. Chief among them: her town's quick move to support her, and her partner's delighted reaction to the news that had frightened her so much.

I am going to have a baby, Nikki thought. *And that's wonderful!*

Chapter Twenty-Seven

Rosemary

The temporary barn was garish next to her beautiful old bank barn, but it would get the job done. For a little while, anyway. Rosemary led the last of the snorting, reluctant Wayne horses into the big white tent, past his stablemates, and into a clean, freshly bedded stall. With the sides tightly staked down and the north and west entrances zipped up against the wind whistling out of the Catoctins, the temporary barn was a surprisingly cozy place. The other horses were already warming it up with their bodies and breath.

"You guys will be a lot more comfortable here," she told the horse, unsnapping the lead from his halter and backing out. "And tomorrow you can go out in a real field, not a muddy farmyard."

He snorted and went to pacing his stall, pawing at the fresh shavings on the floor. The other horses had already realized if they dug far enough, they'd find grass underneath, so everyone was quietly riffling through their bedding with their noses and hooves, pulling up the shavings to find the buffet waiting for them.

Rosemary figured that was as good a way of helping them settle in as any other.

"They're already looking better," Nadine said, pushing a wheelbarrow loaded with timothy hay into the tent. "It only took what, a week of steady care to start putting some gloss back on their coats?"

"Yes, thank goodness." Rosemary sighed as she looked the horses over. "And no one has any underlying health conditions that the vet could find. It looks like we'll be able to adopt out most of them. Except for the gray mare and that chestnut gelding at the end. I think we'll be keeping them. They're seniors."

"You have a thing for the old men," Nadine joked, tossing hay over the stall bars.

"I just don't trust the world with them." Rosemary looked into the chestnut gelding's stall. He had all the hallmarks of extreme equine age, with a prominent nasal bone streaked by white hairs. The hollows above his eyes were dark pits. This horse was probably thirty years old or more—a centenarian, in horse terms. Rosemary had been watching his chewing with a little anxiety, hoping his teeth were good enough to handle his hay. "Old horses have a tendency to get kicked around. I'd rather know they spend their last years in peace, not worried about new barns or new people."

"So this place will still be a sanctuary at heart," Nadine said. "I was wondering."

"Well, over the summer, every time I adopted out a horse, a new horse just kept showing up to take its place." Rosemary shrugged. "I figured it was a sign that it was time to diversify. But I won't turn my back on a horse who needs a safe harbor for the rest of his life."

"And so the new barn fills up before it's built." Stephen came into the tent, a smile on his face, a suit under his coat. He was heading up to New York for a few days to meet with business partners. "Oh good, I see your babysitter is here. Nadine, we talked about this. There are enough horses for a while. You have my permission to tell Rosemary no."

"Nadine?" Rosemary and Nadine exchanged amused glances. "You think *she'll* stop me from bringing home more horses?"

"Shhh," Nadine hissed in an exaggerated stage whisper. "He doesn't have to know."

Stephen shook his head, but he was still smiling. "Horse girls never change. Look, I've just come down to make sure everything's okay before I hit the road? My train leaves in two hours, so I'm cutting it a little close."

"We're fine," Rosemary assured him. She gave him a tight hug and a lingering kiss that had him pulling her closer until they heard Nadine snicker in the background. "I'm just going to head over to Sean and Nadine's and heckle them for being in love, so my evening plans are all taken care of."

"Perfect," Stephen said gravely. "It's about time someone did it."

"That's the thanks I get for leaving my own horses and coming over here to help Rosemary," Nadine muttered. "Typical."

Stephen gave Nadine a kid-sister kind of hug, pulling her close with one arm, then shoving her away. "Thank you for helping Rosemary handle this," he told her. "Seriously. This was a big ask at first, twelve extra horses, but I think we've gotten it down to a manageable number, right Rosemary?"

"Oh sure," Rosemary laughed wearily. *"Nine* new horses is a piece of cake."

"I mean . . ."

"It's fine." She waved him away. "Go to New York and get your meetings out of the way. The sooner you're gone, the sooner you're home. And don't forget to bring back bagels."

Stephen looked put upon. "Anything else?"

"Yes," Rosemary said, putting her hands on his shoulders. She looked deep into his eyes. "I love you."

Late afternoon began to give way to the early November evening over Notch Gap Farm, but Rosemary was still working as a yellow and purple sunset swirled dramatically over the Catoctins. She had been turning her horses out in the north pasture for a long time, ignoring the south pasture as it was mostly wooded and didn't offer a lot of grazing, but at this time of year neither field was good for grass, so it didn't matter much where she put the horses. Fence repair hadn't been top of her mind while she hadn't been using the field, though, so Rosemary had to pile fence boards in the back of the truck and drive it slowly along the fence lines in the south pasture, patching any holes in the old fence. Nadine came along, and she brought Addy, who had been to town on a school sanctioned visit that day and was full of gossip she figured the older women hadn't heard yet.

"So did you hear about Kelly O'Connell?" Addy asked, handing down the box of nails to Rosemary. "The reporter? Apparently, she came back to town after her little disappearance in the woods and she isn't leaving to go home. They say she was with that guy who lives alone in some old mansion on the mountainside. What do you think they got up?"

Nadine, holding up the new fence board, shook her head. "Let's not gossip about Kelly. She's a nice girl, from what I know."

Rosemary glanced at her. "Have you met her, too? I didn't realize."

"A few days ago, actually, when I was minding the cafe. She apologized for sending me that random email about Monica before she got up here. Apparently she was chasing a bad lead."

"Well, I don't think she's chasing any leads now," Rosemary observed. "I was texting with Nikki earlier and she said Kelly was just hanging out in the cafe, looking at her laptop and drinking tea. Not exactly running around on assignment anymore."

"She's taking leave from her job," Nadine said. "At least, that's what she told me."

"Really! That's the last thing I expected. She seems like a very driven person."

Addy wasn't finished yet. "Kitty Yu says that the reporter and that guy got up to some real kinky stuff up there in the mansion."

Rosemary raised her eyebrows. "Kinky stuff? And how does Kitty Yu know that?"

"She heard it from Bentley, because Bentley's cousin knows Ruthann Routzahn, and the Routzahns live next door to the mansion," Addy informed them triumphantly.

"No one lives next door to Hilltop House," Rosemary said. She hammered a nail home as Nadine held a board flush against the post. "It's extremely isolated, plus it borders the state park on two sides. And the Routzahns live two miles away from the Cunningham driveway, and they live back in the woods themselves. I can assure you they're not hearing anything going on up at Hilltop. Don't be too quick to believe your friends, Addy, most of them are making stuff up to get attention."

Addy made some grumbling noises, and Nadine shot Rosemary a look which said, *Please don't upset the Addy.* Rosemary shrugged and mouthed back, *Sorry.* What could she do? Let the kid spread rumors about Kelly and William?

Something had definitely happened between those two, though. Rosemary had helped Nikki at the cafe this morning and Kelly had come in for breakfast. She'd been . . . different. Not that she'd been exactly bubbly before, but she'd been at least a little outgoing. Rosemary figured she'd have to be, if she was going to be a reporter and bounce around talking to strangers all the time. The Kelly who came into the cafe seemed sad, and suspicious, and glanced around her constantly as if she was waiting for someone to jump out of the shadows. She'd bought a latte and a muffin, and taken home a loaf of bread she'd said was for her supper—and that was what Rosemary found *really* suspicious, because in her experience stick-thin, TV-beautiful women didn't eat loaves of bread for supper, however nice the loaves of bread might be.

As for William, well, he hadn't come in at all, which Rosemary supposed wasn't surprising, but she'd still wondered what he was up to. Clearly, something had gone down between the reporter and her old friend. Maybe not "kinky" stuff, but *something.* Rosemary was mulling over the possibility of driving up to Hilltop House herself, once the fence was done and the horses were fed.

"That's the last fence board, I think," she said finally, straightening up. The dark fence was a patchwork with pale new boards. Not exactly a great look, but it would get the job done, and maybe in a few months when things settled down, they could come up and paint everything a uniform color. "Thanks for your help, girls. I imagine you have to get back to your own horses now."

"Yeah and I have an English paper to write," Addy sighed. "On *Hamlet,* of all things."

"You love Shakespeare," Nadine reminded her. "You said so last week when you were trying to get out of mucking stalls. You said, 'I wish I was working on my Hamlet paper.'"

"What do you have, a photographic memory? Jeez." Addy shook her head. "That was before I had Bertha, okay? I didn't know I was going to have a horse to take care of that was like, just my responsibility. I want to spend more time with her."

Nadine gave Rosemary a significant look over Addy's head.

"Well, part of having horses is learning how to budget your time," Rosemary suggested, handing up the tool-belt and the box of nails. "You'll learn that lesson soon enough, trust me. Okay, all done here. You want to ride in the back of the truck on the way back to the barn? Nadine and I won't tell anyone."

It was an easy but effective way to give Addy a special treat. Kids weren't allowed to ride in truck beds anymore. Addy bounced with excitement as Nadine slid into the passenger seat next to Rosemary. "So you're going to turn out all the horses by yourself?" Nadine asked.

"Not until the morning," Rosemary said. "Don't worry about it, I'll manage. They can stay in tonight. I hate to leave them in one more minute, but it's been so cold at night, and they've had a rough time. I think they still need the warmth of the barn." She turned the truck and slowly began to bounce down the pasture, which sloped steeply towards the house and barn. "Or maybe I just need the security of knowing they're in there."

"The tent barn was a good find. You had enough in the emergency fund for it?"

"Oh, I got a little help from a certain husband's Amex," Rosemary said, laughing ruefully. "He said to call it a donation from his company, but I don't know enough about the IRS rules. I'll refund him once the carnival money comes through. Assuming the carnival money comes through, of course."

"I think it will. Everyone's getting really excited." Nadine glanced in the rear-view mirror, making sure Addy was still sitting down and not bouncing around the truck bed. "Addy's been spreading the word already. She's a very effective loudspeaker, that girl."

"And it's working out with the mare?"

"She's obsessed. It took about five minutes. She named her after her grandmother. Bertha, if you can believe it."

"Oh." Rosemary was speechless for a moment. "That's the sweetest thing I've ever heard."

"Yeah," Nadine nodded. "It's pretty darn cute in there. I think we're going to have to keep the mare. And the other horses are just fine. Settling in perfectly. Sean and I will make time next month to figure out what they know, but for now, they're just going to eat and fatten up and get used to how loud a barn full of girls can be."

"Hopefully they're all saddle-broke and can make useful additions to the barn for you."

"Well, even if they aren't, some of the advanced kids can help us get them ready to adopt out, and that will count towards community service hours for them or something. We'll figure it all out."

Rosemary pulled the truck carefully through the deep ruts around the gate. "We need clay for that spot," she fretted. "Always something."

"Maybe the carnival can be an annual thing," Nadine suggested. "If it goes well. Then every year you'd have some extra money coming in."

"I was kind of hoping so myself," Rosemary admitted. "Hey, getting back to that whole Kelly thing . . . what would you think if I went to see William tonight?"

Nadine looked startled. "Like, drive up to his house? But I heard he was a total hermit. Would he even let you in? Is he even *safe?*"

"Oh, I know him. Trust me, William's a softie. He went to school here his junior and senior years, and he used to come every summer and Christmas before that. He used to come and play here with Nikki and me. William's an old friend. And I'm worried about him, really."

"What do you think could be wrong?"

"I think something happened between him and Kelly, to be honest."

"Really?" Nadine lowered her voice. "Like Addy was saying?"

Rosemary laughed. "I don't know if they were getting freaky up there, but I know William. He falls in love *hard.* If he saw something in Kelly, he wouldn't wait a couple weeks to be sure it was more than a crush. He'd go all out."

"That's sweet, actually," Nadine said.

"Sure, it's sweet. But it gets you hurt." Rosemary sighed. "I don't know. Maybe it's not my place. I barely know Kelly. She could have been awful to him."

"Except that she's sad, too," Nadine pointed out.

"Yeah." Rosemary parked the truck. "And what about you? How's everything in Nadine's world? I feel like we're hyper-focused on Nikki and a million other things right now, and you're just plugging away."

Nadine's smile was rueful. "Oh, that sounds about right. I'm just plugging away."

"Forget William," Rosemary said, making up her mind. "That came out wrong. I love William. But after I feed tonight, I want to talk to *you*. Sound okay?"

"Yeah," Nadine agreed, and Rosemary knew she wasn't imagining the relief in the younger woman's voice. "That would be great, actually."

Chapter Twenty-Eight

Kelly

*Y*ou've been placed on suspension with pay, pending the results *of our investigation.* Kelly looked at the words on the email again, biting down on her inner cheek with a slow grinding motion that seemed to satisfy some inner demon.

She'd told everyone she was taking leave, but the truth was much more official. It was odd to think her job could suspend her for going hiking and not coming home on time. But of course, there had been certain expectations for her, going off to a small town in the grip of a national news story. She was supposed to send in taped reports or go on-air live with breaking news, not vanish and create her own news story—and choose not to check her email for a few days, while she was at it.

She put the phone into her pajamas pocket and climbed down the little ladder from the loft bed to the apartment floor. She was starting to like this place; it was so crazy that Nikki from the cafe used to live here. She imagined Nikki had decorated it a little more smartly than it was now; the studio furnishings screamed IKEA's cheapest floor models, with a lot of muted grays and blues. But the afternoon light, streaming through the French doors lining the front of the studio, was plentiful and warming, and the long, galley-style kitchen running along the back wall was excellent, with sturdy professional gas burners on a gleaming stainless steel stove, and a funky vintage fridge with a creamy paint job which constantly made her think of diner desserts, pies heaped high with whipped cream and a cherry on top.

Yeah, she decided, a girl could get used to a place like this. So, why not stay on for a while? And since she wasn't working right now, maybe for an extended period, she thought she would.

And so she'd stay here and . . . then what would happen? Kelly looked into the mostly empty fridge, sighing at her own lack of groceries. She had bread, but no butter. No eggs. No milk. This wasn't her fridge. This wasn't her home.

Fine, not a problem. So she'd go to the market. She'd fill the fridge. She'd hang out in this old garage in Catoctin Creek, and then what? She had no work here. There was her great-grandmother's diary, but that was back at her condo in Arlington. She wasn't about to drive down there and get it.

It's not like this was springtime and everything was in bloom and the mountains were calling and she must go. It was *November*. The town was gloomy; the weather was worse. Everyone was still obsessed with missing Monica. And she hadn't managed to find her. She'd come up here for one thing—*one thing*—and she'd failed. Her ex's girlfriend was still out there, her whereabouts were still a mystery.

And then there was William.

The thought of William made her heart pound like crazy, her fingers tingle with the memory of his skin, her lips form a taut bow as they recalled the force of his kiss. Every single part of her, in fact, had a very specific memory and association with William, and they were *all* positive—except for her actual mental memories, which were decidedly mixed.

Kelly took the half-loaf of sourdough out of the fridge and tore off a chunk, popped it into her mouth. Chewed moodily. Remembering William.

She and William had gone a little crazy, she supposed, and it was possible William was simply a crazy person, as she'd suspected from the very start, and this kind of ending had been inevitable.

But that didn't make missing him any easier.

So if she stayed—what happened to that wound? Was she just supposed to risk running into him at the cafe or the market or the diner, or driving past him and seeing his face behind the wheel? Was she supposed to just live down here in the foothills, knowing that he was up on that mountainside alone? She couldn't deal with that; the knowledge he was alone, and hated being alone, and couldn't *admit* to how he hated being alone—that was the worst part of all.

The empathy was killing her.

It was all too much.

She should leave. *Soon.*

But Kelly didn't know where to go.

So she did the next best thing. After all, she was hungry. And she had no coffee. And the sourdough loaf had evolved into some ridiculous salt and flour and water representation of her craptacular love life.

"When one can't decide, one should eat cake," she told herself, and she tugged on some clothes, the last wrinkled remnants of the bag she'd lugged up here, and went to the Catoctin Cafe & Bakery.

The bell jangled as Kelly opened the door, and the first thing she saw was that the cafe was half-full, people talking at tables, a friendly buzz of conversation rising over the usual hum of the bake case cooler. There were definitely more people here than she remembered from the past week.

The second thing was the Christmas decorations. This place was a holly jolly holiday if she'd ever seen one. There were pine boughs on the mantel of the unlit fireplace against the far wall, lending their spicy scent to the already aromatic cafe. Tiny white lights twinkled through wreaths and garland on the windowsills and along the front of the counter. Small red ribbons grabbed her eye wherever she looked, and a parade of tall silver deer paced down the broad sill of the big front window overlooking the front porch and yard. A tinkly classical version of *Jingle Bells* floated from some hidden speaker.

"Oh my," Kelly breathed, pausing in the doorway to take it all in. The door clicked shut behind her, shutting out the raw November day, and she had a sudden sensation of warmth from head to toe—but it was more than just the difference in temperature.

Something about this cafe in holiday garb just grabbed her.

Nikki was perched on a stool behind the counter, nibbling on a small pile of saltines. The stool was also a new development; Kelly was used to seeing Nikki on her feet. Something was different. "Hey, Nikki," she said cautiously. "How are things?"

"They've been better," Nikki admitted with an expression that was half-grin, half-grimace. "The cafe picked an awkward time to get popular, let's just say that. Well, Kelly! I'm a little surprised you're still hanging around town. Everything okay with work?"

Kelly felt her cheeks flush. "Well, my leave just got a little more long-term, so . . ."

Nikki nodded and picked up another saltine. She bit into it carefully: a tiny, mincing bite from the very edge of the cracker, as if she was trying not to taste it at all. After a moment, she said, "If you're sticking around, we could use your help at the Christmas carnival. It's not until next month, though, so you'd have to be pretty long term."

Kelly, working at the Catoctin Creek Christmas carnival? Suddenly, she wanted nothing more. Sure, it would be free labor, but to be part of Catoctin Creek? This was an invitation she might never get again. From *any* town. Kelly nodded carefully, restraining herself from an effusive agreement as she replied, "Wow, I might have to take you up on that. I'm not really sure what I'm going to do with myself while I'm not working."

Nikki shrugged, as if it didn't matter either way. She picked up a saltine and put it down. She was being really odd, Kelly thought. Something was up. Finally, she asked, "Don't you miss your work? I'd have thought something like that was a calling."

Kelly shook her head. This, at least, was an easy question to answer. "Not at all. I hated that job." She said the words out loud for the first time and liked the way they felt. *I hated that job*. It was the truth. And it felt good to say it past tense, for the first time ever. *Hated*. It was over. "The truth is, I have a personal project I want to work on, so maybe during this leave thing, I can figure out how to work on it." As soon as she said it, she decided. She'd have to go back to Arlington and retrieve the diary.

"Oh yeah? What kind of project?"

"My great-grandmother's diary," Kelly explained. "I've always wanted to prep an annotated version of it for publication. With like, commentary, you know. On the historical context. Clothing and food and . . ." She had never told anyone about this before, and she quickly realized she didn't have an elevator pitch. A project for another day, she figured.

"Well, that's impressive," Nikki said, looking at her with what seemed like actual admiration. "I hope you can do it."

"Me, too." Kelly hadn't realized until this morning that she might have finally reached the crossroads in her life where she could put her accidental career behind her and embark on her real passion. The idea was thrilling. For a moment, Kelly forgot she was supposed to be holding up half a conversation. She was too busy realizing her life might actually be changing. At last.

Nikki put another saltine to her mouth and carefully chewed around the edges. A silence stretched between them. Then she said, "Ordinarily, I would stand up and get your order, but at the moment I really don't think I can stand up without doing something I'd regret, so could you be a dear and get it yourself? All the plates and mugs are right behind me, there." She shifted her head slightly to indicate the rows of shining white porcelain.

Kelly nodded vigorously. "Of course, yes, I'll just—are you okay? Can I get you anything?"

Nikki put down the cracker and closed her eyes. "No. Thank you. I'm just doing my best not to—puke."

"Oh!" Suddenly, Kelly saw everything clearly. "Oh, gosh. Let me make you some tea. Very weak tea," she added, seeing Nikki's coloring fade. "Honey and lemon. You take just the littlest sips and you should feel better. You need the sugar, I think."

"Okay," Nikki whispered through bloodless lips. The nausea had clearly come on pretty quickly. "Thanks."

Kelly settled herself behind the counter, finding everything neat and stowed in intuitive places, a testimony to Nikki's excellent organizational skills. She switched on the electric kettle, knowing that freshly boiled water would make better tea than the scalding stuff that sat in the coffee maker tank, then located the tea bags and set one out on a plate.

She was pulling a fresh lemon from the bowl in the refrigerator when she heard the bell ring and a new customer came into the cafe. Kelly glanced at Nikki; the other woman's eyes were still closed. Kelly didn't hesitate—she stepped up to the bake case and put her elbows on top, the picture of a country baker. "What can I get for you this morning?" she asked the newcomer.

The customer, an elderly woman, beamed at her through several layers of coral lipstick. "Good morning, dear. I think maybe we haven't met? I'm Iris Routzahn."

Nikki raised her head slightly at the sound of her voice. "Morning, Miss Iris," she murmured.

"Oh, goodness," Iris exclaimed, catching sight of Nikki for the first time. "Look at poor you. Is this nice girl taking care of you, Nikki?"

"Yes," Nikki said faintly. "Be fine in a minute."

"You just let your helper handle things," Iris advised her. She turned back to Kelly. "Earl Grey tea, dear, with lemon. To stay."

She took a few dollars out of her purse and put them on the counter, then walked over to a table near the big front windows and sat. Kelly watched, bemused, as the elderly woman took an iPhone out of her huge purse and started playing a game, her frail fingers zipping across the screen.

Behind her, the electric kettle began to chatter, reminding her that now she had *two* teas to prep. She turned off the kettle, then turned and cut the lemon into wafer-thin slices.

By the time she'd given Iris and Nikki their teas, a second customer had walked in, and another couple was hot on their heels. Nikki was sipping slowly at her tea, but she still looked woozy. The new customer stood by the counter, gazing at Nikki with a slightly appalled look—an expression which told Kelly this person was from out of town and didn't have the neighborly tolerance level of a local. That settled it. "Nikki," she whispered, "I want you to go up to your bed."

"No, morning rush—I'll be fine in a second—"

"Nikki, I promise I will not burn down your cafe. Let me help you with this." She hadn't worked behind a counter since her stint as a barista in college, but coffee and cake slinging couldn't have changed much in the ten years she'd been away.

"Burning down wasn't my chief concern," Nikki said dryly, opening her eyes. "But now it is."

"Go on, just get upstairs," Kelly chided, and turned to the new customer. "Good morning, ma'am. What can I get for you?"

An hour, six gingerbread lattes and an endless succession of coffees and teas later, Kelly sank onto the stool Nikki had recently vacated and bit into the cake she'd been dreaming about since she left the apartment. Coffee cake, with a crumbly, buttery streusel topping, so it was borderline acceptable as breakfast food—but cake, nonetheless. She followed up each bite with a sip of the excellent coffee she'd just brewed, using beans which she'd signed for when a delivery from a local roaster showed up, toted by a pony-tailed young guy in denim who said he lived on the other side of the mountains and asked her if she liked to hike.

Kelly felt a gentle contentment ripple through her consciousness. There was something to be said for feeding a lot of hungry people and then enjoying the silence left in their wake. And getting hit on by a twenty-something guy with a gentle get-stoned-and-stare-at-trees vibe.

Time sure rushed past, though. The clock was already pointing towards eleven, and she supposed she'd have to think about a lunch rush arriving in the next hour. She'd better familiarize herself with the sandwiches in the case, and was there a panini press? The point of sale had been easy enough to figure out—every small business seemed to use the same tablet with the same program these days, so all she'd had to do was find the password where Nikki had taped it to beneath the counter and she was good to go. Most people just tapped their credit card to the reader and wandered off without even needing a receipt printed, and for the few who used cash, Nikki left her the key for the cash box under the counter.

Running a cafe with no training was simple. Who knew?

Kelly finished her cake and did a slow lap around the cafe, checking the tables and floors for crumbs and spills. She paused at the front windows, gazing out at the view. The sun had finally emerged from behind the clouds for the first time in days, and golden sunbeams were playing across the front yard, dancing through the bare arms of the elm tree in front of the house. In a couple of hours, bold afternoon light would shine through the dining room windows and sparkle on the buttery wooden floors. Kelly found that she could hardly wait to see it. It was hard to believe the promise of sunshine could be so exciting, but maybe priorities changed in the countryside. For the better.

And she figured she'd be here all day—Nikki had no employees she was aware of, so who would come to relieve her? No one, unless Nikki magically felt better.

She was just finishing her cake when a new woman waltzed into the cafe, a woman who was tall and slim and quietly glamorous. A woman who looked quite out of place in Catoctin Creek—much as Kelly suspected she had on the day she'd arrived.

"Hello there," she called. "Welcome in."

The woman's eyebrows went up to her hairline. "Well! Where's Nikki?" she asked, not bothering with a hello.

But Kelly wasn't bothered; she was getting used to a certain straightforwardness in the way people behaved out here. Clothes and good hair couldn't disguise this woman—she was a local through and through.

"She was feeling sick, so I told her to go take a nap," Kelly explained. "That was about an hour ago."

The woman sighed, shaking her head as if she'd suspected as much. "And you are?"

"I'm Kelly O'Connell." Kelly waited for recognition.

"Ah, of course. The reporter." There it was. "Done playing house with William?"

Whoa, things got personal *fast.* Kelly stood up from the stool, hearing it slide roughly back on the wooden floor. "Excuse me? What do you know about—"

She shut her mouth quickly as Rosemary came into the cafe, concern etched into her forehead. "Caitlin!" Rosemary said to the rude woman. "Did you come to check on Nikki?"

"I came in for a coffee," Caitlin said, shrugging. "I didn't know Nikki was doing worse."

"You know how queasy these early weeks can be," Rosemary sighed, pulling off her red knitted hat. "She's just trying to push through it. But she called me and asked if I could take her to the doctor—they made room for her right before lunch. I was trying to get hold of Nadine to run the counter, but I couldn't, so I thought I'd lock up—" Rosemary's eyes shifted to Kelly. "I didn't expect to see you here!"

"I made Nikki go to bed," Kelly explained. "Then I just kind of took over. I used to work at a cafe in college. So it's second nature, I guess."

"It's just giving people coffee," Caitlin said dismissively. "Not exactly rocket science."

"Sure," Kelly agreed, her teeth just grazing the inside of her cheek before she stopped herself from biting down. "I'm basically a drone."

"Don't mind her," Rosemary advised, giving Caitlin a stern look. "She doesn't even know she's doing it."

"Doing what?" Caitlin demanded.

Rosemary laughed and shook her head. "You see? This is just her personality."

The door to the stairs opened slowly, and Nikki emerged. Her face was white as a sheet. "Rosemary?" she croaked. "I'm ready."

Ready for the grave, Kelly thought. Nikki looked like she had the flu and food poisoning and a severe head cold all at once. Even her usually curly hair was wan and lifeless, the auburn coils hanging down her neck in lifeless waves. Kelly had a sudden vision of herself running the cafe for months to come. But no—this was just early pregnancy stuff. She'd be fine in a few days, a week at most.

Maybe, Kelly thought, she could stay on and help Nikki part-time, anyway. Worth a thought. She was having a really nice morning, apart from Caitlin.

"Come on, you," Rosemary fussed, putting an arm around Nikki. "Let's get you to the doctor. I was going to close the place, but, Kelly? Are you good?"

"I'm good," Kelly said, pleased to be allowed to stay. "I didn't have anything else to do today."

"You're a lifesaver," Rosemary assured her. "We'll be back shortly."

Caitlin watched them leave. When she turned back to Kelly, she had an odd expression on her face. Sort of impressed. Sort of annoyed. A bit like a villain who has been outsmarted, Kelly thought. "I wouldn't have expected it of you," she mused.

Kelly was wary. "Expected what?"

Caitlin shrugged. "For you to fit yourself right in. You don't often get the exact right puzzle piece without even looking for one. Anyway," she went on, her tone going cool again, "can I get an Americano? You *do* know how to make an Americano, right?"

"I think I can manage espresso and hot water," Kelly informed her dryly, and she made Caitlin's drink, all the while thinking about what the odd woman had said.

Did she fit in here?

If she did, there was just one problem.

William was here, too. And frankly, Kelly didn't know how she was supposed to coexist with him.

Chapter Twenty-Nine

Nikki

Rosemary was hassling her to hustle up. "Would you please get into the car? I'm freezing, sunshine and all."

"Okay, fine, I'm getting in," Nikki grumbled. She settled into her seat and Rosemary closed the door. She pressed a hand to her forehead. "I'm always a furnace all of a sudden."

"A healthy furnace," Rosemary reminded her. "And that's what matters."

"You say that, but I'm roasting with the way you want to run the heat in here." Nikki decided she'd complain just a little more, while she had the license to do so. "Didn't the doctor say I should relax and try to stay comfortable?"

"She didn't say anything about your normal friends with normal body temperatures freezing to death," Rosemary grumbled, but she turned the heat down a notch.

Nikki unzipped her coat as best she could beneath the seatbelt and let her complaints subside. It was only a few minutes' drive to get home, anyway, and she knew Rosemary was probably genuinely freezing. Well, it wasn't her fault Nikki had gone and produced a heat-generating being that was apparently going to be her personal fireplace from now until July.

Ugh, this wasn't going to be pleasant in July. She wished she'd made an effort to get pregnant with a more convenient and less sweaty due date. They'd have to finish the air conditioning installation by late spring, or she simply wouldn't make it.

But according to her first official prenatal doctor's appointment, timing was the *only* issue with the future child of Kevin and Nikki, so she had that going for her. The doctor said the nausea and dizziness should pass in another week or two, and in the meantime, she should just take it easy and let her body adjust to its new job. "Everyone has a breaking-in period," she joked, handing Nikki a lollipop like she was ten. "Take it easy on yourself."

Nikki hadn't taken it easy on herself since she really was about ten, but she resolved to handle her pregnancy the way she did everything else in her life: with relentless organization and attention to detail. And since the baby was going to need a lot of stuff, she'd use her downtime to consult the internet and make some spreadsheets and budgets to handle her future as the mother of a newborn.

And figure out what she was going to do for extra help around the cafe.

"Why did we leave Kelly running the cafe?" she asked suddenly, glancing at Rosemary. "Shouldn't she be thinking about getting back to work?"

Rosemary shrugged. "Maybe she decided to extend her leave?"

"To work in the cafe? I feel bad. She came in for a cup of coffee and ended up running the place. We have to find someone else. I'll ask Lauren to look in the applications file at the Blue Plate. Maybe there's someone who will fit the bill in there.

"Well, maybe it's not a problem for Kelly," Rosemary suggested. "She didn't look like someone who was eager to get back to her real life."

"Isn't it funny the way we say that?" Nikki mused. "As if we have fake lives and real lives. All we have is the life we're living, Rosie-marie."

"Then I suggest you tell her that," Rosemary said, pulling into the parking lot behind the cafe. "It should help her make up her mind."

—ele—

Nikki sat at a small table near the back of the dining room and watched Kelly interact with the latter half of the lunch trade. The young woman definitely looked tired, but she kept her smile pasted on as she walked an older couple through the sandwiches available. The couple, unfortunately, were having issues grasping how a cafe sandwich worked.

"But they're *cold,*" the woman protested. "You can't make them fresh?"

"No, no, I heat them on the panini press," Kelly explained patiently. "You just have a seat and I'll bring them out to you, nice and warm. They were made fresh this morning, you see."

"That sounds good, Carol," the man said to the woman. "Let's just do this for lunch."

"Jim, you'd eat anything."

"Now, Carol. Order a sandwich. She said it was made this morning. You think this girl would lie to you about a sandwich?"

"It has to be warmed up thoroughly," Carol warned Kelly. "I can't eat a cold ham and Swiss sandwich. It will be soggy."

"Of course it will be warm. I promise." Kelly leaned forward, her expression conspiratorial. "This is how they make sandwiches in *Paris,* you know."

"Paris! Oh!" Carol was suitably impressed.

The couple ordered their lunch and paid. Nikki watched Kelly put the cash in the box and lock it, tucking the key on its little springy bracelet back to her elbow before she started fixing the sandwiches. The girl knew her way around a cafe, that was for sure. And she didn't seem to mind the work.

But who would give up reporting the news on television—an actual paying gig in show business, the way Nikki saw things—to stand behind the counter of a country cafe and talk the Jims and Carols of the world through how to order a panini sandwich?

Nikki picked at a bowl of soup and a chunk of bread that Rosemary brought over to her, and waited for the lunch rush to settle down. When the cafe had resumed its usual sleepy demeanor, she asked Kelly to come and sit with her. "Take a coffee break," she suggested. "You got a tough day to start running the show."

Kelly made herself a cup of coffee and settled down across from Nikki. She brushed sticky hair back from her face and smiled. "It certainly keeps a person busy," she said, her voice a little hoarse from constantly talking over the sound of the humming refrigerated bake case. "I don't know the last time I worked this hard."

"It's no reporting gig, that's for sure. I should be back at it in another few days, but I won't be able to go all day and night like I was." Nikki stirred the lukewarm tea she'd been nursing. "I don't know how long you're planning on staying, but . . ."

"A while," Kelly said quickly. "If I can, I mean. I have to work out a place to stay. I tried to find the owner's information for the apartment, but my company made the reservation and—"

"I know the owners," Nikki said. "I could talk to them if you want to stay on. But what about your job? Is that for sure over? I thought you said before it was just leave."

Kelly laughed. "You know how sometimes you hope something will end so you don't have to do it yourself?"

Nikki raised her eyebrows. "So you're quitting? Or—"

"I'm *mostly* fired," Kelly said. "I'm on leave while they investigate, which means HR is making sure they don't have to keep me on for any kind of liability protection. But they don't owe me anything. And I've hated that job for a long, long time. I was just staying on to pay my student loans off. And guess what I paid off three months ago?"

Nikki couldn't help smiling back, even though she hadn't asked the biggest question yet. "So you're staying in town, and you won't have a job. But before I ask, I know that you didn't quit so you could work in a cafe."

"No, I didn't. Or, I *haven't.*" Kelly laughed again. "But I want to work on a personal project. The diary I mentioned earlier. And I won't make much money from it for a long time . . . if at all. So I do need a little something to keep me going. And I can freelance on the side, too. I have other skills. This doesn't have to be full-time—if you're offering me a job, that is."

"I am, and it wouldn't be full-time, because I couldn't afford it," Nikki admitted. "But I can find the budget for part-time, and some extra hours when I'm not on my feet, like this week. If you're not sure, I can send you to the Blue Plate to talk to the staff there, learn what it's like working for me. I *think* they'll give me flying colors."

"I'm sure they would," Kelly said. "But there's no need. I accept."

"The job?"

"Yes, please."

Nikki sipped her tea, her stomach feeling better than it had in days. "I don't know how this all worked out so nicely," she admitted. "Rosemary would probably say everything happens for a reason. She's full of grandma sayings like that."

Kelly glanced around the cafe, then out the big picture window, as if she was looking for something—or someone, Nikki supposed. "I think she's right," she said eventually. "It doesn't always feel like it, but it seems that way a lot of the time."

Nikki wanted to ask Kelly what she was looking for, what she thought she'd found in Catoctin Creek. But it wasn't really her business . . . and anyway, she had a feeling she knew.

Chapter Thirty

William

E very night since Kelly left the house kept William awake, as if he'd never slept alone in a house before. It was absurd. He was angry at himself. Real anger, berating himself, both silently and out loud, although he tended not to speak harshly to himself, because it upset the dogs.

Still—how could he miss a person so quickly? This house had been empty for years. He had learned to live with its creaks and groans, the mysterious taps and odd drafts of a house which had developed its own life outside of the humans who occasionally dwelled in it. At this point, the house should be all the company he needed.

It certainly shouldn't feel like a tomb just because one new person had arrived and, just as quickly, left.

One new person with one bright, energetic spirit that felt like the antithesis of his own . . . *No.* He flipped over in bed, tossed a pillow onto the floor, and winced when he heard Lola yelp in surprise. He had to get it together. He'd sleep a little more—in fact, he'd sleep *late,* because what was he getting up for, anyway?

—and then he'd fix himself a big breakfast and spend the rest of the day working on the kitchen. Maybe his ghost-filled home seemed more haunted than usual, and there was nothing he could do about that, but he could still control the interior, and surely if he brightened up the surrounding rooms, the atmosphere would lighten as well. New appliances, new paint, new lease on life, right?

It was that simple.

It had to be.

Go to sleep, William commanded himself. He was good at falling asleep; it was one of his talents.

But this time, it didn't happen.

He opened his eyes, already frustrated, already finished with a day that hadn't even begun yet. Predawn light lapped lazily at the bedroom window, making looming shadows out of his bureau, the desk, the floor lamp. This was as bright as things would get in this room at the back of the house, north-facing and deprived of real sunlight until summer. It wasn't his usual bedroom; he'd left the bed they'd slept in unmade, the door pulled shut. That room got the morning sunshine. All of it, no matter the season.

The winter ahead of him stretched out, formless and unhappy, a night without a moon. His skin hungered for Kelly's soft warmth; his heart did a painful little sideways leap every time he pictured her face or imagined the sound of her laugh. He had to get her out of here; out of his head and out of his home. He couldn't let his aching heart add another ghost to the army of spirits already living in this house, haunting him and only him.

He wouldn't. He would go back to his plans, the ones she'd interrupted so briefly. Renovate the house. Spend the winter working, getting blisters, falling asleep from sheer exhaustion. Let the world beyond Hilltop House spin as it pleased. And maybe once he'd revived the house, people would come back.

It was worth a try.

William laughed to himself. Worth a try? It had been his only dream for so long. Spoil this house like a beautiful woman, then use her renewed charm to lure back the family he had left. He didn't care about their secrets; he didn't want to know about their feuds. He just wanted his family back.

"A woman gets in the way," he reminded himself. "Okay, that sounds chauvinistic. Maybe the wrong wording."

Lola stood up, stretched, and shook, her collar jingling. She gazed up at him with her moon-like eyes.

"You're right," he told her. "I'm sorry. This is not about women. It's about . . . well, damn, Lola, it's about a lot of things."

She wagged her tail hopefully.

First things first, William thought. He'd deal with the elephant in the room. Or the woman in the dairy, as the case may be. He flung back the duvet. The other dogs looked up, instantly ready for breakfast and a run in the yard.

He busied himself in the kitchen, making coffee and toast and bacon. The dogs went for a quick run, ate their kibble in a rush, and then watched him cook, their eyes laser focused on his every move, ready for anything edible on offer. He tossed everyone a slice of bacon, then told them they weren't coming outside with him.

William poured coffee into a Thermos, wrapped toast and bacon in foil, and slipped it all into the pockets of his heavy canvas coat. Noses on paws, the dogs pouted in silent disbelief as he closed the kitchen door on them.

He stood at the mudroom door for a moment, looking into the misty back yard. The heavy gray clouds of the past few days were finally gone, but the sky still felt opaque, somehow. As if there would be no morning, as if the sun wouldn't be allowed to shine. But that was dramatic; it was all in his head. William squared his shoulders and stepped out into the frosty world.

The dairy was a dark square in a gray landscape. He walked around to the front door and squinted at the base of the door, looking for a seam of light, however faint, to indicate someone was in there. He saw nothing. He started to turn away, frustrated— what was he supposed to do, throw open the door and yell *ah-hah!* ?—when he saw it.

The faintest shadow passing over a glow he hadn't noticed until it flickered. Footsteps, a person passing through the space in front of the door. He waited, counting to himself. Ten seconds, and the footsteps passed by again. Someone was in there, pacing the tiny space.

This was the *ah-hah* moment, but he found he couldn't do anything about it. A person didn't lock themselves up into some abandoned outbuilding and then spend the predawn hours pacing its confines if they were in a good state of mind. There could be an insane person in there, the serial killer Kelly had frequently asked him not to be, or at the very least, a person who was going through some very serious emotional hardship. William wasn't interested in a stranger's trauma—no offense, but he felt like he had enough on his own—and again the urge rose up in him, stronger than ever, to leave this person alone to fight their own battles, make their own decisions, leave on their own terms.

You can't be afraid of other people's messes, Kelly told him.

I'm not afraid, his inner voice argued, petulant to the last.

Prove it, he seemed to hear Kelly saying. *Deal with the problem. See if you can fix it.*

William took a breath and knocked on the door.

The pacing footsteps stopped. He counted. Ten, twenty, thirty seconds went by. The faint light under the door didn't waver. And then—it went out.

The light had barely existed, but now that it was gone, the absence was impossible to miss. William stared at the dark ground, trying to remember what the ribbon of light had really looked like.

He was still looking at the ground when the door slowly began to open.

The door *had* to open slowly; the hinges were about a hundred years old and they hadn't been oiled recently. In known memory, actually. He felt his heart hammering in his ears, making his hearing unreliable, making the screech of the ancient hardware almost, but not quite, out of reach for him, and then he was looking at the pale, worried face of a woman.

William felt the air slowly leave his body. He had been holding his breath for goodness knew how long, not even realizing it.

She blinked.

"Uh . . . hi," he faltered.

The woman tilted her face at him. In the darkness, her luminous skin was all he could see, and William was not altogether certain he hadn't just disturbed a ghost who hadn't bothered to materialize below the neck. He'd heard of that kind of thing in Catoctin Creek before. There was a Union Army captain in the Fishbaugh house who never showed more than his head. It was very disconcerting, especially when he turned up in the guest room and appeared to folks who weren't used to him. William had always been thankful that most of the ghosts of Hilltop House seemed to live in his own head. He got tired of their clamoring, but at least they didn't jump out of the shadows—or lurk in them—to frighten him.

The ghost opened her dark lips. "Hi," she said, in a surprisingly earthbound voice. "You probably wonder why I'm here." Her chuckle was rusty.

"I—uh—yeah. But I brought breakfast, so . . ." He started emptying his pockets, pulling out the Thermos, the foil-wrapped bacon sandwich. "I thought you might be missing warm food."

Her eyes went hungrily to the parcels in his hands. "Do I smell bacon? And is that—actual coffee? Oh my god, you're a saint." She looked around, then opened the door wider. "I should be concerned you're going to kill me, but I'm like, *really* hungry and I haven't had coffee that isn't instant in two weeks, so like—please, come in?"

She gestured to the tiny space around her, but all William could see was darkness. He squinted, trying to peer at the interior of the dairy in an obliging kind of way, but the contrast between the slowly rising light outside and the shadows of the dairy was too much for him. "Is—uh—there anything in there?"

"Oh my god. Of course." She reached behind the door. A faint light suffused the little room, revealing the heavy sleeping bag and hiking pack inside. "The solar lamp is mostly done by morning, and it didn't soak up much light yesterday, obviously, with all that rain." The woman stepped back and sat down on the sleeping bag, patting the space beside her. "Come on in, and I'll explain myself."

William ducked through the low entry of the dairy and sat down on the sleeping bag. It was surprisingly warm and soft; he couldn't even feel the cold stones beneath it. His feet dangled off the wide shelf where the milk pans had once rested, waiting for the cream to rise; the toes of his boots just brushed the packed earth floor. In the wan glow of the solar lamp, he saw a tiny heater, just enough to warm one's hands (or maybe one's toes) and a few camp kitchen essentials laid out on the opposite shelf. He could just about reach over and pick them up without having to get up. There was also a little pile of paperback books, the small, fat ones that he used to buy at supermarket checkouts as he passed through quiet western towns.

The woman—Monica, she had to be Monica Waters, right?— was already working her way through the bacon sandwich, trying to keep a lid on the ecstatic moaning she couldn't quite help between each bite. William swung his legs and waited, feeling out of place. When she'd swallowed the last of the sandwich, she sighed and turned to him. "I can't describe to you how good that was. If you're going to murder me, I'm ready."

He recoiled. "You have got to stop saying that." Now he understood why Kelly didn't like him making jokes like that. It was entirely too macabre for the types of conversation they needed to be having.

Monica laughed. "Sorry. I'm renowned for my inappropriate gallows humor. Anyway, hi, I'm Monica Waters, and I've been hiding in your little outbuilding here for the past two weeks."

"Hi Monica, I'm William," he replied automatically. "So, uh, you know the whole world wants to know where you are, right?"

Her eyes widened slightly. "Oh. I thought it might get a little attention. But I did leave a note. So it shouldn't be *too* bad, right?"

"Excuse me? No one has said anything about a note." William was ready to believe her; it wasn't like he was following the news. "I think it might have been missed. Because from what I hear, everyone thinks you're dead."

"But—that's impossible. I left a note." Her voice rose a little, trembling with anxiety. "I put it under the windshield wiper on my car, back at the trail parking lot. It said *Please don't tow, I will be gone for a few weeks on the trail.* I mean, sure, I left the trail, but that shouldn't have mattered. I could have connected with the Appalachian Trail and been gone for months . . ." Realization clouded her face. "Oh no, they towed my car, didn't they?"

"I assume so," William said. "I was up there a few days ago, and I didn't see anyone else's car." The thought of the trip to the Cascade Falls parking lot filled him with misery. He tried to shrug it away. "The note must have gotten lost," he continued. "Someone probably just swept it up, thought it was trash."

"God." Monica shook her head, took a long soothing sip of the coffee. "Of course they'd think my note was trash. No one pays attention to anything. No one listens anymore. That was part of it, you know? I just wanted to get away from the *noise*. I felt like all I could hear in my head was screaming. All the time. I just had to find some silence."

"Well, you found it here," William said, his voice grim now. "Doesn't get much quieter than Hilltop House."

"Hilltop, that's what this place is called? It's pretty. I thought it was abandoned, not gonna lie." Monica shifted to look at him. "I didn't mean to trespass. I mean, I honestly thought no one lived

CHRISTMAS AT CATOCTIN CREEK   289

here, and this little building just seemed perfect. I'd been planning on camping but it's November, right, and this just seemed to make more sense. A roof, walls. Something to keep out the rain. Anyway, I was all settled in when the dogs showed up, and then there were lights in the house, and I thought I'd better hunker down and stay out of sight. I was planning on leaving, and then the rain just kept coming . . ." She shrugged. "It was easier to stay."

William shook his head. She made it all sound so simple. "You really didn't know the entire mid-Atlantic is looking for you?"

A sharp intake of breath. "I didn't. That sounds bad. Is it bad?"

"It's pretty bad. They questioned your boyfriend," William added, hating to break the news to her. "But he's not a person of interest anymore."

"Oh. Oh, god. He must have been—that's not good."

"Yeah. I'm sorry."

There was silence for a moment. Then: "I have to go back out there, don't I." A statement, not a question. But William suspected it was also a plea for help. *Don't make me go home.*

He used to say it, too. He wanted to stay up here on the mountainside forever, too. This was something he understood, too intimately, and yet he was relieved, because at least he could give her real, true advice. "You do have to go back and clean up your mess," he told her, "but you don't have to stay. You just have to leave in the right way."

She laughed, the sound harsh. "What does that even mean?"

William shrugged. "More than a note on a windshield on a windy day, I guess." He shifted on the sleeping bag. The stone shelf beneath was finally making itself known. "Listen, you want to move up to the house to figure this out? It's slightly warmer, and there's working plumbing, and the seats have cushions in them."

Monica looked at him from over the Thermos. "There's still a decent chance you're going to murder me, though."

"And there's more coffee," he added. "Lots more coffee."

"I never thought I'd give up my freedom for brewed coffee," Monica sighed, slipping down from the shelf. "But yes. Yes, please."

Chapter Thirty-One

William

A lot of things can come out over coffee. William found that hot drinks made people comfortable, ready to spill their stories—even more so than alcohol, which might loosen tongues but rarely loosened hearts. Over tea or coffee, two people could bond without being coerced by slipping inhibitions. So William settled Monica in the living room, made sure the fire was roaring, and then poured them both more coffee.

He knew he ought to be calling the police right away, but he figured his big find was nothing that couldn't wait another hour. So he sat down at the opposite side of the sofa, giving her plenty of room to stretch out, and asked her to tell him what had landed her in the dairy, and what on earth she planned to do next.

"Honestly?" Monica smiled ruefully. "I just flipped out. I'd been having a rough year—a rough couple of years, really. And this year everyone seemed to think I should be thrilled with my life. I was with a steady, successful boyfriend, I had a good job on paper —I'm putting everything in past tense because I assume it's over now. I *hope* it's over now."

"Ah." William understood that. "You wanted things to end themselves."

She took a sip of coffee and held it on her tongue for a moment before swallowing. "Yes," she admitted finally. "I wanted things to end themselves. I couldn't quit my job. I couldn't dump my boyfriend. But I could let those things collapse on themselves."

"Do you think they have?"

"It's hard to say, since I've been out here the whole time. No phone signal, but I take it you're aware." She stretched her legs and looked at her toes, wiggling them inside thick wool socks. "I just figure the sympathy vote might screw me, you know? Like people going, 'Oh, Monica, we had no idea you were having such a hard time.' That kind of thing. People might give me a pass."

"The police questioned your boyfriend, though," William pointed out. "He might find that's hard to get over."

"I guess. If he really loved me, maybe he'd forgive me. But does he? Maybe that's what I wanted to find out." Monica shook her head, her dark hair falling over her face. "No, I'm just coming up with excuses. The fact is I was a coward, and I wanted out of the world I'd made for myself, and when push came to shove, I couldn't even *find* the Appalachian Trail so I could disappear on it, so I found a little stone hut and walled myself in there, instead. As if that was a valid replacement for some life-changing walk in the woods."

"A dairy," William said. "It's a dairy. For storing milk and butter."

"A dairy, then. I locked myself in a dairy. Either way . . ."

"I know. I get it."

She looked at him, skepticism in her dark eyes. "Do you really?"

William gestured to the surrounding room: the moth-eaten curtains, the drafty windows, the peeling paint on the walls. "See where I live? I know a thing or two about locking myself away from the world."

She laughed without any real mirth. "Yeah, maybe you do."

They were silent for a few minutes then, listening to the flames snapping in the fireplace, the dogs snoring on the threadbare Persian carpet. William thought about Kelly, who didn't want to be forgotten by the world. She took a night to gather herself—to spend with him—and then she went straight back and told everyone where she was and went on with her life. Right now she was probably back in Arlington, back at her important reporter job, to her life spent on other people's televisions, in other people's living rooms, every night.

He'd been so foolish to think she'd see anything in his way of life, holed up in this house as it fell down around him. She must have thought he was such a coward.

William ran his hand slowly down his face, from forehead to chin, wishing he could just clear his head of her smile, her laugh, the warmth in her blue eyes as she looked at him, waiting to see if he'd follow her lead.

He felt like he'd do anything to stop thinking about her. Anything. Some things simply did not end on their own. They had to be ended.

Or repaired?

"I have to go back," Monica said eventually, breaking the silence. "Right? I made a huge mistake, and now I have to face it. Fair's fair."

"People will be glad you're okay," William said. "Like you said, there will be a big sympathy vote. People will be so glad you made it through, they'll forget to be mad at you. Most people."

She winced. "At first. But they'll remember. This is going to be impossible to live down. But on the other hand, it means I can't possibly stay on at my job or even with Grayson. Even if they decide to make it easy for me. How could I face those people every day? And to think it all started with a horse."

"What?"

Monica laughed dryly. "Oh, this is embarrassing. But you're really nice and you could have had me arrested for trespassing by now, so I'll tell you. I was probably on my way towards a breakdown for a while, but it was losing my childhood horse that absolutely sent me over the edge."

"Did he die?"

"No! That's the thing. I could have handled that. No, my parents sold the farm where I grew up. A big Standardbred farm, trotters and pacers, you know. Not that Standardbreds make a ton of money racing, but it was a family business, went way back. So they want out of the business and meanwhile I'm busy, off being a big-shot lobbyist, showing everyone that girls can play with politics and money just like boys, and so they get an offer on the farm the moment they put it up for sale, and they take it. They don't even *ask* me about it. And I just assumed I'd inherit it along with my brothers, so like, it's gone. My childhood home is gone. Can you imagine?"

William remembered the day he'd learned his grandparents had died. The crushing guilt, when he realized his first thought was, *What will happen to Hilltop?*

He hadn't just meant the property, of course. He'd meant the way they'd lived here. Later, he'd realize that his love for his grandparents was so wrapped up in the life they shared at Hilltop, the question had been perfectly logical, completely acceptable. But at that moment, it had felt callous and frightening, as if he cared more for the family house than for the family who would never see it again. The family he'd never see again.

"I can imagine," he said, keeping his complicated thoughts to himself. This wasn't about him.

Monica stared into the fire, reliving painful memories. "But worse than that, of course, was my horse. I had this old bay horse. His name was Boo. He raced for a while and then he retired and he became my horse. I rode him like, every day from the time I was twelve into my early twenties. He was old. *Old.* And my parents sold him. They said they didn't know I still wanted him around! I was like, this was my *horse!* And they apologized, but it was too late. And where did poor Boo go? He was twenty-two years old. That's elderly in horse years. He didn't deserve to get shipped off the farm he'd lived at his entire life."

She looked at the ceiling, as if seeing the horse she used to love. And then she blew a gust of breath out. "Someone said there was a farm in Catoctin Creek, a place I'd never heard of, where they thought Boo had gone. So I came up here and looked around. I thought it had to be the school, because they'd just bought a bunch of new horses. I'd sent an email or two to different people I found on the website, but no one answered, so then I went and talked to the receptionist. And she was really nice, but when I came up and we looked through files, we didn't come up with anything matching my description. So then I called that big place south of town, Elm Lake, or whatever it's called? And they didn't know anything about Boo, either. That was my big dead-end." She laughed. "So then I just said forget it. I'm leaving. There was nothing to stay for. I had my hiking gear, I was ready to just disappear. I've gone on long hikes before. I thought I could deal with the weather. It's been really cold, though. You know that. You're here." She gestured at the surrounding room.

William assumed she was referring specifically to the lack of an operational furnace. Something he'd have to get cracking on, he supposed. Not that anyone else was going to live up here with him, but . . .

Just in case.

She could come back.

Monica, having said her piece, went quiet. The dogs sighed and stretched, the logs shifted and sparked, and the coffee grew cold in their cups. William wondered, uncomfortably, if he ought to offer her a ride into town, or if she wasn't ready to go back yet. He sipped at the dregs of his coffee. It was bitter at the bottom.

She stirred.

"Can I intrude on your kindness two more times?"

He nodded. "Of course."

"Can I take a shower? And then can I get a ride back to town? I'll have to face the music sometime. Might as well be today. And," she added, face falling, "I feel bad. My parents must be really worried. I swear, I thought everyone knew where I was."

William showed her to the bathroom upstairs and made sure there was a warm bedroom for her to change in. Not his bedroom, not the room where he'd put Kelly for the night. He led Monica to the guest room, flicking on the space heater so she wouldn't freeze when she dried off from her shower. It wasn't that he wanted her in the space where he slept. It was that he didn't want her in the space where Kelly had slept.

He could admit that much to himself.

———— *ele* ————

He left the dogs behind for the drive to town, which meant there were four very reproachful faces watching him from the mudroom as he pushed the door shut. Monica laughed and said she didn't know how he could bear it, but William was able to shrug off his dogs' accusing expressions. He knew they'd go straight to sleep and be in a perfectly good mood when he came back. "It's nice to give them something to anticipate," he joked, carrying her hiking kit to the truck.

Monica seemed to be anticipating something herself, judging by her silence and stoic expression as he navigated the twisting roads into Catoctin Creek. The trees had finally shed their leaves, as if shaking off the last vestiges of autumn with one hard shake, and their bare branches bent against the blue skies shimmering overhead, while crows flapped black wings for balance as they rested before launching another gleaning assault on the stubble cornfields. The day was beautiful, but bleak, one of those frosty days which reminded a person how far away spring blossoms and summer showers were. Hard to believe the holidays were coming, but as they coasted in Catoctin Creek, he saw lights and pine garlands in many windows. Thank goodness for Christmas, he thought.

"Where should I take you?" William asked Monica, realizing they had no destination in mind.

She sighed, as if she hated facing the idea of an actual plan. "Is there a police station here?"

"Nope. I guess we could go into Frederick."

"I hate to ask you to take me so far," she said. "But I don't know where my car is."

"Probably at the county sheriff's lot, wherever that might be."

They were passing through the town; it would be gone in another moment. The Blue Plate slid past, a full parking lot and the signs of packed booths through the windows, evidently doing a brisk trade in pancake stacks and Western omelettes.

"Why did I think a note would solve all my problems?" Monica was still stuck on that subject. He could imagine the way her brain was circling around and around her own foolishness; his brain was similar.

"Other people go hiking for weeks on end," he offered. "I guess you figured you could, too."

Half an hour later, he parked the truck outside the county sheriff's office. Monica took a deep breath, then smiled at him. "Here goes nothing," she said, conjuring up some false bravado. "You know, I just wish I'd found my horse."

"You got a picture of him?" William asked. "I see horses from time to time. Maybe I'd recognize him."

"Of course I do." Monica flicked through her phone, then held it out to him. William looked over the plain bay horse. He didn't know much about equines, but he knew horse-people saw the differences between every horse, the way identical twins had a million differences that only their close family could spot. "Want me to send it to you?" she asked, probably realizing he had no idea what he was doing.

"Yeah, I'll show him to my horsier friends," William offered, thinking of Rosemary. "Someone might know him."

"Man, I hope so." Monica texted him the photo. Then she opened the truck door. "Okay. See you on the other side."

He wouldn't, he guessed, unless he caught the local news. He waved goodbye to Monica Waters. Another short story in his life had come to an end.

Or so he thought.

There were questions. He realized, as he sat behind the wheel, that there would be questions. Monica went inside, then popped out again a few minutes later. She sheepishly beckoned him to join her.

He brushed off her assurances that he wasn't under any suspicion and answered the deputy's questions patiently, explaining how he'd ignored Monica's presence in his outbuilding until it finally weighed on his mind too much to let it go on another day. "So I offered her coffee and breakfast, and then I brought her to town at her request."

The deputy nodded and thanked him for his time. But as he stood to leave, the deputy plucked at his sleeve. "Sorry," she said. "But did you also have Kelly O'Connell at your house? The reporter who went missing overnight?"

"I did," he admitted, sighing. This probably looked like a very weird pattern. "But she wasn't missing overnight. Just for an afternoon. The rest of the time she was staying with me, and I let the park rangers know she was safe that night. Man, I guess my house is more convenient to the state park trails than I realized."

The deputy shook her head, making a note on her pad. "These tourists. You ought to put up a hostel or something."

"Are you going to be okay?" William asked Monica, who was sitting in the waiting room with her feet on her hiking kit.

"Fine," she said, giving him a brave smile. "They're bringing my car over. I guess I get to be a free woman and go home to my problems, so that's great."

"Keep in touch," William suggested. "Let me know how things go."

"Sure, I will," Monica said.

But he didn't think she meant it.

"I'll look for your horse," he promised.

She smiled at him. "Thank you."

Chapter Thirty-Two

Nadine

"So, uh, you want all of this for the carnival?" Sam the firefighter asked. He was a big, burly man of about forty, a third-generation dairy farmer, and a second generation volunteer fireman. His pale blonde hair and tan cheeks gave away his German heritage; Sam was a Fishbaugh from Rhinelander Farm on the east side of Catoctin Creek, and Nadine knew Rosemary and Nikki still privately called him The Fish. "Leftover high school stuff," they'd explained after she caught them giggling over the nickname as they set up her meeting to go over the carnival layout plans. "Please don't tell him."

The Fish, Nadine thought now, trying to keep her face in straight lines. They never should have told her! Those two could be real trouble when they were left alone long enough. And now that Nikki was getting some actual sleep, thanks to hiring Kelly to help her at the cafe, she was getting back to her old self, full of stories and snarky comments that just made everyone love her more.

"Yes, this is the whole carnival. No surprises are going to show up later," she promised Sam, tapping the paper spread out between them. "Here, let me run you through each row."

Nadine had spent a lot of time on this map to the forthcoming Catoctin Creek Christmas Carnival, drawing out the rows of booths, the midway rides, and the exhibition stands they'd have to put together in the next four weeks. She'd made sure to match up the necessary utilities and hook-ups, so everyone would have electricity if they needed it, or space for a generator if they brought their own power. The work had cost her several evenings, but she'd found a way to connect it to her community service credits at the local college, so all in all, things were working in her favor.

"Here's the fast food row, where all the typical midway food goes—you've got your baked potatoes, your spiral fries, your pizza, whatever. And here's the artisan row, where all our local food trucks are going. They'll bring generators, too. Down here are the tents for the women's associations, because we can't have a fair without French fries and pies, right? And back here we have the corral for the horse and cattle exhibitions, and then all this space is midway." She tapped the back half of the map. "Make sense?"

"It does," Sam agreed. He rubbed at his face and studied the paper a moment longer. "It looks real good. Now I just have to get my guys building as fast as they can go. They like a challenge, though."

"I know it's really late notice," Nadine said apologetically. "Is there anything I can do to help?"

"Just don't set any fires," Sam said, standing up and folding the map into a square. "We don't need the distraction."

Nadine left the volunteer firefighters' hall with a smile on her face. The carnival was really coming together, and she was playing a much more active role than she'd expected. And all of this organization felt good. Nadine had always enjoyed setting up procedures, doing things in their correct order. Her barns ran like well-oiled machines; no reason why her carnival wouldn't, either.

Now, though, it was time to head back to Long Pond for her two o'clock lesson with Addy and Bertha. Then the kids in the horsemanship club came down to work on their barn skills for two hours. Then dinner, then she had an English paper to write. Nadine's smile faded just a little as she climbed into the car. A lot to do, but that was okay, she reminded herself. Having too much was better than nothing at all.

Long Pond was bustling with this week's burst of late season sunshine and unseasonable warmth, all the girls heaved outdoors to take on their various sports or work on projects tangentially related to their core studies. Parents loved to hear their studious girls were getting outside and kicking a ball around or shooting an arrow or something else suitably athletic, and the parents of the girls with less than stellar grades tended to be relieved their daughters were showing aptitude for anything at all. She knew the barn would be full, and Sean would be on his feet all day, teaching lesson after lesson. Darby would be running around the barn, helping girls with tack and sweeping up and being a general wonder woman. Nadine did a mental check and decided she could give Darby a quick lunch break before she had to handle Addy's lesson.

But when she walked into the barn aisle, Nadine was surprised to see her assistant wasn't alone. Addy was diligently sweeping the mess left behind in a grooming stall as a rider led her horse away, calling, "Sorry, sorry about that!" over her shoulder.

"It's no problem!" Addy called back. "Go enjoy your lesson!"

Nadine stopped at the grooming stall and watched her sweep. She showed good form, actually. Something strange Nadine had learned over the past few months: sweeping was not a talent all people were born with. "What's this?" she finally asked, when Addy didn't look up right away.

"Oh, Nadine! I'm so glad you're here!" Addy leaned on the broom, a smile splitting her narrow face. "I wanted to ask you about working in the barn. Like, extra. Not just with Bertha. I know it's good for the phys. ed credit and community service, but my parents still want me to play soccer. But then I told them about Bertha and that we were doing so well together and I really like horses now, and they were like, yeah, if that's what you want to do, so like, can I? Join the horsemanship club and work down here in the afternoons?"

Nadine stared at Addy for a moment. Suddenly, all she could see was the girl who had sulked in her office and refused to touch a horse on the first day of her barn rotation. For some reason, she'd thought horses might stick with this girl. Pretty exciting to realize her instincts had been correct.

She was impressed with the girls' parents for playing it so cool. She decided she better do the same. "Yeah, if that's what you want," she told Addy, keeping her voice flat even though she was turning mental cartwheels in celebration. "I guess we have plenty of room for extra help in the barn. What did Darby say?"

"Darby just handed me a broom and told me to keep the aisle spotless," Addy said, gesturing to the grooming stall. "It's funny how dirty everything gets while you're getting a horse clean, right?"

"It sure is," Nadine agreed. "Well, if you have an arrangement with Darby, I'm not going to take you away from it. Listen to everything she says and you'll do just fine. And meet me for our lesson at five minutes to two, okay?"

"Great!" Addy went back to sweeping, then paused, looking at Nadine with deceptively innocent eyes. "Thanks for teaching me how to work with horses," she said.

"You're welcome," Nadine told her, feeling a suspicious burning at the back of her eyelids. "I'm glad you're here."

Nadine sat down at her desk, flipping through the lesson book to see if Sean was going to need lunch brought to the barn later. Some days he could eat back at the house or even go to town, but this wouldn't be one of those days. Booked solid; he'd have a fifteen minute lunch break today. She glanced at the dining hall menu, considering what she'd order for him.

"Knock-knock," said a voice at her open door, and Nadine looked up. She was astonished to see Caitlin, holding a coffee cup from the cafe, along with a brown bag with some suspicious grease stains on the sides. "I brought muffins," she said, waving the bag.

"Anyone with muffins is welcome in my office," Nadine said, although she knew Caitlin never appeared without a favor or a command in her pocket. "Come in. What's up?"

"Just wanted to check in on the carnival," Caitlin said, taking a seat across from Nadine and passing the bag her way. "With Nikki so rough last week, I was worried some of the planning might fall through the cracks. But Rosemary says you're kind of in charge of everything now." Caitlin's eyes were amused. "Look at my former barn manager, all grown up and running town fairs."

"Well, someone had to step up," Nadine said, feeling oddly defensive. "There didn't seem to be anyone else able to do it. Rosemary has all those horses, and she was helping Nikki just get through her days for a minute there. At least I've got plenty of help here. Speaking of which, did you see my new working student?"

"That's one of the girls that got sent down here to see if she'd straighten up, right?"

Nadine winced, hoping Addy wasn't nearby. Caitlin *never* lowered her voice. "Her name is Addy. Started out nurturing the rescue horse and now she's down here working in the barn, by choice. Pretty great, right?"

"Well, we know horses are magical," Caitlin said, but her voice had gone a little dry, as if she was repeating a rote saying that didn't mean much to her. Nadine knew the whole issue was a sore spot with Caitlin, who had simply not inherited the horse gene from her mother—which was unfortunate, since she *did* inherit a beautiful equestrian center—so she moved on quickly.

"Anyway, I met with Sam up at the volunteer fire department and they've got the plans for the site. Everything is booked or under construction as of today, so I'd say we're good to go."

"Thank goodness." Caitlin nodded, looking impressed. "You've done a good job on this."

"I like being busy."

"I know it. You never stopped at Elmwood. I thought you were going to kill poor Sean when I brought him on." Her gaze, from under her eyelashes, was all studied innocence. She reached for a muffin and peeled back the paper. "I'm glad that worked out."

Nadine shrugged, knowing Caitlin was setting the stage for whatever favor she thought Nadine owed her. "Sean wasn't bad. Just lazy and out of his depth. He needed a little fire lit under him."

"And look at him now, out in the arena bringing these girls into line." Caitlin gave her an appraising look. "You're going to turn into quite a mover and shaker in these parts, Nadine. I hope you plan on staying in Catoctin Creek."

"Of course I am," Nadine said. "That's why I came back in the first place."

"But with your mother gone . . ." Caitlin lifted an eyebrow, questioning. "I thought she was part of the reason, too?"

"Well, she'll come back for the summer. And anyway, now that she has her life straightened out, I don't feel like I have to stay just to keep an eye on her." Nadine could speak frankly about her mother to Caitlin. There was a shared history there.

But Caitlin was done with the small talk.

"Listen, I want to ask a favor," she said, leaning forward, and Nadine braced herself for the real reason her old boss was visiting. "You know William Cunningham, right?"

Nadine shook her head. "Only through brief meetings. But between the stories Rosemary and Nikki have told me, and the whole thing with him finding Monica, and Kelly, I definitely *feel* like I know him."

"Yeah, he got himself a spotlight he didn't want, didn't he?" Caitlin laughed. "It's always the quiet ones."

"I guess." Nadine found herself glancing at the time on her phone, willing Caitlin to hurry up and come out with whatever she wanted. She still had to order lunch for Sean, pick it up for him, and get on with her day. With this much on her plate, she definitely didn't have time for any town intrigue.

"Here's the thing about William." Caitlin chewed at her lip, and her indecision sparked Nadine's curiosity. What could slow down Caitlin the steamroller? She found herself on the edge of her seat as Caitlin searched for the words to continue. "He's dealing with a lot of baggage," she said finally. "His family summered at Hilltop House for generations. Like, huge extended family. They used to order extra produce and meat at Trout's just because the Cunninghams were coming to town. Then, his parents had a falling out with the rest of the family—I don't know what it was about—and they stopped coming. It's a long story, but eventually William ran away from home and spent his last two years of high school here, living with his grandparents. But while he was away at college, his grandparents and some of his extended family died in an accident. They left him Hilltop House, which caused *another* rift in the family. The summers and holidays here stopped, and he's just never been the same."

Nadine stared at Caitlin, but she was really seeing the sad-eyed man she'd met at the cafe. You never really knew what a person was dealing with, and Nadine had dealt with her share of family nonsense, but William had some real tragedy to contend with. "He really shouldn't be living up there alone," she said, and Caitlin nodded.

"You're damn right he shouldn't, but William has never listened to anyone. Not even when we were kids. Anyway, now that you're the official carnival captain, can you find a role for him? All you have to do is call him up and tell him he has to help, and he'll do it. He needs to feel like he belongs to something."

"I don't know that I'm carnival captain," Nadine began. "I'm just sort of standing in—"

"Oh, yes you are," Caitlin informed her. "This is it. You're in charge now. Nikki is dealing with this pregnancy, Rosemary is dealing with everything on her plate, *plus* Nikki, and I don't have the time. You kind of volunteered yourself, my dear. I hope you're not regretting that now."

Nadine considered the amount of schoolwork she had left undone over the past week. She'd figure it out. The nice thing about online school was that the due dates on projects weren't hard and fast. Because this was important. "I don't regret it," she said.

"Good. And William will help you. I promise he will. Go deputize him." Caitlin's phone chimed, and she sighed as she looked at it. "I have a meeting in Frederick I have to get to. Keep the rest of the muffins—the girls look like they could use a break."

"Always," Nadine said wryly.

Darby poked her head in almost the moment Caitlin left. "Caitlin said there were muffins?"

"Right here. And holler for Addy to have one too."

Darby shouted down the aisle and got a reedy reply. She came in and threw herself in a chair. "That Caitlin. The devil works hard, but Caitlin works harder, you know? Always cutting a new deal. I kind of admire her."

Nadine raised her eyebrows. "I didn't have you down as a mogul, Darby."

"Oh, you know." Darby took a bite of muffin. "A girl can like nice things and not mind having to work for them. I don't want to muck stalls for a living *forever.*"

Addy came swinging into the office just then, her face brighter than Nadine had ever seen it, and Nadine let the subject drop. She couldn't see the point of a life that wasn't lived with horses, and she had a feeling that if she played her cards right, Addy would feel the same way.

Chapter Thirty-Three

Rosemary

Rosemary was finishing up evening feeding when she heard footsteps outside. She slid the barn door open, expecting Stephen. Seeing Nadine on her doorstep was a big surprise. The hangdog look on her face was a bigger one. For the past two weeks, Nadine had been handling the carnival planning with incredible aplomb. Tonight, though, Rosemary suspected everything had fallen apart. "Is everything okay?" she asked, tugging at the younger woman's hand. "Come in and warm up."

Nadine allowed herself to be dragged into the warm barn. She glanced around, and Rosemary shrugged at the mess. The horses had been outside all day, and their blankets, necks, and manes were muddy. The latter half of November was proving as wet as the first. "I know," Rosemary sighed. "I have to get them out of those dirty blankets, but they'll have nothing else to wear tonight. I'm going to see what extras I have, then check underneath to see if anyone's damp and needs a change-out."

"I'll help you," Nadine offered. "That's a big job. Are the other horses in the same mess?"

"Kind of, but they don't have spare blankets, so I just took them off everyone and flipped them upside down to air out. I'll rug them up again before I go in for the night. Winter's *hard* isn't it?" Rosemary was babbling a little, trying to deal with Nadine's obvious disquiet. What had brought her over here tonight, without even texting ahead?

They worked in silence for a quarter of an hour, ducking into stalls, unbuckling blankets, pushing their hands beneath to make sure the mud puddles every horse delighted in so much hadn't worked their way through blankets which were supposed to be waterproof. Even horse clothing could only take so much abuse before it started leaking. The work wasn't without its dangers: static crackled as they lifted the sides of the blankets, and a few of the horses reacted, stomping and even kicking out. Rosemary couldn't blame them; no one wanted to get a shock while they were trying to eat their hay. It was even worse when a blanket had to be pulled off, snapping and popping while the horse's hair stood on end, sizzling with enough charge to light a lamp.

Fortunately, Rosemary only found two blankets which needed changing out. Finished, she straightened the damp ones, flipped over to dry on a pair of empty wheelbarrows. On the other side of the barn, she heard buckles clink together as Nadine tugged a new rug into place on one of her horses.

Finally, the chore finished, Nadine walked over. She had a small blanket held out in front of her, dripping wet with mud.

Rosemary cracked a smile. "Mighty-mite really likes his mud baths."

"Disgusting," Nadine said, grinning at the mess. "I think this needs hosed off."

"I'll do it in the morning," Rosemary sat down on a hay bale, sighing. "I'm too tired to stand out in the rain anymore today."

"Oh, I'll handle it." Nadine did a quick about-face.

Rosemary hopped up just as quickly. "Oh, no you don't! You're going to sit down over here and tell me what's wrong. You didn't come over here because twenty-five horses weren't enough to keep you busy."

"Twenty-five horses, a barn full of students, a Christmas carnival, and a holiday-crazy boyfriend," Nadine corrected her. She tossed the mini horse blanket against the barn wall, where it could wait for the morning, then sat down on the hay bale with Rosemary. She rubbed her muddy hands against her jeans and sighed. "Rosemary, are you and Stephen planning on having kids? Can I ask that?"

Rosemary glanced down at her. She wasn't particularly surprised by Nadine's question. She just wished she'd made time to talk to her a few weeks ago, when she'd first noticed Nadine was a little off. She'd meant to, even said she was going to sit down with her, but life got so busy, so quickly. The date had been put off, again and again.

Now she put one hand on Nadine's tightly gripped fists. "We haven't decided yet," she said. "I think we might. If we hurry up and get off the fence about it, we might even manage to have two."

Nadine turned a surprised face to Rosemary. "You haven't decided? But you two are married, and, well, you're older . . ."

"Old enough to know life is full of surprises," Rosemary replied. "Not too old to still not be sure about parenthood, though. Have you guys—has Sean been asking about it?"

"No." Nadine looked down again, her hair falling across her cheeks. "But . . . I think . . . I think I want kids. Maybe soon."

Rosemary opened her mouth, but couldn't think of anything to say. That wasn't what she'd expected Nadine to say. It was hard to give advice with completely new information.

"Sean—I don't think Sean does. When you texted a couple weeks ago, told me Nikki was pregnant, Sean said . . ." She swallowed, as if admitting something horrible. "He said, 'Better her than you.' And I just, I like, I didn't even realize until that moment that maybe this weird, lost feeling I get sometimes, that I like to fill up with work? It might be that I want a family. A big one."

"Like, the opposite of the way you grew up," Rosemary realized.

"Exactly."

"You know who that reminds me of?"

Nadine giggled suddenly. "You're going to say William."

"I mean, yeah. He's another one who would probably love a million kids. Maybe you should try to figure things out with him, instead."

Nadine glanced at her. "So you don't think Sean wants kids?"

"You're asking me what your boyfriend wants?" Rosemary shook her head, although she was careful to keep smiling. She didn't want to hurt Nadine's feelings. "When are you going to ask him yourself?"

She shrugged. "I don't want to freak him out. You know how guys are."

Rosemary considered this for a moment. She looked over the stalls in front of them, the backs of her horses as they worked through their hay. What made Nadine think she knew anything about men? She knew about horses, and not much else. "Honestly, Nadine, I don't. I know how Stephen is, and I know if I had a problem upsetting me this much, he'd want me to tell him about it."

Nadine groaned. "I don't know how to bring it up."

"I guess you're just going to have to straight up ask him how he feels about having kids. Like, in the future. I don't think either of you could be in the position to start a family right now, right?" Rosemary put an arm around her shoulders, squeezing Nadine in a friendly hug. "But you might be in a couple of years. And you'd know each other better, and you'll be done with your college degree, and be ready to take on a new challenge."

Slowly, Nadine nodded. "That makes sense. Thanks, Rosie-marie. You give really good advice. And hugs, too."

Rosemary smiled to herself. The sound of Nikki's nickname for her coming from Nadine's lips was charming. Somewhere along the way, they'd assimilated this tough young woman into their little gang of two.

And if she wasn't very much mistaken, there was a fourth potential member out there, just waiting to be let in.

Chapter Thirty-Four

Kelly

The bell rang at the cafe and an older woman's face peeked through the door. "Yoo-hoo," she trilled. "Are you still open?"

Kelly smiled and put down the pastries she'd been wrapping for the night. "For you, of course, Mrs. Baughman," she said warmly. The grandmother of three had recently become obsessed with croissants, and she could barely keep away for an entire day. Kelly knew if she didn't come in for breakfast or an afternoon snack, she'd sneak one in before dinner.

"Oh, you're a dear. I just want to grab coffee and a croissant. I've been craving them all day, and Henry's got his Elks Club meeting tonight, so supper will be late."

"What will you do with yourself while he's gone?"

Mrs. Baughman pulled a plastic bag from her voluminous purse and slyly showed Kelly the half-clad woman on the cover of her new paperback. "Just me and a dangerous Scottish duke for a few hours," she confided, winking.

"You have to watch out for those guys in kilts," Kelly laughed, pouring coffee into a to-go cup. "Always making promises they won't keep and rolling those r's."

Mrs. Baughman was a real card, a regular that Kelly hadn't had any trouble remembering after a few days of serving her. She wasn't so great with the other customers; remembering names wasn't her strong suit. She was used to notepads or cue cards, the names of subjects or interviewees carefully printed so she wouldn't get things wrong, and she supposed the entire face-to-name corner of her brain was atrophied. But she was hopeful things would get better. She'd only been a fixture in the cafe for a few weeks, after all. Someday, all these local folks and their many German surnames would click with her.

"Thanks, honey," Mrs. Baughman said, dropping a few dollars on the counter. "You keep the change, and have a real nice night, okay?" She took her croissant and coffee and whirled out of the store, ready for her evening with her imaginary duke.

"I should get myself a few paperbacks," Kelly sighed, continuing to close up shop. "Better than watching YouTube videos and not starting on my diary." She'd gone down to Arlington and retrieved her great-grandmother's diary, along with some fresh clothes and other essentials from her condo, but she hadn't yet opened it. Now that she had some time to work on the project which had haunted her for years, she had no idea where to begin.

Closing the cafe five evenings a week was much easier: the routine was well-established, and all she had to do was follow the steps Nikki had perfected before she'd even arrived in town. The coffee grounds in their special bag were tied up and put into the steel bin where they awaited pickup by the company which took them away for composting. The dishes were put into the sanitizer and set for their final steam-bath of the night. The leftover pastries, which had another day's freshness in them, were carefully wrapped, with toothpicks to hold up the plastic whenever frosting was in danger of being crushed.

When the door opened again, she was prepared to make the customer one last cup of coffee, but that was it. The note on the door about early closing was posted. She looked up, ready to start her speech.

Then she closed her mouth, shock running through her system.

William was in the doorway.

He looked as she remembered him—of course he did, it had only been a month, not even a month, she scolded herself—and yet he did look different. He looked drawn, he looked tired. He looked as if things were not going well for him. She wondered with sudden shock if he'd been alone at Hilltop House all this time. Surely he'd seen other people.

Please, may he have seen other people.

"Hi," she said faintly, when it became evident he wasn't going to say anything first.

"Hi," he echoed. He took off his knit cap and wrung it between his hands.

The nervous gesture was enough for Kelly to realize she'd have to take charge. William had been so masterful and in charge on his own turf, but something told her that things were different for him once he came down from his mountain. "Come out of that drafty doorway and warm up."

William obliged, his eyes turned towards the floor as he crossed it, as if he was afraid he would trip. Kelly wondered what she'd do if he couldn't find something to say once he was standing in front of her. But he must have something to say—clearly he'd come here to see her, hadn't he?

His eyes sought hers as he stood in front of the counter, but he was still silent.

After a long pause, Kelly leaned on the counter, palms flat, and looked up at him. "William, did you come here to buy something or did you come to see me?"

He opened his mouth, closed it, then tried again. "I came to see you," he said finally. "Is that alright? I didn't know you were still in town. I hadn't left the house for a couple of weeks. Then today, I was helping Nadine with carnival set-up, and she said something about you working here . . . and I hadn't realized . . ."

Well, that explained one thing. Kelly had wondered if he'd been avoiding her. But no. He was just avoiding the entire world. She supposed that was a little better.

"Let me make us some tea, and we can talk," she suggested. "Can we do that? Are you in a hurry? Do you have to get somewhere?" She knew the question was absurd; William had nowhere to be but home with his dogs.

William shook his head. "No, tea's good. I'd like that."

While he settled into the corner table closest to the counter, Kelly flew through the movements of making tea, thankful she'd left the kettle on for a last minute cup to warm her hands on her walk home. Sugar, spoons—she thought about it a moment, then added a carton of milk in case he liked his tea with it—along with the full mugs, it all went onto a tray that she slid onto the table between them. She had never been so grateful for proper tableware. A buffer for their hands, and their gaze, while they figured out what the hell they were going to say to each other.

And what was she going to say? That she couldn't stop thinking about him? That one of the main, unspoken reasons she hadn't been able to leave Catoctin Creek was knowing that he was up there in that house, alone?

That she was in love with him?

Too crazy, she told herself, sitting down at the table. Too crazy, she told herself, sliding her hands across the wood.

Too crazy, she told herself, as she took his hands in hers. *Way too crazy.*

But there were other things she could say to him.

Like: "I have really, really missed you."

She hadn't even realized his shoulders were so tense until they dropped a full three inches. "Really?" he asked, and the hopefulness in his tone was so disarming she wanted to push the tea things aside and leap onto the table, closing the space between them once and for all. "I didn't know," he continued, his eyes boring into hers with sudden intensity. "I've missed you so much. But we barely knew each other. I thought maybe . . . maybe it was just the moment, you know." He'd started strong, but he finished on a weaker note, as if losing his nerve. His eyes fell back to the table.

"It was the moment," Kelly said, "but I don't think we barely know each other. I think we understand a lot about one another. And the parts I don't understand about you?" She gave a little laugh, remembering how angry she'd been with him about ignoring Monica's presence on his property. "Well, I'm not perfect.

I don't know the best and only way to live. You might have noticed I'm not on TV anymore, and I'm working in someone else's cafe? Not exactly the success story everyone thought they were getting."

He smiled, his gaze flicking up to hers again. "Yeah, why *are* you working here?"

"Nadine didn't tell you?"

He shook his head. "We were sorting decorations for the carnival. Like *big* decorations, huge trees and wreaths and things. An entire mountain of plastic gingerbread men. It wasn't exactly a good time for conversation. The gingerbread men might have been listening. They had very lifelike faces," he added, grinning.

"Well, I'm going to leave the big reveal up to Nikki, then. It's not my place. But," she added, as William's eyes got big, "it's nothing *bad*. Everything is good. And I like working here. I'm really, really glad I'm here."

William squeezed her hands. "I'm glad you're here, too."

"How about Lola?" Kelly asked, smiling wickedly. "Want to find out how she feels about it?"

"She'll be happy when she finds out," William said. "But let's keep this between you and me at first, shall we? My dogs get really attached, and right now, I need them to keep liking me the best."

"Afraid I'll steal your dogs?" Kelly pretended to consider the idea. "Maybe it's time for *me* to take to the roads with a van and four wolf lookalikes. I could be an Instagram sensation."

William squeezed her hands again, so tightly she thought her bones might crack. She let him do it—something was bothering him enough that he forgot his size, compared to her. "Don't take to the road," he said. "Stay here a little while. With me."

Chapter Thirty-Five

Rosemary

Rosemary was nervous. The kind of nervous where her palms were sweaty, her mouth was dry, and her stomach was churning. The kind of nervous where she couldn't decide what to wear, because one minute she was roasting hot and the next she was absolutely freezing, almost shivering. The kind of nervous where she was pretty sure she should just stay home and let the carnival go on without her. It was opening night, but really, who would miss her?

"Everyone will miss you," Stephen told her. "Because everyone loves you. Now, put on a sweater and jeans and let me take you to your carnival, my love."

That was helpful for about thirty seconds. She let Stephen go downstairs to start the car while she looked at herself in the bathroom mirror one more time. With her cherry-red knit hat on her dark hair, and a navy blue sweater and jeans, she looked just fine for a day at the fair. And of course, no one would really see anything but her wool coat and scarf around her face; it was *freezing* out there. So far, her prediction of a warm December was coming up woefully short.

Eventually she gave in to the inevitable, heading downstairs, out the door, and into the car. Stephen patted her knee. "You're not getting stage fright, are you?"

"I think I am," she confessed. It shouldn't come as a surprise to anyone that she didn't want to be the guest of honor at a carnival, even a carnival she had helped dream up, a carnival she had helped plan, a carnival that was literally to benefit her own non-profit. After all, she was Rosemary: the woman who didn't like crowds, or even vaguely busy public spaces, who had literally run away from fundraisers before, even when the people surrounding her were people she'd known all her life.

"Is there anything I can say to make you feel better? Or should I just offer you a nip from this flask I've got in my pocket before we go in?"

"Maybe that will be enough," she said, laughing nervously. "I didn't realize you were packing whiskey for this thing."

"Strictly medicinal, my love." Stephen put the car in gear. "Keep talking while we drive. That always seems to take your mind off things."

"Okay." Rosemary cast around for something to say. "Um, well, I know I don't have to do anything but show up, but it still feels like I'm putting myself on display tonight. This whole dedication and formal opening thing feels over the top."

Stephen guided the car down the driveway. A yellow moon was rising over the farm across the road, so big it seemed closer than the lonely farmhouse in the distance. He said, "Rosemary, first off, everyone knows you. It's not like this is a big reveal of the secretive recluse who is behind the carnival." He laughed. "That would be William, right?"

Rosemary laughed too. "Oh, but he comes down more often now! Because he's seeing Kelly."

"Well, I'm sure we can acquire another recluse somewhere. No respectable small town can get by without one." Stephen grinned at her. "And second off, Rosemary, no one is asking you for a speech. No strangers will come and clutch at your skirts. If someone happens to tell you they're donating a little extra to the rescue, you'll be able to say thanks, because you'll know who the person is. Trust your town, honey. They love you."

Stephen was right. He was right, and she was lucky. "Okay," she agreed, taking a deep breath. "Let's go to the carnival."

"We're halfway there, so I'm glad you agreed."

Over the past few weeks, a combined force of hired vendors and volunteers working under Nadine's formidable leadership and William's rather more gentle suggestions had transformed the barren field next to the fire station into a Christmas wonderland. And although the December evening light was wan and the carnival's true holiday spirit wouldn't properly show up until after sunset, Rosemary could already feel the festivity pouring into her spirit as Stephen parked the car. There were colored lights everywhere, brilliant displays that would light up the night in just an hour or so. As she got out of the car, a jangling, old-timey version of *Jingle Bells* was playing over the loudspeakers. She breathed in, and the sugary smells of funnel cake hit her nostrils.

Rosemary felt a surge of nostalgia rising, all these hits on her system combining to bring back wonderful memories. "Oh my goodness, Stephen, you have no idea! This is just what the Christmas carnival felt like when I was little girl."

Next to her, Stephen was brushing at his eyes. "You know, Rosie, I have a *little* bit of an idea. This just took me back to our old neighborhood street fair. For a minute I thought I was six years old and about to get sick on cotton candy and candy apples."

Rosemary glanced at him. "Did you grow up in the nineteen-thirties?"

He grinned and tugged her close. "Yes, wise guy. I'm ninety-five years old and I grew up barefoot in Brooklyn."

"Explains a lot," Rosemary laughed.

They walked up to the carnival entrance, where a lanky teen from the high school was installed in a plywood booth, taking tickets, tucking cash into a box. "You're one of the first ones here," he said, taking Stephen's money. "Kinda quiet right now."

"We're doing the official opening," Stephen told him.

The kid looked at them. "Oh, cool," he said finally.

Rosemary laughed as they fell into step, walking along the frozen path between the food trucks that lined the front of the carnival. "I thought you said everyone would know me," she teased.

"I guess you better start volunteering at the school. Your message is missing our town's youth."

"Rosemary!" Nikki waved to her from the stage just past the food trucks. It faced a clear patch of brown grass between the riding ring and the animal tents, where the local 4-H was exhibiting some of their winter projects. Rosemary could smell goats on the cool evening breeze. It mingled oddly with the funnel cakes and pizza coming from the food vendors, but she supposed that's what country fairs were all about. Nikki hopped down the stairs with her usual spryness; her body was evidently okay with the pregnancy now. "I was almost ready to say you weren't coming."

Rosemary felt her cheeks redden. "Oh, come on, you knew I'd come."

"Well, it's a big deal. And not your usual thing. But we'll make it quick, I promise. Then the school horse show team goes on. So it's a good thing if we gather everyone over here for the official opening. I want a good turnout for Nadine and Sean."

Rosemary would barely remember the next few minutes: the announcement over the loudspeaker, the faces turning to the stage, Nikki dragging her up the steps and over to a microphone. Saying words she would never, ever recall, getting a big cheer from the small crowd. And then, nearly collapsing into Stephen's strong arms with the stress of it all. He hugged her close, off to one side of the stage, as the lights went up to full strength, the crowd cheered again, and Nikki invited everyone to stay to see an exhibition of horsemanship with one of the very horses they were donating to help tonight.

"It's happening," she whispered, as the lights over the riding ring turned on and the crowd wandered over to the bleachers set up around it. "I can't believe it's all real."

"Well, you guys did it," Stephen told her, pressing a kiss to her temple. "And I'm pretty damn impressed. But I hope everyone took notes."

"Why's that?" Rosemary craned her neck to look up at him.

"Because something tells me that this carnival is going to become a staple of Christmas in Catoctin Creek."

Chapter Thirty-Six

Nadine

"You've got this," Nadine said.

Addy took a deep breath. She could tell the girl didn't *feel* like she had this. The pep talk had been going on for fifteen minutes, but Addy's face wasn't shifting from its unfortunate shade of puce.

Beside Addy, Bertha shifted. The black-and-white mare was feeding off the girl's nervousness. Nadine had been trying to explain how this worked, but she was afraid it made the whole situation feel like a self-fulfilling prophecy: Addy was afraid of upsetting Bertha further, which made Addy more nervous, which made . . . Nadine sighed. "Look, first horse shows always make everyone nervous. I was nervous at my first horse show. And so was Rosemary, and so was Sean, probably, and so was every single girl on the horse show team. But there's nothing to be afraid of. I promise you, Addy. You're just going to walk Bertha out there, do the same routine you've done a thousand times at home, and—"

"It's not a thousand times," Addy interrupted. "It's sixteen times. We've done the routine sixteen times. That's nowhere *near* a thousand."

"Seriously, you're going to nitpick on me now?" Nadine looked around. Sean's students were all in better shape than hers; they were experienced equestrians, and horse shows were old hat to all of them. They had tacked up their horses and warmed up before the fairgrounds opened, and now they were just standing around the tent talking, their horses hanging out by their sides on loose reins. She wished there was a way to make this first time in the show-ring easier for Addy, but was there anything simpler than an un-judged exhibition at a small town fair?

The girl was just going to have to take deep breaths and get through it. Some things couldn't be taught. They had to be experienced.

"Addy, you're up!" Sean appeared in the tent, walking through the gaggle of horse girls looking like a circus ringmaster in his polished boots and gleaming white breeches. He'd even donned an old-fashioned velvet hunt cap for the occasion. Nadine found the whole get-up very dashing, but she knew now was not the time, so she bit her tongue before she made a cat-call that embarrassed them both. Sean looked over at Addy, then glanced at Nadine and cocked an eyebrow: *Is she okay?*

"She's ready," Nadine said, gripping Addy's shoulder for a moment. She hoped she could infuse the girl with the strength she'd need as a horsewoman, giving her a bit of the spirit she'd acquire over the years. She knew that if Addy stuck with it, horses would be the making of the girl. But for the moment, borrowed bravado would have to get her through.

"Okay, let's go." Sean started walking, expecting Addy to follow. With a last anguished look over her shoulder, Addy took

Bertha's reins and clucked gently. Nadine felt her heart thumping; she was as invested in Addy as a parent would be, and the feeling was so big and painful, she wasn't sure how a person managed to deal with this all the time, their flesh and blood walking around in the world, trying not to get hurt. For a moment she thought of Nikki, already looking bright and hearty again now that she'd passed that first month of nausea and adjustment, and wondered how she and Kevin would fare as parents. On the outside, they'd be amazing, she had no doubt—but what did it feel like on the *inside*, constantly wanting the best and fearing the worst?

Nadine had been agonizing over this unspoken longing for weeks, but now, she realized, she was not ready to find out yet. Someday . . . but not now. There was time for everything: to finish her degree, to spend one-on-one time with Sean, to keep growing this program that would either enrich their lives for years to come, or send them rocketing towards some bright new future.

She had been in a hurry for a minute, but if there was one thing horsemanship reminded a person, it was that nothing was more important than patience.

Addy went into the riding ring, her chin held high, her hands shaking ever so slightly on Bertha's lead. And Nadine watched as the girl put her rescue horse through all the paces they'd practiced at home.

That sense of pride—that was as big and powerful as the fear she'd felt a moment before.

Amazing, the way life balanced itself out.

Chapter Thirty-Seven

William

William sat in the truck outside the cafe, waiting for Kelly. She was running late closing things, but she'd told him not to come in. "The floors are already clean," she'd protested when he'd knocked on the door. "And I know your boots are dirty."

"They're not dirty," he said.

They both looked at his boots.

"Well, it was raining all morning," he said.

"Just wait. Just wait ten minutes and I'll be out. *Please.*" She closed the door on him, and when he heard the lock turn, he knew she was serious.

So he went and sat in his truck, and pondered his own good luck.

It was weird to think of his life that way, of things going right, of things going his own way. Especially in his truck, if he was perfectly honest with himself, because this beat-up pickup with its torn seats and dusty dashboard and half-broken radio was kind of the perfect testament to the life he led. The fact was, William

8

1

could afford a new truck. He could afford several new trucks. He was a senior board member of the Cunningham Foundation, his grandparents' non-profit organization, and he had a generous salary. Usually, he pushed most of it straight back into the foundation, where the money went to any number of his grandparents' favorite causes—they were partial to children's hospitals, and land conservation, and William was happy to fund these causes, too.

But this year, he'd kept a little more than usual. He was finally making some heavy-duty modifications to Hilltop House. Fixing the furnace, for starters. Repairing the windows and doors, which let in half the weather every time the wind picked up. And he was installing a few ceiling fans, too. There wasn't much chance of putting air conditioning into that gracious old house, but he had to get the place livable for a hot Maryland summer.

Because he wasn't going to leave this year.

At least, he didn't *think* he was.

It was early yet. He could acknowledge this, and still feel like these investments in the house were all worthwhile. He was tired of wandering public land in his truck, listening to his dogs pant in his ears, looking for water and gas as his reserves grew low, looking for a safe place to stay when the mountain winds howled and heavy rains threatened to bring down entire hillsides on his chosen routes.

William wanted to stay home. With Kelly.

She appeared in the cafe doorway, waving to him before she turned and locked the door. He turned up the heat a little; he'd noticed she liked it warmer than he did, that she shivered a little when he was perfectly comfortable, and he was willing to be a little hot if it meant she was cozy. She ran to the truck, hauled open the door, and hopped in. He leaned over to kiss her, and she ran her fingers through his hair as she kissed him back, adding a little extra heat to the greeting.

"Easy there," he laughed, pulling away. "I thought we were going to a nice, wholesome Christmas carnival."

"Entirely too wholesome," she said, buckling her seat belt. "I think Nadine booked an actual church choir for the entertainment tonight."

"I think that'll be nice," William offered. "I'm not a religious man, but a choir singing Christmas carols is better than a bunch of forty-year-old guys covering Led Zeppelin, which is what passes for live music in the boondocks most of the time."

She laughed at that, a dimple he'd never noticed before flashing in one cheek. Kelly had put a little flesh on her taut bones, the result of working in a bakery filled with things she simply couldn't resist, she claimed. But William had his own private theory about that. His mother had always said happy people put on weight.

She was rarely right, his mother, but he'd love for her to have nailed this particular situation on the head.

He'd love to have a little hand in Kelly's happiness.

"How's the house going?" she asked, tipping her head against the headrest. "I haven't been up there in a while now."

"The kitchen is about done. I look forward to showing it to you." He paused; he hadn't invited Kelly back up to Hilltop since they'd started seeing each other again. For the past few weeks, they had been moving slowly, keeping things light and sweet. He was pretty sure if he took her home with him, that would change. *Quickly*. And William wasn't willing to risk their budding relationship by giving into the humming physical attraction which had drawn them together in the first place. They were more than just bubbling chemistry. So much more. He wanted to make sure they got this right.

"I'm taking it slow," he went on, referring as much to the house renovation as to Kelly, although she'd probably only catch the first meaning.

"That's always best," she agreed. "Oh, I see the carnival lights!"

They didn't have far to go—nothing in the town of Catoctin Creek was more than a few blocks apart. As William pulled into the grass parking area across the street from the fairgrounds, he noticed just how many cars were already there. "Looks like it's a hit from opening night," he said. "Thank goodness. I had to sort a *lot* of plastic gingerbread men into piles to get this thing properly decorated."

They waited in a short line to get in, then headed to the back of the fairgrounds to catch the equestrian exhibitions. Most of the crowd—which appeared to be literally everyone from town, according to Kelly, who saw more of the local folks than he did— had already filed to the back, where they were watching Addy put her black-and-white mare through the little routine they'd worked up. It was cute, and when the crowd applauded at the end, Addy burst into tears—which was also cute, once William figured out that she was also smiling.

"Happy tears," he said, wrapping an arm around Kelly, and she leaned her head against his shoulder. "Do you do that?"

"What, cry when I'm happy?" She thought about it. "I guess maybe I have. Not much, though. Why?" she added, grinning. "You want to make me cry? Are you one of *those* guys?"

William didn't even want to know what she was talking about. "I'm not one of any guys," he told her. "I'm just my own personal disaster."

"Wrong," she said. "You're also my personal disaster."

"You're the clean-up crew," he guessed.

"I have federal funds," Kelly said gravely. "And a mandate from the people."

"You guys have the weirdest conversations ever," Nikki said from behind them.

"Nikki!" Kelly reached around and gave her a hug. "How are you feeling?"

"The same as I felt today at lunchtime when you came into work and said, 'Nikki, how are you feeling?' " Nikki made a face at William. "This girl thinks I have to be monitored constantly. I *told* you, all that stuff is done. I'm fine now. Nothing a little extra napping can't fix."

"Which I am thrilled to provide to you," Kelly said. "Please don't fire me now that you're having a good pregnancy."

William's pulse quickened; was there some chance Kelly's job wasn't secure? He'd thought—

"No chance," Nikki answered. "I'm obsessed with naps now. I am never going back to staying awake all day."

They shared a laugh at that; of course, there was a lot anyone could say about a baby on the way, sleeplessness, the whole exhausting process of becoming a mom and dealing with motherhood for the next eighteen years, for *life*. But the horse show team was entering the ring behind them, and anyway, William thought as they turned to watch the show, it wasn't any fun to bring up harsh reality. Might as well just engage with the fantasy for as long as they possibly could.

For life, he thought, if that was even possible.

After the show team, the church choir took the stage. William thought they sounded pretty, but Kelly dragged him away after just a few songs. "Come on, I can't listen to all that holy music on a date," she laughed, tugging him into the lights and blaring music of the little midway. "Win me a goldfish or a teddy bear or something."

"Oh, you don't want a goldfish," William teased. "Too much responsibility for you in your little vacation rental."

She snorted and shoved him. "What makes you think I'm going to live in a vacation rental forever? I'm thinking of asking the owners for a lease."

He stopped walking and Kelly was a few paces ahead of him before she noticed. "What's wrong with you?" she asked, turning around. "Did you twist your ankle or something?"

"No," he said. "I just—I wasn't really sure how long you were staying for."

Kelly walked up to him and placed her hand on his chest. He clutched at it, feeling her warmth beneath her leather glove. The same glove, he realized, that he'd given her that first night at Hilltop House.

She'd kept them, and he hadn't even realized.

"I'm staying in Catoctin Creek long term," she told him. "I'm giving up my condo in Arlington. I've just been messing around with my diary project, and I think it's because I haven't made things permanent. I need to commit to staying here and setting up a work schedule, or I'll never get anywhere with the project. So, I'm going to move here. Completely."

"Completely," he repeated. He thought of the work he'd been doing, all in the hopes she might decide on something like this. "You're really staying here?"

"Yes," she said, tilting her chin up to look into his eyes. He could see the carnival reflecting there, the gentle twinkling of Christmas lights, the frantic sparkling of flashing midway bulbs. He felt like it was a perfect combination of the two of them, although he wasn't quite sure who was which. "I'm staying," she said again, frowning as he didn't reply right away. "Is that what you want? Or were you hoping I'd move on?"

"No." His voice came out raspy, and he cleared his throat, trying again. "No, I don't want to move on. Don't want—*you* to move on. Listen, I don't know what tore my family apart, and sometimes, I don't care. There was a disagreement, and they're proud people, and it wrecked my childhood, and that's all I know. But I'm not going to let pride ruin the second act of my life, okay? So I'm not too proud to tell you that I'm in love with you, right now, and that I want you to stay here."

"Good," she whispered, and he didn't know how he could hear her, over the crackling loudspeakers playing yet another round of *Jingle Bells*, over the carnival barkers calling out their challenges to the teenager wandering the midway, over the thudding of his own heart. But he did.

So he bent his head and kissed her, softly at first, and then with all the passion in his lonely heart.

And he felt the pinprick of tears beneath his closed eyelids. Happy tears.

Chapter Thirty-Eight

Kelly

Her senses were singing, her body humming, and Kelly felt more alive than she'd ever experienced. Her hands were in William's hair, tugging at his long brown hair, sliding along the sensitive skin beneath his ears. She felt him shiver, heard his moan pressing against her mouth, and her passion flared in response.

A carnival barker shouted into his microphone, *"Get a room, you two!"*

Kelly's heart stopped; she pulled her lips from William's with a smacking sound that made her wince. William's hands tugged through her hair, but he straightened, looking around with a bemused expression.

Kelly laughed and turned around, flipping off the carnival barker. He laughed back at her.

"Kelly!" William sounded horrified. "You can't do that at a *Christmas* fair."

"Oh, we all speak the same language," she chuckled, turning back to him. "Listen, do you want to get out of here?"

"I do," he said. "But I think we should stay a little longer, for Rosemary's sake. And Nadine's—I'm sort of on-call in case she needs me."

"What? You didn't tell me that. Well, I'm proud of you," she declared, taking his hand in hers again. "The carnival co-captain. *My* boyfriend." Her heart thudded in her chest as she said it, and she glanced up at him to see how he'd take it.

His dark, molten gaze told her everything she needed to know.

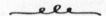

They wandered the rest of the carnival together, hand in hand, looking at each other every few seconds like they were sharing some incredible secret. Something felt more real now that they'd said those few magic words, since she'd told him she was staying, since she'd called him her boyfriend. "Girlfriend," he started saying instead of her name. "Hey girlfriend, look at these wreaths. Hey girlfriend, do you want some cider?" He had her shaking with laughter and dizzy with happiness.

As full darkness fell over the carnival, the lights of the midway and the Christmas decorations blazed brilliantly against the night sky. Kelly thought she'd never seen anyplace as pretty. The sunsets in Catoctin Creek were famous, but the moments after sunset and the velvety night were just as beautiful. She said as much to William, and he nodded. "You should see the sunsets from Hilltop House," he told her. "My grandmother used to say she should sell tickets."

"Oh really?" Kelly raised her eyebrows. "Because Rosemary told me the best sunsets in town are actually at her farm. But I haven't seen either."

"That's unacceptable," William growled. "That's misinformation on Rosemary's part, and an omission on mine. I think you should come back to Hilltop House with me tonight so that you can test it out yourself."

She stared at him. "But William, the sunset *already happened.*"

"Well, I mean, you'll want to have your stuff there already. So you can enjoy tomorrow night's sunset."

Kelly laughed and tipped her head against his shoulder. "I think that's a fine idea, Mr. Cunningham. Yes, I'll come back to Hilltop House with you—but *only* to watch tomorrow night's sunset."

"I can think of a few things we can do in the meantime." He wrapped an arm around her.

This was it, Kelly thought, watching the carnival spin around her, then letting her gaze wander over the little crowd of locals who had turned out for the first night of the carnival. This was the life she was signing up for: a little town, a quiet man, a second chance.

This was everything she wanted.

Chapter Thirty-Nine

Nikki

"I've got Christmas coming out of my ears," Nikki grumbled, as yet another Bing Crosby carol warbled out of the cafe speakers. "I can't believe we have another week before this holiday is out of the way. I just want to listen to normal music again. And get rid of all these pine garlands. And walk down the street without people saying, 'Merry Christmas,' to me every ten seconds like we've forgotten how to say a normal hello. I get it! You want me to have a merry Christmas! What should I say to these people? 'Here's hoping!' might do it."

"You've gotten really grumpy since you got pregnant," Rosemary remarked. "Not sure if you were aware."

"I'm aware, I just don't care," she snarked, and Rosemary laughed. Perks of having a best friend from childhood, Nikki reminded herself. They could be honest with each other. Even when it involved grousing about the most beloved holiday in the year. The truth was, she didn't have much to gripe about right now. Yes, Kevin was still working crazy hours, but he'd worked out an agreement with Gus for when the baby came in the summer, and the old man was leaving semi-retirement for a while —to the reported joy of his wife. And by then, he'd have improved that much more as a farrier. His work would already be taking a little less time, she figured.

And between her two businesses, things were fairly stable as well. Lauren was still happily managing the Blue Plate; Kelly was still cheerfully working evenings at the cafe, and she'd added a high school boy to the weekend line-up, and was looking for a weekend dishwasher, too. Sometime in January, she'd have an actual staff at this place. It was pretty exciting.

But not too exciting that she didn't want to keep moping about the over saturation of Christmas in her life. She rearranged chocolate peppermint cupcakes on their plate. "I guess it was just a lot, with the carnival going for a week and all the music every night, nonstop with the choirs, and now it's playing in the cafe, and we have all these tourists moving through town to see the decorations..."

"In January we'll all be bored to death," Rosemary reminded her. "So just live it up, mama." She put down the basket of bread loaves she'd been sorting, placing the fatter, stuffed loaves towards the back, and the thin breadsticks towards the front. "Of course, I'd love for the year to just skip straight to spring so the barn construction can get underway." She tugged her phone from her jeans pocket and flicked through some pictures, holding out one of the horses in their tent stabling to show Nikki. "They got a break from blankets for a while! They manage to keep the temporary barn really warm with their heat, but then, it's damp, too."

"Everything's going smoothly now, though, isn't it?"

"Yes, Nadine's sending Addy over twice a week to help me with them, and she has a few more students interested in doing rehab as their community service. So once I have them trained up, we'll be in business." Rosemary looked at the pictures a moment longer. "Basically, all the horses have good manners and seem like they have been trained. I still wonder what the Waynes were doing with them in the first place. Of course, Ethel's their only relative around here and she doesn't care to find out."

"I heard Caitlin's serious about buying the farm."

"Yeah, she just has to get the zoning board to agree to consider five-acre farmettes." Rosemary shrugged. "I don't think she'll have any problems pushing that through, though."

"It'll be good for the town," Nikki said.

"You think so?"

"I do."

The bell on the door announced a newcomer, and they looked up to see William, his coat buttoned to his chin. Nikki grinned. "Kelly's not here, Willy boy. She doesn't start work until one o'clock."

"Oh, I know. I'm going to take her a latte, if that's okay. She's working on her diary project now, and it's tough getting started. She says caffeine helps her organize her thoughts." He kicked the mud from his boots and walked over. "Whatcha got there?" he asked Rosemary, glancing at her phone.

"Oh, these are the rescue horses. Looking good, aren't they?" She held up the screen for him.

Nikki watched William's brow scrunch up. "Everything okay there, buddy?"

"Yeah, it's just . . . I don't know much about horses, but I completely forgot about this and—" He pulled out his phone and flicked through it, then held it up. "Doesn't *this* horse look like *that* horse?"

Nikki looked at the picture and thought she could see a passing resemblance. She glanced at Rosemary, and was startled to see the other woman's face lose color. "What's up, Rosie-Marie? You think that's the same horse?" she asked, incredulous.

"I'm *sure* it is. Look at the shape of the head, and that cowlick, and the marking over the nose, like he had a tight noseband once— I wish I could see if he had a freeze brand." Rosemary looked back at William. "Who is this? Why is it on your phone?"

William shrugged. "You're not going to believe this," he said. "But this is the horse that gave Monica Waters a nervous breakdown."

"What?" Rosemary's voice was nearly a shriek. "I mean, what do you mean? This horse belongs to Monica Waters?" She pointed at William's phone. "How do you know?"

"She sent me this picture," William said, as if he exchanged horse photos with girls all the time. Nikki snorted, and he glanced at her reproachfully. "When I dropped her at the police station, after I found her."

"Why did she show you this picture?"

Nikki thought Rosemary was being wonderfully patient, considering how slowly William was telling this story.

"That was her horse. She said her parents sold the farm and her horse without asking her about it. And that was what pushed her over the edge when she was already on the verge of a freak-out. She came up here because someone said the horse might have been sold to someone in Catoctin Creek. When the school was a dead end, she ended up taking her gear and going on a long hike." William gave a shrug that said, *And the rest is history.*

"Nikki," Rosemary said, "I think Monica Waters is the key to what the Wayne horses were doing here."

"Or at least her family knows," Nikki agreed. "How do we get hold of her?"

They looked at William.

He held out his phone. "Already dialed."

Chapter Forty

Rosemary

Rosemary made William make the call; he seemed embarrassed to do it, but she couldn't possibly cold-call someone she'd never spoken to *and* do it from his phone number. Of course, she didn't know William's phone number, either; he only had hers because she'd sent him the photo of her horse, so that made a momentary muddle. But once it was cleared up, William told Monica why he'd called, then passed the phone over to her.

"Hello, Monica?" she asked, feeling weird to be speaking to the woman who had caused them so much anguish and speculation. "Rosemary from Notch Gap Farm here, I take in rescue horses?"

Monica's voice seemed strained. "Oh . . . yes?"

"Yeah, hi, so William showed me this picture, and—I think—I don't want to raise false hopes, but I *really* think I have this horse in my barn."

There was a gasp. "You have *Boo?*"

"I think so? I—you'd have to see him to be sure—"

"I can be there in two hours," Monica said.

"Yes, okay—" She held the phone to her ear a moment longer, then passed it back to William. "I think I better head back to the ranch and get this horse cleaned up for his poor old mom."

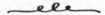

Rosemary was filled with misgiving as she finished spiffing up the bay Standardbred's coat. What if she'd gotten this woman all worked up for nothing? What if this wasn't her horse, just a doppelgänger? Horses so close in appearance were pretty common, especially plain bay ones. And she'd forgotten to ask about his freeze brand, but she couldn't read this one, anyway.

And Rosemary liked to think she'd been around horses long enough to appreciate their differences more than anything, and she really, truly thought the horse in William's photo and the bay horse they called Judge, for no particular reason other than he was the oldest horse in the herd and it seemed like a cute name for an old man, like he was a character in a black-and-white TV show.

Car doors slammed outside the tent, and she felt her heart rise in her throat. But it wasn't Monica walking inside—it was William, followed closely by Kelly. Stephen, Kevin, and Nikki weren't far behind. Her phone buzzed: Nadine, saying, 'I'll be right over!' Apparently everyone wanted to see if Rosemary's horse-identifying skills were as good as she made them out to be.

This is awful, she thought. Even though they were her best friends in the world, Rosemary thought she could happily sink through the earth and disappear forever. She led the horse out and let him crop at the dry grass in the front yard while her friends gathered around and said sympathetic, encouraging things—words she couldn't even really hear, she was so worried.

But her misgivings were swallowed up as the next arrival nearly tumbled out of her car before she even had it in park.

"*Boo!*" Monica shrieked, stumbling across the grass. "Oh my God, it's *Boo!*"

And then the horse lifted his head, flared his nostrils, and whinnied.

Rosemary nearly fainted dead away.

Stephen came up behind Rosemary and laid a hand on her shoulder while she gave the lead rope to Monica, letting her hug and kiss her long-missing horse.

"I knew she had something to do with horses up here," she heard Kelly saying. "I just had it wrong. It wasn't the school. It was *next door.*"

Chapter Forty-One

Nadine

"**B**ut why did the Waynes have all those horses to begin with?" Addy asked, bringing her brush through Bertha's long tail again and again. "I mean, it's clear they weren't going for racehorses, because Bertha here is no Standardbred."

Nadine smiled at the authoritative way Addy spoke. A few weeks ago the girl wouldn't have been able to tell an Arabian from a Standardbred, and now she was talking like an encyclopedia of horse breeds. "Well, we haven't figured that part out yet," she said. "And I'm not sure we ever will. That's the thing about secrets. You can literally take them to the grave."

"Well, someone can figure it out. If you guys all figured out that one of the horses belonged to Monica. Or even that Monica was found at all."

Sean poked his head into the grooming stall. "Nadine, my love, can I borrow you for a second?"

She eyed Addy. "Don't do anything stupid."

Addy made an elaborate face.

Nadine followed Sean down the aisle, wondering what was up. Then she gave up wondering and just focused on admiring his tight little butt in breeches. When he stopped at the end of the aisle, he whirled around. "A-ha! Gotcha!"

Nadine held out her hands in the universal gesture of total innocence. "I'm not doing anything!"

"You were watching my butt," Sean informed her. "Again."

"Wait—are you saying you don't watch mine?"

He hesitated, then grinned. "Hazards of wearing spandex to work, I guess."

"Call it that," Nadine laughed and crossed her arms over chest, letting one hip jut saucily. "What did you really want to tell me?"

"This horse," Sean said, pointing into the last stall before the closed barn doors. The chestnut mare with one blue eye that they'd brought back from the Wayne farm was inside, nosing through her hay. "I found a horse missing post on Facebook that matches up with her description. She wasn't stolen, but she was sold at auction instead of going back to her previous owner, which was against the sales contract."

Nadine gasped. "Are you sure that's her?" They hadn't done much with the chestnut mare yet, but Nadine had been secretly hoping to spend some time working with her once the Christmas break brought a little peace to the school barn.

"Pretty sure," Sean said. "That squiggly blaze of hers is awfully distinctive. And the time frame for when she went missing is about the same as when Monica's horse was sold—*and* the horse was from Pennsylvania, about thirty miles from her family's farm. They probably went through the same sales ring."

"So, the Waynes bought a bunch of horses at auction, it sounds like." Nadine didn't get it. There was still no reasonable explanation for how all those horses had ended up at the Wayne farm. Just none.

"Yeah. We just don't know what for," Sean said, echoing her thoughts.

"And so, you contacted this horse's last owner?"

"I'm afraid so. They're coming down this weekend to take a look. I know you like her. I'm sorry, if this means she's leaving."

"No, it's for the best," Nadine sighed. "If she was sold wrongfully, then she's not ours. I just . . . man, that's two horses. I really hope this doesn't happen with Bertha. That would be awful for Addy. She's put so much work into her."

Sean hesitated. Nadine saw his face fall, and she felt a stab of fear. "What? What do you know?"

"I think I found out where Bertha's from, too. But they haven't called me back yet."

"Crap, Sean, I need that horse in the barn! She's made a huge difference in Addy!"

Sean shrugged, his face miserable. "I'm really sorry. I did what I thought was right. I think you would have, too."

"I wouldn't be out on the internet turning over rocks that could be left alone," Nadine grumbled. But she knew he was right. Horses didn't just magically appear. They had histories. And often, they had people who loved them.

And who wanted them back.

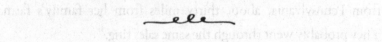

"That's not our horse," the man from Pennsylvania said, shaking his head. "Sorry we took up your time."

Nadine found she couldn't speak.

"Well, I'm sorry, Mr. McNamara," Sean said. "I sure thought it was the same horse."

"Call me Silas," the man said. "And I appreciate the effort. Oh, and I did what you asked—I talked to the Whitneys about the paint mare you got there."

Nadine buried her hands into the chestnut mare's mane and waited. She'd been glad she hadn't named the mare when she was afraid she couldn't keep her around the barn, but now she thought she would. And if this guy would just come *out* with it already about Bertha . . .

"They said that ain't their horse, either."

Nadine sighed.

"A wasted trip," Sean said, but he didn't really sound sorry.

"Well, you know how it is." Silas shrugged. "Anyway, I heard there's a real good bakery in town now. So I'll take the wife in there for a treat."

"I hope she's not too upset," Nadine ventured. "About the horse."

"Well, we all hope Goldie's okay," Silas said. "But to be honest, if you don't keep your horse in your own backyard, you never really do know where they'll end up, do you? It's the risk we all run when we go selling these creatures. I did wonder all the way down here how she might have wound up with the Waynes. It was odd, because I knew the Waynes, and they were pretty strange people, but they were real good about the horses they rescued. I think they woulda told us if they thought they had our mare."

Nadine, who had been blinking back some grateful tears, swallowed the lump in her throat to ask, "I'm sorry—they rescued horses?"

Surely she'd heard that wrong.

"Oh, yeah. They started buying horses up from auctions two years ago, when Mrs. Wayne had a health scare. She told my wife she was so lucky to live, she decided to give back to the world. That was just how she put it. And she always loved horses, so Mr. Wayne told her to buy as many as she wanted."

"Oh my god," Nadine murmured. "And she did, too. They had twelve."

"Twelve!" Silas chuckled. "I'm not surprised. He always did spoil the little woman. Probably never once told her no, in forty years of marriage. Those two were their own world, y'know. They didn't need anyone else."

"I admit we were all pretty confused about finding twelve horses on their farm," Sean said. "And when two of them looked so similar to these missing auction horses, I was a little nervous . . . I was wondering . . ." He trailed off, looking almost embarrassed.

"You wondered if they was horse thieves?" Silas slapped Sean on the back. "Nothing like it. They were good people. Strange, but good. If Mrs. Wayne wanted a horse, Mr. Wayne bought it for her. Without even asking. I reckon most of these horses were at auction because they weren't wanted anymore, and they gave them a good home. Or pretty good, I guess. You said they was in a messy state, so."

"They were well-fed," Nadine assured him. "I think the real problem was just that they died without securing their future."

"Yeah," Sean agreed. "Well, Silas, I hope you find your horse someday."

Silas nodded. "Me, too, son."

Sean turned to Nadine after Silas left, his eyes wide. "So, that's the Wayne story. They were running a rescue."

"They were *hoarding,*" Nadine sighed. "But the idea behind it, that was sweet, really. That her husband would just buy her whatever horse she wanted, to help her fulfill her promise."

"I think we did the Waynes a disservice by calling them crazy for gathering up all those horses," Sean said, ruffling his hair the way he did when he was annoyed at himself.

"Probably everyone has a good reason for the things they do," Nadine agreed. "They surely didn't know they were leaving the horses without a caretaker if they passed. After all, they had someone they were paying to care for them."

"You can't be too careful about your help," Sean declared, his voice oddly hearty. He made a quick gesture with his head and Nadine realized that Addy had walked out to join them, her face full of questions.

"What's up, Addy?" Nadine asked, turning to the girl. "Did you get out of class early?"

"Yes," Addy said. She squared her shoulders and looked at Sean. "And I've made up my mind about something."

Nadine felt her breath catch.

"I'm ready to learn to ride."

They toasted the triumph of little Addy's first ride at William's house that night, the first get-together the house had seen in decades. Kelly acted as hostess, serving champagne and orange juice and sparkling cider, while William set out a magnificent charcuterie board, and then they counted down in a darkened living room while he and Stephen fumbled with the lights for the Christmas tree. At approximately negative six, he finally got the electricity working and the massive fir tree he and Kelly had dragged in from the old pasture burst into spectacular light.

"Bravo!" Sean called, clapping, and Rosemary cheered, and even Nikki looked happy, despite her recently declared war on Christmas, and the rest of the friends joined in with their own applause, until William had to ask them to stop stomping on the floors before they went right through them.

With the fire snapping and the friendship seeming to warm the room, Nadine felt a swell of joy for all they'd accomplished this holiday season. Now, maybe, they could relax and have a little fun. For a week or two, anyway.

She settled down onto a settee and Sean sat beside her, nudging her with his knee. "What do you want?" she laughed, pushing at him.

"I've been thinking," he said, and turned a serious face to her.

"Yeah?"

"Yeah," he said. "I want to buy a new horse."

Nadine narrowed her eyes at him.

"Kidding! Kidding." Sean clutched her hands suddenly, and her heart rocketed into her throat. "Actually, I was thinking, maybe . . . maybe I'd ask you to marry me."

Nadine did her best to stay calm and cool. "Is that what you were thinking?"

"Yeah," Sean said. "That's what I was thinking."

"Have you decided yet?"

"Almost," he said.

"Almost!" Nadine was indignant. "What's the hold-up?"

Sean laughed at her reaction. "I wanted to be sure you'd say yes. But since you just gave the game away . . ." He stood up and clapped his hands, drawing the attention of everyone in the room. "Hear ye, hear ye! I'd like to do something public and embarrassing, if that's okay."

There was a general murmur of assent. "Go for it, buddy!" Kevin hooted.

"Thanks, Kev." Sean turned back to Nadine, considered her a moment, then dropped to one knee.

Nadine couldn't breathe. She hadn't expected this—hadn't even *thought* about this. But when he asked, simply, without poetics or grandstanding, she knew exactly what to say.

"Of course I'll marry you, dummy," she told him, and cupped his face in her hands.

Another cheer, another toast, hands clapping her on the back and arms squeezing her tight: Nadine turned her face towards the light of the tree, and felt the siren song of belonging drawing her in. Catoctin Creek was more than a place with beautiful sunsets and graceful old houses. It was the place which had gathered these fantastic people together. And for that, Nadine was grateful.

The End

Secret Santa

Read more love, laughter and Christmas cheer: visit
nataliekreinert.com/bonus-content to access an exclusive Catoctin
Creek short story, *Secret Santa*.

Acknowledgments

The fourth book in the Catoctin Creek series comes close to the end of a second crazy pandemic year. I started Catoctin Creek as a getaway when we were all stuck at home in 2020, and boy, it has been that and then some!

I appreciate everyone who has come to Catoctin Creek with me. It's been really fun to receive messages from readers who recognized the region and even figured out that yes, geographically, Catoctin Creek is Woodsboro, Maryland, where I lived for a while in high school. Hello, Woodsboro locals! It's great to have you in Catoctin Creek!

Now I plan to step away from this town for a little while, but that doesn't mean I won't be visiting again. I hope to see all of you there when I return.

Many thanks as always to my fantastic Patrons, who help sustain the ups and downs of an author's life with their monthly subscription at Patreon. This includes: Gretchen Fieser, JoAnn Flejszar, Nancy Neid, Elizabeth Espinosa, Renee Knowles, Libby Henderson, Maureen VanDerStad, Genevieve Dempre, Jean

Miller, Susan Cover, Sherron Meinert, Leslie Yazurlo, Nicola Beisel, Mel Policicchio, Harry Burgh, Nicole, Alyssa, Kathlyn Angie-Buss, Amelia Heath, Katy McFarland, Peggy Dvorsky, Christine Komis, Annika Kostrubala, Thoma Jolette Parker, Karen Carrubba, Emma Gooden, Silvana Ricapito, Risa Ryland, Sarina Laurin, Di Hannel, Jennifer, Claus Giloi, Dana Probert, Heather Walker, Cyndy Searfoss, Kaylee Amons, Mary Vargas, Kathi LaCasse, Rachael Rosenthal, Orpu, Diana Aitch, Liz Greene, Zoe Bills, Cheryl Bavister, Sarah Seavey, Megan Devine, Mara Shatat, Tricia Jordan, Brinn Dimler, Lindsay Moore, Princess Jenny, Caitlin Harrison, Rhonda Lane, C. Sperry, Heather Voltz, and Kim Keller.

Wow, what a list! I am so thankful for you all, and hey, I bet you're excited to start working on *Home* with me next!

About the Author

I currently live in Central Florida, where I write fiction and freelance for a variety of publications. I mostly write about theme parks, travel, and horses! I've been writing professionally for more than a decade, and yes...I prefer writing fiction to anything else. In the past I've worked professionally in many aspects of the equestrian world, including grooming for top eventers, training off-track Thoroughbreds, galloping racehorses, working in mounted law enforcement, on breeding farms, and more!

Visit my website at nataliekreinert.com to keep up with the latest news and read occasional blog posts and book reviews. For installments of upcoming fiction and exclusive stories, visit my Patreon page and learn how you can become a subscriber!

For more:

- Facebook: facebook.com/nataliekellerreinert
- Group: facebook.com/groups/societyofweirdhorsegirls
- Bookbub: bookbub.com/profile/natalie-keller-reinert
- Twitter: twitter.com/nataliegallops

- Instagram: instagram.com/nataliekreinert
- Email: natalie@nataliekreinert.com

CPSIA information can be obtained
at www.ICGtesting.com
Printed in the USA
LVHW090429170323
741772LV00003B/560